VALLEY

OF

SHADOWS

BOOKS BY RUDY RUIZ

Valley of Shadows

The Resurrection of Fulgencio Ramirez

Seven for the Revolution

Going Hungry

¡Adelante!

VALLEY

OF

SHADOWS

A NOVEL

RUDY RUIZ

**BLACK
STONE**
PUBLISHING

Copyright © 2022 by Rudy Ruiz
Published in 2022 by Blackstone Publishing
Cover and book design by Kathryn Galloway English
Illustrations on chapter headings by Joe Garcia

Printed in the United States of America

First edition: 2022
ISBN 978-1-9826-0464-6
Fiction / Magical Realism

Version 1

CIP data for this book is available
from the Library of Congress

Blackstone Publishing
31 Mistletoe Rd.
Ashland, OR 97520

www.BlackstonePublishing.com

For Heather, Paloma,
Isabella, and Lorenzo

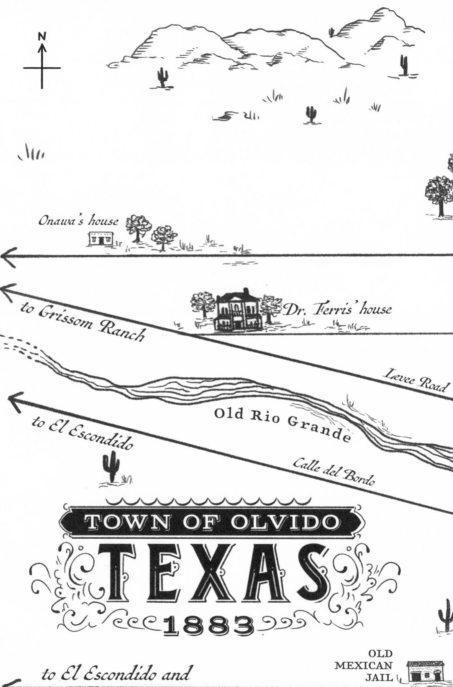

N

Onawa's house

to Grissom Ranch

Dr. Ferris' house

Levee Road

Old Rio Grande

to El Escondido

Calle del Bordo

TOWN OF OLVIDO
TEXAS
1883

to El Escondido and
Santander Ranch

OLD
MEXICAN
JAIL

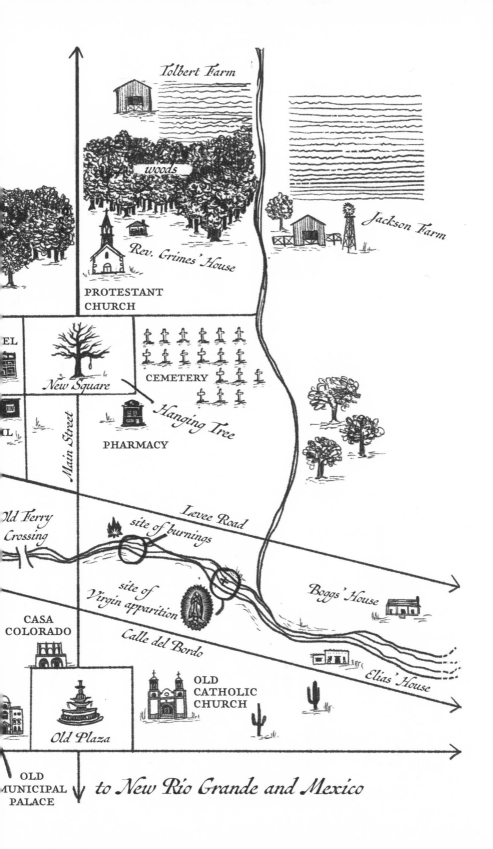

Tolbert Farm

woods

Jackson Farm

Rev. Grimes' House

PROTESTANT
CHURCH

EL

New Square

CEMETERY

Hanging Tree

IL

Main Street

PHARMACY

Old Ferry
Crossing

Levee Road

site of burnings

site of
Virgin apparition

Boggs' House

CASA
COLORADO

Calle del Bordo

Elias' House

OLD
CATHOLIC
CHURCH

Old Plaza

OLD
MUNICIPAL
PALACE

to New Río Grande and Mexico

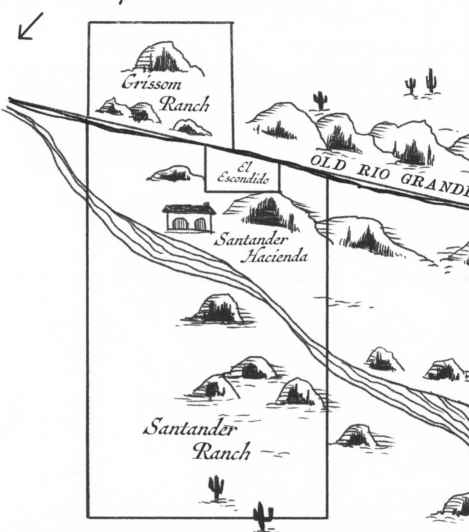

To old Apache ancestral lands

Grissom Ranch

El Escondido

OLD RIO GRANDE

Santander Hacienda

Santander Ranch

OLIVIDO, TEXAS
AND
CHIHUAHUA, MEXICO
LATE 1800s

PROLOGUE

Frankie Tolbert pouted at the dinner table, staring down at his half-eaten beef and potato stew. Tiny carrots floated in brown gravy like miniature orange islands. He imagined himself marooned on one, all alone. His checkered napkin was stuffed into his collar to shield his white T-shirt and denim overalls from the sauce. Mother forced him to put it there as if he were still a little kid. He despised having to stay behind with her and his little sisters while his father and older brother tended to men's business. It wasn't often that someone knocked at the door in the middle of dinner after the sun had set and dusk had fallen. He figured something exciting must be going on, and he wanted to be part of it. After all, he had just turned ten. He was only three years younger than his older brother. Why did Johnny get to have all the fun? Would he always be left behind with the women? He brooded as his mom glanced anxiously out the window.

"Y'all keep eating. Don't let your food get cold," she said.

His sisters, Abigail and Beatrice, raised their forks in unison, their golden curls bouncing up and down as they bobbed their heads. "Yes, ma'am," they chimed.

How was it fair for him to be treated the same as an eight-year-old and a six-year-old? They were practically babies, and girls to boot. He stared longingly at the front door. His father had left it slightly ajar, and the buzzing of cicadas drifted in with the evening breeze. They sounded like a never-ending chorus of rattlesnakes to Frankie. Rattlesnakes were dangerous, like the night itself. That's why his dad had charged him with staying with the women. When his dad and older brother weren't around, it was his job to protect them. He tried to reconcile his symbolic position with his authentic desire to know what was happening out back in the barn, where the men had circled moments earlier.

His mother's eyes flicked from the window to the front of the house. Then the familiar-faced man reappeared in the crack between the door and the frame. He nudged the door slightly with his boot and called out to them in the dining room. "Mrs. Tolbert, your husband says y'all should come on back and see this too. It's quite fascinating."

Abigail and Beatrice wiggled with excitement in their pink-and-white gingham frocks. Frankie yanked his bib off, jumped to his feet, and was at the door in a flash. Their mother brought up the rear as the four of them followed the tall man, who sauntered slowly toward the closed barn door.

It was dark outside, the clearing between the farmhouse and the barn barely lit by the glow of the oil lanterns inside the house spilling faintly onto the ground. Up in one of the trees, an owl hooted. The night was otherwise eerily quiet.

When they reached the barn, the heavy door groaned on its rusted hinges as the man pulled it open, motioning for them to enter first. It was pitch black inside, and when he closed the door behind them, they couldn't see a thing. For the first time that night, Frankie was suddenly not frustrated or excited. He was afraid. He could hear his heart thumping fast in his chest. In the dark, he reached for his mother's hand but instead found Abigail's, the elder of his two sisters.

"Mom?" the girls whimpered.

Frankie heard the sound of a match being struck against a rough surface. A single flame illuminated a strange shape looming at the back of the barn. Feathery protrusions bristled out from its sides, like spikes. And it was crowned by a wild mane. Was it a man or an animal? Or was it something else altogether?

"What's going on?" Frankie's mom asked, her voice quivering. "John?" She called his father's name, but there was no response.

A second match was struck, and another lantern lit by a man Frankie did not recognize. He had gray hair and looked distinguished, dressed in a fancy suit.

As the meager light diffused through the barn, Frankie's eyes adjusted to his surroundings. Then he saw his father, lying in the straw, his shirt covered in blood. His brother, Johnny, was not far, also on the ground motionless.

His mother shrieked. Outside, a heavy flapping could be heard as the owl in the tree took flight. She wrapped her arms around the children and tried to back out of the barn, but there were two burly men blocking the way, the lower halves of their faces covered by dark bandannas.

"What's happening?" she cried, but the men shoved her onto the ground and one of them straddled her like a calf being tied and knotted.

The man forced a bandanna between her teeth and pulled it around the back of her head tightly. She squirmed and tried to fight back but it was no use. The girls cried but were quickly silenced. Frankie leaped onto the assailant's back, kicking and clawing, but soon all three of them were bound with rope and gagged, sitting against posts that reached up to the rafters. From there, two ropes dangled down menacingly.

Frankie and his sisters watched in horror as their mother's wrists were fastened. Kicking and grunting, she was hoisted up into the air by the two masked men, pulling on the ropes that had been flung over a crossbeam.

Frankie looked away as the men stripped his mother naked. Why was this happening? These kinds of things didn't happen to good people. The preacher's wife had said as much in Sunday school. Had his father done something wrong? What had any of them done to deserve this? He strained against the ropes, but it was useless.

A large blade gleamed in the lantern's glow. The well-dressed man clutched the knife in his hands, his knuckles bone white, as he neared their mother. The monstrous shadow at the back of the barn rustled, the sound of dry leaves shaking and a low murmur of unrecognizable words rising forth as the creature inched toward the light.

"Don't look, don't look," Frankie whispered to his sisters. It was the least he could do. He'd failed miserably in his charge of protection. "Close your eyes. Keep 'em closed." He squeezed his eyes shut as tightly as he could and prayed silently until his mother unleashed a blood-curdling scream.

PART I

ONE

1883

Solitario Cisneros squinted across the golden plains at the growing cloud of dust. He stood out on his porch, sipping his bitter morning coffee from a hot tin cup, just like he did at the start of every day, the new sun peeking over the vast blanket of creosote-dotted desert.

He reckoned there were at least three riders, and they were moving fast judging by the rate at which the dust cloud mushroomed, battling the orange glow of the rising sun. Between him and the interlopers stood a scattered regiment of cattle, motionless, oblivious to the intrusion. The cows didn't even bother to raise their heads from the sparse clumps of grass they grazed upon.

You're about as much use as my comrades were, back when I was with the Rurales, Solitario mused at the cattle, his dark eyes smoldering as he maintained his steady stare toward the east. The outlines of three horses emerged from the swirl of sandy particles churning across his land. Two gringos and a Mexicano. He could tell by the types of hats the riders wore on their heads. Soon they'd be able to spot him there on his wooden porch. Even though he was dressed in black, they could probably already make out the flash of the sun glinting off his tin cup. After all, the sun was behind them. He took a final sip, setting the cup down on the rustic table next to him. He stared down at the weathered wood. It blended into the floorboards beneath it and the wall next to it. All had been painted gray at some point and now sat faded and covered in layers of sand. The whole place yearned to blend into its background, featureless, nearly invisible unless you knew where it was, who you were looking for. That was not only how Solitario felt, it was how he preferred things. Simple. Sparse. Subtle. Pensively, he stroked his long full mustache before ducking into the front room of his house, reaching for his gun belt, and slinging it around his waist in a fluid motion. It was tooled from black leather, just like his boots. And it sat below a turquoise belt buckle exquisitely fashioned into the shape of an eagle. A silver revolver gleamed below each hip. Glancing outside, he surmised he did not have the luxury of time to wrap his ammunition belts over his shoulders or to throw his jacket over his frayed vest. Instead, he pulled his broad-brimmed black sombrero off its hook, lowered its midnight-blue underbrim over his wavy black hair, and stepped back outside, waiting at the top of the stairs as he observed the approaching intruders. Visitors were rare in these parts, at least for him. At least these days, since the river had changed course.

When the riders reached the clearing in front of the low-slung house, the sun was directly behind them, and all he could make out were their dark silhouettes, their outlines sizzling deep orange, like the yolks of frying eggs.

He stared at them impassively, his hands at his sides, not threatening but ready.

"Jefe." The Mexican man removed his sombrero as he spoke. "¿Me permite desmontar para saludarlo como debe ser?"

A wave of relief washed through Solitario as he recognized the man's voice, but outwardly he betrayed no signs of either having been alarmed or of letting down his guard. Besides, for all he knew, the man might be performing under duress. He could still not make out the two gringos who flanked him. "Claro, Elias," he replied.

When the man dismounted and approached, the girth of his belly and the dearth of his stature both became evident. While Solitario looked no different than he had during their fighting days together, his comrade had grown stockier, and white stubble populated his chin like the prickles on cholla. Solitario fought back the urge to smile in recognition as the man stretched out his weathered hand. Shaking firmly, he scanned Elias' eyes for any hint of trouble. He read worry in them for certain, but not panic, not urgency, not the darting sideways glance that would have been code for immediate danger. Whoever the gringos at his side were, the stout man in denim pants and a tan work shirt did not seem particularly afraid of them.

"What brings you out here, Elias?" asked Solitario, his eyes trained on the rifles holstered to the flanks of his companions' horses.

"It's been too long, Jefe. You look the same. Pero está muy flaco. Are you eating enough? I know you never eat breakfast, but how about lunch or dinner?"

"I'm sure you're not here for breakfast or to check on my health."

"No, Jefe. I remember your cooking. And, no offense, but my Otila's huevos rancheros are much better." The man wiped his forehead with the red bandanna tied loosely around his thick neck. Already the heat was rising, promising that the day would be a scorcher.

"¿Entonces?" Solitario nodded. "Who are your compañeros?"

"They are from the village. They asked me to guide them to you. I hope you don't mind. They promised to pay me well. This is Mr. Stillman, the mayor." He pointed at a tall man sitting stiffly in his saddle. "And this is Mr. Boggs, the banker." He motioned toward a shorter man with a bowler hat perched awkwardly on his horse.

Solitario squinted up at the men, still rigid on their steeds. "How can I help you?" he asked, his English flowing with the phonetic rhythm of a tongue dipped in the Rio Grande.

Mr. Stillman spoke with a southern drawl. "If you come with us, we'll compensate you handsomely as well."

"What for?"

"There's been a murder in the village."

"There are murders in the village often," Solitario responded in a measured tone as if this was merely a natural part of life, which it was, "and nobody comes out here to interrupt my morning café."

"I remember your café, Jefe." Elias grinned, shaking his head, his ruddy cheeks inflating like those of a well-fed chipmunk. "Being interrupted might not be such a bad thing."

Solitario scowled at Elias. A few years out of service and people quickly forgot their place. He stared with suspicion at the mounted men. It was hard to assess a man's intentions when you could not look into his eyes. "Like I said, killing is as common as coyotes and cactus. Why do you need me?"

The tall southerner shifted in his saddle. "Because this here murder is . . . well . . . let's just say it is highly unusual. And we have no idea who might have committed it."

"I am not the law around here anymore. And I don't get involved in matters of vengeance," Solitario replied, regret tingeing his gravelly voice. "I'm sorry my old sergeant wasted your time bringing you all the way out here."

"It is no matter of revenge or anything of the sort," Mr. Boggs finally spoke, his voice quivering as if it took a lot out of him to pipe up. "We just need help ascertaining who has committed this terrible atrocity, bring them to justice so they don't do something ungodly again. The towns-folk are petrified. Some are talking about packing up their wagons and leaving. You must come. At least come bear witness with your own eyes."

Solitario could sense the fear in Boggs' voice. He had seen something that had shaken him to the core, his voice still trembling from the after-shocks. Out in these far reaches, it took a lot to unsettle a man, even those wily or naive enough to abandon the safety of their northeastern cities for the uncertainty of the frontier, the way he figured Boggs had done.

"I'm sorry to hear it. But I'm not the one you should be looking for anyway. Go find your sheriff, Tolbert. He'll help you."

"That's the problem," Stillman explained. "Sheriff Tolbert is pre-cisely the one that has been killed."

"And you are the only other lawman within a couple days' ride that can take stock of the crime scene . . . well . . . before it's too late," Boggs added.

Bodies rotted fast in this heat. Evidence disintegrated. Bandits es-caped into the chaparral, wound into the mountains, and vanished across the Rio Grande as nimbly as the puma that roamed the lands.

"I'm sorry about your sheriff," Solitario said, removing his sombrero, its silver embroidery glittering in the sunlight. "He was un hombre decente, a decent man."

The two mounted men removed their hats in unison, bowing their heads.

"His wife and children must be grieving. Perhaps it's best to leave things alone," Solitario said, still hoping to avoid the journey into town. "Widows and mourners don't welcome people like me picking over their dead. What's done is done. They should bury him and be finished with the whole business. No amount of meddling will bring Tolbert back to them."

"You see, that's the other half of it," Boggs replied, his voice faltering. "Whoever killed the sheriff, they killed his wife and family too."

"They've done it in a way that doesn't seem human, Jefe," Elias added. "You have to come see for yourself. Es una barbaridad."

Solitario's gaze dropped to the faded porch step he stood on and then to the cracked earth that spread out below. A heavy weight threatened to descend upon his broad shoulders. He felt despondent. He wasn't sure if it was for the sheriff and his family, whom he'd respected but hadn't known all that well, or for himself. He rarely left his ranch, hardly ever dealt with other people anymore. Cows didn't ask him questions or expect much of him. Cows didn't cry when he failed. He furrowed his thick eyebrows as his eyes stalked a trail of fire ants marching across the parched ground between him and his former sergeant. Sighing, he turned and followed his own shadow into the sparsely furnished house. He strode through the front room, which contained a settee upholstered in faded blue velvet and a rocking chair that had belonged to his parents, may they rest in peace. Past the small kitchen with the wood-burning stove, in his bedroom, against one wall, sat the bed where he rested at night. Across from that stood a simple table with a mirror and the lone decoration in the room, a sepia photograph of a newlywed couple in a tarnished silver frame. A gentle breeze flowed through the windows, tattered gauze curtains billowing inward like ethereal fingers yearning to caress him. Standing out of their reach as he got ready, he watched Elias saddling his horse, Tormenta, a black mare with a reputation for moving as swiftly as its namesake squalls, startling bursts of ferocity that occasionally flashflooded the arid valleys carved between the

Trans-Pecos Mountains. He beheld himself in the mottled mirror, lowering his desolate eyes to the picture taken thirteen years ago. She looked so joyful, so lovely in it. Luz, in her white wedding gown, her black tresses draped in long braids over her petite shoulders, dimples on either side of the upturned corners of her full lips. Ruby, they had been, not shades of ash as they were in the image. Alive, she had been. Not translucent and monochromatic like the sheers wafting in the wind. A lover and a beloved. Not a ghost or a memory. And he, well, people said he never changed, but he noticed the creases grooved into his face by the unforgiving sun and the desert wind. He could tell the difference between the optimism brimming in his eyes on those church steps in the photo and the reluctant, hollow stare that met him in the mirror. He had always been good at observing the minute discrepancies that escaped others.

When Solitario emerged, he wore his black jacket, his ammunition belts crossed over his chest, and a yellow bandanna knotted at his throat. In addition to his revolvers, he carried a rifle. Donning his sombrero, he rose up onto Tormenta and nodded at the men.

"So you'll help?" quivered Mr. Boggs.

Finally, Solitario could see the fear in the man's eyes. He knew at once that this small portly man with flushed cheeks and fogged spectacles sliding down a nose slick with sweat should have never left the city where he had been born. He should have never followed whoever led him out west in search of whatever fortune would elude him before he met his premature death.

Go back home, he wished to advise Mr. Boggs. *Take your wife and children back to safety before it's too late*, he thought, glimpsing the gold wedding band on the man's left hand. *Don't let greed or ambition or misguided boyhood dreams rob you of what you have at hand.*

"I'll take a look," Solitario answered in a noncommittal tone. He felt sorry for Mr. and Mrs. Boggs, and what he calculated must be two to three Boggs offspring.

He was even sorrier for the sheriff and his family, but he was grateful for the long ride into town. He would need the time to harden his soul against whatever carnage awaited him there.

TWO

Olvido was a town cartographers forgot to put on maps. Fittingly, Solitario often wished he could erase the memory of everything that had befallen him there. But he could not escape those recollections, just as he had so far proven incapable of evading that which had driven him from his birthplace seven hundred miles southeast along the Rio Grande. Back then he'd been a wide-eyed seventeen-year-old with delusions of being able to outrun his fate. He had even dared to believe he could make some sort of difference in the world.

Olvido was a one-road pueblo torn in two by a deep trench that gaped hollow, a crunchy, cracked, and forsaken riverbed that wound through the cluster of dwellings and trading posts along its banks as a constant reminder that even the Rio Grande had wished to wipe the town from its history. Along both the elevated banks, north and south of that scar, rows of houses sprung like weeds. The humble structures along the southern bank were made of adobe and coated with sun-bleached stucco long ago painted in fuchsia, lime, turquoise, and marigold. Now the colors were faded, like the mariachi music that had once filled the streets. The modest wooden houses across the vanished waterway slumped in tones of gray-and-brown wood, savaged by the persistent sun and weathered by the desiccating winds. Before the Rio

Grande had shifted south, this had been a bustling pair of border villages, divided by the water but united by the trade of two nations and
the blood of shared families. Now that the two villages had become one
town, there was no water and little commerce, but there still seemed to
be an abundance of blood spilled rather than celebrated.

Solitario and the men reached the town after traversing the valley,
following the ancient river's abandoned course, the mountains' shadows
dancing about them almost imperceptibly. The sun was high overhead
as Solitario and his entourage approached from the southern bank; they
rode first through the main thoroughfare of what had once been the
Mexican side of Olvido. Their horses kicked up dust as a string of grimy,
barely clad children shuffled barefoot in their wake toward the riverbed
while the adults watched from behind the shuttered windows. Their
lips moved silently, but Solitario knew they were whispering his name.

The horses balked and snorted at the edge of the chasm, where the
ferryman's post sat empty. The collapsing planks of a wooden landing
had tumbled downward into the ravine. The posts that anchored the
once-teeming dock leaned precariously askew. A frayed rope dangled
from one of them, leading down to the smashed ruins of a massive barge,
which had once carried families and merchants, crates and barrels, even
livestock, back and forth countless times a day.

A makeshift set of rickety wooden steps had been installed at some
point, alongside a ramp sloping down into the riverbed. This arrange-
ment was mimicked by twin structures on the opposite side of the
gaping gorge. Tentatively at first, the horses skittered down the ramp
and then scrambled up the other side. Once perched on the northern
bank, Solitario turned back to see the throng of sunbaked children
standing across the crevasse at what had once been the river's edge, as if
what now flowed between them was molten lava which would inciner-
ate them if they dared to follow.

Passing the general store, the feed shop, the saloon, and the bank,
frightened pale faces peeked behind curtains. The group rode quietly
past the whitewashed Protestant church, toward the northern edge of
the American side of Olvido. It had borne a different name back then,

an Apache word assigned to the place by its first inhabitants, but when the river had shifted, the Anglo settlers had voted to expunge that name and go with Olvido. They couldn't agree on which defeated Confederate general to honor, and they somehow found it less offensive than the Apache alternative. After all, Mexico had lost the war, and fortune had rerouted the Rio Grande southward, so now they could appear generous to their Mexican neighbors by adopting their pueblo's name while divorcing them of their rights and their lands as quickly as possible. The Apache, on the other hand, were still a problem. Why give them any ideas or—far worse—hope?

When the group reached the Tolbert farm, they paused at the wooden gate, where two young men in matching snap-button shirts stood guard. They looked remarkably alike, fresh-faced and flush-cheeked, perspiring heavily in the afternoon sun without any shade beyond that of their Stetsons. Each wore a shiny silver star over his left chest pocket. Their gun belts were tied tightly around their waists, the guns positioned high on their hips. Solitario instantly surmised they'd not pinned those badges to their shirts prior to that morning. Nor had they ever fired a pistol at anything but a bottle perched on a fence post.

"Anyone been here nosing around?" Mr. Boggs asked.

"Just the preacher," one of the guards answered.

"And his wife," the other added. "She brought a covered dish."

Mr. Stillman frowned, shaking his head and spitting his chewing tobacco onto the ground in disgust. "Some people never cease to amaze. Please tell me you had the good sense to turn them away," Stillman lamented.

"Yes, sir," the first guard answered. "We followed your orders, sir, just like you told us."

"Good man, Dobbs," Stillman nodded. "Pay the boys, Mr. Boggs."

Boggs fastidiously rifled through his saddlebag, extracting two shiny silver coins and placing them in the palms of the young mens' outstretched hands.

The two youngsters glanced at Solitario sideways with their sky-blue eyes, shifting back and forth on their boots like two cowhands about to mount a bucking bronco for the first time. *Twins*, Solitario mused. You didn't see the likes of them too often in these parts. They usually died at childbirth along with the mother. Nature was harsh that way.

The Dobbs boys opened the gate so the men could ride down the caliche path to the farmhouse, which was tucked beyond a row of mesquite trees, spindly leaves drooping like a poor man's weeping willow.

The Victorian farmhouse was fronted by an ample porch guarded by six white rocking chairs. Tying their horses at the porch steps, Mr. Stillman motioned for Solitario and the others to follow him around the house, where a large red barn stood. Beyond that, a patch of shoulder-high corn grew next to a creek. Solitario walked slowly, his boots crunching over the caliche scattered along the path. He observed the mesquite trees, the expansive field of brown grass adjacent to the homestead, the dense woods across the way.

Before Stillman pulled the barn door open, Solitario pointed across the barren field at the woods beyond. "Who owns that property?" he asked.

"I believe it belongs to the Protestant church," Stillman replied. "They're the nearest neighbor."

Solitario nodded.

Stillman pulled on the door, motioning for him to enter. "We'll wait out here. Once was enough."

Gritting his teeth, Solitario stepped into the shadowy interior of the barn, dimly lit by intermittent shafts of light sifting through upright wall planks. Straw rustled beneath his boots as he moved slowly but deliberately, his eyes adjusting to the darkness as the stench of freshly rotting human flesh seared his nostrils. The first thing he noticed were two puddles of vomit on the ground, which he sidestepped. Flies swarmed as the scene came into view like a nightmare taking shape in the midst of a tortured night.

A disrobed woman hung from the rafters, her arms outstretched, wrists tied to a horizontal beam overhead. Her pale body was smeared in crimson fluid that had flowed from a cavity gaping between her breasts. Her freckled face was forever twisted into a grotesque expression of horror.

She appeared to be smiling despite her obviously anguished state preceding death.

Solitario paused as he looked up at her. She nearly resembled a statue of Christ nailed to the cross, except she hung suspended by ropes. No crown of thorns. No loincloth to preserve her modesty. No other stigmata, except the hole where her heart had once beat.

Scanning the ground from the spot where he stood, he mentally cataloged the scene. The sheriff lay on a thick layer of straw, faceup, his throat slashed, a pool of blood still drying beneath and around him. No hat anywhere nearby. No gun belt. No holster. No badge on his chest. A barefoot boy in his teens was sprawled between the door and the center of the barn where his mother dangled. He wore dungarees and a white T-shirt stained by crimson. His face was bruised, his lip split, blood crusted his chin and matted in his blond hair. Around the boy, the straw was broken and disturbed, patches of dirt peeked out from beneath it, and numerous boot tracks encircled his body.

Stroking his mustache, he took mental notes regarding the height of the structure, the length of the ropes, and the other objects scattered about the space. He did all of this without moving from the spot where he stood. Then, after he had committed the scene to memory, he approached the sheriff's inert form. Sheriff Tolbert's eyes were still open, glassed over, but he read the expression immortalized on his face as one of surprise rather than terror. His death had been quick. Solitario knelt down and peered at the sheriff's hands. They were clean, showing no signs of having put up a fight.

When he was finished scrutinizing the sheriff's remains, Solitario walked gingerly over to the boy, following the same process. The boy had been beaten badly, and in the end, a brutal blow with a metal object had cracked his skull. His hands were black and blue, and his nails were encrusted with dry blood. He'd fought back, that was for sure, Solitario thought as he avoided the boot prints, noting that at least one of the boots—but not all—had borne an *X* in the center of the sole.

Solitario shook his head and rose to his full stature, retracing his steps backward toward the door in order to avoid further disturbing any of the evidence. Closing the barn door behind him, he turned to face the other men.

They all stared at him expectantly. It had always been like this, the pressure threatening to crush him.

"Any thoughts?" Mr. Boggs broke the silence.

Solitario reflected before answering, "I would like to see the inside of the house."

Stillman led them to the front porch and opened the door, following Solitario like a shadow as he stepped through the house. Inside the neatly appointed home, there were no signs of any kind of altercation. The sheriff's gun belt hung on a hook near the entrance, revolvers neatly tucked into place. Dinner sat half-eaten on the table. Meat and potatoes suspended in a thick—but now congealed—brown gravy. Solitario hesitated, narrowing his eyes as he stared at a family portrait in the hallway to the bedrooms. He recognized Sheriff Tolbert and Mrs. Tolbert, as well as the teenage boy lying dead in the barn. But in the black-and-white photo, there were three additional children, a boy a couple years younger than the first and two little girls with freckles like their mother's, wearing polka-dotted dresses with their light hair in pigtails.

After walking through the rest of the house, which seemed undisturbed, Solitario and Stillman regrouped with the others beneath the mesquite trees in front. They all stood in a row, gazing at the house as if by staring at it long enough they could will it into divulging the details of what had taken place between its walls.

"Any ideas?" Mr. Boggs tried again.

Solitario squinted at the house, thick lines etched into his cinnamon skin. Without turning to Boggs, he answered, "My principal thought, Señor Boggs, is the same one I stated earlier. That I am no longer a lawman."

"Surely, we can convince you to investigate further, or to at least provide us with your initial assessment of what might have happened here," Mr. Stillman pressed.

"Like we said, we'll pay you good money. The going rate for a Texas Ranger," Mr. Boggs added.

Solitario knit his eyebrows together, at last turning to face the men, who were perspiring profusely despite the dry climate, the shade, and the breeze beneath the mesquites. He marveled sometimes at how these people could earnestly believe they belonged out here.

"What do you say, Jefe?" Elias chimed in. "I can help you. It will be like old times."

"We can pay your sergeant too," Mr. Stillman piled on.

"Money is of little use to me," Solitario answered slowly. "You do not have to pay me for coming out here and witnessing this calamity."

"Won't you give us anything? Not even a hint or a clue?" Mr. Boggs pressed, urgency tightening his facial muscles.

"Where are the other children?" Solitario asked.

"We don't know," Mr. Stillman replied. "Nobody has seen hide nor hair of them. We've got a man knocking on every door in Olvido in case they ran somewhere out of fear and are hiding out, laying low."

Solitario considered that possibility. It seemed unlikely to him. "Do they have any other family in town?"

"No. They're all back east," Stillman said.

"No ransom note?" Solitario asked.

"Nada," Elias chimed in.

"Have you talked to the preacher, the one that lives nearby?" Solitario queried.

"Yes, but he didn't know a thing," Boggs answered. "He hadn't seen the children recently. He says he didn't hear any noise last night."

"And those twins out front discovered this?" Solitario asked, thinking of the two duplicates he'd encountered near the entrance.

"Yes, the Dobbs twins did," Boggs said. "They do odd jobs for the sheriff. He liked them. They came late last night to put some tools in the barn and bring the milk cow inside and, well, they found them."

Solitario mulled over the myriad of possibilities, imagined himself questioning the various parties, tracking down those children. Were they dead already? Was there any saving them? A part of him that felt nearly as dead as the victims rustled deep within his mind, but already he could feel the gravitational pull of his ranch tugging at him. He'd been gone only a few hours, yet he already missed being near Luz, being near what remained of her.

"What kind of person would do something like this, Jefe?" Elias asked, wiping his brow with his red bandanna.

"I'll tell you two things, and then, lo siento, but I'm done. I've got animals to tend to back on my ranch. And I don't have the time or inclination to do this kind of work anymore."

"But you're young. You could be the sheriff here . . . again . . . if you play your cards right," Stillman urged.

Solitario stared back at him. "Do you want to hear the two things I have to say? Or do you want me just to go back home?"

Stillman and Boggs appeared crestfallen, sighing in dismay.

"Tell us," Boggs pleaded.

"First, there is not a kind of person that did this. It is a kind of *people*. It took more than one man to commit these crimes."

"And second?" Boggs asked, leaning in, his eyes bulging.

"Second, the kind of people that would do something like this— leaving no ransom note, not stealing a thing—weren't looking for money. That makes things worse because it means the kind of people they are is the evil kind. And, if I had to provide an opinion, I'd say they're not finished with what they've started." Solitario reached for a silver canteen in his black leather saddlebag and took a long swig of lukewarm water. He wished it were tequila, given the circumstances. Without another word, he climbed back on his horse and rode toward the gate, leaving Stillman and Boggs scratching their heads beneath the trees.

Elias chased after Tormenta and his former boss on foot, reaching them at the gate. "Jefe, won't you wait and come with me to eat at the house? Otila will cook a good meal so you won't go hungry on the long ride back to your ranch. And you can see Elena and Oscarito. It's been a long time since you've seen your goddaughter. They've grown. It would do you good to sit down and spend time with people . . . living people." His voice trailed off, trepidation rattling his eyes.

"No, gracias, Elias. I've lost my appetite. Please send my saludos."

Elias nodded sullenly. "Bueno, pues hasta la vista. Que Dios lo guarde."

Solitario nodded, "Igualmente," and rode back up the dusty road toward the white church. At the fence line between the Tolberts' farm and the woods that separated their land from the church grounds, a flash of gold caught his peripheral vision. "Whoa," he pulled on the reins, bringing Tormenta to a standstill. They were far enough away from the gate and the farmhouse that the men he had come with were out of sight. He peered over the fence into the woods and tangled brush. Tormenta snorted, pawing the ground with an impatient hoof. She was ready to get back to the ranch, to their hiding place. There was evil in the world all right, Solitario thought, and life had taught him to stop fighting it and to take refuge. He looked at the road ahead, at the town he must cross to reach the valley and follow the dry riverbed back to El Escondido, as he had aptly named his ranch after what had happened to Luz. He didn't relish having all those probing eyes trained on him. Yet, his curiosity rustled like a hibernating bear stirring in the cobwebbed recesses of a long-unused portion of his mind. Sighing, he dismounted and approached the fence. He scanned the edge of the woods. Behind the dense barrier of juniper and chaparral, he could spy the babble of a creek.

Must be the same one Tolbert used to irrigate his small crop of corn, he thought. Following the sound, his body leaning against the fence, he peered a little deeper into the brush. And then, there was the flash of gold again. His eyes followed the trajectory of the movement toward the field of brown grass that stretched from the woods back to the farmhouse. And then, suddenly, he sprang back as he saw a boy standing there, about ten yards away. One foot in the woods, one in the field. His hair shone gold in the full sun. He stood barefoot in the crumbling grass. Same dungarees and white T-shirt Solitario had witnessed in the barn. But his hands were clean. His lips pristine. His skin unblemished, peppered only with freckles from working in his father's corn patch. Full of sadness, his blue eyes gazed at Solitario. And then, just like he had appeared, he was gone in the blink of an eye.

THREE

On the way out of town, Solitario rode back into the Mexican portion of Olvido, past the ruins of the Catholic cathedral where his wedding picture with Luz had been taken. He slowed Tormenta to such a measured pace that she snorted in disapproval, but still she relented and abided by his request. She had known Luz. She knew what Solitario was thinking and feeling. She even paused for a few moments when he was ready to press on, just to be sure he'd relived his memories sufficiently.

After they left Olvido, they reunited with the dry riverbed and rode over its veined surface beneath the growing shadows of the observant canyons. Halfway back to El Escondido, Solitario paused and dismounted in the shade of one of those towering rock outcroppings. There, where once water would have lapped at his feet, he chewed on a strip of jerky, then drained the last drops from his canteen, sharing them with Tormenta.

She whinnied in gratitude as the breeze flowing through the canyon brushed her black mane and cooled her sweaty hide.

While Solitario sat on a rock, staring south toward where Mexico had retreated, Tormenta heard the same whispered phrase that he did. It was the voice of that Tolbert boy at the edge of the woods. It was as if he had spoken to Solitario back when he was standing at the fence, but only now had the words reached his ears.

"Save my brother and sisters, please, sir," the Tolbert boy said.

Tormenta's ears prickled as she turned her head to the east, toward Olvido, toward where the boy remained. Then she flicked it back toward Solitario, wondering if he'd heard the boy too.

Of course, he had. She knew. He stared at his half-eaten jerky and dropped it onto the parched earth for the lizards to consume.

As he approached Tormenta again, he appeared disconsolate to her. She wished she could lower her body to make his ascent easier, but she couldn't, so she rustled between the cacti, snorted restlessly, and pointed her nose west, toward home. He stroked her neck and slipped his left boot into her stirrup, rising into the saddle.

When they reached El Escondido, the sun was setting behind the ranch house. He dismounted to open the gate beneath the sign forged in metal. After they passed through, he descended again and closed it behind them. Then they rode to the clearing, where he unsaddled her and led her to the trough, pumping fresh water into it from the well. It was cool and she drank it up thankfully.

The house was divided by a breezeway that ran from the front porch to the back one, which was adorned by a row of vacant wrought-iron birdcages. In the evenings, after he dunked a bucket of water over himself and changed into his cotton pajamas, he relaxed his tired frame into one of the two rocking chairs out back, watching the sun set over the distant desert horizon.

After she drank and ate her fill, Tormenta circled back and kept him company, resting beneath a cluster of mesquite trees not far from the house. She stood behind the tombstone both she and Solitario knew all too well. She had watched Solitario irrigate the harsh land before the grave with his tears.

As he sat there, he sipped his tequila and thought of things only he could remember, only he could conceive of, but Tormenta knew he was thinking of Luz.

Solitario sipped smoky liquor from a small glass as he squinted toward the amber sky. And when that sky turned turquoise and then purple, and pinpricks of light poked through its black, Tormenta faded into the darkness. It was then that from the gravestone a delicate figure draped in flowing white gauze stepped forth. Her raven tresses hung like vines over her shoulders and breasts. Her lips gleamed like rubies in the rising moonlight. Solitario's eyes met hers through the ink of night, and he smiled wistfully as she stood there gazing at him with love and longing.

FOUR

Caja Pinta was a rectangle of land inscribed on a map in Spain but found near the edge of the Gulf of Mexico. That box, that caja, straddled the Rio Grande and for the better part of two centuries belonged to the Cisneros clan, as assigned by the king of Spain for very particular reasons. The most notable of those reasons being the memorable deeds of a long-deceased ancestor in the battles between the Catholic monarchs and the Moorish khalif in Granada. Since the 1700s, Caja Pinta had been passed down to the family's eldest male heir from generation to generation.

Solitario had been born on Caja Pinta, his father's land and his slightly older twin brother's inheritance. In the river itself, he'd been cut from his dead mother's womb in the spring of 1850. He had known this as far back as he knew he had been alive. It was a story told over and over across those lands. When the river had become the border, his father's ranch had been divided, and not long thereafter Americans had seized the territory to the north. His father, Mauro Fernando Cisneros, had gone to fight for what was his, against his pregnant wife's wishes. When the gringos had ambushed and killed him, Solitario's mother, Soledad, had hurled herself into the waters and drowned. Solitario and his older twin, also named Mauro Fernando, had been rescued by a woman from a nearby ranch on the shoals of the river. Then, their unlikely savior had relinquished the crying infants to live with their distracted uncle, Juan Nepomuceno Cisneros, at his neighboring hacienda, Las Lomas.

There, Solitario had been reared in the shadow of his older twin, Mauro Fernando, who was destined to rule over the family land. While Solitario received the same thorough education in the languages of Spanish and English as his older brother and was fully trained as a charro, he was otherwise left to his own devices. While his uncle roped his brother into endless social obligations, Solitario freely roamed the lands, riding bareback on horses from childhood. His favorite trek spanned the Rio Grande's banks to the mouth of the river, where it emptied into the Gulf. There, he would visit his abuela, Minerva, his mother's mother. She was a strange woman, always robed in black, her hair a tangle, her home a collection of branches and twigs crowned by dried palm fronds, the windows mere holes cut open to let the sea breeze flow through the jacal. She cooked her food over driftwood, hung bushels of herbs from her thatched-roof ceiling, concocted potions and salves for the women of the surrounding ranches, and spun an eternity of tales for him that seemed as magical and incredible—yet as real—as the sea. Whereas his father's family had come from Spain with parchment scrolls signed by kings and their own delusions of grand destinies in the New World, she had hailed from a different stock, one of humble people persecuted for their beliefs and for their incantations and divinations. Now, she still clung to life like the sea oats sprouting resiliently from the silky dunes.

"Abuela," Solitario asked the wizened Minerva, "Why did my mother have to die?"

"Because she loved your father," Minerva answered.

"And why did my father have to die?"

"Because of his pride."

"And why do the people say that we are cursed, my brother and I?"

His abuela stared out through one of those crude holes she herself had cut out of the wall of her hut, her eyes following the waves as they rocked toward the seashore. And she didn't answer his question.

But it was true, as Solitario learned running wild across all those endless fields of wispy grass. The people that hailed from those lands all spoke of a curse that had befallen his family, one brought on by their own angry and spiteful kin, one that was yet to wield its might but was likely to hobble the dreams of the Cisneros men. They referred to the hex as "la maldición de Caja Pinta." They whispered that his mother, Soledad, haunted the dunes overlooking the river, waiting eternally for her husband to return from what was now America.

Once, when Solitario was twelve years old, in the plaza in the nearby border town of Nueva Frontera, an old woman had pointed her trembling finger at him as he licked his mango ice cream cone and forbade her granddaughter from ever speaking to him, not that he would have been interested. He was already sweet on a girl from the neighboring ranch. Gloria was her name. Her auburn hair tumbled to her waist and her honey eyes reflected the gold of the sun. And he spent countless hours riding across the fields with her, exploring and adventuring.

On one of those trips, they stumbled across a sand dune by the river where a lonesome woman stood facing north across the water, her long chestnut mane flowing in the breeze. Gloria had tried to speak to the woman, but she had not responded. It was almost as if she could not see the young girl.

Then, Solitario had climbed the dune and stood directly in front of her, waving his hand to block her view. For a moment, he caught her eye and she looked down at him, a faint look of recognition softening her lovely face.

"Hola. Who are you? What are you doing here on my family's land?" Solitario asked, grinning at Gloria and giggling. Was the woman crazy, lost, confused?

The lady, who was dressed in gossamer the color of the sand she stood upon, gazed down at him, tears glistening at the corners of her eyes. "I am waiting, m'hijo," she replied softly.

"Waiting for what?"

"For your father," she answered.

Taken aback, Solitario felt a shudder ripple through him as his eyes opened wide. He reached out to touch her, but his fingers felt nothing, passing right through her hand. A brief chill shot up his arm. Startled, he stumbled backward and slid to the foot of the dune. Gloria scrambled to help him get up. When they both turned to look at the crest of the hill, Soledad Cisneros was gone.

FIVE

Elias sat in the cramped kitchen of his adobe home overlooking the vestiges of the vanished Rio Grande. When he had first followed Solitario here, a decade and a half earlier, a cooling breeze had flowed through the kitchen window, the river babbling in the background. Tall green reeds sprung from the banks. Children laughed as they fished with their abuelos, perched on rocks like waterfowl. Now, nada. No water. No relief. No life. Only dry earth. Only heat. And death. He stared glumly out at the brittle grass that clung to the edges of the ravine.

Otila rustled in the corner, crouched over her metate, rolling the smooth, heavy stone over boiled kernels of corn to make the masa for the tortillas. He remembered how those moist morsels used to melt in his mouth. Now, every time she brought him another tortilla, it seemed to crumble, grinding like silt between his teeth.

When Otila's stew of dried beef and beans was ready, she set the cast-iron pot in the center of the table. As Elias sprinkled crushed chile colorado into it, the children filed in and sat at their places. Elena was twelve and Oscarito was nine. Elena was slender and wore her black hair in two long braids. Oscarito was short and pudgy, just like his father. They were good children, well-behaved, disciplined. After all, he had served as a sergeant in the Rurales. He had kept order among grown men fighting for their lives and their patria. The bare minimum he could accomplish now that his military and peacekeeping career had ended was to raise children in an orderly fashion. Otila was an excellent partner in the matter. She cooked and cleaned religiously. She taught the children how to read and write, which was uncommon in these parts. And in the afternoon, they went to a one-room schoolhouse across the riverbed to learn English. They had to; they were Americans now.

Meanwhile, Elias repaired carts and wagons and worked with the blacksmith to fit shoes and bits for the horses that pulled them. It was a simple trade that he had learned in the army. It had been handy then, but he never had imagined it would become his paltry livelihood. He had never looked past the excitement of adventuring at Solitario's side, riding with the Rurales, fighting the French invaders to restore Benito Juárez to the presidency, and later fighting bandidos and keeping law and order in Olvido back when it was booming and the river flowed right through it, like blood in a body's arteries. Life took unexpected twists and turns, he mused, just like the river had.

After they ate supper, spooning stew from the communal pot with small pieces of tortilla, the kids went outside to play.

"Come in as soon as it starts to get dark," Otila cautioned them.

In his mind, Elias heard the rest of her thoughts. She had been about to add something about what had happened to the sheriff's family and it not being safe outside in the dark. But she had thought twice about it. Sometimes, when your life was all toil and suffering, you wanted your children to experience a sliver of peace and joy while they could, before the realities of adulthood set in. She was kind that way.

When Elena and Oscarito ran outside and met up with their friends, Elias smiled faintly at her. Out of a cabinet near the old pipe stove, she produced a bottle of mescal and poured it into two small cups made of barro. At last, she sat. It seemed she never got to sit down until the meal was over. They both sighed as they raised their cups, toasted each other silently, and took their sips.

"¿Qué cuentas?" she asked.

"Nada nuevo."

"What are the people saying?" Otila pressed.

"You tell me," he replied. They both knew quite well that what really mattered was what the women of the village were whispering to each other.

"Everyone has el susto. Some cannot sleep because they are so frightened," she said, following his gaze out the window to the barren landscape, peering beyond the desiccated weeds to the faded clapboard houses of the gringos across the way. "They say the gringos are blaming us for what happened to el sheriff and his familia. They're worried that they'll come after us."

Elias nodded. It wouldn't be the first time. And it certainly wouldn't be the last.

"Some of the women say they've asked their husbands if this might be the time to leave, to go back to Mexico."

He understood this was her way of asking him the same question but without actually doing so. She was wise, his Otila.

"Well, we never left Mexico. It left us."

She nodded in agreement, pouring another round. "I worry about the children. Do they have a future here?"

Do they have a future anywhere, he asked himself. "I wish Solitario had taken the job. It would have been good money for both of us. We could have saved up and then maybe moved, but as it is, we have no money. We're stuck here, mi amor."

She savored the fiery golden fluid, letting it roll over her tongue, closing her eyes for a spell. "It's not so bad," she finally conceded.

They sat and drank quietly for a while. Then he reassured her, reaching out across the table and taking her hand. "Whatever happens, I'll protect you."

She nodded. "I know you will."

After another round, she asked him, "Do you blame him? For not accepting the offer?"

"No."

She did not seem surprised.

"He always made good decisions," Elias added.

"Except for that once."

He shook his head and stared out into the uncompromising darkness. "Yes. Except for that once."

SIX

As much as he wished to avoid any involvement or further human contact, Solitario could not expel the apparition of the sheriff's son from his head. He'd been keen to spirits since his childhood out on Caja Pinta, but he'd never witnessed a gringo one. He didn't know it was possible, but he now supposed that it had been mere stupidity or prejudice on his part. After all, despite the frequent violence of their actions toward the Indios and the Mexicanos, the Anglo people had souls too, didn't they? In his experience, spirits clung to places for a reason, manifested themselves because of something unfulfilled that kept them anchored to this plane of existence. That boy was trying to tell him something. Didn't he owe it to him, having seen the terrible way in which he and his parents had died, to listen to what he had to say? What if the boy had overheard something that might help rescue his little brother and sisters?

Solitario stood on his front porch sipping his coffee and squinting at the rising sun, orange like the yolk of a freshly laid egg from one of the hens in his coop. The only thing he could imagine might taste more bitter than the murky black brew in his tin cup was the mere idea of exiting El Escondido, of shedding the safety and consolation of her largely unseen presence. Luz. She only appeared at night. She never spoke. But still, he could not bear the thought of leaving her, of forgoing a glimpse of her even once at twilight, of missing her reaching out for him with her pale hands.

Tormenta whinnied by the open gate. It was almost like she was exhorting him to leave, to follow this one instinct as it reared against an even deeper one.

"I will be back tonight, Luz," he whispered into the arid air, his gut churning in rebellion as he set his cup down on the weathered table, pulled down the brim of his sombrero, and descended the steps to the dirt clearing.

The town was even quieter than it had been a couple days earlier. Riding past a somber row of burros loaded with firewood, Solitario passed into the Anglo part of Olvido without speaking to anyone. When he reached the Protestant church, he saw the Anglo preacher and his wife staring at him from the vegetable garden they kept out back. He wondered if they knew anything they might be keeping to themselves.

Once he arrived at the Tolbert fence line, right after the tangle of woods that separated it from the church's land, he slowed Tormenta and dismounted, leaping over the fence. He walked slowly along the edge of the uncleared area, poking through the juniper bushes, waiting for a flash of gold dashing through the mottled sunlight beneath the trees, but—this time—he saw nothing.

He looked back at Tormenta. She waited patiently at the fence, watching him with one slick almond eye, as horses did, flicking a fly off her flank with her flowing tail. She didn't paw at the ground impatiently as she had during their previous visit. Solitario stroked his mustache, removed his sombrero, and ran his hand through his wavy hair. It was getting long. He couldn't remember the last time he'd cut it. He'd been alone for so long. Soon it would reach his shoulders. He'd have to do something about it, he noted. After all, he'd been taught to always maintain his appearance. Even if he was an orphan. Even if he was the younger son with no inheritance. He had been indoctrinated as a caballero, a gentleman, a way of life he'd sworn to adhere to in honor of the father he'd never known.

He squinted into the woods, looking for a path inward through the thick vegetation. There were likely rattlers hiding there. He walked farther from the road, searching for an opening, the sound of the creek growing louder as he reached the back of the property. Finally, he discovered what might have once been a narrow path, now overgrown, and ducked between two mesquite trees, disappearing into the woods. Dry leaves crunched beneath his boots. It was cool in the shade, and the farther he pried through the shrubs, the darker it grew, the dappled sunlight giving way to continuous cover. He wasn't sure what he was looking for, but he pressed on, letting his instincts guide him.

Suddenly, he heard a branch snap behind him. He turned, crouching slightly, his hands in front of him for protection. Was it the boy? He peered into the shadows. Was it a possum? It smelled musty and damp, and all sorts of night critters would take up residence in this environment. He felt as if he were being watched but could not see by whom. His right hand shifted down to his gun. He unsnapped the holster, felt the reassuring ivory in his palm. He was ready. But no one came, nothing emerged from the murky woods.

Resuming his course, Solitario found the creek. It ran between the Tolbert ranch and somebody else's land, he surmised. It was common for neighbors to share sources of water out here. In the manner of the original Spanish settlers, they often built small ditches called acequías to route water from the creeks onto their properties to irrigate their crops. From the banks, he could make out the outline of a house in the distance, beyond knee-high reeds of grass and a row of desert willows. There were no fences here, and it crossed his mind that it would have been easy enough for someone to sneak onto the Tolbert's farm unseen from back here, avoiding the road altogether. He wondered if that had been the case.

The creek was only about ten feet wide and ran shallow this time of year, so much so that by the time it emptied into the old riverbed, it was just a muddy trickle. He followed it up to the corn patch, scrutinizing the ground as he went. Right before reaching the crops, he noted boot marks imprinted on the muddy banks. Kneeling down, he measured them mentally, counted how many different pairs he could identify. Three, four, maybe five. One with an *X* on its sole, just like in the barn, in the dirt, next to the boy's body. Johnny was his name, he recalled, the sheriff's eldest. So they had crossed back here. He rose and squinted at the distant house. He'd have to figure out who lived there. Not that he could assume they were guilty, but maybe they'd seen or heard something that night. Maybe their dogs had barked and they'd looked out the window.

The corn patch was fenced by wooden posts connected by barbed wire. He opened a flimsy gate, gliding through the rows of corn. He rubbed the green leaves between his fingertips. Dried blood was smeared across one of the stalks. At the end of the corral closest to the barn, there was another gate. There, a scrap of pink-and-white checked fabric fluttered in the breeze, pinned to one of the barbs. They'd come in through here and they'd left the same way, taking the missing children with them.

Back at the barn, he peered into the darkness. The bodies had been removed since his last visit. Traces of blood remained on the straw. The two ropes still hung lifeless from the rafters. He sat on a bail of hay, waiting—to no avail—for the boy to appear. Shivering despite the stifling heat, he glanced over his shoulder. He sensed an uneasy presence, not the boy. The boy had seemed placid and resigned. This was a residue of whatever horrors had transpired in this place. Shaking his head, he walked to the door and stood outside beneath a tall live oak. Up in the tree, he could make out the shape of an owl.

Where are you, boy? Last time you seemed so eager to make yourself seen and heard.

Sometimes it was like that. A soul made a brief appearance before forever vanishing from this world never to be seen again. Maybe they were confused, searching for their bodies or their loved ones, lingering momentarily around their homes. But other times, they kept coming back, driven by a sense of purpose. The boy had indeed harbored motivation powerful enough. Surely, he would muster a return, Solitario reassured himself. Perhaps it was merely a matter of time. Unfortunately, time was probably something that Johnny's siblings had in short supply.

In the afternoon, Solitario walked out to the road and regrouped with Tormenta. The sentries that had been posted at the front gate of the Tolbert's farm were nowhere in sight. And he hoped he might have a chance to steal back to his ranch without having to exchange words with anyone. Talking to the dead was tolerable but dealing with the living was always more laborious for him.

He had almost made it out of Olvido when he heard Elias' familiar voice hailing him from behind. Turning, he saw the retired sergeant approaching, his sombrero in hand.

"Jefe, I heard you were in town. Twice in the same week! Es un milagro," Elias smiled, catching his breath as he approached.

Tormenta turned around of her own volition as Solitario shook his head in barely concealed dismay. *So close.* He was itching to return to his hideaway, to gaze upon Luz beneath the trees behind the ranch house, to feel her proximity, if nothing else.

"Ahora sí. You have to accept my invitation, Jefe. Come to my house and have supper with us."

As much as he didn't want to do so, Solitario pondered the possibility as a way to facilitate staying in town overnight and trying one last time to find Johnny.

"Ándale, you can spend the night. I've got a hammock out back beneath two mesquites," Elias added, practically reading his old chief's mind.

Solitario assented with a shrug of his shoulders, following Elias to his pink-hued stucco casita. As he watered Tormenta out back by the trees, Solitario apologized to Luz for not returning home as he'd promised. Meanwhile, Elias announced to his family that his legendary jefe was honoring them with a visit. Otila and Elena began cooking, and Oscarito followed Solitario about like a miniature shadow. When Otila presented her pollo en mole, Solitario ate heartily, praising her cooking.

"Is it true you saved my father's life during the war against the French?" Oscarito asked wide-eyed.

Solitario chewed quietly, finally replying, "I suppose we both saved each other's lives many times."

The children's eyebrows arced in awe, appraising their father in a new light.

"I want to be a soldier like my father and you when I grow up," Oscarito proclaimed.

Solitario and Elias exchanged knowing glances.

"War is not fun," Solitario summed up. "But, if your dream is to be a soldier, you'll have to fight as an Americano. This is your home."

Oscarito frowned. "But they stole all this land from Mexico. If they hadn't, it wouldn't matter that the river changed course."

The adults nodded, keeping their eyes down on their plates.

Even though the wars Oscarito referred to had been waged before his birth, Solitario—along with most Mexicans—still struggled to accept the magnitude of the loss. But for the kids, it was a side note easily brushed aside as they went back to peppering Solitario with questions about what their father had been like back in the days of fighting the French imperialists in defense of Mexico.

Solitario kept his answers as short and as vague as possible, preferring not to plumb the depths of those memories, but he couldn't help but sprinkle in an elbow jab at Elias. "Your father was a good fighter in a gun battle, but he was easier for the enemies to miss back then . . ." He glanced at his sergeant's belly.

They all laughed.

"There's no denying it." Elias grinned, stuffing another corn tortilla into his mouth. "Your mamá's cooking is just that much better than anything I ever ate before I met her."

When the children finished eating, they cleared the table and asked if they could go outside and brush Tormenta's mane. Solitario smiled and nodded his approval.

As the grown-ups sipped their mescal, Solitario watched through the window while Elena and Oscarito pampered his horse. Dusk had fallen, and it was growing dark quickly.

As Otila washed the dishes in a metal tub, Elias asked, "I suppose you're going back to the Tolbert farm tonight?"

Solitario nodded.

"I figured you didn't take me up on my offer just to socialize." Elias smiled. "Always working, even when you're not officially on the job."

Solitario shrugged, sipping the golden fluid.

"You saw something out there, didn't you?" Elias probed.

Solitario finally met his eyes, "Sí."

Elias cocked an eyebrow. "You should take the sheriff job. Right now, the Anglos are blaming the Mexicanos for what happened, but I don't think it was one of us."

Solitario shook his head. "Has there been a ransom note yet?"

"No note. Nada. What did you see?"

"I'll tell you if it comes to something," Solitario answered.

———————

At the edge of the woods between the Tolbert farm and the church, Solitario sat on a smooth boulder with his elbows perched on his knees and his chin resting in his hands, listening, waiting. The moon was waning and its light was dim. Tormenta stood by the fence. He could see her outline against the night sky. He watched her ears. If they perked up, he'd know either she sensed something or someone was approaching.

The rock was hard, and the wait was long. The rhythm of the cicadas lulled Solitario, and he began to doze off, catching himself a couple of times to stop from slipping off his seat onto the ground. Rubbing his eyes, he whispered into the murky maelstrom of the trees and shrubs, "Johnny? Can you hear me? I saw you the other day. I'm here to listen. I want to help. Maybe you know something that could save your brother and sisters."

He stopped and listened intently, his eyes boring into the thicket of trees, his body leaning forward into the forest.

Then, suddenly, the hair on the back of his neck prickled to attention like soldiers did when a commanding officer walked into a room. Tormenta snorted. He turned toward her, and there was Johnny, standing in the field between them, his skin like alabaster glowing in the silver light of the moon.

"Johnny," Solitario whispered. "Talk to me."

Johnny's mouth began to move, but Solitario didn't hear the words until after it stopped, as if there were a strange delay, a long distance between them over which the sound had to travel to reach his ears. Johnny said, "Please, sir, help my brother and sisters."

"I am Solitario. What are their names?" he answered gently.

"Frankie and Abigail and Beatrice."

"Did you see who took them?"

"It was dark, and I didn't know the men. Except for one, he looked familiar, but I don't know his name."

"I know you can help me find them," Solitario said, urgency seeping into his voice. Spirits never stayed for long. He wondered if it took too much energy or if time moved differently for them and a prolonged conversation could not hold their attention span for long. "Tell me what you know."

"I saw my own body lying there in the barn. And my mother and father . . . It was like a horrible nightmare, but I understood I would never wake up." He paused. "I followed the men. I was floating over them. I couldn't hear what they said but I saw them hike into the mountains south of the town. They put Frankie in a cave. They holed him up in there. They took my sisters with them, but I stayed and walked through the stone. I saw Frankie curled up in a ball on the ground. He was crying like a baby, but I told him he had to grow up and be strong and get out of there so he can help our sisters."

"Good," Solitario said. "You lent him courage." He paused to think, rubbing his temples. "Johnny, did you hear the men say anything about where they were going next or their plans? Were they going to ask for money in exchange for your brother and sisters?"

Johnny shook his head.

"Did you see anything inside the cave or in the mountains nearby, anything strange or peculiar that might help me find Frankie?"

In his mind, Solitario received an image from Johnny. It was a faded drawing on a cave wall. It looked like a long white snake surrounded by tiny masked dancers. "That's good, Johnny. You can rest now. I'll go looking for him."

Johnny stared at Solitario. He looked weary. His mouth moved again. "I won't rest until I know they're safe. Promise you'll come back and tell me. I don't know why, but this is the only place I can wake up in now and I can't seem to leave again."

The boy was stuck in a familiar place. He couldn't find his way back to that cave in the mountains. Or could he? "Have you tried going back to your brother?"

"Yes. It's useless. I wish I could help him and my sisters, but I can't do a thing but talk to you."

"I'm sorry . . ."

"Promise you'll come back and tell me when you find them. I can't rest until I know they're safe. After my dad . . . died, that became my job. Now it's Frankie's. But still, I can't rest. I'm tired. I want to sleep. But I keep waking up here, fretting and worrying."

"I promise."

Solitario blinked and when he reopened his eyes, the boy was gone.

SEVEN

Growing up on Caja Pinta, Solitario wasn't sure if seeing the dead and being able to talk to them was a blessing or part of the curse that supposedly afflicted his family.

After discovering his mother's ghost on the dune overlooking the Rio Grande, he asked his grandmother to tell him about her.

"She was a passionate woman," Minerva recalled as she walked with Solitario along the beach near her hut, her wild gray mane whipping in the Gulf winds. "Her heart was bigger than her head."

"What do you mean by that?"

"If she'd followed her head, she'd still be alive. She couldn't bear the thought of living without your father. She was so in love with him that she preferred to drown than carry on without him."

"Why was it my father's pride that caused their deaths?"

"Because she begged him not to go fight for his land once the Rio Grande became the border, but he was vain and arrogant and he thought he was bigger and stronger and more powerful than he truly was. You must never overestimate your abilities. If you do, it will get you killed. That's what happened to your father."

"So he was cursed already? When did this maldición de Caja Pinta begin?"

"You could say in a way he was already cursed by his character, as we all are," Minerva replied, stooping to gather some shells scattered around their bare feet on the wet sand. "But the actual maldición people speak of came after his death, when I cursed all the men that would follow in the Cisneros clan. I wove it in anger and grief over losing your mother. Now I regret it—mostly because of you—but I cannot undo it."

"So I will suffer because of it?"

"You already have. You just don't know it."

"How?"

"Well, you can see how your brother is favored as the eldest, and this has come between you. You see your mother and you talk to her, but she only repeats the same things over and over. You wish she could hold you in her arms, but she cannot. It is harder to experience loss when that loss is visible to you, and it never fully fades away. And, maybe worst of all for me, you will live knowing your own grandmother put a hex on you. And someday this, too, will drive us apart. You see, la maldición means that all of the male descendants of Mauro Fernando Cisneros will be cursed to lose what they love most."

"But you're sorry?"

"Yes."

Solitario mulled the dilemma. "And how is my brother cursed? He will inherit the hacienda and the lands, and everybody loves him."

"Oh, you'll see. Already, one can see it in him. The arrogance of his father. The headstrong impulsiveness of his mother, magnified by the curse. He will break hearts and squander his fortune and drink himself into an early grave. And all those people who love him now will grow to despise him and blame him for all their woes."

"He's your grandson, but you don't sound like you like him very much."

She smiled. "He reminds me too much of the past."

"And me?"

"You remind me of the future."

Back at her jacal, she perforated the corners of the shells she had collected with a needle and strung them like beads on a thin strip of leather, fashioning a necklace. She then sprinkled it with holy water and spoke over it in a language that sounded familiar to Solitario, although he did not comprehend a word of it. He watched intently, feeling an invisible buzz of energy vibrating between his grandmother, the necklace, and himself. When she finished, she raised the necklace off the table with both hands and offered it to him.

"It will protect you, m'ijo."

"Against the maldición?"

"No. Against other things. Against the maldición, I can do nothing but work with the years I have left to make seeds that hopefully someone, someday, can sow and reap to eventually be fruitful in breaking the curse."

"Maybe, someday that will be me. Maybe, I'll break the maldición," Solitario said.

She smiled sadly at him as if she knew better. "Wear the necklace," she implored, rummaging through a set of drawers. "And cover it with this"—she handed him a bright yellow bandanna—"so nobody will see it and try to steal it from you."

Solitario wore his necklace, hidden behind the yellow bandanna, on the day he understood that the maldición was real. He and Gloria were nearly seventeen years old. Instead of embarking on imaginary adventures across the windswept grasslands of the ranches along the river, they often spent languorous afternoons hidden in plain sight, deep within the dense thickets of mesquite trees that dotted the fields. There, Solitario would unroll a blanket he carried attached to his saddle, and they would while hours away slowly disrobing each other, savoring the taste of each other's salty skin, exploring the sensations of their lips and bodies interlocking in a heated embrace. As Solitario hovered over Gloria, his rhythmic motion caused the necklace to swing back and forth, the shells rustling musically against each other. As she moaned in ecstasy, Gloria cupped her hands around his cheeks, gasping, "Te quiero tanto."

Solitario told her he loved her too, more than he could put into words. "Marry me," he whispered into her ear.

"Claro," she answered. "We'll always be together."

That night as they rode inland from the sea, following the southern bank of the river, a torrential storm swept across Caja Pinta from the west, bringing with it a surge of water that caused the Rio Grande to flood. They rode as fast as they could, away from the powerful currents, but their horses could not find purchase in the mud and they were all carried, tumbling head over heel and hoof toward the Gulf. In flashes, Solitario saw Gloria reaching out for him desperately, her curls clinging to her cheeks. Her horse's hooves rising from the tumultuous waters toward the angry heavens. The neighing horse's head appearing for a moment, its eye wide with terror. Solitario was unsure which way was up or down. He stretched with all his might toward where he'd last seen Gloria, diving in search of her, but his head was dealt a powerful blow by an uprooted tree trunk rushing toward the mouth of the river. When he awoke, coughing up salt water and seaweed on the beach, Gloria was nowhere to be found. He ran to his grandmother's hut and together they kept vigil until her body washed ashore the next day.

Bereaved, he wept in Minerva's arms, bathing her in tears. Together, they carried Gloria's body to her parents' house. That night, his grandmother told him he should run away as far as he could from Caja Pinta. "The maldición is too strong here. Perhaps if you distance yourself from its source, you will have a chance at life."

"But you're all I have, Abuela," he mourned.

He was all she had too. He knew it. But his grandmother insisted. "I've lived my life and caused too much pain. You must live yours and try to ease the suffering, others' and your own. Away from here. I want you to stay, but I also want you to survive."

The next morning, he left the ranch with his horse and a small knapsack. He rode into Nueva Frontera and joined the Rurales, which were fighting in the resistance against Maximilian's French invaders. He'd never returned home, but he'd heard that his mother Soledad still gazed forlornly toward America from her desolate dune. And his grandmother Minerva was still out there, working her magic while ruing the curse she'd created.

EIGHT

Solitario stood on Onawa's doorstep, his fingers rubbing a delicate neck-lace strung with seashells that peeked out from beneath the open collar of his black shirt.

She smiled instinctively upon seeing him, yearning to fling her arms around him and welcome him into her small adobe home at the north-western edge of the village. But she resisted the urge, knowing he was a man who kept his distance from others.

"Hola," she said, her full lips curving upward, her copper skin glow-ing. "What a surprise!"

Solitario fidgeted with his seashells as he looked at her. He had always appeared handsome to her, rough yet gentle, peaceful yet brooding, simple but complicated. On the surface he appeared mysterious and inaccessible, but—from the first time she'd seen him—she had discovered a knack for intuiting his thoughts. That day, eight years ago, when she'd stumbled across him sitting on a boulder by the river with a gun in his hands, his eyes closed in contemplation, she had known what was on his mind. Just like she knew now what he was thinking, except this time his thoughts pleased her. He was marveling at how quickly she'd developed into a woman. She'd been but a fifteen-year-old—in the midst of her Rite of Passage ceremony—when she had saved his life. Now her body was not only lithe and graceful like the pronghorn antelope that streaked across the desert, but also curved and soft. Her hair was straight and smooth as the surface of a lake and black and thick as a raven's feathers, hanging down to her waist. He looked at her for brief spells and then turned away like he was afraid of her. But his fear didn't come from her magic, or the fact she was Apache like her father before her, or even the nagging truth that she was Mexican like her mother, may she rest in peace, but rather from her very womanhood.

"Hola, Onawa," Solitario finally uttered, as if each word were a drop of blood wrung from his body.

"Are you here to see my father?"

"You, actually," he replied.

Caught off guard, she felt her cheeks flush. "Well, come in and say hello to him first."

He removed his black sombrero as she led him into the shadowy house. It was remarkably cool given the infernal heat outside. In a small room at the back of the structure sat her father. He was as ancient as time, his white ponytail reaching the floor as he sat on a brightly woven cushion.

Solitario nodded respectfully to the elder. "Buenos días, Aguila Brava."

"It has been some time, amigo." The elder motioned for Solitario to sit on one of the other cushions on the floor.

Onawa boiled water in a kettle over the hearth. From a small cloth sack, she shook out broken stems of ephedra, stirring them in. When she brought the tea to the men, they sat in silence sipping it.

"So what brings you out of the safety of your home?" Onawa's father finally inquired.

"It is this matter of Sheriff Tolbert's family."

Onawa stood in the doorway, listening intently, as she always did while the men conversed. She'd grown up spying on her father and the other tribe elders, back when her father had been a revered chief, before their tribe had been defeated and dispersed by the army, its scattered remnants left to age and languish in a quasi-limbo of weakened irrelevance at the edges of towns like Olvido that didn't know if they were American or Mexican.

"That is an evil business," Aguila Brava said. "Nothing good can come of it."

Solitario silently agreed, nodding his head.

"Are you investigating? Have you accepted the white men's offer?" the elder asked.

"You've heard?" Solitario's expression betrayed surprise.

Onawa chuckled, causing them both to whip their heads in her direction. She had been so quiet they'd probably forgotten she was still there.

"He seems to know everything before he even hears it," Onawa said.

"Surviving as many years as I have is costly," her father explained, "but it also yields certain rewards. When you raise a child, you can anticipate their next move. When you lead a tribe, you can sense their fears and wishes. When you live among the white men, you can likewise guess what they'll do next."

Solitario stroked his mustache thoughtfully. "I'm not sure if I . . ."

"Trust them?" Aguila Brava finished his thought.

"Never!" Onawa scoffed.

Both men looked at her. She knew they thought she was being impudent, but she was too excited by Solitario's rare appearance to sit silently in the kitchen or to continue with her chores outside.

"As you see, Onawa has become outspoken. She has a strong spirit, like her mother."

"Sí," Solitario said. "She is also correct."

Onawa smiled at him, an overture he resisted mirroring.

"My daughter believes that the white men offering you the sheriff's vacated post smells like a trap," Aguila Brava concluded. "I must say, I concur with her instincts."

"The Anglo townsfolk are already blaming the Mexicans for what happened to Sheriff Tolbert," Onawa sighed. "If you accept their offer, it will be a no-win situation for you. If you arrest a Mexican, your people will think you've sold out to the white man. And if you apprehend an Anglo, the white people will turn on you and claim you were unfair, that you were biased and protected your own kind."

Aguila Brava cocked an eyebrow, beaming proudly.

"You've taught her well." Solitario at last smiled.

"Sit with us, child." Onawa's father patted the cushion next to him.

Giddily, she joined them. She wore a buckskin dress, and as she crossed her legs on the floor, she sensed Solitario's gaze. When she sought out his eyes, however, they were trained respectfully on her father's weather-beaten face.

"Tell us why you are here, Spirit Talker." Aguila Brava spoke in a hushed tone.

Solitario at last met Onawa's eager eyes, "Onawa, do you still . . . see things . . . things that others do not?"

"Yes."

"She has only grown stronger, clearer in her visions," her father confessed.

"I do not wish to accept the sheriff position, not only for the reasons you have so accurately described but also for my own personal . . . misgivings. However, there is a young boy and two young girls missing, the Tolbert children. I have spoken to the brother who died at the farm. He told me that his younger brother is in a cave, in the mountains south of Olvido. I was thinking maybe you could help me find him. And, who knows, maybe he will have a clue about where his sisters were taken."

"It would take weeks to search every cave in the mountains," Onawa said. "I'm not sure my vision would be of much help."

Her father raised his hand. "Wait, child, there is more."

"Sí, there is more," Solitario said. "The boy showed me a picture on a wall in the cave where his brother is trapped. It looked old like it was perhaps painted by your ancestors."

"What was it?" Onawa asked.

"A white serpent surrounded by masked dancers," Solitario explained.

Onawa looked expectantly at her father. He nodded at her, giving her permission to offer her help.

"The snake is an omen. I don't think you'll need my vision to find the cave," Onawa said, "but I'll gladly help you look for it."

"There could be at least three, maybe four, caves with that kind of glyph on the wall," Aguila Brava spoke. "It may take a couple of days for you to visit them all."

"I'm not sure the boy has that much time," Solitario said. "Maybe you could use your vision to help us pick the right one."

Onawa smiled at him, then glanced at her father, who appeared perturbed, the lines carved into his forehead deeply furrowed.

"I would join you," Aguila Brava said somberly, "but my knees will not carry me that far anymore."

"Otherwise, he'd probably be fighting alongside Geronimo right now." Onawa's eyes glimmered with admiration and encouragement for her father.

"I will take good care of your daughter," Solitario assured him, glancing at her with a look she read as trepidation in his eyes.

Onawa relished the opportunity to leave the house, to ride south into the mountains next to Solitario, this wounded soul she longed to soothe.

"Do not worry, father. We will find the boy and return as quickly as possible. Once we are up in the mountains, I will divine in which cave he is hidden."

She had wished to put both their fears to rest, but she realized she had failed miserably. Solitario stared at her as if she were a white serpent herself, coiled and poised for the attack. And her father harbored clouds of doubt in his misty eyes. He had given his consent, but she knew he was more worried for her than he was for the boy.

Onawa spied on Solitario through the small window in the front room of her father's house. He was busy packing provisions into the leather saddlebags on Tormenta's back. Her father had insisted they take enough cured meat and water to ensure they would not go hungry or thirsty during their search. Her horse, a golden palomino named Invierno, stood next to Tormenta.

They were a strange pair, she thought. Tormenta was the mare, but she was tall, muscular, and powerful. Invierno was a stallion but he was shorter and lighter, probably faster and more nimble too. As Solitario patted the horses, she recalled their first encounter.

When she cleared the reeds and saw him hunched on the boulder by the river, she balked. Was he a bandido? Might he harm her? She'd been instructed all her life to steer clear of any man not from her tribe.

He seemed so immersed in his own thoughts that she thought perhaps she could retreat unnoticed. She was about to slip back into the vegetation unseen when she sensed that he was not a danger to her but rather to himself. He was dressed all in black. His face drooped with dismay. His eyes stared at the revolver cradled in his hands as if he were pleading for mercy.

Her instinct was not to run but to help. Still, she hesitated. She wore a white buckskin ceremonial dress, which draped down to a pair of white moccasins, and she worried about getting dirty on the muddy banks. She wasn't supposed to be here anyway, but the Rite of Passage ceremony lasted four days, and halfway through she was already exhausted from the endless rituals and dances and intense attention. It was a miracle she'd managed to slip away. If she returned disheveled and muddied, the elders would be incensed at her disrespect.

Still, she felt drawn to him. The fact that he was Mexican stoked her curiosity. After all, her mother had been Mexican, too. She took a tentative step toward him, praying to her mother's spirit for protection.

He looked up slowly, meeting her eyes with a pained expression.

Without a word, she glided gracefully to him, her hands outstretched as if his gun were an offering she had long been expecting, just another symbolic gift on her route to becoming a woman.

"You have always been drawn to him." Aguila Brava interrupted her dazed reverie at the window.

Embarrassed to be caught staring at Solitario, her cheeks felt hot to the touch as she covered them with her hands.

Aguila Brava gazed through the window, watching as Solitario whispered to his horse. "Do not be ashamed of your instincts," he said. "Although it is wise to be aware of them."

Onawa joined her father in looking at Solitario. She could feel a yearning deep inside her body. Were her instincts purely physical? And, if so, would that be wrong or simply natural? Had she and her father still lived in the tribe, perhaps her marriage would have been arranged. Or if her mother were still alive, she might have borne a strong opinion, served as a matchmaker. Instead, Onawa found herself somewhat unmoored, on the fringes of society, unsure how or when or even if she might find a suitable companion. Was she destined to be a lonely spinster caring eternally for her aging father? That which she most wished to see—her own future—remained a mystery to her.

"Just remember, Onawa," her father added, "to always look beneath the surface, let what lies within guide you."

"You mean on this journey?" Onawa asked. She would rather her father be concerned about her safety on her first trip without his supervision than her keen interest in her travel companion.

"I mean in all respects, even when it comes to men."

"You mean Solitario?" It would be the first time since the day she saved his life that they would be completely alone and unchaperoned together.

Aguila Brava nodded. "He is a handsome man. He is young still. And if he accepts the sheriff's badge, it will shine on his chest. But what is more important is whether he can shine inside. Or whether his darkness will consume him?"

"But he is your friend . . ." She was confused by his seemingly contradictory advice.

"Yes, he has been, but every relationship is its own world."

Outside, Solitario brushed past the window frame and knocked lightly on the door.

"Venture into this world with caution," Aguila Brava concluded, his gaunt hand reaching for the doorknob.

As she followed him outside, Onawa felt disconcerted. Did her father not trust her? Was he afraid she would dishonor him, or herself? And might all the worry be for nothing? After all, Solitario seemed as afraid of her as she was intrigued by him.

Solitario seemed oblivious to her troubles as they bid Onawa's father goodbye and mounted their horses, heading south through Olvido toward the mountains.

Before crossing the dry riverbed, they passed Mr. Stillman on the town's main road.

"Señor Cisneros," Stillman nodded from his horse.

"Señor Stillman," Solitario replied.

The mayor acted as if Onawa were invisible to him. He was the kind of white man that she had grown to despise. Just the sight of him stirred an anger inside of her that quickly dispelled her previous concerns.

"Have you thought more about our offer?" Stillman asked Solitario.

"My position has not changed," Solitario answered.

"Where are you headed?"

"To search for the missing Tolbert boy."

Mr. Stillman seemed taken aback. "But I thought you were not interested."

"My friend and I will look for him, but it ends there."

"I see." Mr. Stillman maneuvered his horse closer to Tormenta, lowering his voice so that no passersby could overhear him. "The townspeople are getting restless. There's a great deal of finger-pointing going on. Boggs and I are worried that an armed posse could be formed, and that our Mexican neighbors could be in danger. We could use someone like you in charge."

Solitario glanced sideways at Onawa and then back at Stillman. "I might only make matters worse, Mr. Stillman. Have you been searching for another lawman?"

"No takers so far."

"Well, no amount of lawmen will bring back the dead," Solitario said. "For now, we will focus on the living."

"You think the boy and his sisters are alive?" Stillman asked. "Where would you even begin searching?"

"I don't know if they're alive," Solitario answered, evading the second question.

Stillman eyed Onawa suspiciously, but she did not elaborate on Solitario's response, pretending instead to be distracted by a cluster of children passing by on foot. She knew that the mayor was wondering whether there was any truth to the rumors about her visions. She was not about to volunteer any hints as to the true nature of her abilities. The less they knew, the more they feared.

"Well, keep me informed," Stillman answered. "Surely, if you found the Tolbert kids, there would be a collective sigh of relief across town. Do you want us to send some men with you to help? I could get the Dobbs twins to join you."

"We travel alone," Solitario said. "It's simpler that way."

Onawa relished his defiance, grinning slyly as they left the dumbfounded mayor in a cloud of dust.

NINE

Frankie was cold and he was hungry. The cave was dark. Only a tiny bit of light peeked through around the edges of the giant rock blocking the entrance. He sat huddled in the farthest recesses of the cavern in a tiny smooth crevice. He shivered, grimacing in pain as his belly grumbled. He wondered where his sisters were now. They had always seemed like such a nuisance, but now he would give anything to be with them again. And where was Johnny?

Johnny's spirit had appeared to him in the cave, looking sad and distant. He had kept him company and they had talked. His older brother's presence had frightened him at first, but then it had given him strength. Where had he gone? Would he ever see him again?

He was so thirsty too. At first he had yelled as loud as he could at the entrance to the cave, hoping somebody would hear him and rescue him, but eventually, he had grown exhausted and could scream no longer. His throat was raspy and ached.

In a dark corner of his stone prison, something rustled. Every muscle in Frankie's being tightened with fear. Was it an animal? He couldn't see a thing, but he heard a repetitive scratching against the rock, a rustling of feathers, a low chittering sound that sent electric shocks up his spine. Closing his eyes, he prayed for Johnny to come back, for God to protect him, for the sound to go away. Then, as suddenly as it had begun, it stopped. He exhaled in relief, but his heart was racing in his chest. What had it been? Where had it gone? And what if it returned?

TEN

South of Olvido, the plateau extended to the distant foothills of the Chisos Mountains. They rode silently for the rest of the day across the scalding sands, heat rippling upward, a hypnotic, undulating tapestry of creosote and agave dotting the Chihuahuan Desert as far as the eye could see.

When the sun was low in the sky, they stopped to rest. It was pointless to go on. Soon it would grow dark. Solitario built a campfire while Onawa watered the horses. When they were both finished, they sat next to each other on sarapes and watched the flames dance.

He remembered watching her perform on the last day of her sacred ritual when he had been invited to attend as an honored guest. The ceremony had symbolized her journey into adulthood, but she was still an innocent girl. Her kindness and hospitality toward him had been rooted in sheer goodness and a desire to save him from his inner demons. He had never thought of himself as someone needing help, but that was indeed what he had become at that point in his life. And he owed his ongoing existence, for whatever it was worth, to her, Onawa, the seer, and to her father, Aguila Brava, the brave eagle.

She smiled in his direction before biting into a piece of jerky and chewing it in as small bites as she could.

He extracted a silver flask from his leather pouch and offered her a sip of mescal. She took a cautious draft and returned the container to him, squinting into the fire as the fluid scorched her throat.

They sat silently as the sun painted the sky in broad strokes of garnet and amethyst. After the sun ducked beyond the horizon and the sky settled into an ever-deepening blue, Solitario retrieved his guitar from a large leather sack that had hung on Tormenta earlier. Tormenta sniffed in approval as she watched him tune it during his slow saunter back to the campfire. Onawa peeked sideways at him, struggling to conceal her pleasure.

He picked at the strings and twisted the keys on the guitar's neck, tuning the instrument as if it were a singer clearing his throat. The tarnished silver buckles along the sides of his black pants regained their luster in the light of the fire. And then, slowly, he began to strum, staring into the fire as sparks danced in the darkening night. His eyes fluttered shut. He could sense that she yearned to hear him sing, but he remained silent. The guitar strings slipped through his fingers with a delicate power, and she was lulled into a drowsy state, leaning toward him, her head coming to rest gently on his shoulder.

When he stopped playing, he kept the guitar in his lap and looked down at her, whispering, "Why did you come?"

After a long pause, she whispered back, "To save the boy."

When Solitario roused from his slumber, he looked across the smoldering campfire smoke and saw her sitting cross-legged on her blankets facing the eastern horizon, which was splintering like shattered glass in an array of colors signaling the new day. He could tell she was divining. She stared not at the horizon but down at a clay bowl she had carried in her satchel. He knew the bowl was filled with water, and in its reflections, she hoped to see where the boy was hidden. He measured his breathing and strained to stay as immobile as he could in order to avoid disrupting her concentration. He stared at her long black hair, draped down her back smoothly like a sheet hanging on a wire. At last, when she was done, her face tilted up toward the cornflower sky. And he slid out of his sarape gratefully, ready to face the day.

They stood at the base of the mountain range, piñon and juniper pines spreading out and rising before them in every direction. Facing a choice, he asked her the question that had led him to bring her here against all of his hesitations, trepidations, and better judgments. "Which way should we go?"

She turned east and stared toward that blazing horizon whence Solitario himself hailed. Across the mountains, the Rio Grande flowed in that direction, draining into the Gulf where Solitario had been born and run as a child. He felt the magnetic pull toward home, toward everything he had run away from so many years ago, and he yearned for her to say that the boy was in that direction. He wished he could ride to that cave and then keep riding and never turn back, but he knew that could never be. And then she turned west, raising her right index finger toward the opposite horizon. "That way," she said.

Solitario nodded in a heartfelt mixture of relief and disappointment, pointing Tormenta in the prescribed direction and leading the way upward into the mountains as the sun arced overhead and the temperature rose.

Halfway through the day, as they wound into the mountains, they stopped at a creek for the horses to drink. Sitting on two rocks opposite each other, they chewed on strips of jerky.

Onawa asked him, "Why are you doing all of this? It is not like you to leave your place, your rancho."

"I don't know," he answered honestly. "I feel obligated."

She nodded. "Obligation is important."

"Sí."

"Es bueno."

He looked up at her, a chunk of salty dried meat in his hand. Sometimes he forgot she spoke Spanish as fluently as he. She smiled at him, enjoying his gaze.

"What are you thinking?" she asked.

Pondering her question, he answered slowly, "You have many talents."

"We will see," she replied.

"I am confident," he said.

"Then why have you not come to see me sooner?"

He stopped chewing and shifted his line of sight to the creek and the horses drinking, tails swishing, the rippling water reflecting dazzling light. He wasn't sure he knew how to answer her question without offending her. Sometimes people did things for you and then expected or desired something in return. And when Luz had died, she had taken everything he had with her. He had nothing left to give. But how could he say that to her? He glanced back at her, perched gracefully on her rock, her long smooth legs propping her up. She was young. She was full of promise. She deserved someone who wasn't broken, someone unlike him. But it was hard to convince people that what they most desired was not in their best interests.

"We should keep riding," Solitario said. "The boy is suffering."

Her eyes bore into his as she dropped the last piece of jerky in her hand. "Yes, there is much suffering in the world."

"This is the way," she exclaimed as their horses cleared a stand of piñon trees halfway up one of the mountains. The air was growing cooler and drier, and their water was running low.

"Are you sure?" he asked, taking a sip from his canteen.

She hesitated and looked the other way. "Do you doubt me?"

"No."

She smirked and huffed, then squeezed her ankles against Invierno's flanks, spurring him upward, rocks sliding beneath hooves as Solitario followed on Tormenta.

Moments later they stopped at a pile of boulders along the side of the mountain.

"The cave should be here," Onawa stated, staring at the rocks.

"It is," Solitario replied. "It's been sealed off."

Descending from their horses, they approached the obstructed cave entrance.

Peering between the cracks, Solitario called out, "Frankie! Can you hear me? Frankie? We're here to help you."

Nothing but a sharp echo came back to them.

"Can you see anything in there?" Onawa asked, crouching down to peer through another opening.

"It's too dark."

One by one, they worked together to remove the rocks, starting from the top and working their way down. Once they had cleared a large enough hole, Solitario climbed through, and Onawa passed him a torch.

Solitario whispered, "There is something on the wall."

"What is it?" she urged, impatiently.

"The white serpent."

Onawa followed him inside, where they searched the cavern for the boy, but he was nowhere to be found.

Crestfallen, Onawa apologized. "I was wrong. It cost us the day coming up here. The poor child."

Solitario strained his eyes to discern the farthest reaches of the cave as it narrowed and the ceiling sloped down to meet the ground. "We need more light. Let's finish clearing the rocks."

They climbed back out and continued the laborious task of jointly removing one rock at a time and completely clearing the opening. Drenched in sweat, they stood at the center of the cave. As Onawa studied the wall painting, Solitario knelt on the sandy ground and crawled toward a far corner of the space until his body could fit no farther. He asked Onawa for the torch, shining it into the dark crook, but there was nothing there except more rocks. On one of the stones rested a blue feather. Solitario picked it up and examined it. Then he backed out of the cramped tunnel and rose to his feet, dusting himself off.

"Anything?" Onawa asked.

He shook his head but held up the small plume.

She took it, staring at it quizzically. "I do not recognize it."

"Me neither."

She sighed, handing the feather back to him and hanging her head as she turned to exit into the waning daylight. He stood alone for a moment, closing his eyes and sniffing the air. It was dank and clammy. It smelled of having been inhabited, which of course it had been, hundreds of years earlier, but this was more recent. Could it have simply been an animal? Why the wall of rocks? Opening his eyes, he walked slowly toward the opening. The next cave would take at least a day to reach. They would need more water, he thought. And then, right before he reached the mouth of the cave, he saw Johnny standing there in his dungarees for an instant, his hand held up, gesturing for Solitario to stop. Solitario stopped in mid-step, turning slowly around and peering again into the darkness behind him.

"Onawa?" he called out hesitantly.

When he felt her standing next to him, he pointed down the crawl-space he had explored. "Since you are smaller, you could fit in there and remove the rocks at the end. Pass them back to me, see if there's anything behind them."

It was strenuous work, even for someone as dexterous as Onawa, but she forced herself into the crevice as far as she could and scratched at the rocks, shaking them loose, passing them back as Solitario loomed behind her, torch in hand. In the low, flickering light, they both struggled to see, and the air was dense with dust and a musty odor.

"What do you see behind the rocks?" Solitario asked.

"More rocks."

"Don't give up. You brought us here for a reason."

She grunted as her hands slipped off a large fragment striated with calcite and quartz. Her blood streaked across the craggy surface like an extra layer of red granite. Determined, she pried it loose and rolled it backward. The torchlight caught a flash of white where the rock had been moments beforehand.

Onawa gasped, "There's something here." Reaching out, she touched the white fabric, pressed against it. Reinvigorated, she clawed away at the other rocks to reveal a mud-streaked face, eyes closed, golden hair. "It's the boy."

"Is he alive? Is he breathing?"

"I don't know," she answered, feeling his neck for a pulse. "I can't feel a heartbeat."

As Solitario leaned in for a glimpse of the boy, the torch blew out and they were plunged into absolute darkness.

ELEVEN

Elias recited his children's prayers and tucked them into their small beds in the cramped room they shared. Outside their open window, it was dark and quiet except for the solemn song of the cicadas. He tiptoed to the adjacent room, where he joined Otila in their bed. She was already asleep, and the creaking of the frame as he lowered his girth into it disturbed her only slightly as she grumbled and turned on her side to face him. Usually he fell asleep in an instant, but tonight he lingered awake, staring at the ceiling. He could not put his finger on why, but he found himself on edge. He had heard that Solitario and Onawa were out looking for the Tolbert boy. He'd been upset that his jefe had not asked him to join in their search. Otila had urged him not to take it personally, but it stung that his old capitán would prefer to go it alone with an Apache woman than to bring his trusty compadre along. Had he become so old and useless?

Eventually, he slipped into a troubled sleep. His dreams were invaded by French imperialist forces, as they frequently were, memories that instead of fading over time only seemed to mushroom larger and more menacing in proportion. Fighting in the mountains south of Mexico City, combat in the cobblestoned streets of Puebla, at times firing rifles from straight lines of infantry, squinting after pulling the trigger, bracing himself for the fire of incoming bullets. At times, thrusting his bayonet or in close combat having to pull his saber out, standing back-to-back with Solitario, who snapped commands over the thundering cacophony of gunfire and cannons, men's anguished screams and moans as their bodies were punctured and pierced and blown apart, the acrid stench of gunpowder filling the smoky haze, searing his nostrils.

In his recurring nightmare, he found Solitario cornered by three enemy soldiers in a dead-end ravine. They wielded bayonets and advanced slowly toward his capitán, who brandished his sword defiantly. Elias came upon them from behind and took aim with his carbine. In real life he had shot one of them in the back. And, in that moment of surprise, the other two had hesitated and whipped their heads around to see where the shot had come from as he reloaded. In that instant, Solitario had run one of them through with the saber in his right hand and sliced the other's throat with the dagger in his left. But in the recurring nightmare, Elias' rifle jammed, and they advanced on Solitario, slaying him mercilessly before turning on him, which was when Elias awoke in a panic, gasping for breath, beads of perspiration dripping from his forehead and stinging his eyes as he lurched upright in bed.

Otila murmured something about the children and flopped herself over, turning away from Elias' constant perturbations. Elias sat there for a moment, regaining his senses, reminding himself that the war was long over, that he had survived. When his breathing slowed, he rose from the bed as carefully as he could in order to avoid rousing Otila, and he made a quick tour through the house to check on the children and look out the windows. Fear was not something that ended with the execution of tyrants or the signing of treaties. Fear was something that followed you the rest of your life, Elias thought. Was that why Solitario had not called on him to serve again? Was it because he knew that Elias was afraid for himself and for his family? Or was Solitario himself frightened that Elias would fail him, that he had grown too fat and too slow? Standing in the kitchen, Elias looked out the window into the night. A firefly buzzed by, meandering in the evening breeze like a drunken vaquero wandering home after a long night at the cantina. A branch cracked. The sound startled him.

Barefoot and wearing only his loose and frayed pajama pants affixed to his waist by his trusty federal army belt, he opened the door, looked both ways, and tentatively stepped outside. The outhouse was a short walk away, outlined in the paltry moonlight. As he walked toward it, a hush fell over the trees. He paused halfway to his destination, sensing that he was not alone. The shadows of the mesquite trees shifted like sinister spirits across the ground. He was a grown man. He'd fought in countless battles. Yet he could still feel like a child, like the orphan he had once been. Peering into the darkness, he could see no one, so he continued. When he reached the outhouse, he grabbed the door handle. As he was about to pull on it, the door sprung outward, slamming into his face. In a flash, a tall, hefty man overpowered him, wrestling him to the ground, knocking the wind from his lungs. He didn't stand a chance against his assailant's massive weight and superior strength. In moments, he was bound and gagged as several others surrounded him. They made no noise, and he could not distinguish their features in the darkness. When he grunted, his initial attacker silenced him with a sharp kick to the groin. Then they dragged him back toward the house.

Not my children, not Otila, Elias' mind raced. How could this be happening? But it was, unfolding before his terrified eyes. He watched as first his wife and then Elena and Oscarito were gagged and bound in their beds. *Solitario, where are you now?* He prayed to the Virgencita de Guadalupe for a miracle, but as the four of them were dragged toward the dry riverbed, he did not hold out much hope for divine intervention. Six tall posts had been erected in the basin. As Elias and his family were strapped to them, he saw the carnicero and his wife and son already tied to stakes as well. He grimaced at the thought of what was sure to follow. Then it dawned on him that there was one stake fewer than there were hostages. He scanned his surroundings desperately. Who would be spared? That was when he noticed Elena still being held by one of their attackers, being forced to watch as her family and neighbors were doused with lantern oil. Elias yearned to scream for help, but he could not. He wanted to tell Elena to look away. But the dirty rag tied through his jaw prevented him from making any significant sound. A match was struck.

A torch was lit. In the flickering firelight, it became clear that kindling sat beneath their feet. *Look away, Elena*, Elias pleaded mentally. And then he prayed with all his remaining energy, knowing it would be the last thing he would ever do. He asked not for forgiveness, not for salvation, not for a quick death. Instead, he begged for vengeance.

More torches were lit, one for each of the six prisoners. In the light, Elias could nearly discern the men's faces, but not clearly enough to recognize any of them. And then the flames shot up around his feet. Heat seared his legs as an unbearable pain shot through him, obliterating his thoughts as the fire blinded him completely.

TWELVE

Solitario awoke with a sense of urgency in the middle of the night, a knot in his throat, a burning deep in his belly. Lying on the cooling sand, wrapped in his sarape, he wondered if something was wrong with Onawa or Frankie. When he twisted toward the smoldering campfire, in the orange glow of its embers, he saw Onawa and the boy asleep through the serpentine smoke.

The boy was barely alive, but his state did not seem to have worsened. Worrisome as Frankie's condition seemed, that was not what had roused him. No. It was something else. Something different and equally urgent. He tasted mole on his tongue. Mole poblano. Roasted chile, sesame seeds, chocolate, and almonds. He grimaced. He was repulsed by sentimentality. But all he could think of was Elias. They had once eaten mole in Puebla at a convent they'd liberated from occupying soldiers, and it had tasted like manna from heaven after not eating properly for weeks. He knew this was why Otila always prepared chicken mole on the rare occasions when he joined them for dinner.

The smoke from the dying campfire scorched his nostrils, and his eyes watered. He rubbed at his eyes and looked up at the starry sky. What did God have in store for Frankie, for Elias? Why did he have to feel responsible for their well-being? He had given all of this up long ago and yet here he found himself again, fretting for other people's lives. For what? It was so much easier to stay put on his ranch and get lost in Luz's fleeting apparitions.

He sat up, gazing at the sparks that danced over the vanquished fire. *Tomorrow will be different,* he thought. *I'll go into Olvido and I'll return this boy to the authorities. I'll visit Elias and his family. And all will be well,* he reassured himself. *And then I'll go back to El Escondido and resume my peaceful life.* That was all he wanted or needed out of life at this point. It was better to stay out of the way than to get trampled over by the stampede of time and fate.

As he sat there staring at the fire, Onawa stirred. Her eyes split open and locked onto his. In her giant pupils, he saw the dance of sparks reflected.

"What is wrong?" she whispered, her vocal cords parched from two days in the desert without sufficient hydration.

"Something."

"What?"

"I don't know what."

"The boy?"

"No, he looks the same."

"Then something in the desert?" Her expression turned apprehensive, her body tensed as she reached for the rifle lying beside her.

"No." He waved the notion away.

"Should we ride?" she asked.

"Not yet," he answered. "It's not safe. We wait until daybreak."

She nodded and her eyes closed as quickly as they had opened.

He watched over her and the boy, waiting for the sun to bleed over the horizon.

———————

When they rode into Olvido, they could smell the smoke and the stench of burned flesh. Solitario and Tormenta led the way. Onawa carried Frankie across her lap on Invierno. The streets were emptied by dread. Threads of smoke curled through the streets like sinister roots of carnage.

At the dry riverbed, a crowd had gathered. Mounted on his horse, Solitario could see over their heads. There stood six charred monuments, blackened remains twisted upon them, steam mingling with the last remainders of smoke rising into the baking sun. Women fell on their knees in prayer. Children wept.

Onawa averted her gaze as Solitario maneuvered his horse through the crowd, and the rest of the throng parted for him to pass. He rode down into the voided channel and stopped before the row of smoking, unrecognizable effigies. The odor of burned flesh made him cringe and nearly convulse, but his stomach was empty and there was nothing for him to regurgitate onto the cracked ground. He descended from Tormenta, his black boots crunching over the crumbling soil as the crowd watched from behind and up on the banks. He sifted carefully through the ashes at the feet of the vertical pyres, coming upon a blackened hunk of silver in the rising morning sun. Clearing the embers with the tip of his boot, he reached down to pick up the metal object. It was still hot in his fingers as he raised it, blowing the soot off to reveal the seal of the Mexican Republic, the eagle perched on the cactus with the serpent writhing in its talons and beak. There had been only one man, other than himself, who possessed such a belt buckle in the village.

Mr. Stillman called out to Solitario from the northern bank of the fugitive river, "Might this be enough, Capitán Cisneros, to convince you that it's time for you to return to duty?"

Solitario turned the warm buckle in his calloused hands, staring at the charred corpse sagging before him. With every passing second, it increasingly resembled his sergeant, Elias. After the crowd's hushed murmurs subsided, he at last turned his gaze upward at Stillman.

He considered speaking but decided—as was usually the case—that it was best not to. He placed his left foot into Tormenta's left bootstrap and hoisted his right leg and body over the steed. Fluidly, he scaled the riverbank to the northern levee, coming up alongside the mayor. Then, they rode together to the town jail, where they tied their horses outside and proceeded inward, followed by Onawa, who carried the boy.

"The boy needs a doctor," Onawa said.

"He is alive?" Mr. Stillman asked, clearly surprised by the news of Frankie's survival.

"Yes," she answered. "Barely."

Stillman nodded at Boggs, who rushed to fetch the town doctor.

Inside the small building that served as town hall, sheriff's head-quarters, and jailhouse, Solitario stared sullenly at the grimy stucco walls. He had once toiled in a place just like this south of the river, struggling to keep the peace and maintain the order. And here he was again. He stared at the desk in the corner, covered with Sheriff Tolbert's personal items.

"We need you, Captain Cisneros," Stillman said. "I reckon I don't need to tell you who those people were, burned down where the river used to run."

Solitario looked up at him slowly, "I reckon you do."

"The butcher, Lopez, his wife and son," Stillman divulged. "And, of course, your old friend Elias, his wife, and . . ."

"Son . . ." Solitario finished.

"Yes."

"And his daughter?" Solitario asked.

"Missing."

Solitario's eyes darted to Onawa, who gazed back attentively.

"They are taking young girls," Solitario surmised.

Stillman stared sternly at Onawa and then back at Solitario, "I'm afraid so."

They all stood like chess pieces in a stalemate until Boggs burst back into the office, flustered and flushed. "It's getting bad out there, Mr. Mayor. The town's a powder keg if ever I saw one."

"What's happening, Boggs?" Stillman asked.

"I'm worried our once-peaceful municipality might explode at any moment. The Anglo townspeople claim the Mexicans killed the Tolberts. The Mexicans say the Anglos torched the Elias and Lopez families. And everyone else is blaming it all on the Apache," Boggs blurted out.

Solitario turned to Onawa, whose expression was clouded with worry. He knew just as she did that if the town rose up against the

Apache, her father would be in danger. He'd be the first they'd seek out. He was not only knowledgeable, but also old, weak, and vulnerable.

"Will you help us?" Stillman asked Solitario. "Will you wear the badge?" He extended his hand, a shiny silver star resting in its palm.

He didn't want to. In fact, it was the last thing he had ever hoped— or expected—to do. It went against every instinct in every bone and every cell of his tired body. He had given up fighting for justice when Luz had died. But he thought of Elias and Otila and Oscarito writhing in flames within the void that once divided America from Mexico with a churning torrent of cooling water. And he thought of Elena and the Tolbert girls still missing and possibly alive. And he worried for Aguila Brava sitting in his adobe home waiting to die, with either dignity or shame. He looked at Frankie, lying unconscious in a cot in the corner of an open jail cell, waiting still for the doctor, and he met Onawa's beseeching eyes, and—as much as he searched—he couldn't find a way to say no yet again. Still, saying yes felt like climbing a mountain whose peak was concealed high above a layer of clouds.

Without a word, Solitario stepped past Mayor Stillman and strode down the hall to the back door.

THIRTEEN

When Onawa stepped into the clearing behind the jailhouse, she spotted Solitario standing at the fence, staring out toward the mountains to the north. Standing next to him, she followed his line of sight.

"I once knew a man who said mountains don't have feelings," Solitario said.

"I'm not sure I agree," she replied.

He sighed. "Me neither."

"I just think their emotions are buried deep and slow to surface."

He nodded, squinting into the distance.

"What will you do?" she asked.

"I don't know," he answered.

"Yes, you do. Just look inside yourself for the answer. That's the advice my father gave me before we left to search for the boy."

"Wearing the badge goes against everything I swore to myself I would never do again," Solitario said. "That life is in my past."

"Maybe it's not a life, but a job," Onawa pondered. "What if avoiding it is actually keeping you trapped in your past?"

He studied her.

"On the other hand," she continued, "I don't trust the Anglos. Why should you help them?"

"You don't do the right thing because it's easy. You do it because it is right."

"Is it right?"

"I owe it to Elias. I owe it to my goddaughter, Elena. And to the other children too. They are innocent. They know not of my troubles or our endless wars and our tangled histories."

She suddenly saw him in a different light. It was as if the sun had shifted from behind a cloud. What drew her to him was not what she had always believed it to be. It was not how he looked or walked. It was not the Spanish he spoke, which reminded her of her mother and a side of her heritage she longed to know better. No, it was an unspoken compass within him, an invisible code he followed.

"You remind me of my father," Onawa revealed in that moment of realization, surprising even herself.

"I'm honored," Solitario managed to respond.

"You will do what must be done, even if you don't want to."

PART II

FOURTEEN

Solitario sat on his flat boulder at the edge of the Tolbert farm's woods. He'd been waiting for Johnny for a couple of hours, but the boy had yet to show himself. To pass the time, he'd let himself back into the barn and sifted through the hay, searching for anything he might have missed. Blood-caked dirt still hid beneath the straw. Now that the silver badge was pinned to his shirt, he felt more comfortable taking his time. He was no longer an intruder. He belonged here. And that gave him a strange sense of peace despite the turmoil the walls had witnessed. Carrying his lantern from corner to corner, he probed the darkest shadows, urging his mind to imagine what might have taken place within that godforsaken place. There had been a group of men. One had been familiar to the boy. Others had not. The killing had been brutal, sadistic, prolonged. The sheriff had gone out back unarmed, so he had reason to trust the men, yet there he had swiftly met his fate, leaving his most cherished souls to suffer without him. His poor wife had not been violated but she had been savagely brutalized. Her honor may have been spared, but not her heart. It had been torn out of her chest. The entire scene playing out in his mind, it had the makings of some kind of ritual, a performance. The children had even been forced to serve as spectators. When he had been about to leave the barn, a hint of color had caught his eye behind the door. Crouching down, he held the lantern over the spot. Was he seeing things? No, there it was, a turquoise shimmer. He reached for it. It was a delicate plume, similar to the one he'd encountered in the cave. Tucking it into his pocket, he had returned to the boulder.

He sat there still, when he heard horses approaching. Tormenta snorted by the fence. Two identical shadows loomed against the moon-lit sky. They still wore their cowboy hats even though it was dark.

"I'm out here, boys." Solitario spoke in a low voice, watching them start and then dismount.

The Dobbs boys climbed over the fence and came out to meet him at the rock by the tree line.

"Sheriff Cisneros," one of them said, slurring the letters together the way gringos did.

Solitario squinted through the dark. "Which one are you?"

"I'm Blake, sir," he answered. "And this here's Michael." He nudged his brother. "But there ain't no way you'll be able to tell us apart, Sher-iff," he added. "Don't feel bad about it though. Even our own parents used to get confused before . . ."

Solitario nodded. They had been orphaned in an Apache raid. He'd heard the stories. Tolbert had taken them under his wing. They were better farmhands than they were deputies, but they meant well. "I have my ways, Blake."

"How?" Michael asked.

"I can hear the difference in your voices." Blake was braver. Thus, he always spoke first and with more confidence. Michael was more curious, more thoughtful, so he listened and then asked questions with caution. Besides, Blake had a tiny scar in his right eyebrow where the hair had never grown back. "You'll see. And just call me 'Jefe.'"

"Jefe," the Dobbs twins repeated, grinning.

Solitario figured Tolbert would always be their sheriff. It would be easier to gain their trust and loyalty this way. He was not a replacement, just the best alternative, the only alternative, really, for the moment.

"Now, why are you here?"

"We came out to see if you needed any help," Blake explained.

"What about Frankie?" Solitario asked. "You didn't leave him alone at the jailhouse, did you?"

"No, sir," Blake answered. "Dr. Ferris came, and we helped him take the boy over to his house. He and his missus are going to watch over him."

Solitario nodded in approval. "Good. Did you tell him what I told you?"

"Yes, sir," Blake said. "We told him the moment Frankie wakes to send word."

"The boy might have clues," Solitario whispered, turning his gaze onto the dark woods.

"Is that why you're here?" Michael asked. "To search for clues?"

"You could say that," Solitario replied, knowing he would never find what he'd come looking for if the Dobbs twins lingered around. "But you best leave me to my own devices. Go home and get a good night's sleep. Tomorrow, we'll start asking questions. I'll need you alert."

"Yes . . . Sheri . . ." the Dobbs twins started and stopped in unison, ". . . Jefe." They chuckled at the strange sound of the Spanish word rolling off their tongues.

When they were gone, he lay down on the rock and stared up at the stars. The breeze was cool, rustling through the trees. Night had long been his favorite time of day.

―――――――――

Solitario woke from a dream in which a disembodied Sergeant Elias had been calling out for his help. His voice had sounded desperate but distant, and his face and body refused to materialize, just like Johnny's tonight. Where was Elias' smoldering spirit waiting? Would Solitario come across him in the dry riverbed, the arroyo seco, standing by the charred ruins of his pyre, or might he find him sitting at the kitchen table in his small adobe house, forever waiting for Otila to place another steaming tortilla on his plate? Or would he appear only in the surreal confines of his commanding officer's dreams?

Propping himself up by the elbows, Solitario peered into the forest, whispering Johnny's name to no avail.

Beyond the woods, a flickering light beckoned from the preacher's house behind the church. If Johnny wouldn't talk to him, maybe the reverend would.

Solitario rose slowly and walked out to the road, patting Tormenta's neck softly. "Wait here," he told her as he ambled past those woods where Johnny's frightened spirit now took refuge, to the neighboring homestead.

He entered the grounds through the gate in front of the church. He stood below the looming white spire for a long moment, craning his neck to look up at the pointed top. The lights were all out inside the building, so he circled back to the preacher's home, where the flicker of candles filtered out onto the porch.

As he approached, he heard the creaking of a rocking chair. He paused to listen for it, but then it stopped too. Even the cicadas seemed to hold their breath, their shells shushing their incessant susurrations. He could barely discern the dark figure of a man sitting on the porch.

"We don't do confessions here." The preacher's gravelly voice cut through the sudden silence of the cicadas. "You may as well be on your way."

Solitario took a few more steps forward, nearing the porch's outer railing. "Why do you say that, Reverend Grimes? Do you think I suspect you have something to confess?"

"Heavens, no!" the preacher scoffed. "I assumed you were here to spill your own guts. Whenever one of your kind comes here, it's usually because they wish to unburden themselves of some sin so terrible, they wouldn't dare tell their own priest."

"My kind?"

"Mezcun."

"I see." Solitario nodded, glad again to be wearing the silver badge over his left chest pocket. He felt for it. The metal was cold and smooth beneath his rough hand. "And you don't listen to their confessions?"

"Lord, no. This isn't a Catholic church. We're Baptists. We don't drink. We don't smoke. We don't dance. And we don't confess."

"Does that mean you don't sin?"

"Oh, we all sin, Cisneros. As different as we may be, White, Black, Brown, Red, and Yellow. We all have one thing in common. That's the worst in each of us. Sin. But we believe God is the only one that can forgive us for those sins."

"So you cut out the middle man."

"You could say that."

"So then what do you do for your flock if not absolve them so they can sleep well at night?"

"I lead them in prayer and reflection. I inspire them to be good."

"How many of 'my kind' do you inspire to do good in your congregation?"

"Hmm, let me see . . . that would be none."

"I heard you didn't let anyone come here to worship when the Catholic church burned down."

"We built this house of God with our own hands. It is for our families. We must protect it, keep it clean."

Solitario shook his head. "And Sheriff Tolbert? Was he in your flock?"

The reverend paused for a long while, his chair creaking again. "The sheriff and I didn't exactly see eye to eye."

"Speaking of seeing, did you happen to notice anything that night that the Tolberts were murdered?"

"No, I did not. I already told Stillman and Boggs that."

"They're not the law."

"No, no they're not."

"That's why I'm asking you. You see, if you lie to them, it's a sin. But if you lie to me, it's a crime," said Solitario. "What was your dispute concerning?"

"The woods between the church's land and his farm."

"I see. What about the woods?"

"Where exactly the dividing line was."

"Is your problem over now?"

"Well, that depends," Reverend Grimes answered.

"On what?"

"On who stands to inherit the Tolbert farm and what they plan to do with it."

"Who gets the land if nobody from the family survives?"

Another long pause, a hem and a haw. "Well, I believe the way the wills were written, the sheriff left it to his wife and the wife to their children . . ."

"And on the off chance the children were to be gone too?"

The reverend vacated his rocking chair and reached for the screen door. "I'm feeling mighty tired, Cisneros. I didn't expect the Spanish Inquisition to come to my door tonight. If you want to know more about Tolbert's will, you'll have to check the county records to see if it's registered there."

"I'll do that," Solitario nodded, touching the brim of his hat in the dark as the reverend closed the door and stared at him from beyond the screen, his stern, bearded face now faintly illuminated by the dancing flame of the lantern hanging in his foyer. "Funny thing about confessions."

"How's that?"

"Well, your kind don't do them in church. You prefer to reveal them to lawyers and file them with clerks."

"Good night, Cisneros."

It irked Solitario that this man of the cloth did not deign him worthy of using the prefix "sheriff" when addressing him. But he was accustomed to such slights from the gringos. That was their way. They raised themselves above others by denying them the deference they themselves required. Yet, they expected the opposite of people like him.

"Good night, Reverend Grimes," Solitario intoned respectfully, even though doing so caused a sharp pang in his belly.

The reverend sighed, closing the door and leaving Solitario alone in the dark.

───────────

As Solitario approached Tormenta, he noticed she was standing at attention, her ears perked up, her eyes trained on the Tolberts' woods. Johnny was back. Solitario hastened, hopping over the fence and picking up his pace. A flash of golden hair moved through the trees, reflecting the moonlight. Plowing into the brush, dry branches scratching at his face, Solitario pursued the boy.

"Johnny, it's me, Solitario," he called out. "Don't be afraid, Johnny. I'm the one you talked to before, remember? I'm trying to help."

The boy froze in his tracks. When Solitario reached him, they stood in a small clearing, the moonlight filtering down through the opening overhead.

"You came back," Johnny whispered, the sound of his voice finally syncing up with the movement of his pallid lips.

"I promised I would."

"Did you find Frankie?"

"I did, Johnny," Solitario replied. "You were a great help. My friend and I found the cave with the painting of the snake and the dancers on the wall. Your brother's alive. You saved him."

Johnny smiled. "What did he say?"

"He's unconscious. The doctor is taking care of him now. Hopefully, when he wakes up, he can tell us more about what he saw."

Johnny nodded and gulped. "Sorry I was scared tonight."

"Did something happen?"

A troubled expression fell over Johnny's face. "I saw my sisters, Abigail and Beatrice."

"They're still alive?" Solitario asked.

"Yes," Johnny answered. "They are very frightened. I was asleep and I was dreaming and suddenly I was standing in a small room with them, a room in a house where they are being kept. They were crying, but when they saw me, they ran to me and hugged me. I told them to try and stay calm, told them help is on its way."

"That's good, Johnny. Had they been hurt?"

"No."

"Did you notice anything else about the room or the house, maybe where it was located? Is it in town or out on a ranch?"

"It felt like a big farmhouse, on some land. I didn't get a good look outside, but I thought I heard a cowbell clanking in the pasture."

"That's good, very good. Anything else?" Solitario's eyes glimmered with a familiar hunger for knowledge, any hint that might put him on the right track to saving those girls. "What do you remember about the room they were in? Was there any furniture? Did it look simple or fancy?"

"It was a bedroom," Johnny recalled, scratching his head. "It looked like a girl's room. It was nice and comfortable. And they were not alone. There was another girl with them, an older girl with dark skin and long black braids."

Solitario rifled through his shirt pocket, pulling out some photographs. Sifting through them, he showed Johnny the image of his goddaughter, Elena. "Was this the girl, Johnny?"

He nodded. "She was there. She was brave."

"Why do you say that, Johnny?" Solitario asked. "How was she brave?"

"I could tell she was just as scared as my sisters about being trapped there in that stranger's house, but she didn't seem put off by me at all, even though she knew I wasn't like them anymore. I think she's brave because she promised me she'd look after Abigail and Beatrice. When I couldn't stay any longer, she put her arms around them and held them tight. I'm glad they're not alone."

Solitario gazed down at the photo of Elias' daughter in his hand. She was alive. He allowed himself to sigh with momentary relief. He'd failed to protect Elias and his wife and son but he could still do something right for their family. He owed it to his old sergeant. If only he could figure out where the girls were being held captive. If only Johnny could remember something else, another clue. He looked up to ask the boy more questions, but his golden hair and freckled face had vanished without a trace.

FIFTEEN

Elias had been scrawny back when they were in the Rurales, fighting for the Republic. His loose vaquero pants barely stayed in place above his hips, where he tied them with a frayed rope. His beard was as dark as his eyes shaded by his sombrero.

He stood by the campfire next to his brother, Efrain, who was older and taller. Efrain was also faster and more handsome, but Elias tried not to dwell on those inequities, of which the only one that mattered under the present circumstances was Efrain's superior speed. Because of his agility and swiftness, Efrain had been given the job of scout in the regiment commanded by Colonel Luis Terrazas. And, most importantly, since he required energy to roam the mountains searching for imperialist forces, Efrain was served a double portion of beans at lunch and dinner.

Elias eyed Efrain's second bowl of frijoles enviously, then he turned, squinting at a cluster of uniformed officers about thirty feet away. The smoke stung his eyes, and the sun baked his arms, and the sweat made his dirty shirt cling to his skin, but that wasn't what bothered him most. He sniffed the air like a hungry hound. Through the smoke he detected a hint of bacon and it cut straight to his stomach, which twisted painfully in response.

"The officers have bacon," Elias informed his brother beneath his breath.

"Of course they have bacon," Efrain confirmed. "They're officers."

Elias shook his head disdainfully. Nothing was ever going to change. No matter how many wars and how many battles and how many different presidents or emperors took power. "No matter what, it's always the same." He spat into the embers at their feet, causing a momentary sizzle as his saliva evaporated. "Look at them with their clean blue uniforms and their shiny gold buttons. And here we are dressed in rags, our skin blistering under the sun. Them with their bacon and their wine and us with our meager ration of beans and mescal."

Efrain stared at the remnants clinging to the clay bowl cupped in his hands. "I would give you the rest of my frijoles, but I have to go out on another patrol."

Elias shrugged, eyeing a lone soldier off to the side, away from both the enlisted men and the officers. He sat alone in front of his tent on a folding chair made of wood and leather. He wore a black uniform that was different from everybody else's. Silver buckles studded the outseams of his pants. His black jacket was short and embroidered. A saber dangled at his side, as did two guns, one on each hip. Around his neck, he wore a yellow bandanna. His head was crowned by an elegant black sombrero.

"What do you make of the charro?" Elias asked Efrain.

Efrain chewed as he looked across the clearing at the solitary man. "He keeps to himself. They say he's better with horses than with people."

Elias admired the muscular black stallion poised next to the man's tent. "I wonder if he gets bacon," Elias mused.

The regiment was encamped west of Ciudad Chihuahua in the arid Cerro Grande, a sprawling mountain range between whose peaks stretched vast cactus-studded valleys roamed by cougars, Yaqui Indians, and French imperialist interlopers. They were a far-flung fragment of the Republic's exiled army, scraped together from army troops loyal to the Mexican President Benito Juárez and Rurales. Under Colonel Terrazas they'd been biding their time to gain reinforcements and retake the region's capital, which had fallen into the enemy's hands.

"Why don't you ask him?" Efrain dared his younger brother.

"No. He wouldn't even talk to me. He's one of them."

"You think?" Efrain stared at the charro. "Maybe. Maybe not. He looks different."

Elias shrugged again. Maybe some other time. His stomach rumbled with disappointment.

That night, Elias was stirred from sleep by his brother. "¿Qué pasa?" he asked, sitting up on his petate beneath the stars as the other men around them remained asleep.

"I saw something over the crest of the hill," Efrain whispered.

"Should we wake the men, alert the officers?"

"I don't know. It is some of the officers. They're doing something they shouldn't," Efrain said, fear flashing in his eyes.

Elias stood up quietly. "Show me."

Efrain put his pointer finger over his lips, urging his brother to be as quiet as possible.

Pulling his pants up and fastening the rope as tightly as he could, Elias followed his brother into the foothills. Beneath the starry sky, the sand felt cool on his toes as it sifted through the leather straps of his sandals. Approaching a ridge, Elias heard laughter intermingled with muffled cries.

In the cobalt light, he and his brother could make out four uniformed officers. They'd tied a trio of barely clad men to a row of tall saguaros. The captives struggled against the ropes binding them to the trunks, their exposed arms and legs slashed by the cacti's prickly spines. Helplessly, the prisoners watched as the officers took turns crouching over a pair of women on the ground. The women wrestled futilely as the officers had their way with them.

"They're Yaqui," Elias said, his heart pounding. "They must have been passing through and got caught."

Efrain frowned. "What do we do?"

"What *can* we do?" Elias whispered back, acid scorching his throat. "They're officers. What they're doing is wrong, but if we try to stop them, they'll tie us to the saguaros too, or worse."

Before they could turn to head back to the camp, however, Elias and

Efrain heard a sudden thundering of hooves as a rush of black stormed past them, the displaced air blowing their hats off their heads.

As his eyes adjusted to the swiftly moving shape, Elias saw the charro galloping over the summit and streaking down toward the clearing.

Efrain asked, "Do we help him?"

But Elias was already scrambling down the hill in hot pursuit. He hoped to help the horseman, but in the time it took him to reach the base of the hill without tumbling down the slope, he saw the man dispense with the officers.

First, as the charro charged in, he targeted the two officers standing watch. Riding between them, he swung left and then right, his saber gleaming in the starlight. He didn't impale them, simply knocked them unconscious with precise blows to the head from the broadside of his sword. Then as his horse whinnied and reared, he maneuvered the steed in such a way that the great beast used its forelegs to batter the two men crouched over the Yaqui women.

When he reached the charro's side, all Elias could do was help the women cover themselves with the sarapes lying beneath them. As he finished, the horseman threw a coil of rope to him and instructed him to tie up the officers.

Hesitating, Elias gawked fearfully up at the charro still in his saddle.

"Don't worry, if anyone asks, you tell them Solitario Cisneros gave the order."

Elias nodded and began tying the men with the help of his brother.

Solitario, meanwhile, positioned his horse alongside the row of saguaros and—with a flick of his saber—deftly sliced the ropes that held the Yaqui men in place. The men thanked him and embraced the women before fleeing into the night.

As the sun rose behind them, Elias and his brother stood next to Solitario, who remained mounted on his horse. Between them and the colonel's tent knelt the officers they had apprehended.

"What is the meaning of this?" Colonel Terrazas asked, squinting into the rising sun as he emerged from his tent in his pajamas. "Why are my officers on the ground?"

Elias gulped with apprehension as his pulse raced. He wasn't sure what he and his brother had gotten themselves into, but he feared that they would soon regret it.

"With all due respect, Colonel Terrazas, these men aren't worthy of the uniform or the rank," Solitario said.

"What have they done?" the colonel kicked the sand in frustration.

"They have dishonored Yaqui women, violating them in front of their men. They were found doing this last night."

The colonel shook his head in disgust. "How many times have I told you? No. We cannot deviate from our mission. We cannot bring shame to our uniform." He spat in disgust at the ground. Then he looked up at Solitario, sitting tall and straight on his horse.

"Bien hecho, Capitán Cisneros," the colonel said. "Take them away. Place them in the stockade. They will be put on trial and they will lose their rank. And when I reclaim my city, they will wish they were back out in the desert as they stare at the prison walls."

Solitario nodded, glancing at Elias and Efrain to his side.

"And these men, the scout and the starving one, they helped you?" the colonel asked.

Solitario nodded. "They are the ones that discovered the crime."

"Very well," the colonel said as he assessed the pair. "Tonight, the three of you dine in my tent. Adelante." He ducked through the flap, disappearing into his canvas headquarters.

Elias and Efrain took turns scrubbing each other in the nearby creek. When Solitario found them, he dismounted and approached with a bright white bundle in his hands and a subtle smile on his face. He stood with his shiny black boots in the shallows, surveying the brothers' tattered shirts drying beneath the sun on a boulder. They had tried washing out the stains but only succeeded in making more holes in the disintegrating fabric.

"I brought you these shirts to wear," Solitario said, placing the clean clothes on a rock.

Elias grinned broadly. "Gracias."

Solitario placed a small silver blade atop the white bundle. He didn't need to say anything about it, but Elias knew it was meant for them to shave.

"Meet me at my tent later," Solitario said, excusing himself. "Con permiso."

Elias and Efrain were giddy as they shaved and trimmed their mustaches and beards, combed their hair, and got dressed. At sunset, when they appeared at Solitario's tent, he acted as if he barely recognized them.

Staring at the rope around Elias' waist, he shook his head, "Wait here." After rustling about in his tent, he emerged holding a black leather belt with a silver buckle engraved with the insignia of the Republic, the eagle perched on the cactus in the Valley of Mexico. He handed the belt to Elias, who quickly changed.

"These are hard to come by," Elias commented as he tightened the belt, admiring the silver buckle. "How do you have two of them?"

Sorrow flickered across Solitario's features, the corners of his lips twitching downward for an instant, but beyond that he did not answer.

When Elias had centered the buckle, he and his brother followed Solitario to the colonel's tent. The brothers were nervous, but Solitario seemed unfazed in the presence of wealth and power. Was he accustomed to it? Was he unimpressed by it? The brothers had wondered aloud and speculated wildly all day long. Now, however, as they ducked into the spacious headquarters behind Solitario, Elias could think of only one thing: the air inside the colonel's tent—it smelled like bacon.

———

"Tiene los ojos más grandes que la boca," chuckled Colonel Terrazas, alluding to Elias' defeat at the dinner table. Various nearly finished plates sat arrayed before Elias, whose eyes were glassy from the red wine he was unaccustomed to consuming.

The men laughed and raised their crystal goblets, which—glinting golden in the dim light cast by the kerosene lanterns—seemed way too fragile and dainty in their rough hands.

Elias could still not believe he was sitting at a table draped in white linen in the commanding officer's tent, feasting on delicacies ranging from a salad of fresh radishes sprinkled with lime, queso fresco, and sea salt to grasshoppers fried in chile oil. He thought perhaps he had died and gone to heaven when the colonel's cook brought out a discada, a dish prepared on a searing-hot, black iron disk. Sizzling on that disco were chopped-up bits of beef, tomatoes, onions, peppers, jalapeños . . . and, of course, bacon. Each ingredient was cut into precise pieces and seasoned with salt and pepper before being fried in butter. The traditional Chihuahuan dish was served with steaming flour tortillas and their choice of red wine or cold cerveza.

Throughout the meal, Elias and his brother watched Solitario diligently, mimicking his use of the silverware and napkin. That night, Solitario removed his broad-brimmed sombrero at the entrance, along with his yellow bandanna, which he draped over the sombrero on a table where they also laid their weapons. As they ate and made polite conversation with the colonel, Elias' eyes landed on the delicate necklace of white shells, juxtaposed against Solitario's brown skin. What a strange man, this charro, who spoke little yet accomplished much.

The colonel seemed equally entranced, presiding at the head of the table, swishing his special reserve of Rioja from Spain in a large glass. "So, Capitán Cisneros, now that you have thinned out my officer ranks, how do you propose to compensate me for my loss?"

Solitario leaned back and stroked his mustache pensively. "With all due respect, Colonel Terrazas, it sounds like you've already made up your mind on that matter."

The colonel drained his glass and smiled. "You are wise for your years, joven. I'm glad to have you here. You may not realize this, but I knew your father well, many moons ago."

Suddenly, Elias understood there was more to Solitario's rapid ascent through the hierarchy of the Rurales and his distinctive position separate from the Republican Army officers than his masterful horsemanship and fine attire. He should have known, he chided himself, Solitario was an authentic charro, and charros were gentlemen of noble Spanish ancestry, trained and raised as the heirs to knights like Don Quixote and conquistadores like Hernán Cortés, Juan Navarro, and Diego de Montemayor. But Elias had always imagined those fair-skinned tyrants as arrogant invaders, the kind of men that might have joined—rather than arrested—the officers shuffling in the sands with their pants down, in the foothills. Solitario Cisneros was a different kind of man, one on a trail of his own blazing. Elias and his brother sensed that about him, and it rekindled something inside of them they had not felt since they had been children and taken up arms to defend their country.

Solitario fell silent and stared into the murky depths of the crimson wine in his glass. "Colonel Terrazas"—he looked their leader in the eye—"that makes one of us."

Taken aback, the colonel leaned back in his carved wooden armchair. "I'm sorry, m'ijo. For a moment, it slipped my mind, the fate that befell your good father when the Americanos extended their territory to the Rio Bravo."

Solitario's lips formed a tight line. Then he took a long sip of his wine.

"Well, your father was much as I am, a direct descendant of the original hacendados of our respective regions in the fronteras. I have had to fight—just as he did—to protect my lands along the border. I am lucky that I'm still alive . . .

"We all are." Efrain smiled, trying to lighten the mood.

"Are you from Chihuahua, Colonel Terrazas?" Elias asked, attempting to build the momentum back toward festivity.

The colonel stared back silently as if Elias had thrown his discada onto his impeccable uniform, decorated as it was with gold medals and colorful ribbons in green, red, and white. All of them stared expectantly at the colonel until at last he spoke.

"Yo no soy de Chihuahua," he intoned somberly. "Chihuahua es mía."

He was not of Chihuahua, but rather Chihuahua was his.

They respectfully toasted to his sense of ownership, rustling uncomfortably in their chairs. And then they listened to the colonel pontificate about the evils of the imperialist French invaders, Maximilian and Carlota, and their cowardly French overlord, Napoleon III. Then there was the long list of treacherous conservative Mexican generals that had joined their side to drive the democratically elected Benito Juárez from the presidency. But soon, he swore, General Porfirio Díaz and the Republican Army would retake the major cities and drive the French out to the sea. It was only a matter of time, he pledged. But it only could be achieved with men like them fighting for freedom and justice and a more equal world, one ruled by people elected by their peers rather than appointed by their monarchs. Solitario nodded quietly as Elias and Efrain imitated his gestures.

When they were finally dismissed and the colonel walked them out into the clearing in front of his tent, the colonel asked Solitario, "So now that you are a capitán, who will you designate as your sargento?"

Without hesitation, Solitario placed his hand on Elias' shoulder. "This man will be my sergeant."

The colonel nodded. "Good, and this one?" He gestured toward Efrain.

"He is your best scout, Colonel. I don't think you want him doing anything else."

"Bueno. It is good that not all of you have your eyes larger than your mouth," he said, pointing at Elias' belly. "Sleep. Tomorrow, you work harder than you ever have before. Buenas noches, hombres."

They bid the colonel good night and sauntered back to Solitario's tent. Standing at the entrance, Solitario served the brothers tequila in small tin cups he extracted from his saddlebag. Then he stood quietly, patting his horse's neck as the men sipped the fine liquor, closing their eyes as its oak fire rolled over their tongues.

Finally, Elias cleared his throat and spoke in a hushed tone as to not rouse the soldiers sleeping nearby on their petates beneath the open sky. "I did not know you were a capitán."

Solitario stroked his horse's mane and gazed up at the myriad points of light overhead. After a while, he met Elias' gaze and answered, "Neither did I."

Remembering the belt Solitario had lent him, Elias began to unbuckle and remove it, but his new captain gestured for him to stop.

"Keep it," Solitario said.

"Muchas gracias, Jefe." Elias beamed, tugging at his drooping pants and tightening the belt back into place.

Savoring his tequila, Efrain asked, "Why did you do any of it? Saving the Yaqui, giving us credit? Letting the colonel invite us to dinner? That's not the way people are."

Solitario wrinkled his eyebrows quizzically. "I only did what seemed fair."

"But life is not fair, Jefe," Elias said, placing his hand on the horse. "What is your horse's name?"

"Oscuridad," Solitario replied.

The brothers nodded in affirmation. It was a good name and the stallion lived up to it. "Como la noche," Elias acknowledged.

"The night is dark, but it is also full of light," Solitario said, drinking from his cup.

"Why do you seek fairness?" Elias boldly pressed.

Solitario was quiet for a long time. He poured another round of tequila. Then, he looked up at the sky as he answered, "I have witnessed much injustice in my life. Some say it is a maldición. I am running from it. I figure if I'm running from something, I must seek out the opposite: what is right, what is just, what is fair."

Elias and Efrain looked sideways at each other. They did not say anything, but Elias knew that his brother was thinking the same thing he was. After floundering for years, lost in an army barely concerned with feeding them, fighting futilely against an ever-changing list of enemies they weren't exactly sure why they were supposed to kill, they had finally found someone to follow.

They'd been chasing a scattering of imperial units patrolling the mountains to the west of Chihuahua for weeks, working to winnow them out of the way before mounting what the colonel hoped would be a decisive assault on the capital. In the wake of Oscuridad and Capitán Solitario Cisneros, Sergeant Elias and their soldiers had succeeded time and again, diligently minimizing casualties, capturing prisoners, and treating them with dignity as Solitario insisted.

"This is noble work," Elias told his brother.

Efrain agreed. "For once, I feel like I'm fighting for something worthwhile."

At dawn, the brothers embraced by the campfire before Efrain scurried into the foothills to perform his routine reconnaissance. Elias watched as his older brother climbed to a crest, standing against the lightening sky like a lone saguaro jutting defiantly toward the heavens. Then, Efrain sank behind the jagged mound interrupting the horizon.

Later that afternoon, an order came in for the sergeant to take a group of men into the mountains as several scouts and cavalry members had not reported back at lunchtime.

Elias sought out Solitario for guidance, but he could not find his capitán. Was he one of the missing horsemen? He chided himself for not having kept closer tabs on his commander. How could he become so complacent so quickly? He rubbed his belly anxiously as he led a group of four men into the hills on foot, carbines in hand. About an hour into the hinterlands, shots rang out from a ridge above the ravine they were crossing. Two of Elias' men fell dead on either side. *Sharpshooters*, Elias thought. *Frenchmen. Or French-trained.* He ducked for cover behind a terra-cotta-colored boulder as shots whizzed by, chips flying off the rock, bullets grazing the straw of his sombrero's brim.

Another one of his men grunted as his torso was punctured by gunfire. And then the last one fell facedown, his arms sprawled out as if the dry earth was his mother and he was hugging her upon returning home. Blood oozed out of his back as more holes appeared in his shirt. The gunshots echoed through the canyon's steep walls. The imperialist shooters were perched high above.

Elias made the sign of the cross, clutching his gun tightly and casting his telltale sombrero aside. As it spun through the air, it was perforated three times by bullets from the unseen gunmen. Elias crouched behind the large rock, beads of sweat bulging on his forehead until they burst and trickled down, burning his eyes and bathing his hot cheeks with salt.

He heard the enemy soldiers calling out to each other as they descended from both sides. *There is no way I can get out of this*, he thought. *Efrain, where are you? Why didn't you see this coming? It's a surprise attack. The campground will be next. Colonel Terrazas himself could be captured or killed.* And then what? Chihuahua would never be liberated from the imperialist forces. He heard the crunching of caliche beneath the enemy soldiers' boots. The pounding of his heart shook in his ears. *So this is how it ends?* he wondered. He had never thought he'd make it to sergeant. Maybe he should be proud, maybe he should be glad, thankful even. At least there had been that dinner in the colonel's tent. He'd tasted not only bacon but steak and fresh vegetables and Spanish wine. He'd served under a worthy capitán. If this was time, he should go out guns blazing, he determined. Gritting his teeth, he thanked God for his life and stepped out, ready to shoot with guns in both hands.

As he did so, bullets whizzed by him, ricocheting off nearby rocks. He fired in the enemies' direction, but it was hard to tell where they were hiding. He was terribly exposed, and the seconds seemed to stretch into eternal valleys of seductive time. As the bullets kicked up the dust, they created a sandy miasma around him, cloaking him protectively. And then, through that chalky cloud emerged a thundering, massive shape with a rider mounted upon it. More shots rang out. Steel glinted in the sunlight as a saber flashed in arcs about the snorting beast. Hooves kicked up more sand and dirt and gravel. Enemy soldiers grunted, their bodies tumbling down the hillside. One of them rolled right over Elias, pushing him to the ground.

As the dust and gun smoke cleared, Elias gazed up and saw a charro clad in black talking in hushed tones to nothing but the filthy air itself. He couldn't make out the words. But as the man descended from the horse, he knew without a doubt it was Solitario dismounting from Oscuridad.

Silently, lying as still as he could in case there were still snipers with guns trained on him, Elias observed as Solitario stared mournfully at the men he'd slain, scattered lifeless across the ravine in their red pants and navy-blue coats. Solitario had shot them to save his sergeant, but he seemed to look at them a great deal longer than anyone else would have. What if there was someone else hiding, waiting to shoot?

As Solitario strode toward him, Elias remained focused on the dead soldiers at eye level. Beyond Solitario's dusty boots, he saw the green stalks and white blooms of calla lilies sprouting from the sand to cloak the bloodied cadavers.

SIXTEEN

Not an hour earlier, Solitario had leaned over an expansive map spread across a table in the colonel's headquarters. The map was covered with tiny multicolored wooden blocks, representing the regiments of the Republican Army and Rurales as well as the imperial forces. He was listening to the colonel's strategy for retaking Chihuahua when his concentration was interrupted by a familiar voice. Turning around, he peered at the flap that covered the entrance to the tent, but the man he had expected to see was not there. The voice had been Efrain's. He could have sworn he had heard him warn, "Peligro, Capitán. Venga rápido," but he wasn't there. The colonel carried on with the full attention of the other officers as Solitario silently collected his guns, sombrero, and bandanna, ducking out into the sun.

Outside, two sentries stared toward the mountains in the west.

Solitario holstered his pistols and knotted his bandanna around his neck. "Did one of the scouts just come by here?"

"No," the guards answered, looking at him with perplexed expressions.

Solitario hurried to Oscuridad, mounting him in a smooth motion. They were in the foothills before Solitario could even remember which sector of the mountain range Efrain had been deployed to, but soon he found his way, winding through the trails between thickets of prickly pear, ocotillo, and barrel cactus.

Solitario scanned the landscape, searching for movement, but all was still. Then he paused, reining in Oscuridad as he spotted a swath of purple nearby. For some indescribable reason, the color slowed his heart. Inhaling, he proceeded slowly. As he reached the patch of purple sand verbena blooms, a breeze that was too cool for midday washed soothingly over his face, like a gentle wave back home on the coast during an otherwise merciless summer day.

He brought his horse to a halt and dismounted. Removing his hat, he stood at the edge of the wildflowers, the tips of his boots nudging up against the silvery oval leaves dusted in reflective grains of sand. As the fragrance of the flowers calmed him, he closed his eyes for a long moment. When he reopened them, Efrain stood before him, looking just as he'd seen him at the break of dawn.

"Warn the colonel," the scout implored. "It's a surprise attack on two flanks."

Solitario stared at him, knowing full well this was not an Efrain made of skin and hair and flesh and bone. "Where are you?"

"It's too late for me."

"No."

"Tell the colonel and save my brother."

Solitario unlocked his gaze from Efrain's spirit, squinting into the desert, searching for his fallen body amid the endless speckling of cacti across the plain, up the slopes of mountains rising and falling like waves of earth moving at an infinitesimally slow speed. "I'm sorry." He could not spot Efrain anywhere amid the terrain. The scouts wore khaki pants and matching shirts to blend into the scenery. Camouflage, the French called it. They'd invented the term. Now it was used against them by the Mexican resistance, which was superior at guerrilla warfare in its native habitat. Soon they would drive the French emperor out. Benito Juárez would be reinstalled in Mexico City. And everyone would find something new to fight about, or another foreign power would decide that Mexico was vulnerable enough for them to feast on her weakness. And more Efrains would die. "Ride with me then," Solitario murmured to Efrain. "Help me find your hermano."

They shot through the mountains, Oscuridad churning the sand beneath his hooves with a hunger to put distance between his master and the encroaching enemy. Solitario warned the colonel and snapped commands to his troops. Then, he told Efrain to point him in the direction of his brother.

Speeding through the foothills into a steep canyon, Solitario spied enemy soldiers up on the ridges, shooting down into the ravine. He pulled his pistols and fired, Oscuridad rushing into the fracas. Assailants wavered and tumbled into the gorge, rocks sliding alongside their bodies. In close quarters, he unsheathed his saber and swung to both sides, not sparing the enemy the tip or the sharp edges. Blood splattered across his black pants and jacket, spurted onto Oscuridad's hide.

Dismounting, like the eye of a swirling hurricane of dust and smoke, Solitario spoke in hushed tones to Efrain. "¿Donde está?"

"He is playing dead with that imperial soldier, over there by the boulder." Efrain pointed toward his brother.

"You've saved him," Solitario assured the scout. "You can rest now."

"But now I won't be able to protect him anymore. He is my little brother."

"I will take care of him for you," Solitario promised.

"I was to be the godfather to his children someday."

"I will see to that in your honor."

Efrain nodded as Solitario strode across the scalding sand toward Elias, who was sprawled facedown next to a fallen enemy.

Along the way, Solitario paused, staring at the dead imperialists splayed at his feet. Their bodies were crumpled awkwardly, and they rested faceup, their eyes vacant, blood trickling from their noses and mouths, holes perforating their blue jackets, gold buttons glinting in the sun. As he looked at them, he recalled learning how to shoot out on Caja Pinta and El Dos de Copas. As a shadow to his older brother, he had merely watched and listened and learned everything his brother took for granted and then went out on his own to practice it. He had lined up green glass bottles on gnarled fence posts, blasting them to smith-ereens. And, when that had become too easy, he had tied the bottles' necks to ropes and hung them from tree limbs, pushing them so they would oscillate like pendulums. Aiming at them from afar, he watched them explode as they arced toward the blue sky.

He stared at the dead men, seeing their bloodied faces and broken bodies, scraped and crushed from the long spill down the canyon walls, and he longed to see them made of broken glass rather than rotting flesh. With a brush of his hand, he flicked a rare sprinkle of tears off his cheek. Where the salt water landed, green seedlings sprouted from the canyon floor, enveloping the dead. Solitario barely noticed the calla lilies blooming as he hoisted Elias over his shoulder and carried him to Oscuridad.

Halfway back to the camp, Elias sat up and asked, "Who were you talking to back in the canyon, Jefe?"

"Your brother."

Elias didn't say anything else. He didn't ask any questions.

Solitario gritted his teeth as he listened to his sergeant sniffling behind him.

SEVENTEEN

Solitario stared at the adobe wall in the jailhouse. It wasn't much to look at. It wasn't like the cave art he'd witnessed with Onawa or the Virgen de Guadalupe he'd seen emblazoned on Juan Diego's tilma in the Basilica of Mexico City, but it had potential. It could be his own work of art. He could arrange his thoughts on it and make it into an image of something that always seemed to elude his grasp just as his fingers closed over its essence. Truth? Justice? Fairness, perhaps?

He sighed as he pinned another photo to the wooden board he'd hung up to organize his thoughts around the victims and the suspects. Who would commit such atrocious acts? And why? What motivation could anyone have? As he thought of the Tolbert, Elias, and Lopez families, he could not detect a clear connection between the three. He needed more information. He had already visited Elias' house to feed his horse, look for clues, heck, to look for Elias himself, but he had found nothing on the first try. And Frankie remained in a coma at Dr. Ferris' house. Spirits had always been his best informants, so he decided to give Elias another try, this time bringing his guitar to draw him out.

Riding through the slumbering town, Solitario whispered to Tormenta as they crossed the gorge. "You'll be happy to see your amigo," he said, approaching Elias' vacant home on the levee.

Beneath the large mesquite trees between the house and the dry riverbed, a tobiano-patterned pinto horse waited for his rider to return, his white coat glowing in the moonlight that filtered through the mesquite fronds. His brown patches blending into the darkness, he looked as if he were only partially there.

Tormenta whinnied softly in greeting as she approached her old friend. They sniffed each other calmly, snorting in approval as Solitario dismounted.

Solitario stroked the pinto's mane and fed both of the horses from a sack inside a wooden shed near the outhouse. Then he unstrapped his guitar from Tormenta's flank and sat beneath the tree, with his back to the rough trunk, strumming lightly, the sounds of the guitar strings blending into the song of the cicadas. He closed his eyes and let the music wash over him. He recalled riding over the northern desert plains of Chihuahua toward Olvido with Elias at his side when the war with the French had come to its gruesome end. He'd been filled with hope that at long last he might have outrun the maldición de Caja Pinta.

A creaking sound roused him from the depths of his remembrance. Opening his eyes, he saw the outhouse door slowly swing open. The evening breeze rustled through the mesquites, dispersing leaflets in a gentle drift. Had the wind pushed the door aside?

Elias emerged tentatively. "Last time I came out here, things didn't go so well."

"You've been in the bathroom a long time," Solitario smiled at his sergeant, still plucking at the guitar strings.

"That's what Otila used to say," Elias murmured, walking toward the horses. He glanced over his shoulder, wary of being ambushed again. "I miss her and the children."

"You haven't seen them?"

"No," Elias glumly patted his horse. The pinto responded by snorting softly and bowing his head a couple of times.

Solitario had never fully understood how it all worked, who got to come back and who didn't, where they went when they disappeared. Did the spirits end up on another plane with their loved ones? Or did they simply dissipate into the ether like a morning mist burned off by the rising sun? "I'm sorry," Solitario concluded. What else he could say?

"Who will take care of Caballo Sin Nombre now?" Elias asked, referring to his notoriously nameless pinto.

"I will take care of him," Solitario replied, putting his guitar down, propping his arms on his knees as he stared at Elias. "But first we must worry about Elena."

Elias suddenly seemed to remember more details of what had transpired. "She survived."

"Yes, she is being held somewhere, along with the two Tolbert girls."

"That's why you're here, doing what you do . . ."

"Doing what I do."

"I don't remember anything." Elias rested his head on his hands, rocking it back and forth as if stirring its contents might produce a different result.

"Tell me what you do recall."

"I had a bad dream. I was out here. It was in the middle of the night. I didn't even see who hit me, but they dragged us down by the river. I saw the carnicero and his family. We all went up in flames, except for Elena." He paused, his face contorting in anger. "Venganza was my last thought, Solitario. And you know, I was a peaceful man. If I could find a way out of trouble without violence, I was happier for it. But this cannot be forgiven. You need to save my daughter and avenge Otila and Oscarito's deaths for me." He spat on the ground. Sensing his rage, the horses rustled uneasily, their hooves digging into the loosely packed dirt.

Solitario rose to his feet, "Show me where they came at you."

Elias pointed at the outhouse, "Right as I walked out to head back to the house."

"I need to look at it in the daylight," Solitario surmised. "I do not want to disturb any traces by accident in the dark."

Elias nodded, "So then, why are you here now?"

Solitario's eyes narrowed into long slits and his mustache dropped, "To see you."

At Elias' invitation, Solitario spent the night in his house, sleeping in Oscarito's bed. Before lying down to sleep, he examined the family's personal items yet again. Aside from some overturned tables and bed-sheets strewn on the floor, nothing seemed to have been disturbed or removed. Robbery was not the motive, clearly. At a small vanity where Elena kept a row of combs, brushes, and hair ribbons, Solitario picked up a brush entangled with her long black hair. Turning it over in his hand, he stared at it glumly. His stomach rumbled not with hunger but with anger. Somewhere out there, Elias' daughter was in grave danger. He was her padrino. It was a sacred duty. Not only had he accepted the responsibility of looking after her in the absence of her parents, now he might be the only person standing between her and a horrible, pre-mature death. Shaking his head in frustration, Solitario put the brush back in its place. He owed it to Elias to make sure Elena would some-day pick up that brush again, run its bristles through her hair, have a chance to salvage the wreckage of her young life.

After a fitful night, dreaming of Elena lost in the desert, Solitario rose with the sun. He brewed his morning coffee in Otila's eerily empty kitchen. When he sat at the table to savor the steaming salve, Elias stepped through the kitchen door to join him.

"I miss Otila's cooking," the sergeant said. "Her breakfasts were reason enough to get out of bed in the morning."

Solitario nodded, sipping in silence, not knowing what he could possibly say that might assuage his friend's suffering and loneliness.

"You can stay here as long as you want," Elias offered. "It will spare you the long ride back to El Escondido every night and morning."

"Gracias," Solitario answered. "There is no time to waste, not to-morrow and not today. We must find Elena. Let's start by taking a closer look outside."

The men sauntered toward the outhouse, where the door was bang-ing in the wind. Dust blew in their eyes. The horses hoofed the ground restlessly. There was a wildness in the morning gusts, the kind that usually blew in something unpredictable and—in these parts—typically unwanted.

Solitario crouched at the perimeter of the clearing surrounding the outhouse, where the brittle grass disappeared. In the dirt, he could make out various sizes and types of boot prints, but the powerful winds were erasing them.

"There," he pointed at a faint mark, and just as he did, it vanished from sight. "Did you see it?"

Elias nodded. "An *X*."

"Just like at the Tolberts' barn."

The cornstalks were withered and brown in the field out front of the Jackson homestead, which rose from a plot of churning dust as if it were being conjured up from some dark depths beneath the ground. It was a two-story house painted white long ago, the wooden planks peeling and gray underneath, a rusted rooster weather vane creaking atop the high-pitched Victorian roof.

Solitario stared at it from his saddle, raising his yellow bandanna over his nose to avoid inhaling dust into his lungs. His eyes burned. After seeing the *X* in the ground at Elias' outhouse, he'd fetched the Dobbs twins so they could tell him more about the property adjacent to the Tolberts'. Then, much to his chagrin, they'd insisted on escorting him.

"This is the Jacksons' place," Blake Dobbs said, his eyes clouding over with suspicion as he looked at it. "The Tolbert farm is over yonder." He pointed beyond the house. In the distance, the land sloped down to where the creek ran between the properties and then sideways into the woods that separated them both from the church property.

"Where is everybody?" Michael Dobbs wondered aloud.

"Looks like someone gave up on the crops a while back," Blake said.

"How many people live here?" asked Solitario.

"They're a big family, but all the kids left already except for the youngest. We used to go to school with her. Gertrude is her name. It's just Old Man Jackson, his wife, and her," Blake explained.

"Did they get along with Sheriff Tolbert?" Solitario questioned.

"I never heard otherwise," Blake replied.

"Pretty much keep to themselves," Michael nodded in agreement.

Solitario's stomach twisted, the way it often did when he was about to find something unpleasant. Frowning, he chided himself for allowing the Dobbs boys to come along. They seemed naively—if genuinely— excited to play detective, but this was no game. And the last thing he wanted on his hands was more innocent blood.

"You boys should head back into town and fetch the doctor," Solitario instructed.

"But, Jefe, we can't leave you here alone. What if there's trouble?" Blake protested.

Solitario glared at him. He knew there was going to be no trouble that he couldn't handle or that hadn't already happened, for that matter, but his job wasn't explaining things to his deputies. His job was keeping them safe. And, sometimes, some things were better not seen by the young because—forever after—they could not be unseen.

"We'll be back right away," Blake said, nodding.

The Dobbs brothers turned their horses around and rode off quickly, leaving a billowy cloud of dust in their wake.

Solitario advanced slowly to the house, circling it on Tormenta. Dead flowers in a couple of pots on the porch. An old mule watering itself down by the creek. A cow in the pasture chewing on cud, staring at him from beyond the barbed-wire fence. As they turned behind the house, Tormenta stopped abruptly, without Solitario commanding her to do so. Surprised, Solitario reached for his revolvers, had them out of their holsters before his eyes could settle on whatever had given Tormenta pause.

Two lifeless forms, clad in black but blanketed in dust, rested on the ground behind the house. Their limbs were splayed awkwardly. Bloodstains had pooled, drying around their heads like dark halos.

Solitario stared at the bodies, holstered his pistols, and dismounted. As he approached the bodies, who he assumed were Old Man and Old Lady

Jackson, he gazed upward at the high roofline, jutting into the sky. Then he looked back down at where the bodies festered, swarmed by buzzing flies. From their position it was clear they had fallen a great distance. Perhaps *fallen* was not the right word, he mused. Rather, the husband and wife had been hurled to their deaths from a soaring, unsurvivable height.

There would be no *X*'s still pressed into the ground here. The winds had been too strong. And even if they hadn't been blowing like they wanted to wipe Olvido off the map once and for all, Solitario suspected that the assailants had not bothered to check on the dead after hearing their bones crack and their necks snap on impact.

Solitario stood over the cadavers for a moment, but the stench was too strong. He raised his bandanna over his nose again, swatted away a fly, and led Tormenta back to the front of the house, where she waited as he climbed the front porch.

Standing in the shade, his eyes narrowed as he spotted bullet holes in the walls. He leaned in to examine them. Splinters jutted out around the small openings. The shots had been fired from inside the house. He removed his sombrero, gritting his teeth. Maybe they'd taken the daughter. Maybe she was with Elena and the Tolbert girls. He made the sign of the cross, took a deep breath, and opened the door.

Keeping the bandanna over his nose with one hand and holding a revolver with the other, Solitario moved stealthily through the home, making sure not to disturb anything that might turn out to be evidence. The house was in complete disarray, more so than Elias' had been. This invasion had been met with some resistance. His eyes landed on bullet holes ripped through the living-room walls, broken glass dispersed across the floorboards, family photos smashed and sprinkled with droplets of blood. A crimson-smeared Stetson sat in a corner, next to a discarded gun. Bullet casings were scattered about. The kitchen was strewn with pots and pans as if Old Lady Jackson had put up a mighty fight with her kitchen hardware in the confined space. A trail of blood stretched down the hallway and up the stairs.

Solitario climbed gingerly along the inner edge of the stairs, clutching the banister to maintain his balance. As he ascended, he scrutinized the bloodstains on the steps. The intruders had stepped on the blood but left no recognizable marks. The bedrooms were in a more orderly state, with the exception of the daughter's room, where Solitario also found signs of a struggle. Gertrude's vanity had been overturned, the mirror cracked, perfume bottles dashed on the floor. The boards creaking beneath his boots, Solitario prowled through all of the rooms but found no more bodies. Standing on the landing at the top of the stairs, he noticed that the bloodstains simply stopped there. Gazing up, he noticed a trapdoor to the attic, red fingerprints smudged around a bloodstained cord dangling down. Pulling on it, he unfolded the ladder attached to it.

Rising into the shadowy attic, he peered through the opening. It was a fully finished space, wide open. A large mirror leaned against a long wall. At the foot of it sat a row of tattered pink satin ballet slippers. Here, Gertrude had danced. For a moment, Solitario closed his eyes and envisioned the slender young woman twirling gracefully before the looking glass. With a long, slow exhalation, he opened his eyes and climbed up, unfolding his frame to its full height. The roof was pitched high indeed, he nodded in acknowledgment.

The bloodstains resumed on the polished dance floor, a large circle slathered in crimson at the center of the room. As he knelt down to examine the markings more closely, he zeroed in on a dash of fine brown powder spilled within the circle. He gathered it together using a small piece of paper which he folded and tucked into his pocket. When he was finished collecting that tiny bit of evidence, he continued his mental cataloging of the space.

A ladder rose up to yet another hatch, leading to the roof. The rungs were bloodied too. He figured the attackers had dragged the wounded parents up there and thrown them down to their deaths. But where was the girl? Where was Gertrude? In the corner of the whitewashed attic, a large wardrobe stood in tight-lipped vigil. Perhaps it contained her dance clothes. What were they called? Tutus? Or something fancy and French-sounding like that. Solitario grimaced at the thought of anything French, even all these years later. Stepping around the circle drawn in blood, careful not to disturb it with his boots, he approached the wardrobe.

Before opening it, he gazed out the window toward the entrance to the farm. At the gate, he spotted the Dobbs twins returning with Dr. Ferris in tow, their three steeds hastening down the dirt road toward the house.

He opened the wardrobe door expecting to see a row of pink gauze skirts, but what met his eyes scorched his soul like a searing cattle iron. He turned away, but it was too late. Stuffed inside the antique wardrobe was the bloodied corpse of what must have been a young woman, devoid of her own skin, with nothing left on the bones—some of which jutted out of place—but blood and exposed tissue. Her head had been removed at the base of the neck. Along with the entire dermis, it was nowhere in sight. Solitario slammed the wardrobe door shut. Fighting a powerful wave of nausea, he leaned with his hands on the sill, raising the window for fresh air. Down below, the twins and the doctor stared up at him quizzically. He squinted into the sun, shaking his head. For the first time in all of his many occupations, he had encountered an evil so dark that he was shaken to his core.

As Dr. Ferris examined Gertrude Jackson's remains in the attic, Michael stood guard outside the house, and his brother, Blake, rode into town to fetch a cart to haul the bodies to the cemetery.

Standing over the doctor, who crouched over the body, Solitario asked, "Would you say that this kind of flaying requires a special skill?"

"Definitely," Dr. Ferris replied, stroking his white mustache. "Most hunters around these parts know how to skin an animal, but they do it in strips, tearing chunks of muscle off the carcass. This here was done much more deliberately, with great precision and care. Very few cuts into the muscular layer."

"It is as if they wished to remove her entire skin in one piece," Solitario assessed.

Dr. Ferris nodded in agreement.

"What kind of person could do that?"

"A madman," Dr. Ferris answered.

Solitario strode to the window and stared down at Michael Dobbs standing in the clearing. "I meant from a perspective of the skills required."

"Oh, I see . . ." Dr. Ferris sat back on his haunches, pausing to consider the question. "I suppose perhaps a butcher would be capable."

"Our town butcher just went up in flames a few days ago. Could this have happened before then?"

"Judging by the rate of decomposition, I would say that this crime happened after the burnings at the stake."

"Who else then might possess the skills?"

"The Apache . . ."

Leaning with his back against the window, Solitario peered down at Dr. Ferris. "What about a doctor?"

Dr. Ferris stared back at him, his Adam's apple rising and falling several times. "I suppose that's also a possibility."

Solitario nodded, crossing his arms and watching intently as Dr. Ferris concluded his examination. Once he was done, they wrapped the body in canvas and hauled it downstairs.

Outside, in the burning light of the sun, Solitario once again approached the bodies of Gertrude's parents. As the doctor turned them over, he was surprised to see a hole in each of their chests.

"Their hearts were removed before they were thrown off the roof." Solitario vocalized his thoughts as they formed.

"How do you know it was before?" asked Michael Dobbs.

"There were no signs of their bodies being disturbed after falling," Solitario answered.

"They were likely dead before they hit the ground," the doctor concluded. "Although if there was still some fresh blood in their brain, then the snapping of their necks would have quickly ended their suffering."

"How merciful," Solitario muttered, spitting onto the ground in disdain.

As Dr. Ferris and Michael Dobbs prepared the bodies for transport, Blake Dobbs rounded the house at an alarming speed. The cart he was pulling nearly tipped sideways due to his haste.

"Whoa!" Blake cried as he struggled to rein his horse to a stop, its hooves sliding across the clearing.

"Careful, young man," Dr. Ferris admonished. "The last thing we need is more dead bodies on our hands."

"I'm sorry," Blake called, jumping down to the ground. "Jefe, there's trouble in town. You've gotta hurry."

Solitario gazed calmly at his deputy. "What is it?"

"People heard about these killings already. Some men have formed a posse and are rounding up suspects. I'm afraid they're planning to shoot them all."

"Suspects?" Solitario mused. "How can that be? We haven't concluded our investigation."

"I don't think they care, sir," Blake replied, panting, his cheeks flushed, sweat pouring down his brow into his eyes. "You need to go before there's blood in the streets."

"Who are they rounding up?" Solitario asked as he strode to Tormenta, fastening his sombrero with the cord that dangled beneath his chin.

"Mexicans and Apaches," Blake answered.

"Help the doctor load the bodies and then hurry after me," Solitario called out, mounting Tormenta and galloping away in a cloud of dust.

EIGHTEEN

As Solitario sped into Olvido, the wind buffeted Tormenta. Tumbleweeds skipped across the dirt roads and took flight, carried high by the gusts. Severed tree branches sailed overhead. Abandoned structures whistled and howled as air blew through their hollowed-out innards, their battered doors banging in the wind. Solitario sensed chaos encroaching. He'd felt it on the eve of poorly planned battles and during the impending invasion of cities harboring too many unknown variables. It was a specific kind of foreboding he did not welcome one bit.

Leaning low over Tormenta's rippling neck, he flashed down the town's main street, coming to a halt in what served as Olvido's new town square, a cluster of commercial buildings built by the Anglo settlers lining four sides of a large square clearing. At the far northern end of the street—about a hundred yards from the square—stood Reverend Grimes' white church. At the opposite end dropped the dry river gorge, beyond which the street stretched through the Mexican part of town.

The squall burst into the square just as Solitario arrived, kicking up dust devils and sweeping up dry leaves in a frenzy of debris. Squinting through the arid tempest stinging his eyes, Solitario knew at once none of the people being held against their will could have committed the complex and heinous crimes in question. Against a long stucco wall, beyond which lay the graveyard, fifteen men had been lined up, tied with rope at the ankles and wrists, their hands behind their backs. They wore the faded and frayed clothing of campesinos, several of them still crowned by sombreros. A few were little more than boys, including a trio of Apache too young to be out hunting or fighting with their fathers. A handful of gunslingers patrolled them, their pistols cocked and ready. The townspeople and shopkeepers had all wisely retreated into hiding behind their shutters.

Solitario resisted the urge to dismount and untie the prisoners. He was fast with his guns but he was also heavily outnumbered. He had never had much use for words, but he had also learned long ago that they were sometimes indispensable to survival. Diplomacy, Colonel Terrazas had called it, an endeavor at which he had considered himself rather competent. It was often easier to acquire vast swaths of land by outthinking and outtalking your opponent, the colonel had taught Solitario, rather than by relying on the sheer brutality of force. Sometimes, the threat of bloodshed was more effective than the act of violence itself. And yet other times, the vague promise of an alluring reward in the future might dissuade a man from choosing to kill in the present.

Moving slowly, Solitario guided Tormenta toward the horseman he deduced to be the posse's leader. The man's face was covered by a bushy red beard, his skin ruddy from sun and alcohol and tobacco. He wore a dusty gray coat and a weathered Confederate cavalry hat.

As Solitario approached, the horseman turned on his tall quarter horse and addressed him. "If I was you, I wouldn't go meddling here," the man grumbled. "¿Habla ingles?"

Solitario sized him up, his fingers itching to reach for his pistol. He knew he'd likely outdraw the man, but it was his four henchmen he was worried about. How would he elude their gunfire in response?

"Yes, I speak English," Solitario said, inching closer.

The man's eyes landed on the silver badge glinting on Solitario's jacket. "I see. You must be the new sheriff everyone's been flapping about. I'm Captain Ringgold. I work for Mr. Grissom."

Grissom was the county's largest landowner. Everyone knew his name if little less about him, except that he was not a man with whom one should trifle. Solitario had heard of Ringgold too, a relic from the Civil War that Grissom had brought out West with him after the Union's victory over the South. Ringgold was known for drinking hard and losing his temper, a combination that usually resulted in innocent people paying the price for his excesses.

"Solitario Cisneros," he introduced himself in response. "Now, tell me, Captain, what is the meaning of all this?"

"These here men are being brought to justice for the gruesome killings that been happening in these here parts," Captain Ringgold answered, spitting a wad of tobacco onto the ground to the right of his steed.

"But how can justice be determined when the investigation is still underway?" Solitario asked. "These men—and boys—do not fit the description of the kind of people I believe may have committed the crimes of which you speak."

"We'll see about that," Captain Ringgold retorted.

"How's that?"

"Well, if we shoot them and the killings stop, then we'll know it was them . . . or some of them at least."

Solitario tried not to scoff at Captain Ringgold's sloppy sense of justice, choosing instead to restrain his instincts and practice the colonel's diplomacy. "So, what evidence do you have against them?"

"Well, they're Mezcun and Apache," Captain Ringgold replied. "Both of which are known to be violent."

Solitario stared back silently, wondering what gave Captain Ringgold the sense that he could dispense justice.

Solitario scanned the immediate area yet again, searching for any hidden gunmen, allied or otherwise. As the captain spoke, a stagecoach lumbered into town, pulling to a stop in front of Olvido's lone hotel, a two-story building with an ornate balcony overlooking the square. Mr. Boggs emerged from the hotel in a shiny purple vest embroidered with an intricate black pattern. He helped two ladies in elegant dresses with flounced, bell-shaped skirts and fancy hats descend from the coach, quickly ushering them into the lobby.

"When are you planning to set up your firing squad?" Solitario asked. "If you are patient enough to wait, I would like for our town's mayor to have a few words with you beforehand. Perhaps the spilling of innocent blood could be avoided. I need more time for the investigation."

"Your investigation," Captain Ringgold sneered, "ain't going too well, now is it?"

Solitario's deadpan face revealed nothing.

"How many dead bodies pile up already? I hear the busiest men in town ain't the banker or the baker, but the gravedigger and the coffin maker," Ringgold added. As he chuckled at his own cleverness, his men guffawed behind him.

Just as the laughter subsided, the Dobbs twins rode into the square, lining up behind Solitario.

Ringgold grew quiet. Solitario figured he was recalculating his odds. It was five against three now, but Solitario knew his deputies looked pretty wet behind the ears, while Ringgold's men were jaded veterans of war.

"Like I said," Solitario repeated, "it would be good if you spoke to the mayor before taking matters into your own hands and facing the consequences of doing so."

Ringgold snickered. "You've got big cojones, lawman, I'll give you that. I don't know if you're more nursemaid than sheriff with those two deputies of yours, but sure, I'll give you ten minutes to turn up the mayor if you can. If you're as good at finding him as you are at solving crimes, I reckon we'll be having ourselves a good old-fashioned firing squad here pretty damn soon."

Solitario let the man talk all he wanted. Every couple of seconds was another breath of life bartered for the men quaking by the graveyard wall, steps away from their final resting place, no doubt eager to run as far away from it as possible.

"Boys, go fetch the mayor," Solitario instructed, his somber gaze remaining steadily fixed on Captain Ringgold's blue eyes. He could see a bloodlust in them, one not quenched by war but rather made stronger and turned into a sickness. Men like Ringgold needed to kill to feel alive. "Hurry."

"But Jefe . . ." Blake began.

"Let's go," Michael interrupted. "C'mon. No time to waste."

As the brothers rode away, Solitario realized what a good thing it was that there were two of them. Blake had been about to protest they had no idea where the mayor might be, but Michael had realized Solitario already knew that and was simply bargaining for time. Maybe his deputies had potential after all, Solitario mused as he stroked his mustache. They made the kind of team he had always yearned for—yet never found—in his own twin brother.

"I'll wait under the tree," he told Ringgold, nodding and guiding Tormenta toward the lone oak that towered at the center of the square. Some called it the hanging tree.

In the shade of the majestic oak, Solitario dismounted. He knew all eyes were upon him, those of the prisoners along the stucco wall, those of the villagers peering out through their shutters, those of Captain Ringgold and his men, edgy and poised to fire their weapons at the lineup they'd assembled in their pursuit of so-called justice. As they all watched and waited, he took a long draft of water from his canteen. He whispered a few soothing words to Tormenta, who could clearly sense the tension. He unstrapped his guitar from his horse's flank.

Sitting against the tree, Solitario began to pluck at the strings, tuning his instrument. He played an old Spanish lullaby, the notes carried on the wind, swirling through the square, providing a rhythm and a haunting melody for the leaves and tumbleweeds to dance. Ringgold's men glanced at each other incredulously, but Solitario played on, the mercurial magic emanating from his guitar weaving a spell over the posse. Even Ringgold himself swayed in the stiff breeze in tandem with the tempo of Solitario's sweet song. The underside of Solitario's sombrero began to glow a deep cobalt blue, its silvery white embroidery glittering as he closed his eyes and let his fingers fly over the strings, summoning notes both from instinct and from memory. It was a song he had learned long ago on Caja Pinta, way before Luz had bestowed the enchanted sombrero upon him. As he played, the hue of the sombrero's underbrim grew lighter, like a night sky shifting toward dawn.

When he finished the song, the blue glow faded from his face. And, when he opened his eyes, he saw Captain Ringgold slumped in a deep sleep over the neck of his horse, his men sprawled unconscious on the ground, snoring beneath the midday sun. As the Dobbs boys returned with Mayor Stillman in tow, Solitario motioned for them to be quiet and untie the prisoners. While they did so, he handcuffed Ringgold and his men. The prisoners all ran as fast as they could out of the plaza, but Captain Ringgold and his posse continued to slumber undisturbed despite the wind and the sun and the heat.

"Load them into the wagon and put them in the tank," Solitario told the Dobbs boys.

"Are you sure about that?" Mayor Stillman asked, his voice quivering. "Captain Ringgold works for Mr. Grissom, our biggest taxpayer."

"Justice is not for sale," Solitario quipped, fastening his guitar back to Tormenta's side.

As he was about to put his boot in the stirrup and swing up into the saddle, Solitario heard a man clear his throat behind him. He reached for his gun as he whirled around. But instead of a surprise attacker, Solitario was greeted by a familiar face from years past.

An elderly man with wavy white hair, dressed in an elegant cream-colored suit, stood before him with a wrinkled, quivering hand outstretched. "M'ijo," he said, "I'm so pleased to see you are still putting the sombrero my daughter made for you to good use."

"Don Miguel!" exclaimed Solitario, giving the man a tight squeeze. He felt smaller and frailer than Solitario recalled. Too many years had passed since they'd last seen each other. It had been easier to ignore his father-in-law's continued existence after Luz's death than to be painfully reminded of her in his presence. Don Miguel's eyes glimmered green in the brilliant sunlight, just as hers once had. "What brings you to town, Don Miguel?"

"Just a bit of business," Don Miguel answered, waving toward the bank. "I hear you've taken up the badge and gun again. That's good. Olvido saw its best days when you were keeping the peace."

Solitario smiled. They had been far better days, indeed, when Luz had been alive, before the river had forsaken Olvido. "We will see what I can do."

"I'm heading back to my ranch," Don Miguel said. "I boarded up the house in the city a long time ago, as you know. Too many memories of . . ."

"Sí." Solitario nodded, growing solemn. "Too many memories of Luz."

"Cuídate, m'ijo," Don Miguel said, walking toward his carriage, which was parked in front of the bank. "And hang on to that sombrero. She made it with love, for you."

Solitario watched as his father-in-law climbed into his carriage and rode away. He mounted Tormenta, touching the now-dark underside of his sombrero. Luz had been magical. She had imbued everything she touched with her spirit. He fought back the sudden urge to weep.

At the town hall, Solitario stood watch over the captives sleeping in their cells. The Dobbs twins stared in disbelief. Mayor Stillman sat at the sheriff's desk, scratching his head.

"I can't believe how you did that," Blake Dobbs remarked for the umpteenth time.

"How *did* you do that?" Michael asked.

"It's an old charro trick I picked up down south of the river. Call it my kind of diplomacy."

"Well, regardless of how you did it," the mayor concluded, "lives were spared and that's what matters. Our town can't afford for its population to keep dwindling. People are getting very restless, very scared. Do you think Grissom sent Ringgold and his posse to kill those men as a way of quieting things down?"

"All I know is if people keep dying, this town's gonna be quiet all right," Blake Dobbs said.

Solitario stared at Captain Ringgold slumped on a bench against the jail cell wall. "I don't know if Grissom sent them. We'll find out when they wake up . . . which should be in a few hours. In the meantime, I have work to do. The reason I know those men we saved were not to blame is because these killings seem complicated and orchestrated. Yes, there are several people working on them, but the crimes themselves don't seem random. They're not robberies either. They are ritualistic. It's not the work of field hands and children. It's the work of educated and skilled evildoers."

"So the Apache?" Stillman asked.

"I don't think so either. But if we don't figure it out soon, people like Ringgold are going to keep blaming every Apache and Mexican they can lay their hands on, until nobody can stop them from shedding innocent blood."

Solitario picked up his sombrero and opened the front door. Looking back, he instructed his deputies to keep close watch over the prisoners.

"And me?" the mayor asked.

"I have a feeling Grissom will show up soon enough," Solitario replied. "Make sure he promises if we release his men, he'll keep them out of our way until we finish our investigation."

The mayor nodded in agreement.

Heading out, Solitario mounted Tormenta and disappeared into the unrelenting dust storm.

NINETEEN

As the sunset submerged her house in a deep copper hue, Onawa dabbed her father's forehead with a damp towel, her eyes tracing the creases in his weathered skin. He had given so much for her and her mother. Now it was her turn to sacrifice for him. She hoped she could always make him proud, but she couldn't help but feel like a disappointment. No marriage. No grandchildren. Time—like her father's life—was slipping through her fingers.

Moving quietly through their low-slung adobe home on the outskirts of Olvido, Onawa paused at a small altar in the front room. A collection of candles and artifacts that had belonged to her mother sat on the rustic wooden table before the lone photograph she possessed of her. In the picture, her mother was dressed in white. Her black braids, one draped over each shoulder, nearly reached the ground. She stood next to Onawa's father, who had been in his prime back then, a feathered headdress crowning him chief. It was not an Apache tradition to maintain such a tribute to the departed within one's home. Quite to the contrary, most Apache believed in disposing of their deceased loved ones' ephemera in order to ward off any unhappy remnants of their spirits. But Onawa's father had allowed Onawa this observance in honor of her mother's Mexican customs.

Onawa peered at her mother's stiff image. Longing rose through her body—the sweet, impossible yearning of a daughter parted too soon from her mother. Onawa believed that her mother's spirit was still with her, stirring the branches in the breeze, bringing the scent of lavender and sagebrush through the open windows at night. But still, she missed her. Some spirits were more visible, more palpable than others. And her mother's had long seemed very much at rest.

For a moment, standing there staring at her altar, bathed in the golden light filtering through the windows, she feared her entire life was suspended in amber.

"I wonder what you would think of Solitario, Mamá," Onawa whispered. "Would you approve of him or urge me to run the other way?" Sighing deeply, she touched her mother's fading face, lost in her loneliness, as her father snored in the back room.

She was startled by a sudden rapping on the front door. Squinting through the peephole, she was relieved to find Solitario standing outside, his familiar face shaded by his broad sombrero.

Opening the door, she smiled, "I already heard about your serenade in the square."

Solitario's poker face was unwavering. "How is it possible that gossip travels faster than the speed of sound itself?"

"Come in," she motioned, stepping back. "My father is sleeping, but he will be glad to see you. He has not been feeling well."

Solitario removed his sombrero.

"Here, let me hang it for you," she offered. As she touched the sombrero her fingers tingled with energy. "So this is your secret weapon?"

Solitario stood awkwardly in the center of the small room.

"You don't have to answer that," she added, placing the sombrero on a peg by the door. "We all need our secrets."

"Onawa?"

"Yes?" she answered expectantly.

"I am actually here to see you."

"Again?" she smiled, a flutter in her stomach buoying her spirits.

"Yes, I need your help."

Her eyes glimmered, landing on the shiny star pinned to his jacket.

It had not been there during their journey to the caves in search of Frankie Tolbert. "Why is it only men get to wear shiny badges glowing with power?"

His mind seemed to wander from the room.

"Solitario?" She snapped him out of his daze.

"Yes," he replied, meeting her eyes. "I am sorry your father is ill."

Onawa turned toward her father's room, tiptoeing to its doorway. He was still asleep. "Are you in a hurry?"

"I'm afraid so."

"How can I help you?" She leaned on the doorway between the two rooms. In between, there was a small alcove where she cooked their meals.

He described the killings at the Jackson farm to her. "Some people are blaming the Apache. One common thread through all of the murders is a sense of ritual," Solitario said, running his hand through his hair. "Do you think anyone from your father's old tribe could be involved in this?"

She gazed through the shadowy alcove toward her father. They had left the scattered remnants of their tribe a few years back to reside in Olvido, ostensibly because her father's failing health no longer allowed them to keep up with the band's swift movements. But she suspected there were other reasons beyond that, differences of opinion between the elders like her father seeking peace, refuge, and an end to the endless wars, and the younger leaders determined to continue fighting alongside Geronimo against the ever-encroaching white man.

"Whenever a white person goes and gets themselves scalped or skinned, people immediately start pointing fingers at the Apache. But I don't think they are correct to assume such guilt. When our people fight," Onawa concluded, "they fight with a purpose."

"Yes, and usually that purpose is very clear," Solitario agreed.

"Not like these killings," she said.

"I agree, but if I don't figure out why these deaths are happening and who is causing them, my songs and my sombrero will not be enough to stop those who wish to blame anyone who looks different from them."

"The rituals you have described do not sound Apache to me," Onawa said thoughtfully, glancing at the photograph of her mother on the altar. "They sound Aztec."

Solitario nodded.

"There is a woman we must visit," Onawa decided. "It is a half day's ride from here to the southeast."

"Near the Big Bend?"

"Yes," she said. "Let's wake my father so he can give us his blessing."

"I'm sorry to take you away from him," Solitario whispered as they inched toward Aguila Brava. "Perhaps you could give me directions and I could go alone."

"This woman will not speak to you if you go alone."

"She is a bruja?" he asked.

"Yes, she was a friend of my mother's," Onawa answered. "That is why I must go."

Solitario nodded as Onawa softly nudged her father's shoulder.

"T'aah," she whispered, "wake up, T'aah. Your amigo is here."

Aguila Brava's eyes snapped open, and a smile curved across his wizened face as he focused on Solitario standing next to Onawa. "Spirit Talker," he said. "Welcome back."

They traveled at night to save time and energy. Departing Olvido at three a.m., beneath the cover of darkness, afforded them a cool breeze as they moved over the vast desert, the sands glowing white in the moonlight. Solitario rode on Tormenta and Onawa on Invierno as they quietly traversed the desert at a steady pace. The landscape was speckled with an infinite abundance of creosote and yucca. In the distance to the south and to the north, they could see the black outlines of the mountains jutting into the starry cobalt sky. They progressed undisturbed, the only sound the occasional howl of a distant coyote. As they rode, Onawa felt strangely at peace, in an unspoken harmony with Solitario and the horses. It was as if she had always known she'd make this journey with him at her side.

Leaving Olvido far behind, Onawa sensed they were not alone.

Glancing back over her shoulder, she could make out a lonesome figure trailing in the distance.

"Why does he follow us from so far behind?" she asked Solitario.

"You see him too?"

"Yes."

"I think he's shy around you," Solitario answered. "He was saddened that I did not invite him to join us when we went to the caves in search of the Tolbert boy."

Onawa wondered if Elias would still be alive had he indeed accompanied them on that trip. Did Solitario lose sleep over the same doubts? Did he blame himself for his old sergeant's untimely demise? Either way, he would have lost his family. And there was still the possibility of rescuing his daughter, Elena.

Onawa tugged at her reins, slowing until her horse stopped completely. Tormenta turned quizzically, hesitating as well.

"Sargento Elias," Onawa whispered into the wind, "come join us."

Elias suddenly appeared halfway to them. Onawa heard his voice, as did Solitario. "I am not sure if I am welcome."

"You are always welcome," Onawa said to soothe his spirit.

Elias stood next to them. "Buenas noches, Jefe. Buenas noches, Onawa."

"Buenas noches," they both replied, glancing at each other.

"Sargento, there is no need for you to be shy around me or afraid of me. This is your battle too," Onawa told him. "Together we will find your daughter and protect her."

"Gracias," Elias replied.

"Walk with us," Solitario added.

"Muy bien," Elias said.

"You can ride with me if you like." Onawa smiled at him.

"Otila would not approve," Elias answered. "But thank you for offering. It is very kind of you."

"Have you seen her?" Solitario asked.

"Not yet."

"Someday you will," Onawa assured him. She thought of adding that he would rejoin his wife when his remaining work was done and he could at last find peace, but she decided against it, figuring he didn't need more reminding of the challenges and terrifying possibilities that lay ahead. What if they failed to rescue Elena? What then? Would he be damned to forever scour the sands searching for someone he could never find or seeking a vengeance destined to elude him?

Onawa kept her worries to herself as the three continued their journey together, occasionally pausing to study the stars and ensure they were headed in the correct direction.

When the sky lightened, they stopped on a ridge and made a small fire, over which Solitario boiled coarsely ground coffee he extracted from his saddlebag. From two small tin cups, he and Onawa sipped the bitter fuel as they sat on the edge of the mesa and watched the sunrise explode over the eastern horizon, the desert burning a brilliant orange beneath them.

As they admired the spectacle of nature birthing a new day, Onawa inched herself closer to Solitario so that their arms could touch. She was about to rest her head on his shoulder when he scooted sideways to reestablish the void between them. Her heart sinking, Onawa sat up as straight up as she could, squinting into the sun, the sting of its fire bringing water to her eyes.

Why does he run from me? she lamented, both her heart and her pride aching as if they'd been speared by the thorns of the cacti surrounding them. But before she could mold her turbulent emotions into spoken words, Solitario pointed out over the flatlands extending below them.

In the distance a thin plume of white smoke curled into the sky.

"Is that where she lives?" Solitario asked.

Onawa fixed her eyes on the rivulet of opaque vapor, nodding and grimacing as she finished her coffee.

As he packed the cups away, she stamped out the fire with her moccasins. "Elias was right," she quipped as she leaped back onto Invierno.

"About what?"

"Your coffee tastes very strong."

"Maybe you could do better?"

She said no more, but she shot him a cocky look that she hoped expressed her genuine feeling that she could do anything better than he could. Her face and arms glowed in the copper light as she bucked her legs around her horse's flanks. Letting out a hoot that resembled an Apache battle cry, she tore out of the clearing, diving down a steep ravine toward the canyon floor. *You want distance between us?* she mused. *Catch me if you can.*

Her heart raced as—behind her—Tormenta whinnied enthusiastically and Solitario gave chase.

———————

The bruja's jacal was built so close to the ground that they would both have to stoop to pass through its threshold. Made of roughly hewn adobe bricks, the roof was fashioned from tightly jammed mesquite branches. A stone chimney pumped smoke into the air from whatever she was cooking deep inside.

Onawa reached the house first, Solitario trailing not far behind. When they got there, the primitive dwelling's sole inhabitant was already waiting outside.

The woman was ancient, probably about the same age as Aguila Brava, or even older. She wore her hair in long silver braids and was clad in a swirling purple robe as she met them in the clearing.

As Onawa dismounted, the woman raised her hands and closed her eyes.

"It is as if your mother is standing before me," the bruja whispered, her voice trembling with emotion.

Onawa smiled, sighing in relief. "Alicia . . ." she exhaled.

"Ven, mi hija . . ." The woman opened her arms wide, the sheer fabric hanging from them flapping in the cool morning breeze.

Onawa shuffled to her, embracing her fragile form. She had shrunk over the years, just as Onawa's father had.

"I have not seen you since your coming-of-age ceremony," Alicia said, clasping Onawa's cheeks in her rough hands, her long nails grazing her hair. "You have grown into a beautiful young woman, just as your mother was when I taught her."

Onawa's broad smile sprung from deep within her own soul. She felt like she had come home, even though she had only been this way once, a long time ago—with her mother—as a child.

"When we return to the places we've known with our loved ones, it is as if they are with us again. It makes us feel whole. Come, mi hija, we will eat breakfast. I am making chilaquiles." Alicia took Onawa by the hand, leading her toward her jacal. Hesitating as she reached the entrance, she turned to assess Solitario. "I remember your compañero. He was at your Rite of Passage too. Do you wish for him to join us? Or shall we bring breakfast outside for him and his amigo?"

"They can both join us, if that is fine with you," Onawa replied, more out of politeness to Elias than Solitario.

"Oh, I no longer allow spirits to enter my home. Not after what happened some time ago . . ." Alicia's eyes glazed over for a moment. Then, she focused on Elias and added, "No offense, Sargento Elias."

Onawa chuckled at the stunned looks on Solitario's and Elias' faces. Alicia was an old and diminutive bruja, but her resources ran deep as the water hidden in channels beneath the desert. Only those who knew where to look could find them.

"Why don't we bring them breakfast out here. You and I can talk inside first," Onawa smiled gently, looping her arm through Alicia's, stooping with her as they walked into her home.

———————

After breakfast, Solitario removed his sombrero and joined them in the house, which consisted of a long, narrow set of small areas designated for working, cooking, and resting. It was clear that she had lived here alone for quite some time. There were no traces of other inhabitants or of the need for things such as furniture and decor to make guests comfortable. They sat on the floor, their legs crossed.

After Onawa laid out the facts of the investigation, they waited to receive the bruja's wisdom. Alicia closed her eyes and breathed deeply. After a while, she reopened them and spoke. "Onawa, mi hija, and Solitario, grandson of Minerva Villarreal of Caja Pinta . . ." Onawa watched as Solitario's eyes widened at the depth of Alicia's intuition.

"Thank you for coming to see me. You are where you are meant to be, and this is always a good thing."

She can help us, Onawa thought. *I knew she could.* In her excitement she nearly forgot the morning's awkwardness. About to pat Solitario gleefully on the knee, she caught herself at the last second, instead running her hand through her hair.

"Your journey is winding and long, one filled with many sorrows and challenges." She looked from Onawa to Solitario to convey that her words extended to both of them. "This particular challenge that you face in Olvido, this effort to save Sergeant Elias' daughter and the other children, it is a worthy cause. We must always strive to live our lives in pursuit of a worthy cause. The series of crimes you describe, they are indeed rituals. I recognize not only their content but their order."

Onawa glanced at Solitario, who nodded.

Alicia rose and retreated further into her man-made cave. In the back, she rustled for a couple of minutes, reemerging with an antique leather tome cradled in her arms. Taking her place on the floor across from them, she swept the dust off the cover, revealing a familiar symbol worked into the leather.

"The Aztec calendar," remarked Onawa.

"Sí, mi hija," Alicia confirmed, laying the book on the sarape and opening it to reveal intricate drawings made with colorful pigments drawn from the cacti of the deserts north of the Valley of Mexico. "This codex has traveled a long distance to end up collecting sand out here in this nowhere land."

"Are they spells?" Onawa asked, leaning forward, curiosity glinting in her eyes.

"Spells, enchantments, history, songs, tales, culture . . . who can tell the difference between one and the other?" replied Alicia.

Solitario watched intently as the bruja leafed through the pages. Onawa wondered if she reminded him of his grandmother, much as she reminded her of her own mother. Women not of war, but of mystical ways. Women not of death and fear, as others often mistook them to be, but rather of love and of creation, of seeking new ways to solve old problems.

"The rituals you describe follow the Aztec calendar and the order of sacrifices that the Aztecs made to their gods as the seasons progressed," Alicia explained. "The first death, that of the sheriff's wife, happened during our July, which for the Aztecs was the eighth month of the year, Hueytecuihutli. The sacrifice took place during a festival dedicated to the goddess Xilonen, the Aztec goddess of nourishment. The attempt to starve the young boy you call Frankie in the cave aligns with the next sacrifice in the Aztec's traditions, which took place during their ninth month, Tlaxochimaco, to the god Huitzilopochtli. The burning of your poor sergeant's family, along with that of the butcher, in the dry riverbed happened in August, during what was the Aztec's tenth month, Xocotl-huetzin, in a tribute to Xiuhtecuhtli, the god of fire . . ."

"What of the most recent crime, that of the Jackson family on their farm?" asked Solitario.

"Paciencia, mi hijo," Alicia said. "This latest rite coincides with the Aztec month of Ochpaniztli, which took place from late August to early September for us. It is a sacrifice dedicated to the mother goddess, Toci, in which people are hurled to their deaths from great heights and a young woman is decapitated and skinned. The high priest would then wear her skin and perform a dance in honor of Toci."

Onawa and Solitario both winced at the thought of poor Gertrude Jackson's skin being worn by a high priest dancing in the ceremony.

"So what would come next?" Onawa asked.

Alicia's fingers moved over the pages of the codex as she translated the ancient glyphs. "More sacrifices by fire are next. Then two noblewomen would be sacrificed to Tlāloc, the god of rain. This would be followed by a death by bludgeoning in honor of Coatlicue, the goddess who gave birth to the moon and stars. Then a larger sacrifice to Huitzilopochtli—of many children, the girls they have taken captive—by extraction of the heart."

"When?" Solitario asked. "How much time do we have to stop them?"

"The next one could happen any day now. The next one, the noblewomen, in October. The bludgeoning after that. And the last one, the girls, during November."

"Why?" sought Onawa. "Why would anybody do all of this?"

"Well," Alicia replied, gingerly closing the ancient tome, "the Aztecs did it all because they believed their gods were controlling everything in their lives, from the rain for their crops to the fate of their battles and wars. Many of the people they sacrificed were enemies they had defeated in battle and enslaved."

"But why now? Why in Olvido?" Solitario pressed.

Alicia smiled cryptically at the two of them. "That, my dear children, I do not know. My hope, however, is that you will figure it out . . . in time."

Solitario turned to look through the jacal's open entrance. Outside, Elias lingered, wringing his hands over his daughter Elena's uncertain fate.

Surfacing from the depths of her thoughts, Onawa disrupted the foreboding silence. "For somebody to perform these rituals now, they must hope to gain something from it."

"A gift from the gods," Alicia agreed. "It was what the Aztecs sought as well. Of course, the Aztec deities have been largely dormant for some time now. When the Spaniards conquered Tenochtitlan and built their cathedrals atop the ancient pyramids and temples, they suppressed the old religion, replaced it with their own idols. Without the sacrifices and the prayers of their people, the gods fell into a deep slumber. Something like this, however, might be enough to rouse them."

"It is a tragic irony that religion can compel its faithful to commit such heinous crimes," Solitario said. "On a less philosophical note, can you help me identify these two items I found at the crime scenes?" From his jacket pocket, he extracted one of the blue-green plumes he had found in the Tolbert barn and Frankie's cave, as well as the folded paper containing the fine brown powder he had collected in the Jackson farmhouse's attic.

Alicia picked up the feather. "This is likely the feather of a tropical bird meant to resemble the mythical quetzal. Whoever is leading the rituals wears a headdress and skirt threaded with sacred plumes and shells, just as the Aztec high priests did long ago." Putting the feather back down between them, she picked up the pouch and sniffed the brown powder. "And this," she concluded, "is ground essence of teonanacatl, a mushroom used in the rituals to induce visions and transport participants to the divine realm of the Aztec deities."

"Thank you for enlightening us," Solitario said. "I found the mushroom powder in Gertrude Jackson's dance studio. Perhaps using the teonanacatl somehow made it more bearable for the high priest to shroud himself in her skin and commune with his spirits."

Alicia nodded, taking Onawa's hand. "I would love for you to spend days here with me. There is so much I wish to pass on to you. You lost your mother too young, before she could teach you what she learned from me. Our ways are being lost, mi hija."

Onawa nodded, tears beginning to fill her eyes.

"But I know you must make haste. You must return to Olvido and prevent more innocent people from dying in these misguided distortions of the rituals of old," Alicia said.

"I will come back when it is over," Onawa promised. "I promise."

Outside in the bright clearing, Solitario thanked the bruja, and Onawa embraced her tightly. Elias had already begun the journey west.

As Onawa prepared to mount Invierno, Alicia clutched her arm and held her back while Solitario waved and rode away. "Onawa, you love him, don't you?" The gravity of her tone of voice made the state of Onawa's heart sound like a penance, a heavy cross to be borne across the desert.

Onawa nodded, looking deeply into the bruja's wobbly, glimmering orbs, set like gemstones within her wrinkled visage. As she did so, Alicia's eyes filled with liquid, like water rising from a well deep beneath the cracked desert floor.

"Ten cuidado, mi hija," the bruja whispered, fear lacing her scratchy voice. "There is a reason he keeps his distance. You know . . . he is cursed?"

—————

As they rode across the desert, Onawa wrestled with her emotions. Her father had spoken of the darkness inside Solitario. Was it this curse of which Alicia spoke? Was that why he always kept his distance from her?

When they stopped amid the vast and scalding plains to eat and water their horses, Onawa stood closer to him than usual. Visibly flustered, he stepped aside.

"Does my nearness repel you?" Onawa asked, probing his eyes.

Solitario stared back, unmoving and silent.

"Do you not see how I feel for you? Do you not find any part of me . . . aside from my skills . . . worthy of your interest?"

Solitario took another step back from her as if he'd spotted a rattler in the sand.

"You act afraid of me." Her voice rose, her frustration spilling out. "But all I've ever done is help you. Is it this curse that people speak of? Or is it me?"

Solitario finally replied, his eyes softening, "Do not blame yourself."

"Then what?" she demanded.

"There is indeed a maldición . . ." Solitario admitted. "I do not like to speak of it for fear that my words will fuel its strength. It is la maldición de Caja Pinta, the place where I was born."

"And? Why does it keep you from letting me into your heart?"

"Onawa, I lost my wife." His voice cracked.

"I'm sorry, but that was many years ago. Isn't it time you carried on with your life?"

"I don't know if I can let go of the past," he confessed. "And, even if I did, la maldición prevents me from ever loving again."

"Why?"

"Because I am cursed to lose the ones I love. If I allow myself to become closer to you . . ." His sad eyes begged for her to not make him voice the rest of his thoughts.

She finished his sentence. "You think if you allow yourself to become closer to me . . . I will die too."

He nodded.

She took a sip from her canteen, then frowned. "Do you have any tequila left?"

He handed her his flask, from which she took a hearty swig.

Looking him up and down, she said, "I've always been happy to see you. As a girl, I let my mind run wild with silly dreams about you. I thought maybe someday when your heart healed and you finished mourning, and I was old enough . . . well, I thought maybe something might happen. I wondered if we could be together—not as a girl and a family friend, but—as a woman and a man. I was deluded. Now I realize the only person in the world who might be more deluded than me . . . is *you*. You break my heart, Solitario Cisneros. Either way, no matter what, I now understand, the future I imagined is dead."

She handed his flask back and whirled around, striding toward her horse. She wasn't sure who she was angrier at, him or herself. Either way, Invierno sensed her rage, whinnying and speeding ahead the moment she mounted, leaving Solitario alone in a cloud of desert sand.

They did not exchange words again, riding in silence the rest of the day. The sun was commencing its long and slow descent when Elias reappeared frantically before them, startling the horses. "Hurry, it is happening again!" he called out. "The next sacrifice the bruja spoke of . . . It has begun."

Onawa and Solitario raced toward Olvido. As they neared the town, descending from the mountains that ringed the surrounding plain, they saw a cloud of black smoke already filling the sky above it, hovering like a persistent thundercloud, casting a wide shadow over the valley and all who dared inhabit it. As they galloped through the valley, the creosote-speckled ground blurred beneath their horses' flying hooves. Blotted out by the billowing cloud of smoke, the sun gave way to darkness and a cooling breeze ushered waves of falling ash. It floated down in shimmering flakes like an early autumn snow, swirling about them as they leaned forward and urged Invierno and Tormenta toward the forgotten city on fire.

TWENTY

The new room in which they were being held captive was a chapel. It was more elegant and ornate than anything she had ever seen in the pueblo of Olvido. The walls were clean and white. The altarpiece was carved from wood, filled with nichos inhabited by statues of saints and the Virgen de Guadalupe herself. Inscribed along the edges, where the walls met the vaulted ceiling, gold leaf curled like wisps of wind ushering clouds across the heavens.

Elena gazed up and wished she could take it all in with awe and wonder, with glee and joy, as she might have expected being welcomed through the gates of heaven might feel. But instead, her heart overflowed with dread. She had preferred the coziness of the bedroom she had shared the first few days with the Tolbert girls. The room had been decorated in a floral print and contained a girl's comforts, some rag dolls, and brushes. It had felt like somebody's home, if not theirs. But this place they had been brought to, beautiful as it was, did not feel like anybody's home. Worse even, it created a sense of terrifying expectation. The pews of the small chapel were not filled with fervent worshipers. They sat empty. And she and the other girls were not there of their own volition, seeking purity and salvation. They were there because they had been dragged by force. The little ones, Abigail and Beatrice, were so frightened their small bodies trembled like leaves in a storm against her larger body. She tried to comfort them as best she could, wrapping her arms tightly around them, telling them that they just needed to stay quiet and pray and soon enough they would be back home. She didn't know if they believed her. She didn't even know if she believed herself. In fact, she didn't think she did. She had seen Abigail and Beatrice's brother Johnny appear and disappear with her own eyes. She knew he was but a spirit now. She figured the girls' parents and other brother were likely dead as well, just like her own were. She'd seen her father and mother and brother burn at the stake in the gorge. Why should Abigail and Beatrice's family be any luckier? But she lied. She massaged the truth as her father, the sargento, had told her he'd seen her godfather, Solitario, and their commanding officer, Colonel Terrazas, do during the war against the French imperialists. If the men could blur the lines between truth and fiction to make survival seem possible for their troops, then why could she not do the same for these two younger girls?

In the chapel, light flickered from candles burning in a wrought-iron candelabra. Stained-glass windows told the familiar story of a bearded man carrying a cross. The translucent fragments colored the shadows in deep hues of blood and sky and cactus. And suddenly, Elena could not contain her tears, soaking the girls' golden curls.

"Why are you crying, Elena?" Abigail beseeched her. "You promised everything would be just fine."

"Yes, Elena, you promised," little Beatrice echoed. "You said we'd see Ma and Pa and Johnny and Frankie soon enough and this would all be a fun story we'd tell at the dinner table for years to come. Why are you crying so, Elena? Why?"

Elena wiped the tears off her cheeks and held the girls tight. She wasn't sure why she was crying. Was it for her parents? For her brother? For these girls? For herself? Or was it simply because she was sad that it took dying to see something so beautiful as heaven itself?

At the chapel door, Elena heard a thumping. Something was struggling to gain access, scratching against the thick carved wood. Was someone— or something—coming to collect its offering? Her eyes flicked to Jesus, hanging on the cross over the altar. He seemed unable to help them. He was covered in wounds and crowned by thorns and nailed to the splintered wood. His sorrowful eyes turned up to the heavens and searched for mercy from his own father. Whatever was beyond that arched door was coming. And Jesus looked like he was crying and forsaken.

Jesus has enough problems without me burdening him with my own, Elena thought, squeezing Abigail and Beatrice.

She stared at the door. She could hear the thing rustling against it. Outside the windows, heavy footsteps sounded, men's muffled voices. Then silence.

"Come, hide with me," Elena told the girls.

They huddled behind the pew closest to the altar, farthest from the arched wooden entrance to the chapel.

She peeked over the prayer bench as the door creaked open. Would a monster step through to devour them? Was the end near? Would she soon rejoin her parents who had burned at the stake? She clutched the Tolbert girls tightly, spying in dread over the top of the pew.

As she looked, she saw not a monster but another little girl—this one with a soot-streaked face and copper curls—being shoved through the crack onto the chapel floor.

The girl gazed up, her green eyes shining in the stained-glass light. She looked straight down the center aisle to the altar, where Elena scrambled toward her with arms reaching out to gather her up and try her best to make her feel safe.

"Are we gonna die?" the green-eyed girl asked, her eyes burning into Elena's.

Elena's response was to grab her and ferry her back to Abigail and Beatrice. Together they clustered behind the defensive barrier of the sturdy wooden pew.

"We're safe here," Elena lied. "There's strength in numbers." She'd heard her father recite that phrase in his conversations with her padrino, Solitario. And now all she could do was repeat it and hope that it was true, hope that her godfather would likewise be true and deliver on the promises her father had professed in his name.

TWENTY-ONE

Solitario watched helplessly, alongside a mass of distraught townspeople, as a large wooden house burned to the ground, taking two adjacent structures down with it. The heat surged in waves, repelling the crowd.

"Another entire family gone," murmured Mr. Boggs, standing next to Solitario. "We're running out of time to stop this insanity."

The pressure to blame someone was mounting. Solitario could sense its burgeoning heft on his shoulders, like a sack of flour that felt heavier the farther one carried it.

Mayor Stillman muttered, "On the other hand, the fire could be unrelated. An accident, perhaps? The town's residents would be glad to hear that. It might keep them from fleeing and turning Olvido into a ghost town."

Solitario figured the mayor would welcome delivering good news to his voters, but doing so would constitute a betrayal of the public trust. "It is connected." He answered the two men's concerns as they stared somberly at the smoldering ruins.

"How do you know?" Boggs asked.

Solitario pointed at the two charred bodies lying beneath white sheets.

"How can you tell?" the mayor probed.

"Their hearts were plucked from their chests," Solitario replied. It had been a good thing that the volunteer fire brigade had managed to extract those two unlucky souls before the fire completely consumed their flesh, for otherwise it would have been impossible to ascertain whether they had died purely due to accidental fire or whether foul play had been involved. "It also fits the order of the rituals that Onawa and I learned about this morning."

"So, you know what is coming next?" Mayor Stillman asked.

"Sí," Solitario nodded, gazing solemnly at Onawa across the crowd. She stood away from the smoke, glowering from the fringes, her long black hair flowing in the wind. "Let's discuss it in private."

The men nodded, following Solitario back to the jailhouse.

Inside, a surly Captain Ringgold stood in the jail cell, scowling at Solitario as he walked in. "I don't know how you did what you did," Ringgold said, "but you're gonna regret it." In disgust, he spat through the bars onto the floor.

Solitario stared at the wad of phlegm bubbling on the wooden planks outside the cell. Without acknowledging the prisoner, he directed his words to the Dobbs twins. "Boys, make sure that before the prisoners are released, Captain Ringgold mops the floors as part of his fine."

"Let's step into my office," the mayor suggested, guiding Solitario and Boggs down a narrow hallway to a room in the back of the town hall.

There, the mayor took a seat behind his desk, motioning for the other two men to sit across from him. Boggs sat, but Solitario stood at the door, where he could keep an eye on the hallway and the jail.

"So what's coming next and how do you know?" Mr. Boggs anxiously asked.

"Onawa took me to a woman who knows about such rituals," Solitario explained. "As we suspected, they are Aztec-style sacrifices. It makes little sense since there are no Aztecs here . . . or really, anywhere anymore, at least none practicing these kinds of violent rituals in the name of forgotten gods. But whoever is committing these crimes, for whatever reason, they are following the Aztec calendar."

"What do you think will happen next?" Mayor Stillman pressed.

"After these deaths by fire, there are two noblewomen in danger,"

Solitario said. "After that, a death by bludgeoning. Then, a final sacrifice of a large group of children. I believe that is why they are kidnapping girls. They are saving them for the climactic ceremony."

"That explains one thing," Stillman said pensively. "When the bodies were accounted for in the fire, there was a young girl missing."

"Now they have four," Solitario said.

"And then what, after all the sacrifices?" Boggs asked.

"As if that weren't enough?" Mayor Stillman huffed. "These people sound completely mad."

"Well," Solitario replied slowly, "best I can figure, there are two possible scenarios. One is that the person behind this wants to scare everybody away for some reason. Maybe he wants all the land for himself."

"What's the other scenario?" asked Boggs.

Solitario shifted uncomfortably on his boots, leaning against the doorframe. It was already somewhat miraculous that these two white men had entrusted him with a position of authority. He was worried that if he said what he was truly thinking, they might lose whatever faith they still had in him, especially since so far, he had failed to put a stop to the string of deaths. Still, his job was to tell them the truth as he saw it. "The other scenario is that the person orchestrating the rituals believes that the Aztec gods will reward him in some way."

"Oh, hogwash," Stillman scoffed.

"It must be about money," Boggs agreed, dismissing Solitario's spiritual theory. "It's always about land or money. And land *is* money, so there's truly no difference. Follow the money, Sheriff. Did the victims owe anyone? Who inherits their land now that they're dead? Is anyone buying up deserted properties aside from Grissom, who's always buying?"

Solitario was surprised by Mr. Boggs' acuity for detective work. "I need your help getting that information out of the county archives. Mortgages, loans, wills, and so on. Also, I would like to look at some of the bank ledgers."

"We'll get on it," the mayor agreed. "I'll do the county work. Boggs, you do the banking part."

Boggs nodded, standing up.

"There's one more thing," Solitario said, looking at Boggs with concern. "Who were the two ladies you welcomed off the stagecoach yesterday?"

"Those are my mother-in-law and my sister-in-law, visiting us from Boston," he answered.

"I assume they are of means?" Solitario asked.

"Quite," Mr. Boggs answered. "In fact, I am hoping to convince them to invest in our bank so that we can finance more of the town's expansion and open branches in other parts of West Texas and New Mexico."

"They seem like noblewomen," Solitario said, thinking they might be the most "noble" women that might be found in their dismal frontier outpost, at least from the perspective of the killers. "We must put them under protection. The Dobbs twins will take shifts at your house."

Boggs gulped. "This isn't going to help convince them to invest."

"Neither would Ringgold's near atrocity in the town plaza," Solitario said. "You should be sure your investors understand we live in a dangerous place, Mr. Boggs. Nothing is sacred here, not their lives or their money."

The moment that Dwight Grissom stepped into the jailhouse, the room suddenly seemed so crowded it might simply burst. He wore a finely tailored gray suit with a black tie and black Stetson to match. His shortly cropped hair and mustache glistened a silvery gray. He was not a man of great physical stature, Solitario noted, but the inflated state of both his bank account and his ego amply compensated to fill the room.

"Where's the sheriff?" Grissom asked gruffly, standing in the open doorway.

"You're looking at him," Solitario replied, nodding. "Solitario Cisneros."

"Ah, yes, there's a new lawman in town. We've met before. Dwight Grissom. I tried to buy your ranch some years back, El Escondido, but you weren't in the selling mood. I also tried to buy your father-in-law's ranch . . ."

"But he wasn't in the selling mood either," Solitario recalled.

"Yes, well, all moods change eventually. Speaking of which, my mood ain't too great about now. You've gone and arrested five of my men, Sheriff Cisneros. I hope you have a good reason why, because my tax dollars pay for your salary."

"I haven't been paid yet," Solitario clarified. "And I don't really need the money. But your men, there," he motioned toward the jail cell, "they were about to murder fifteen innocent men and boys in cold blood, without a shred of evidence against them."

"They were just trying to do what you have been unable to manage so far." Grissom sauntered up to Solitario. The rancher stood about six inches shorter but jutted out his chin and puffed up his chest to make up for it. He carried two shiny silver revolvers in his holsters, which Solitario could tell were more for show than anything else.

"If I need the help, I'll let you know," Solitario replied curtly. "Are you here to bail them out?"

"What charges are you holding them on?"

"Disturbing the peace and conspiracy to commit murder."

"We've got to plea that down," Grissom shook his head. "Disturbing the peace is manageable. We can pay the town a fine and be done with it."

"You'll have to talk to the judge about that."

"Well, the judge also happens to be the mayor, so I'll go have myself a little talk with him then," Grissom smiled at Solitario, heading down the hall to Stillman's office.

When the deal was done, Michael Dobbs opened the jail cell and was in the process of escorting the prisoners outside when Solitario cleared his throat. "You're forgetting something."

"What's that?" Grissom asked.

"Your man Ringgold has a personal fine of his own to pay," said Solitario.

Grissom stared at Captain Ringgold as Michael Dobbs emerged from the back with a mop and bucket.

"The rest of you can wait outside," Solitario instructed, sitting at his desk and putting his boots up on it for good measure.

Ringgold sneered, yanking the cleaning supplies out of Michael's hands. Glowering at Solitario and muttering obscenities under his breath, he mopped the floor as his boss and men watched in shock through the windows.

Late at night, Blake Dobbs was replenishing the kerosene lanterns while his brother Michael stood guard at the Boggs residence. Mayor Stillman and Mr. Boggs sat around a table set up in front of the collage of photos Solitario had assembled on the wall. The table was piled high with leather-bound ledgers and papers.

Solitario stood at the board, pointing at the photos as he spoke. "So, thanks to Mr. Boggs' forensic accounting, we have learned that the Jacksons had borrowed money against their farm, not from the bank but from the Protestant church."

Boggs nodded in confirmation. "Their crop was a total bust too, so they were living on borrowed time. Reverend Grimes could have put them out on the street sometime soon."

"So the reverend is one of our suspects," Solitario said. "He gets the land if the Jacksons aren't around to save it or pay him. He also had a beef with Sheriff Tolbert. And he is a man of religion, so maybe the ritualistic approach appeals to him."

"So you think the reverend is behind all this?" Boggs asked, wide-eyed.

"Not necessarily." Solitario shook his head. "Why would he burn the most recent house down? There's no connection there."

"None that we've found," Mayor Stillman answered. "Besides, he's a reverend for Christ's sake. We can't go arresting the town preacher."

Solitario continued, "He also would have little reason to kill the Elias and Lopez families, except for sheer racism, which—as we saw with Captain Ringgold in the square—can be a powerful motivator in times of trouble."

"It doesn't make sense though," Mr. Boggs interjected. "Why would the reverend want to scare people out of town? Without parishioners, his church goes under."

"Or he gathers up all this land and sells it to Grissom?" Solitario said.

"Grissom could just buy up the land directly himself without all this bloodshed."

Solitario scratched his head, "Grissom could definitely have a motive in frightening the townspeople to leave. With the market flooded with land, he'd get lower prices."

"Something doesn't add up," Boggs said, wiping his glasses and yawning. "Why would a white man, whoever he is, adopt Mexican traditions dating back to the Aztecs?"

Solitario nodded, placing additional cards up on the board. The banker was right. There were many photos on the wall now: the growing slew of victims as well as the suspects—Grissom, Ringgold, Reverend Grimes—along with the new cards, bearing the words *Apache* and *Aztec* followed by question marks, but the extreme nature of the killings and their ritualistic complexity did not point to any of those men or groups either working alone or together. "We should break for the night," he sighed. "Return tomorrow with fresh eyes. And you, Mr. Boggs, need to be with your family. Do you have a pistol?"

Boggs nodded in the affirmative, his cheeks flushed.

As they stood to leave, Mayor Stillman stared at the photos on the wall, focusing on the lineup of victims' photos and names. "Isn't it strange that they're killing all sorts of people?" Stillman pondered aloud. "Mexicans and Anglos, young and old, rich and poor alike? And that our suspects are all over the place too: white, Mexican, Apache . . ."

Solitario gazed back at him, shaking his head. "Discrimination is evil," he uttered in a hushed tone, "but evil does not discriminate."

After the men left, Solitario pored over the bank ledgers by the dim light of the kerosene lantern on the worktable, diligently examining the flows of money among Olvido's various notable residents. A particular name caught his eye as he scrutinized a list of people to whom Dwight Grissom had made payments in recent months. Scribbling the name down, he made a mental note to send a telegram to Mexico City the following morning to check on it. Then he ambled through the darkened streets toward the doctor's house. He needed more information to crack this case. And it was quite possible that Frankie Tolbert held the key.

Dr. Ferris let Solitario in and showed him to the guest room where Frankie slumbered still. The boy looked gaunt and pale.

"He can't go on much longer like this, without nourishment," Dr. Ferris said. "His internal organs will begin to shut down soon."

Solitario stared down at the poor boy he and Onawa had rescued from the cave in the mountains, wondering if they had done him a favor or a disservice. He had promised the boy's brother that he would do his best to save him and his sisters. Frustration swelled inside of him, scorching his innards with a wave of burning acid. As he stared at Frankie, there was a knock at the door. When the doctor returned, he was trailed by the town apothecary. The frail, balding man glanced nervously away as Solitario sought to make eye contact.

"Here are tonight's tinctures, Dr. Ferris," the apothecary mumbled, handing the doctor two sets of vials, one golden and one lavender.

Solitario observed as the doctor first gave Frankie an injection of the golden fluid and then rubbed the lavender liquid on his parched lips.

"What are those medicines for?" he asked.

Dr. Ferris seemed taken aback as he straightened up, still holding a syringe in one hand and a bottle in the other. "These are to help keep him alive. The injections fight off any infection he might have that's keeping him from waking up. And the oral tincture is to help avoid dehydration."

The apothecary nodded. "I must get going now, Dr. Ferris. See ya tomorrow. I'll just let myself out."

Solitario watched the squirrelly man scuttle down the hall. Then he observed as the doctor delicately placed the surplus medicines on the nightstand next to Frankie's bed.

"You'll fetch me the moment he stirs?" Solitario asked.

"Of course, Sheriff," Dr. Ferris replied, staring at him from the other side of the bed.

Between them slept a living witness, one who might shed light on whether any of those men on the suspect board happened to be the "familiar-faced man" that had come knocking that fateful night at the Tolbert farm. They both knew Frankie might be vital to saving the lives of those still at risk. Solitario, however, couldn't help but feel a nagging suspicion that perhaps the doctor might not want the boy to wake up.

When Solitario returned to the jailhouse, he added the doctor and the apothecary to his wall. Pretty soon half the town might be up there, he thought. The more suspects he identified, the further he felt from the truth.

Hearing a creak outside, Solitario stepped onto the town hall's wooden porch. Olvido dozed quietly in the dark of night. The only sounds were those of the breeze rustling through the trees and the song of the cicadas. The streets were abandoned, but Solitario saw a lone figure sitting patiently on the front step. He recognized the burly shape of Sergeant Elias.

"What are you doing here?" asked Solitario.

"I came to make sure you're working," Elias answered. "I was worried you might get distracted by the young Apache lady."

Solitario shook his head, wondering when Onawa might deign to speak to him again. "I don't think you need to worry about that. I won't rest until I find Elena and the others."

"Then come home with me," Elias pleaded. "You can think there just as you can here."

Solitario was about to duck back inside and continue poring over the documents on the table when he caught a glimpse of Elias' sorrowful soul lurking within the eyes of his ghostly manifestation. Elias was lonely. He did not want to be home alone, without his family, without even the sound of his own breath or the beating of his own heart to keep him company.

"Vamos, then," Solitario conceded. He blew out the lantern inside, locked the door, stuffed his keys in his pocket, and motioned for his sergeant to follow. "Tomorrow, we resume the battle."

As they traversed the river gorge, Elias reminisced, "We came here together, Jefe."

"Yes, we did."

"And we're still here even though so many others aren't."

"Yes." Solitario often wished it were different, that he had been the one taken early rather than his wife. He imagined Elias yearned for the same, that he too would have given his life to spare his wife and son. "Perhaps you'd prefer to be at rest?"

"I cannot rest until you rescue Elena."

As they climbed back up to the levee where Elias' house waited, Solitario felt the burden on his shoulders grow even heavier. Beneath the mesquite trees stood Tormenta and Caballo Sin Nombre. They snorted softly as Solitario and Elias approached through the dark.

"Your old friend is still here," Solitario said, patting Caballo Sin Nombre as he watered both horses.

"Still here," sighed Elias, gazing up at the stars.

Solitario wondered how much longer they would still be there, how much time any of them had. Could he get this job done before he himself was rendered nothing more than a restless spirit on the wind?

"Do you ever wish we'd never come to Olvido, Jefe?"

Solitario weighed the question. Not coming to Olvido would have meant never meeting Luz. And never meeting Luz would have meant never losing Luz, but it also would have meant never loving her, never being loved by her. Fleeting as they had been, those times, or his memory of them, had kept his heart beating all these years afterward. "I thought I could outrun the curse." Clearly, he had not done so then . . . and still today it plagued him.

"La maldición de Caja Pinta?"

"Sí." They both well knew he had failed miserably in that endeavor.

Weary, Solitario walked slowly to the house. When he reached the door, he turned back and looked at Elias, standing by his horse. "I cannot wish away what was. All I can do is remember and honor it."

"And keep running . . ." Elias concluded.

Solitario removed his sombrero and disappeared into the dark and empty house, his mind awash in memories, both old and new.

TWENTY-TWO

Toward the end of the war against the French imperialists, Solitario and Elias were part of the force that reasserted control of Chihuahua. Not long after that, the Republic of Mexico was restored under President Benito Juárez. Colonel Terrazas resumed his role as governor of the state of Chihuahua, assigning Solitario to command a unit of Rurales responsible for keeping the peace throughout the vast desert state.

In 1870, after nearly five years serving under the colonel, Solitario was summoned to the governor's palace, which was housed in a former Jesuit college built during the early colonial era. Through its colonnaded courtyard, Solitario paced in his finest charro outfit, velvety black and adorned with sparkling silver embroidery. He wore his yellow bandanna tied around his neck. His heroics during the war were well known throughout the region and everyone who saw him pass saluted him. In the governor's office, he met with his former commander, who sat at an ornately carved desk, behind him a row of colorful flags.

"We have come a long way from that tent in the desert, Capitán Cisneros," Governor Terrazas said.

"Pues sí, Gobernador," Solitario nodded, admiring the art hanging on the walls. "¿Come puedo servirle?"

"I have yet another favor to ask of you," the governor said, running his fingers through his bushy salt-and-pepper beard.

"Fire away."

"The border town of Olvido needs someone to take charge and bring order to the streets. I have a good family friend there who is a rancher like me, Miguel Antonio Santander. He is a bit older than I am, and he was a dear friend of my father's, God rest his soul. He has been trying to build the local economy there, but outlaws and bandidos are making it difficult. He has asked for my help, and I can think of no one better suited than you. After all, you come from La Frontera. You know how complicated it can be, at the place where two nations meet."

Solitario nodded in agreement. "I ask only two things."

"Dígame, Capitán."

"That I can take my sargento, Elias, with me."

"Done."

"And that you convey to your good friend Santander that if I accept the post, he may be the king of Olvido, but my word is the law."

The governor chuckled. "In all these years, you have never wavered, Cisneros. You remain as true to your values as ever."

"It is the only way I know," Solitario answered. It was true. Raised to be the poor younger sibling, he had been taught that he would inherit nothing but his training and his honor. He could never abandon them. With those two, he had to make the most of life.

"The charro is Mexico's answer to the chivalric code," Governor Terrazas said, pounding his curled fist on his desk, startling the pair of guards that kept watch at the door. They reflexively reached for their guns, but the governor waved them off. "And you, my friend, are a true charro."

"From your lips to God's ears."

They shook hands, and as the governor walked Solitario to the door, he counseled him to be careful. "You've been away from the border for some years now. I'm hopeful you've at last escaped that maldición you told me about, but I must advise you to be wary. Remember, on the border, nothing is ever quite as it seems. What you think is on one side is often to be found on the other."

The governor patted Solitario on the shoulder and hugged him goodbye.

A few days later, Solitario and Elias rode north from Chihuahua to Olvido, on the border with West Texas.

They carried their spare belongings in bundles hung over the sides of the burro Elias was assigned, as the army was short on horses.

Solitario led the way on Oscuridad as Elias trailed slightly behind.

"I feel like Sancho Panza," Elias muttered.

"I didn't know you'd been reading," Solitario said as they traveled slowly over the dry mountains beneath the blazing sun.

"I haven't, but everybody knows the story."

"Yes, I'm not sure I want to end up like Don Quixote, although I admire his tenacity," Solitario said.

"Maybe we are both locos for taking this post," Elias wondered aloud. "I'm from down south. There, the land is lush and the fruit is plentiful. If I spend too much more time in the desert, I might just turn into a pillar of sand and crumble away in the hot wind."

"You're just upset they didn't give you a horse."

"Did you even try to get me one?"

"I should have, but it slipped my mind," Solitario admitted. "I thought I was lucky just to have you sent along with me."

"Yes, you are very lucky," Elias chided. "I, on the other hand, got the flip side of that coin."

Solitario smiled quietly, riding on. He knew his sergeant was all bluster, that deep inside he would have it no other way. Horse or burro. They would have a job doing what they enjoyed, keeping the peace, seeking out fairness and justice. They would have a roof over their heads, food, and pay. What more could two soldiers ask for as their country struggled to rise out of the poverty worsened by endless wars?

Overnight, they camped out by the side of the dirt road that stretched through mountains and desert plateaus as it snaked its way north to the Rio Grande. When at last they reached Olvido, they found a bustling border town that instantly reminded Solitario of his home, Nueva Frontera. The principal difference on the surface was that the climate was dry in Olvido, whereas Nueva Frontera, positioned as it was at the mouth of the river by the Gulf of Mexico, was always drenched in humidity as if the air itself were sweating due to the alarming heat.

New buildings were going up left and right, made of adobe and finished in stucco, painted bright hues of cobalt, turquoise, lime, pineapple, orange, and rose. The town radiated a festive spirit brimming with optimism. Solitario found it contagious, smiling broadly as they rode through the dusty streets toward the address he'd been provided, where he was to meet Don Miguel Antonio Santander.

The governor's friend was a rancher by trade, but—like many wealthy hacendados—he kept a residence in the city as well. His colonial home overlooked the plaza on the block between the cathedral and the palacio municipal. It was painted bright red, like a toreador's cape.

"You can't miss it," the governor had told Solitario. "Everyone there calls it La Casa Colorada."

"He wasn't kidding." Solitario pointed at the magnificent house. Its walls soared, its windows protected by wrought iron and framed by skillfully carved stone, its massive wooden doors worthy of a fortress.

Elias grinned. "Do we get to live here?"

Solitario shook his head. "Not even in your dreams, amigo."

At the door, the mayordomo told them that Don Miguel was expected back from his ranch in the afternoon. He suggested they rest in the plaza or have a drink in the café across the square in the meantime. From there, he added, they would easily see Don Miguel's carriage arrive at the house.

Taking the time to familiarize themselves with the town, they hitched their horse and burro behind the house and walked through the streets to the levee. Standing there, they gazed across the swiftly flowing river at a smattering of small wooden buildings across the way.

The ferryman waved and asked if they needed to cross.

"No, just looking," Elias answered. "Is that El Otro Lado?"

"United States," the ferryman pointed. "Used to be just the outskirts of Olvido, but now it's a village of its own. Might as well be one town, but that's where more and more of the gringos are settling when they come from up north to trade with us."

"That's how it was where I grew up," Solitario said. "La Frontera was on the northern side of the river and Nueva Frontera on the south."

"And here?" Elias asked the ferryman. "What do they call the village in the United States?"

"They just call it Olvido Norte or El Otro Lado," the ferryman said. "It doesn't matter. We all know what's what around here."

Solitario wondered if that was true. Sometimes, the border had a way of blurring the lines.

On their way back to the plaza, Solitario heard a distressing sound. Nearby, in a corral across a side street from La Casa Colorada, a horse nickered and neighed, his hooves pounding the ground as two vaqueros covered in dust struggled to break it.

Solitario felt a surge of anger rising up within him, like a wave surging during a storm. The vaqueros were abusing the animal. It was not right. And, if they continued, the horse might accidentally harm himself. He envisioned the rough men having to put the horse down and simply laughing about it, as they did now. The cowboy on the ground was using a lasso to try and control the horse's legs, preventing him from bolting. The rider whipped the horse, clutching onto the horn of the saddle as it bucked under him. It was a pinto horse with white and brown splotches, young and strong but afraid and in pain. Solitario recognized the terror in the horse's bulging eyes as he approached with Elias in tow.

Incensed, Solitario threw the foot gate open and strode into the corral, his hands hovering over his pistols.

"That's not how you treat a horse!" Solitario stated, his voice ringing sharply above the animal's complaints. "Stop at once."

The horse crumpled to the ground as the cowboy with the lasso tightened the rope, forcing its legs closer together. The rider remained in the saddle, facing Solitario. "You don't belong here. And you can't tell us what to do. Get out."

Solitario glowered at them as they continued to wrestle with the horse, struggling to hold it in place. Turning to Elias, he told him, "Bring me two lassos."

Elias hurried back across the street to where they had hitched Oscuridad and the burro.

Solitario watched as the vaqueros continued to punish the animal. "You are going to break its legs."

"Then we'll have to shoot him," the rider answered, laughing as if he looked forward to it.

Solitario shook his head, extending his hands so Elias could place a long coiled rope in each. Taking a step forward, he twirled both lassos at the same time, opening a loop in each of them wide enough for a man. Squinting at the two men, he released the lassos at the same time. The ropes shot forth from his hands so quickly that the cowboys had no time to react. The lassos fell perfectly over them, only a swish of air grazing their faces as the loops fell to their chests, where Solitario yanked them tight. When the lassos closed around them, he pulled with both arms, grimacing from the strain.

The rider flew off the pinto, arcing toward Solitario as the other vaquero released his hold on the rope around the pinto's legs and was dragged across the ground toward him as well.

Solitario could hear Elias laughing behind him, his guns cocked and ready, trained on the fallen vaqueros, who swore obscenities and wriggled like worms on the corral floor as Solitario finished tying their wrists and ankles.

The pinto reared on its hind legs and let out a relieved whinny, to which Oscuridad responded from across the street. The freed pinto then tore into a quick trot around the corral, shaking itself off as if the pain might ripple away like beads of water following a cloudburst.

"He's a pretty horse," Elias smiled. "Now he's happy too."

"He will be," Solitario agreed. "When we get him away from these two pendejos."

The two vaqueros sat in the dirt, glaring at Solitario. The former rider shouted, "You're going to regret this, charro. When our patrón finds out, he will have you put in jail. That's his horse and it's our job to break it."

"That's not how you treat a horse," Solitario replied.

"What's the horse's name?" asked Elias.

"Es un caballo sin nombre," the vaquero who had ridden it answered.

"El Caballo Sin Nombre," Elias echoed. "The horse without a name. I like it. It's catchy."

"Then, it will be yours," Solitario said.

"What? How?" Elias asked.

"You'll see. That burro won't do for a lawman. You'll need a horse. And I'll train this one the proper way."

"You're loco." The rider spat on the ground. "Both of you are locos."

"The horse may not have a name," Solitario replied, "but your behavior does. That name is *cruelty*. And it should not be tolerated, not against another human and not against any living creature."

As he spoke, an older vaquero approached from across the street, fuming. "What is the meaning of this?" he asked Solitario. "You are trespassing on private property."

The vaqueros smiled widely, glancing at each other and back at Solitario.

Unfazed, Solitario assessed the man. He must have been the foreman for the corral or for whoever owned the horse. "Whose property?"

"What?" the older vaquero looked confused.

"Who owns this private property? The horse and the corral? Who is your patrón?"

"Everybody knows that," the older man replied.

"We are new to Olvido," Solitario said.

"I see. That explains a great deal." The old vaquero shuffled back and forth on his boots, his eyes following the glinting metal clasps along the sides of Solitario's pants. "Don Miguel Santander is our patrón and the owner of this pinto horse. I'm afraid you've made a big mistake."

Solitario fought off a smile. "No, señor. The ones who have made a big mistake are these two men. They should not be allowed around your patrón's horses. Sergeant Elias here will keep an eye on these two, while I meet with Don Miguel."

"He is busy with an appointment. I suggest you release the men, and we forget all about this." The old vaquero stared at the guns tucked into Solitario's holsters and the ammunition belts strapped across his chest. "Don Miguel stands by his men."

"His appointment is with me," Solitario stated, leaving Elias in charge and sauntering toward the front corner of the bright red house.

As he crossed the street, he suddenly sensed he was being watched. Glancing up, he spotted a strikingly lovely face in an upstairs window. When their eyes met, she vanished behind a curtain of white lace.

Solitario had never been inside a library as voluminous as Don Miguel Santander's. The books stretched from wall to wall and from floor to ceiling. Diffused light filtered into the darkly paneled room through tall windows set between the massive wooden bookcases built into the walls.

He sat on a soft leather couch across from Don Miguel as the mayordomo served them a té de yerba buena. Don Miguel wore a tan suit and black tie. His sunbaked skin contrasted sharply with his crisp white shirt. Solitario liked the man immediately, recognizing by his appearance that despite his high status and wealth, he did not shy away from work on his ranch beneath the punishing sun.

"You come highly recommended by my friend, Gobernador Terrazas," Don Miguel said. "He assures me you can help bring peace and order to our streets."

Solitario nodded, "I will do my best, that much I can promise you."

As they sipped their tea, Don Miguel described the local politics and cautioned him about who was heading the various gangs of bandidos and contrabandistas terrorizing the region. Solitario listened attentively, taking mental notes.

As they finished their tea, the mayordomo tiptoed into the room and whispered into Don Miguel's ear, cupping his hand over his mouth and glancing nervously at Solitario.

Don Miguel appeared surprised, his eyes widening as he reassessed Solitario. When the mayordomo left the room, Don Miguel knit his thick white eyebrows together and leaned forward. "It appears your arrival has already made an impression."

Solitario replied with his stone poker face.

"I just heard about my vaqueros tied up and held at gunpoint across the street by your sargento?" Don Miguel said, his question begging an explanation.

"I am glad you brought that up." Solitario nodded. "Those men were severely mistreating a pinto horse."

"Is that a crime?"

"Against nature."

Don Miguel frowned. "I was hoping you would focus on criminals, not my hardworking staff."

"As the governor mentioned to you, I will enforce the laws and keep the peace, but I will not spare anyone, including those under your employ. That is, if you will still have me."

Don Miguel scratched his head. "I depend on my vaqueros. I have many cattle and horses. You put me in a difficult . . ."

"Es verdad, Papá," a graceful voice interrupted him from the corner.

Solitario whipped his head around, recognizing the beautiful face he'd seen high above in the window.

"What is true?" Don Miguel asked the young woman, who wore a mint-green dress that flowed loosely down to her feet.

As he rose to his feet in her presence, all Solitario could think of was that she looked like a princess from a faraway, mystical land, a place where everything did not exist blanketed in dust, but rather embroidered in sparkling finery. Not a remote ranching and trading post in the wilderness, but a shining capital where the streets were paved with cobblestones and the altars were adorned in gold leaf. Her skin was smooth, delicate, and radiant. Her features sharp and elegant. Her eyes green like the fabric she wore. Her hair, dark and long, cascaded in waves over her shoulders and down her back. His eyes were riveted to her. He had to remind himself to breathe.

"It is true what this gentleman says," the lady elaborated. "I witnessed the cruelty of those vaqueros from my room upstairs. This man not only saved the horse's life, he probably spared the vaqueros themselves from injury."

Flustered, Don Miguel glanced back at Solitario. "Capitán Cisneros, this is my daughter, Luz."

What a fitting name, he thought to himself as he nodded. Forgetting he had already done so, he reached up to remove his sombrero, grasping nothing but a lock of his own hair.

She giggled at his bumbling maneuver as he blushed and looked down at the splendid Oriental rug beneath his dusty black boots.

"Please, both of you sit. I just wanted to let you know, Father, what I saw, and that the man speaks the truth. I'll leave you to your business. A pleasure to meet you, Capitán."

"The pleasure is mine." He bowed as he watched her go.

"Now you see what I'm up against," Don Miguel smiled, sitting back down. "Perhaps we should conclude our meeting not with more tea but with a little tequilita reposada?"

The mayordomo returned, pouring a golden fluid into two small goblets.

As Solitario sipped, he stared at Don Miguel and waited for further explanation.

"Between our new lawman and my daughter's ideals, I may find my path growing ever narrower and straighter," he concluded.

"Perhaps I can alleviate the challenge in terms of the pinto horse and your vaqueros," Solitario suggested, understanding that keeping the ranch hands and foremen from revolting was a matter of importance to a rancher.

"How might you do me such a favor?"

"Allow me to purchase the pinto from you. Take it out of my pay. Tell them you had sold me the horse and therefore it was my private property I was protecting."

"I see. A way out." Don Miguel savored the fine tequila. "Terrazas taught you well the ways of diplomacy."

"A victory for all," Solitario affirmed. "But those men need to be instructed on how to properly train a horse. Or they should not be allowed near any of your animals."

"I will see to it," Don Miguel agreed, reaching out his hand.

They both smiled as they shook and finished their tequilas.

"I believe this is the beginning of a fruitful partnership," Don Miguel concluded, accompanying Solitario to the foyer.

Solitario glanced up the curving, wrought-iron staircase, picturing Luz up in her room. His breath grew short simply thinking of her again.

―――――――――

Don Miguel and Solitario agreed to meet weekly in the library to review the new police force's progress in establishing order within the booming border city.

"Trade is flowing, just like the Rio Grande itself," Don Miguel said excitedly a couple of months into Solitario's tenure. "We must make sure that all of our townspeople benefit, not just the bandidos who would plunder and hoard the riches all for themselves."

"It seems only fair," Solitario agreed.

With funding from the governor, he and Elias oversaw the construction of a new town jail, which the governor himself came to christen.

During the weekly meetings and planning sessions in the library, Solitario often exchanged furtive glances and secret smiles with Luz, who found clever ways to interject herself into the conversations. Her knowledge was extensive. As it turned out, she herself had ordered and read most of the books in the library. She had even studied in boarding schools in Mexico and Paris after her mother had died young of the cholera. Solitario could not figure out why a lady like her would remain in Olvido, but it seemed that her mission was to keep her aging father company, and in many ways, to exist trapped within a gilded cage of her own crafting, like one of the exotic songbirds she kept in a collection of ornate wrought-iron cages in the courtyard of the colonial mansion.

One day when Don Miguel was late for their standing appointment, Solitario wandered into the central courtyard, drawn by the festive singing of Luz's birds. Leaning in to observe the colorfully feathered specimens, he smiled as he heard them intone their whimsical songs. There were so many different kinds of birds throughout the vine-covered courtyard. Between their birdcages and dovecotes, giant potted palms soared toward the sky overhead. In the center of the courtyard, a stone fountain added to the ambiance.

"This is my little jungle." A familiar voice startled him.

He immediately whisked his black sombrero off his head and bowed slightly, smiling at the sight of her.

She wore a pale pink dress, flowing in the breeze just like all her dresses seemed to do, even when she was inside and the air was still.

The scent of jasmine was intoxicating as starlike blooms floated gently down around them, shaken loose by the breeze from the vines covering the arched colonnade and second-floor balconies.

"You're so beautiful . . . I mean, your birds are so beautiful," he shook his head at making yet another misstep.

She stifled a giggle, brushing his awkwardness aside as she stood next to him, admiring a small green bird with blue-and-red feathers, "This is a conure. It is a miniature parrot. It could learn your name if you taught him."

"Fascinating," he said, his eyes locked on her as she leaned in and puckered her lips, blowing a kiss at the bird. He thought perhaps his heart might be beating even faster than the small winged creature's.

She gave him a tour of her pets, explaining their names and from where they each originated.

"Have you traveled to those places?" he asked, marveling not only at her intelligence but at her affection for the animals. It was a rare affinity they shared in common.

"Oh, yes, with my father," Luz answered. "He likes to take me along on his business trips . . . to the Yucatán and Chiapas, Guatemala, even Costa Rica and Cuba . . . he does not like to be alone. He's never gotten over my mother's passing."

"I am sorry," Solitario replied.

"It was a long time ago." She smiled, gazing up at him with her large green eyes that shone like emeralds.

"One never gets over such a loss," Solitario conceded.

"You speak from experience?"

He nodded, thinking of the father he'd never met, the mother he'd witnessed only as a spirit standing on a sand dune, the girlfriend he'd lost in the flood, la maldición maldita. But something about Luz stirred more than lust or love or desire within him. Like her very name, she spliced the darkness and loneliness of his life like a clear beam of light, igniting a spark deep in his soul that threatened to grow into a blazing fire.

At first, he feared that Don Miguel might not think him suitable for Luz, given that he was not a man of great wealth. He determined to change that so that he could ask for her hand. It was not long after he made up his mind that he captured a band of thieves that had been assailing the new railways carrying goods from the interior to the border. Unbeknownst to him, the railroad company had offered a large reward for the capture of the bandidos. The day he was presented with the sizable check, Solitario opened a bank account, purchased his ranch, and asked Don Miguel for Luz's hand in marriage.

"You have more than proven yourself to me, as a man of character and now as a man of means, a landowner like myself," Don Miguel answered. "It would delight me to see Luz not have to grow old by herself. There has never been another gentleman worthy of her attention in these parts. So, if she says yes, I will give you both my blessing. I ask only one favor . . ."

"Anything," Solitario answered, feeling more joyful and excited than he ever had in his young life.

"That you not take her far away from here, that you stay close so we can live as a family."

"Of course," Solitario answered. "Olvido will be our home."

That evening, Solitario brought a group of mariachis, including a somewhat dissonant Sergeant Elias, and serenaded Luz from the street where he first saw her at the window. She opened the window, smiling as she gazed down at him in his mariachi uniform, the moonlight sparkling off the silver embroidery on his jacket and sombrero. He played the guitar and sang passionately for her, and as she clapped, he knelt on one knee and proposed to her.

"Sí." She smiled from above. "I will marry you, Solitario Cisneros."

At last, he thought, his life would diverge from the destiny hewn into his name. He would no longer be alone.

Governor Terrazas came all the way from Chihuahua for the wedding at the cathedral across the plaza. When the married couple emerged from the arched doorway onto the sunny steps, they were showered with rice grains by the jubilant crowd. A photographer that Don Miguel had commissioned for the occasion took a picture of them together. Then, they celebrated in the courtyard at La Casa Colorada, surrounded by the family's friends and Luz's birds. They waltzed around the fountain as a string quartet from Mexico City performed. And before the evening was over, Luz presented Solitario with a special wedding present. She descended in her flowing white dress down the exterior staircase to the courtyard as the festive crowd cheered her on. In her hands, she carried the most magnificent sombrero Solitario had ever seen. Its top side was black and embroidered in silver, but its underside was a midnight-blue velvet with white patterns stitched into it by hand.

As she gave it to him, Luz whispered, "This is a special sombrero, mi amor. I made it myself. When you wear it and you sing or play your guitar, whatever feelings you wish to express or convey will deeply move your listeners' hearts and minds."

He was not sure what she meant, but he placed the stunning sombrero on his head and thanked her, embracing her tightly.

Don Miguel cleared his throat and raised his champagne flute. "To my daughter, Luz, and her husband, Solitario. Not until late in life did my dearly departed wife and I become parents. Luz was our only child. I never thought she could possibly meet a gentleman that I would deem worthy of her affections, much less her hand in marriage. But the day I met Capitán Solitario Cisneros, I had a feeling about him. This is a man of honor. Today, I am proud to welcome him into our family. Again, to Luz, my beloved daughter, and to Solitario, my newfound son, may your union be eternally blessed."

The guests raised their glasses and toasted the newlyweds. The mariachis played festive music. And at that moment, Solitario made a mistake he still regretted all those years later as he slept alone in Elias' house: he allowed himself to believe that he had finally outrun the maldición de Caja Pinta.

TWENTY-THREE

When Solitario awoke in Elias' small house that Sunday morning, he felt inexplicably drawn to the old plaza in the Mexican part of Olvido. After drinking his coffee with Elias, he rode Tormenta slowly through the dusty streets. The plaza lay in shambles, the trees dry and brittle, drifts of brown leaves rustling through the weeds. An elderly lady pumped water at the well as he stopped to admire the ornately carved facade of the cathedral's charred ruins. He had never considered himself highly religious—spiritual, yes, but not particularly attached to any organized way of worshiping. He thought of his relationship with God as a personal and direct channel of communication, an unseen but vital link. He prayed when he felt grateful or when he required solace, but he had given up on asking for anything since the day Luz died. Still, he found it sad for the town and its Mexican residents that nobody had mustered up the resources or the will to rebuild the decimated cathedral. What did that mean? Had the people of Olvido so resolutely surrendered any hope for the future?

He dismounted Tormenta and stepped through the open threshold into the nave of the church. The pews had been pillaged for firewood or construction material. The roof had largely burned and now gaped open to the heavens above. Nothing but burned beams and crumbling rafters lay strewn across the Oaxacan tile floor. The stained-glass windows had all exploded in the fire that had consumed the building not long after the river had changed course, as if God himself had become enraged at the Rio Grande's fickle abandonment of his flock.

Here, he had married Luz. He recalled her standing next to him at the altar. Stepping over the ashy remnants, he stood at the spot where they had been declared husband and wife. As he imagined her standing next to him, he was startled by a creaking noise behind him. Turning, he saw the old woman who had been pumping water in the plaza. She carried a bucket in each hand and was dressed in a tentlike black dress with a matching scarf over her white hair.

"M'ijo, they don't say Mass here anymore. You have to go down to the dry river gorge if you wish to pray with the other believers," she said.

"Gracias." He nodded.

"They are down there now."

He wondered why she was not there with them but decided that it was none of his business. He typically preferred to avoid talking unless it was absolutely necessary. En boca cerrada no entran moscas.

After the woman left, sloshing water from her swinging buckets, he went back outside to where Tormenta patiently waited. He patted her on the neck and led her around the plaza to Luz's childhood home, boarded up just as Don Miguel had described. It no longer shone bright red as it once had years earlier. Its walls were covered in countless layers of dust, rendering it a chalky pink hue. La Casa Colorada was a lifeless and colorless shadow of its former self. He frowned, shaking his head. It looked the way he felt.

He swung back into his saddle and rode toward the riverbed. Just as the woman had prophesized, a large throng of Olvido's Mexican towns-people filled the canyon left behind by the elusive river. The priest stood on a makeshift altar; his black cassock flapped in the wind as he raised an oversized host toward the sun. The worshipers fell to their knees and bowed their heads, murmuring prayers under their breath. As quietly as he could, Solitario crossed the ditch and continued his Sunday morning ride through the town, a thought crossing his mind.

He headed to the Anglo church and dismounted by the fence out front. The church door was open, and he could hear the congregation singing a solemn hymn in English.

Peeking through the doorway, he saw the Anglo settlers dressed in their Sunday best, little girls and their mothers wearing bonnets over their carefully brushed hair, the boys and men wearing ties, their hair slicked back and shiny with brilliantine.

Standing there, he listened as Reverend Grimes preached his fire-and-brimstone vision of the world. He could tell that the reverend liked to practice the classic fear-and-hope dynamic. He scared his parishioners with all his talk of sin and inadequacy, but then he offered them the succor and salvation of his Lord. It was not all that different from the Catholic approach, Solitario mused. They didn't adorn their house of prayer with statues of the Virgen de Guadalupe or even of saints. They kept things simpler, cleaner, and far less bloody. Instead of a wounded figure of Jesus over the altar, they focused on a simply hewn—if massive—cross, the symbol of Jesus' sacrifice rather than the macabre image of His grotesque suffering. Solitario wondered as he waited for the service to conclude why and how so much blood could be spilled and so much hatred maintained between diverging flocks of faithful over such subtle nuances. Did not everybody yearn for the same things? To know there was more to life than this? To believe in the hope of a reward at the end of years of suffering? To be forgiven for one's sins and mistakes? To feel slightly less alone in the universe?

He listened as Reverend Grimes launched into a sermon about the horrific killings that gripped the townsfolk with dread. After wondering aloud if Olvido had brought on its long run of bad luck through the wayward ways of its own inhabitants, the reverend reassured his followers with familiar words from Psalm 23: "Though I walk through the valley of the shadow of death, I will fear no evil: for Thou art with me; Thy rod and Thy staff, they comfort me . . ."

Solitario recalled the words and mouthed them in Spanish as if he were conjuring up a childhood rhyme. Companionship, discipline, guidance—these were comforts out in the wilderness to most people. They were the alternatives to solitude, chaos, and perdition. His eyebrows gathering like dark clouds, he circled to the back of the church and peered into the woods, hoping for a flash of gold to streak between the trees. He had not seen Johnny Tolbert in a while. Was all of this slipping through his fingers? What if he failed to bring the criminals to justice and save Elena and the other children? Doubt crept through his soul like a slithering serpent.

When the congregation dispersed back to their homes, he intercepted the reverend on the path to his house.

"Working on a Sunday?" asked the reverend, clutching his prayer book to his chest like a shield.

"As are you," Solitario replied, approaching the preacher.

"Yes, the Lord's work never ends."

"Neither does the law's," quipped Solitario. "When the Lord isn't present in the valley of the shadow of death, someone else has to step in."

"That is where you are wrong, señor," Reverend Grimes pontificated. "The Lord is always present. That is the point of the prayer, which I am afraid you missed."

"I was never very good in school," Solitario confessed. "I'm more a person of action. But I will ask you one thing. Where was your omnipresent Lord when the Jacksons and the Tolberts and the Elias and Lopez families were brutally murdered?"

The reverend bowed his head and resumed his walk toward his house. "I'm afraid my wife is waiting for me to eat supper. Perhaps we can continue this debate another day . . . or perhaps never."

Solitario followed the preacher to his front porch. "Funny thing I learned from the county and bank records, Reverend."

"And what might that be?" the reverend turned at the top of the steps, scrutinizing Solitario from up high.

"That the Jacksons' land will go to you and your church, as well as the Tolberts', if there are no survivors among their children. The Jackson farm is mortgaged to you. And the Tolbert farm would go up for auction if there were no heirs, but the church would have first dibs since you filed a dispute over the property line with the county."

"Are you insinuating something?" the reverend retorted, his facial muscles going slack.

"Would you volunteer to let us conduct a search of your house and church?"

"Absolutely not. What will people think? What will they say?" he asked.

"They might say what everybody's already thinking," Solitario replied as he hazarded a guess. "That you had the most to gain from the death of the Tolbert and Jackson families. And that you couldn't care less about what happened to the Mexican families in the river gorge. Maybe you arranged that to throw us off your scent . . . or to spite me."

"You think the world revolves around you," the reverend replied. "That's why you'll never get to the truth. You're too distracted by your own emotions and personal vendettas. You don't like me, so you want to blame me."

"That's not how the law works."

"Exactly." The reverend stepped into his house and slammed the door. After Solitario knocked, he nudged it open a sliver. "Come back when you have a warrant. If I have any clout left in this town, the mayor will never grant you that. And on a Sunday, no less." Reverend Grimes slammed the door a second time for good measure.

Solitario smiled. He had figured it was worth a shot. Now he knew one thing for certain: whether it was related to the murders or not, the good reverend had something he'd rather hide. Perhaps he was not as pure as the gospel he preached.

TWENTY-FOUR

Percy Boggs sat uneasily at the head of the table in his Victorian home. The table was laden with as sumptuous a feast as could be mustered in Olvido. He had spared no expense in celebrating the presence of his wife's mother and younger sister. Roasted pork beckoned from a silver platter at the center of the table. Steaming sides surrounded it: corn, mashed potatoes, carrots, and gravy. His wife, Annie, glowed opposite him, looking lovely in a yellow dress her mother had brought for her from Newbury Street in Boston.

"So Mrs. Lewis, tell us how Boston is doing these days," Percy Boggs asked his mother-in-law, attempting to enliven the stolid atmosphere.

Unaccustomed to the Texas heat, the matronly lady in her elegant purple dress fanned herself with a lace accordion fan. "It is horrid, if one's being honest. People keep coming in hordes from the rural areas and the south. The city is crowded and filthy. Anyone with means escapes as often as they can to the Berkshires or up north to Maine."

"Surely, Beacon Hill is still an acceptable refuge, Mother," Annie Boggs smiled, serving a plate.

Her mother sniffed, gazing about the dining room's finely decorated interior, the elegant furnishings, the silk drapes. "It is tolerable, I suppose, compared to the conditions to which you have chosen to subject yourself."

"Olvido is a frontier city on the rise, Mother." Percy forced a smile as well, raising a glass of red wine and taking a generous swig.

Mrs. Lewis turned to Annie, murmuring beneath her breath, "Why does he insist on calling me that?"

"I like it here. It feels adventurous and new for the making," Annie's younger sister, Georgina, declared.

Their mother pursed her lips. "It's too far away. You missed your sister's coming out," she admonished Annie. "And my grandchildren are growing up like savages out here," she waved dismissively at Percy and Annie's two young daughters, who sat quietly at the table, stiff in their Sunday dresses, afraid to move for fear of offending their fastidious grandmother.

Percy had warned them to behave or else their grandmother would demand they be shipped back with her to attend boarding school in Massachusetts. If only the old bat didn't control the purse strings to the family fortune. Percy gulped more wine as if it were water and he were stranded in the desert.

"It's a sacrifice, Mother," Percy said, "but with great risks come even greater rewards."

"So you say," Mrs. Lewis replied, frowning as she chewed her mashed potatoes. "It's so dry here that the mashed potatoes are crumbling in my mouth."

"The men are rugged and handsome here," Georgina beamed, her golden curls bouncing up and down excitedly. "That guard the sheriff posted outside is a luxury we don't have in Beacon Hill."

Flustered, Mrs. Lewis chastised her, "Georgina, set a better example for the children. My dear, really! We are here to visit family and tend to business, not to flirt with the natives."

"Mother!" Annie protested. "Michael Dobbs is a fine young man. We are fortunate he is here to protect us. Otherwise, who would?"

Percy Boggs drained his glass, placing it down a bit too emphatically. Everyone turned to face him. His face flushed pink with a mixture of frustration and embarrassment. After all, he, too, had a pistol. Sure, he'd never fired it, but he could feel it in his trouser pocket at that very moment.

"I'm sorry, Percy," Annie checked herself. "I am sure you could protect us quite adequately."

Mrs. Lewis sniffed again, putting down her fork and laboriously chewing a piece of pork loin.

"Perhaps I could take him a plate?" Georgina ventured, looking to her sister for permission.

"Who?" her mother asked.

"The guard," Georgina replied. "Michael Dobbs."

Mrs. Lewis rolled her eyes to the ceiling, from which hung an expensive crystal chandelier. "What's the point?"

"The point of what?" Annie asked, as Georgina stood to prepare a plate for the Dobbs boy.

"Everything." She stared at the chandelier. "My eldest daughter and only grandchildren marooned out here in this desert wasteland, pretending to live a civilized life, stringing chandeliers from your ceilings as if anyone here could even begin to appreciate their finery."

Percy could restrain himself no longer. "The future is the point! We must strive to be part of America's manifest destiny. The new fortunes will be minted out here. With your help, Mother, we could put the Boggs . . . and the Lewis families at the forefront of entrepreneurship and wealth."

Mrs. Lewis dabbed the corners of her wrinkled lips with a lace napkin, lamenting, "How gauche."

"Not now, dear." Annie shook her head from the other end of the table, cautioning Percy to let her do the talking later.

Stymied, he sank back into his ornately carved armchair. He eyed the wine cabinet. Was it too soon to open another bottle? Of course it wasn't, he convinced himself. His mother-in-law was in town, and that demanded a high volume of drinking. It was the only way to shoulder the humiliation.

As Percy Boggs stood to free another bottle from the wine rack, Georgina scampered out into the foyer with a plate full of food in her hands.

Percy was in bed next to his wife when a noise downstairs startled him from his slumber. "Did you hear that, Annie?" he whispered, sitting up and rubbing his eyes.

She rustled, mumbling something unintelligible as she turned away.

Percy reached for his wire-rimmed glasses on the nightstand. Standing, he wavered a bit, a sharp pain shooting through his head. *Too much red wine*, he realized, reaching for the small nickel-plated pistol in his drawer. Gingerly, he tiptoed to the door and pried it open. He stuck his head out into the hallway and peered both ways. The corridor was vacant. He walked barefoot to the top of the stairs. There he heard more noise downstairs. Chairs being moved across the dining room floor? What in God's name? He descended cautiously, his gun in his left hand so he could steady himself with his right hand on the banister. As he reached the bottom of the stairs, he turned through the foyer toward the dining room, but before he could reach it, he heard the floor creak behind him. As he whirled around in surprise, all he saw was a large round iron skillet rushing swiftly toward his head. He heard the crunch of his glasses right before the blow rendered him numb and senseless.

When Percy Boggs came to, his headache was unbearable. He squinted, but everything was a terrible blur. He tried to reach for his glasses to wipe them clean, only to find he could not move his hands. They were tied behind him. He couldn't stand either. He was bound to one of the dining room chairs. He tried to talk, to shout, but that was impossible too. A strip of cloth was tightly strapped through his mouth to the back of his head. In the dark dining room, he could discern movement, shadows, but little else due to his abominable eyesight. He could hear the muffled sounds of futile struggle, grunts and squeals of discomfort and pain. His heart thundered. Was this the end? What of his children? What had happened to the guard? Where was the sheriff? He wriggled pointlessly in his seat until a fist pounded into his cheek. Biting his tongue during the impact, Percy winced at the pain, blood pouring down his chin onto his white pajamas.

"Wouldn't want you to miss this," a voice said, gruffly planting Percy's cracked glasses on the bruised and bloody bridge of his nose.

As Percy focused, he saw two intruders, but he could not make out their faces. They wore black hoods over their heads. Sitting bound and gagged on the table were Mrs. Lewis and Georgina in their dark nightgowns. Their eyes bulged with terror as they gawked at him helplessly. Turning sideways, he saw his wife. *Annie, poor Annie.* He had gotten her and their girls, and now her mother and sister, into this terrible mess. All for what? His dreams of success? Where were his children? And where was that damned guard?

The two hooded men arrayed a row of candles at the foot of the table. The flickering light illuminated the pale faces of Annie's mother and sister.

How could he ever face his mother-in-law again, Percy Boggs wondered. She had warned them countless times before they had moved out west. This was the fruition of all she had feared for them.

When they were finished lining up the candles, the two intruders stood at opposite ends of the dining table. Slowly, they unsheathed long, shiny blades.

Annie gasped as Boggs tried to look away. *Don't look, Annie. Don't look*, he thought.

A rustling sound could be heard entering from the kitchen. Against his better judgment, against his will even, Boggs peeked in the direction of the noise. In the fluctuating light, he spied the amplified shadows of long feathers on the dining-room wall. At first he was not sure if he was looking at an otherworldly creature, but slowly it dawned on him that this was a man dressed in some kind of alien garb. His lower half was covered by a skirt construed of large plumes and strings of seashells and beads. His torso was bare beneath a black cape that draped over his back. His face was shielded by a mask with more feathers bristling out from its sides and over his head. Boggs had never seen an Apache dressed like this.

The man spoke in a low, raspy voice, using words that Boggs did not recognize, chanting them as he performed a ritual in front of Mrs. Lewis and Georgina. With a hunk of chalk, the man drew symbols on Mrs. Lewis' terrified face. Boggs strained against the ropes, but it was useless. They were tied too tightly around his arms and wrists.

As the feathered man finished his incantations, he nodded at one of the hooded intruders. The intruder raised his long blade, positioning himself behind Mrs. Lewis.

Annie nearly toppled her chair over, writhing and shrieking through the bandanna in her mouth.

No, please, no, prayed Boggs, closing his eyes. *Do not let this happen, God.*

The sharp metal sliced through Mrs. Lewis' neck, blood spraying across Percy's and Annie's faces as they watched in horror.

The shaman spoke more words, cupping his hands so the blood spurting rhythmically from the elder's severed neck pooled in them. He raised his hands and let the crimson fluid stream down his forearms.

Annie was sobbing. Georgina fainted, slumping sideways on the table, her body leaning up against her beheaded mother's quivering mass.

The shaman nodded at the other hooded swordsman, who clutched Georgina's shoulder to straighten her delicate frame. He lowered the blade toward her neck. Just as he was about to slash through it, a knock came at the door.

Dear Lord, thought Percy. *Please be the sheriff. Somebody has to stop this madness before it goes any further.* What if, after Georgina, his own children were next?

The attackers stood frozen for what seemed like an eternal moment. Boggs grunted, struggling to cry for help through the gag in his mouth.

"Mr. Boggs?" the man at the door called out. "Michael?"

It was the other Dobbs twin. He knocked again, this time louder. "I'm gonna come in and check on y'all," he shouted.

The door handle jiggled in his hand. It was locked.

One of the hooded men put away his saber and unholstered a revolver, stepping toward the window and peeking out from behind the curtain. "I'm going to take a shot at him. That ought to scare him away or make him take cover. Meanwhile, you get out of here fast as you can."

He was talking to the shaman, Boggs realized.

The man slowly opened the window as the jiggling of the doorknob continued. Those Dobbs twins sure were nice, but Percy wasn't too sure how smart they were.

Everyone in the room, including Georgina, who had been unconscious, jumped as a single shot rang out.

"Damn it!" Blake Dobbs yelled, scrambling off the porch. "You done shot me in the arm!"

Blake Dobbs fired back, the window shattering, bits of glass flying through the room, feeling like a dozen bee stings all at once piercing Percy's bare arms and neck.

The hooded man crouched beneath the windowsill, urging his comrades, "Get out! Go now, both of you. I'll finish the girl."

The shaman and the other hooded assailant dashed out the back door.

More gunshots rang out as Dobbs and the remaining intruder continued to trade fire.

Stray bullets blew apart more windows. The chandelier exploded overhead. Georgina wiggled her way off the table and crawled underneath it, doubling over with her head shaking in her lap. Percy's eyes followed the light fixture's skeleton as it swung back and forth overhead. The hooded gunman fired yet again, and Boggs heard a loud groan outdoors, followed by a thump on the ground.

This is it, thought Percy Boggs. *The other Dobbs boy is dead. It's all over. God, just save our daughters. Protect them from harm. May they be hiding under their beds.*

The intruder chuckled maliciously under his hood, "Now where'd you hide, young'un?" he crouched down to find Georgina curled up in the fetal position under the dining-room table, which was covered in broken glass and crystal fragments. He reached down and yanked her by her curls as she let out a muffled screech. Pulling her upright, he stood behind her, unsheathing his blade and raising it to her throat.

TWENTY-FIVE

Solitario heard the shots as they echoed across town. He'd been watering Tormenta beneath the mesquite tree at Elias' house when the cracking sounds disrupted the stillness of the night, shuddering across the blackened sky. Crows flew from the branches, cawing in distress. In a flash, he jumped onto his horse. Riding bareback, he plunged into the ravine toward the source of the gunfire. As another shot rang out, a flash of light caught his eye up on the levee. It was Mr. Boggs' house. *Damn it*, Solitario chided himself. *I shouldn't have left Michael there alone. Faster, Tormenta, faster.*

Tormenta flew up the other side of the gorge, streaking toward the Boggs residence. As they skidded into the clearing in front of the house, Solitario saw Blake Dobbs lying in the dirt behind a sage bush. He was breathing still, but his arm and leg were bleeding.

Solitario dismounted, kneeling next to him.

"Hurry, Jefe," Blake panted, beads of perspiration glistening on his pallid cheeks beneath the brilliant starlight of the vast, open sky. "Something bad is happening in there."

Solitario eyed his deputy's wounds. His leg was bleeding profusely. If he didn't do something, Blake Dobbs would bleed out fast. Untying his yellow bandanna, Solitario fastened it tightly around Blake's thigh, applying pressure to the gunshot wound.

Blake winced in pain, curling his hands into tight balls. "Go, Jefe, go."

Crouching low to the ground, guns drawn, Solitario dashed toward the front porch. He climbed the steps as quietly as he could, reaching the door. Inside, he could hear the muffled sounds of terror. Without hesitation, he backed up, rose to his full stature, and kicked the door open. He barged in prepared to fire.

"Shoot, and I'll kill her," a hooded figure said from the dining room to Solitario's left. The stranger stood behind Mr. Boggs' sister-in-law, pressing a long, gleaming blade against her jugular.

Solitario scanned the room: the matriarch sprawled lifelessly on the dinner table, Mr. Boggs and his wife tied to the chairs. He needed a clear shot, but the room was so dark and shadowy, the man's body shielded by the young woman's. He took a tentative step toward the dining room.

"Don't come any closer, you hear?" the assailant threatened, increasing the pressure of the blade against Georgina's delicate neck. Her smooth white skin began to succumb to the steel's sharp edge, a sliver of crimson appearing at the seam where the two met.

The attacker dragged her along as he stepped backward through the dining room toward the kitchen. Solitario followed slowly, careful not to let them out of his sight, but maintaining his distance until he could get a better view of his target.

"Y'all jis stay put, stay right where you are, right where I can see you," the hooded man said. "Now, I'm going to jis git through the back door, and you wait inside. You don't chase me. If you do, I'll cut her right then and there and toss her onto the ground, jis as dead as her mama."

Mrs. Boggs shook with grief and fear as Mr. Boggs gaped in horror.

Solitario advanced through the dining room, his eyes trained on the intruder and his hostage, who now stood in the doorway to the kitchen. He knew he could not let the man retreat any further. If he let him close that kitchen door or sneak out the back, if he lost eye contact for even a moment, the attacker might just take that chance to finish Georgina off and bolt to his horse. Solitario's breathing slowed. His heart maintained its steady cadence. He knew this man aimed to kill Georgina one way or another, whether it was now or later. Nobody else was coming to help. If he hesitated or let the intruder use his hostage to escape, the girl would surely die. She was part of this sacrifice, a ritual halfway finished, one of the two noblewomen. The bruja had described the act as an offering to the rain god Tlāloc.

His gaze narrowed on the man's hood. At the base of the fabric, he glimpsed a patch of white skin. It was the man's neck, ever so slightly exposed. At last, he had found something on which to focus, a clear target. His hands—and his spirit—as still as a frozen lake in the dead of winter, Solitario fired a single shot.

An arc of crimson fluid floated across the room, splattering across the damask wallpaper as the assailant teetered back and away from his captive, his long blade clattering onto the table as he crumpled to the floor.

Through a serpentine cloud of gun smoke, Solitario saw Georgina's tears glimmering in the candlelight. He hurried through the room to make sure the attacker was dead. After doing so, he untied Georgina. As she collapsed, sobbing on the floor, he released Mr. and Mrs. Boggs from their bindings.

"My daughters!" cried Mrs. Boggs, scrambling up the staircase, followed by her husband.

As Mr. and Mrs. Boggs searched upstairs for their daughters, Solitario moved quickly through the rest of the house, ensuring no other intruders lurked in the darkened rooms. He found the back door ajar, swaying in the cool night breeze. Outside stood a single horse, waiting for a rider that would never return. Circling back to the foyer, he heard Mrs. Boggs scream in anguish upstairs. Craning his neck to look up, he saw Mr. Boggs standing at the upper railing.

"They're gone," Boggs cried, shaking his head in despair. "Our girls are gone."

———————

In the aftermath of the attack on the Boggs family, Solitario removed the black hood from the remaining intruder's corpse. Nobody recognized him. He was a young man with a bushy brown mustache. Nothing about him was distinguishing. And nothing seemed to link him to any of Solitario's suspects. Neither did Mr. Boggs' description of the shaman-like person that had fled the scene along with the other hooded attacker.

Solitario surmised that before the adults had been roused from their sleep, there had been more hands in the invading party. Those additional men had incapacitated Michael Dobbs and escaped completely unseen with him and the Boggs girls before the grown-ups had been awakened to participate in the ungodly ritual that had not only destroyed the Boggs' dining room but also sacrificed their matriarch.

Mrs. Boggs wept on the sitting-room sofa, hanging on to her sister.

"Mother's dead!" Georgina wailed, her body shaking.

As Dr. Ferris tended to Blake Dobbs' injuries on the front porch, he marveled as he removed Solitario's yellow bandanna from the young man's leg, "This is strange. It appears that not only did the bleeding stop, but the bullet has been pushed out of the wound onto the surface." He picked the small projectile up with his tweezers. "Usually, it's quite a painful process extracting one of these from the wound." He stared at the bullet as he held it up with his instrument.

Solitario wrapped the bloodied bandanna around his neck, concealing the necklace his grandmother, la bruja, had given him long ago. He was not about to explain things that the doctor could not begin to understand, but he himself had never imagined that the protective magic emanating from the seashells strung around his neck would rub off on the bandanna after all the years of wearing them together.

"My leg feels fine," Blake Dobbs agreed incredulously.

"Usually a patient would be laid up for days, and I'd be worried about infection, but your injury is basically already healed," Dr. Ferris shook his head in amazement.

"I can't rest. I gotta find my brother." Blake jumped to his feet.

Mr. Boggs sat deflated on one of the rocking chairs arrayed on the porch. His hair disheveled, his glasses cracked, his pajamas splattered in blood, he appeared completely defeated. "We have nothing to go on still. How will we find them? At least your brother's a grown man. My little girls are defenseless."

Solitario mulled over the predicament. Things seemed to only get worse, not better. Was this what failure felt like? He had lost everything in his personal life but never had he lost confidence in his professional abilities. He had never truly doubted himself or his capacity to fight crime and injustice, but he certainly doubted himself now. Had the years of hiding out on his ranch made him rusty to the point he had grown completely ineffective? Why did his lone recourse seem to be the one person he was thinking of calling upon yet again?

"Blake, is your leg good enough to walk and ride?" Solitario asked.

"Yes, Jefe. Tell me what to do. I'll do anything to help my brother."

"I need you to go somewhere for me," Solitario answered, not only thinking of their recent argument but also recalling at whose hands the Dobbs twins had reputedly been orphaned. "I need you to fetch someone. Tell her to come quickly. Tell her it's an emergency."

Before Solitario could finish dispensing his commands, Blake Dobbs was up on his horse, nursing his bandaged arm, ready to ride as if his thigh had never been punctured by gunfire. "Who do you want me to bring, Jefe?" he asked.

"Onawa."

Blake balked, his face clouding over with doubt.

Solitario gazed into Blake's eyes and said, "She can help us find your brother."

Frowning as he nodded, Blake turned slowly and then spurred his horse toward Aguila Brava's house.

———

Dr. Ferris flatly stated that he placed no stock in notions such as magic and Apache mysticism, but Mr. Boggs countered that—at this point—he was desperate enough to try anything. Solitario listened quietly, waiting for Onawa to arrive, his elbows resting on the porch rail as he squinted into the night. When she emerged from the darkness, riding several horse lengths ahead of Blake Dobbs, Solitario gestured for her to follow him to the side of the house so they could speak in relative privacy.

Dismounting, she brushed her hair out of her face and glared at him, still fuming despite the days that had passed since their confrontation in the desert.

After he explained the atrocities that had taken place, she seemed to put aside her emotions to carefully contemplate the events. "This shaman you speak of. His clothing and mask, his ritual, they do not sound Apache."

Solitario nodded. "It sounds like what Alicia talked to us about."

She agreed, glancing at Mr. Boggs on the porch, hunched over his knees on the rocking chair, his head cradled in his hands. "It is unusual to see a white man suffer this much, especially a wealthy one."

Solitario followed her line of sight. He felt sorry for Mr. Boggs and his wife. He had known the moment he had laid eyes on him that he should have never come out west, and he most certainly should not have dragged his wife and daughters along. "We need to find the Boggs girls and Michael Dobbs . . . along with all the other children."

"And you want me to help again?" Onawa placed her hands on her hips, squinting at him.

"People contend that twins have a special connection," Solitario said. "I did not experience that with my own twin brother, unfortunately. Our destinies were mostly at odds due to the circumstances. But we were also not identical twins like the Dobbs boys. And we were not close, the way they are."

Her voice shifted into a more controlled tone. "Yes, twins are often bound together. You think perhaps—through the one that brought me here—we could see where his brother was taken?"

Solitario nodded. She always seemed to understand him without the need for much explanation. He liked that. The less talk, the better. Especially given the tenor of their most recent conversation.

Her eyes landed on his badge. "Again, Solitario, tell me why only you men get to wear the shiny badge?"

Just like the first time she'd asked him, he replied with his poker face until she relented.

"Yes, I will try," she sighed. "Not for your deputies, nor for you . . . but for the children. I will need a lock of Blake Dobbs' hair and a large bowl with water," she commanded. "And I don't want those white men gawking at me from the porch while I do it."

He nodded. "Wait here."

Pulling Blake Dobbs aside, Solitario frowned so intensely that the muscles in his face hurt. For him, the only thing more challenging than asking something of himself was asking it of someone else.

"What is it, Jefe?" Blake asked.

"I need you to cut off a bit of your hair."

"Why?" Blake seemed flustered.

"Onawa will use it to seek out your brother."

Blake glanced in Onawa's direction. She stood alone in a clearing to the side of the house. Then he stared at Solitario. In his blue eyes, Solitario could see clouds of distrust but also rays of fear and hope. "I don't know if I believe in her ways," Blake said. "As you know, my family doesn't have the best history with the Apache."

"You don't have to believe. You don't even have to like it. All you have to do is cut some hair for me," Solitario said, handing him a knife.

Blake accepted the blade and chopped off a small lock of hair behind his right ear, handing it to Solitario.

When Solitario returned to Onawa with the items she had requested, the porch had been vacated, the grumbling men retreating inside, where the Boggs women were still caterwauling over the loss of their mother and the abduction of the young girls.

Onawa flung her shawl to the ground, smoothing it out until it made a neat square. Placing the clay bowl at its center, she knelt over the water. Sprinkling Blake Dobbs' hair into the clear liquid, she closed her eyes and held her hands over the bowl, her lips moving silently.

Solitario watched her intently, admiring her poise and determination, thankful for her help despite her obvious irritation toward him. Her concentration was etched into the curves of her oval face. He could tell she was traveling, present but absent, soaring like an eagle over the desert plains, following some vital link of energy tethering Blake Dobbs to his missing brother, Michael.

She shuddered, cringing. Her eyes snapped open. "I know where he is," she whispered, staring past Solitario toward the south. "We must hurry."

TWENTY-SIX

The place they had taken him was dark and cold. His eyes were blind-folded, his hands tied behind his back, his ankles bound. Michael Dobbs had never felt so much fear, so much pain. He'd also never—not once in his entire life—been so far apart from his brother.

He'd been sitting out front on the Boggs' porch, his mind wander-ing, daydreaming about that pretty girl, Georgina. He sure had been surprised that Mr. Boggs, a somewhat portly and forgettable man, could have such a lovely relative. Of course, she had turned out to be Mrs. Boggs' younger sister. Apparently, Mrs. Boggs was first in line for the inheritance, and—as divine compensation—Georgina had gotten all the looks. Luck had its ways of evening things out in the end. He'd been sitting there puzzling on such things, as he liked to do to keep his brain occupied, when suddenly he felt a pinprick on his neck. It felt like a mosquito bite, but it was past mosquito season. As he slapped at it, he was startled to find a cold hand behind his head. Then, his body had gone numb. His vision blurred. And he passed out.

When he awoke he was all tied up and jostling sideways on the rump of a galloping horse. He could barely breathe. His ribs ached. He thought he was going to die right then and there. When the horse finally came to a stop, he'd been carried like a burlap sack full of sorghum into a cold, drafty structure. It smelled musty, a hint of old and crumbling manure in the air. Straw rustled under the boots of whoever was carrying him in there. He was strung up right quick, his feet and legs roped together and above his head, all the blood rushing down to his brain, giving him a splitting headache.

He tried to yell and scream. It was bad enough to be in this pickle, but for an inquisitive fellow like him, it was even worse not to understand why, or to be able to ask any questions. What was next? Was he about to be sacrificed too, like all the other victims? That poor Jackson girl, Gertrude. He'd overheard the jefe talking to the doctor about her. She'd been skinned alive. A demented madman had performed a ceremonial dance wearing her skin like a sacred robe. What kind of depraved insanity was that? Would the same type of sordid fate befall him now? If he somehow, miraculously, made it out of here alive, he'd have to seriously reconsider this line of work. Sure, he was curious and wanted to do the right thing, and being a lawman fit well with those qualities, but dying like this just didn't seem worth it just for having an interesting job. Besides, he hadn't been looking forward to the prospect of having to shoot somebody dead. He didn't mind running errands for Sheriff Tolbert or helping out Solitario Cisneros. The former had been like a father to him, and the latter seemed like a serious man with good intentions. But killing and dying for a living, he wasn't so sure anymore if he was up for that, if he were lucky enough to escape in one piece.

He thought all this as he hung upside down in that abandoned barn, the rafters creaking as he swung from them, the night breeze flowing through the seams in the warped wood. This place hadn't been used in a long time. How would anyone in God's good earth ever find him here?

After a while, the man came back. He had heard him talking outside and then the sound of horses galloping away. Now it was just them two, it seemed. The man didn't appear all too happy about it, because he kept muttering curse words and spitting on the ground. And then out of nowhere, he hit Michael hard right in the ribs. The man must have been wielding some sort of bat or staff or maybe even a metal rod, because it hurt like hell. And he hit him again and again all over his body.

It felt like he was being broken into pieces with each blow. The pain shot through him like blasts of fire until he felt himself going numb and cold again. He thought maybe he was about to die, but suddenly the blows stopped and the muttering started again.

"Damn sons of bitches," the man grunted. "They're crazier than a coon dog in heat. This ain't no way to kill a man."

Michael heard the man drop his weapon to the ground. He wished he could sigh in relief, but he could barely breathe, being upside down as he was. Then he heard the man mutter at him, "I'll be back, boy. They want me to kill you nice and slow. Three days, they said. So sleep tight, little choice you got. I'll be back for you tomorrow." The man spat in disgust at what seemed like himself and his job and his bosses' proclivities, as it were. Michael just hung there like a bat with his wings tied to his torso, and his ears covered up, too. Blind as a bat, Michael had heard the saying. Well, how about blind and deaf and mute and tied up like a bat unable to move from its perch on the rafter? This was no way to die. He thought of poor Mrs. Tolbert who had also died strung up in her barn. Well, if it had been good enough for her, then it might have to do for him. A good, kind woman, she'd been.

Blake, Michael thought. *If you can hear me, brother, pray for me. Or better yet, find me. Find me, please. Save me, brother. Come here and cut me down and carry me away before that spitting, grunting, evil man comes back to finish me.*

Hanging there, every breath took its toll, especially after the blows. For sure, he had cracked ribs, maybe bleeding inside. Maybe he would die even if Blake found him and spared him another day or two of this abuse. But he'd rather die at home with his brother than alone out here at the hands of a maniac with a blunt weapon swinging at him as if he were some kind of Mexican piñata.

He slipped into unconsciousness but was startled by a sound up above. It sounded like a bird in the rafters. Maybe there was a hole in the roof and a crow had found its way in. What if it was a buzzard and it started pecking at him? Then he heard its cry. Damned if it wasn't a hawk or an eagle of some kind. It called out, shrieked like it meant to convey something to him, and then it took to its wings, which flapped mightily, sounding like big and wide and strong wings, the eagle taking flight, soaring. It called out from up high again. It was the damnedest thing, Michael thought. And then it was gone. He wished he could have seen it, but his eyes were still covered. He could hear his heart beating and ringing in his ears. Had it even been real? What had the eagle meant to tell him, he wondered? For some reason, he hoped it was a message of hope that his brother was already on his way to help him.

TWENTY-SEVEN

Elena stood in line at the outhouse, to which the guards escorted the girls twice a day. The little ones had trouble holding it in that long, so Elena had been pleading for the guards to take them more frequently, but they were having nothing of it. They were wretched men, filthy cowboys who cursed and spat and stank of sweat and whiskey and worse. When they finally took the girls outside, their eyes stung in the sunlight after so many hours of being cooped up inside the chapel. She was tired of that place. They all were. If she made it out of this alive, she wasn't sure if she'd want to see the inside of a church ever again. But then again, there she was praying for a miracle, or at least for her padrino, Solitario Cisneros, to come save them. And if her prayers were answered, then she would feel obligated to go to church. Of course, in Olvido, the Mexican cathedral had burned down anyway, so they held Mass in the dry riverbed. No ceiling. No windows. No stale air.

Her body was sore from sleeping on the hard wooden pews. And she was emotionally spent from trying to comfort the younger girls. Just that morning, two more had been brought, whimpering in their long white nightgowns, their feet bare, their dark curly hair a tangle. They were homely, fair-skinned, and freckled, and she heard one of the guards refer to them as the Boggs girls. The name sounded familiar. She was certain she'd heard her father mention it. Yes, he was one of the men that his father had taken out to El Escondido to try and recruit her padrino Solitario to search for the Tolbert girls and their family's killers. Now, here his daughters were too. Would there be any children left in Olvido when these evildoers were done?

Elena let the younger girls go into the outhouse first. She stood at the back of the line. Abigail and Beatrice Tolbert were the littlest. Then the green-eyed girl—Lavinia was her name. Poor thing had been in a terrible fire. Her whole family had died, but someone had whisked her out of there. She'd told Elena she wished she had died with her momma and poppa. She didn't want to be here, wherever *here* was. All Elena could figure out was they were in a large hacienda complex. The chapel was connected to a big house by a covered walkway with arches. It was all painted the color of clay, blending into the desert and the mountains in the distance. When they took them to the outhouse, all she could glimpse was open ranchland. The desert was dotted with black cows.

The new prisoners, the Boggs girls, stood ahead of her in line, shifting nervously from one bare foot to the other, when movement caught Elena's attention. Not far from where they stood, between the outhouse and the chapel, beneath a cluster of mesquite trees, stood a dark-skinned man dressed in a costume made of feathers and seashells. His back was to the girls as he leaned over a worktable. He was doing something, one of his arms moving back and forth rhythmically. He held something shiny in his hand. Elena squinted in the bright light, trying to make out what the man was doing. He even had feathers on his head. As his arm moved, she heard an almost musical sound emanating from him.

"Hurry," the elder Boggs girl urged her sister, "I'm gonna have an accident."

Elena frowned. These men wouldn't give them a change of clothes, and it was starting to reek in the chapel. Still, she stared at the man, taking one step closer to the outhouse. As she observed him, he suddenly paused and turned, like he sensed he was being watched. When he rotated his body in her direction, Elena gasped. He wore a mask, aqua and cobalt plumes fanning out from the sides, glittering in the severe sunlight. Where his mouth should have been there were jagged white teeth, probably plucked from a coyote's jaw. In the arm that had been moving, he held a long metal rod. It was a sharpening tool. She recognized it because her father had used one in the blacksmith shop. In the other hand, he held a long, gleaming blade. He stared straight at her as she took everything in. Right when it was her turn to go into the outhouse, the feathered man shifted sideways a bit, letting her see what lay spread across the table behind him. It was a frightening display of glistening knives and saws. Gawking in horror, her knees nearly buckled out from under her. She reached for the door to steady herself, but just as she did so, one of the guards shoved her into the outhouse, slamming the door shut and plunging her into the putrid darkness.

TWENTY-EIGHT

Solitario followed Onawa over the pitch-black dirt road, heading south-west toward the Chisos. Their horses moved swiftly, and the going was treacherous in the dark. Blake Dobbs trailed behind them, slowing them down. It would be easy to lose him. He was not as skilled a rider, nor was his horse an equal to Tormenta or Invierno, but he had insisted on coming. Solitario had assented because, after all, his brother's life was at stake.

"You should not have let him come," Onawa snapped when Blake Dobbs had fallen so far behind he was out of earshot.

"Why?" Solitario asked, gliding up next to her.

"For starters, he does not trust me," she said. "And in these situations, distrust among partners can get people killed."

He could not deny her wisdom. It was as if she—not he—had spent half a lifetime at war. Come to think of it, he chided himself, she had indeed spent her whole life at war. She was half Apache, half Mexican.

He couldn't help but wonder if she still trusted *him*. Was her statement aimed at him too? Would she ever smile at him again with those welcoming, joyful eyes? Or would she retreat forever, allowing the distance between them to grow until the maldición was no longer a threat?

He mulled over her comments as they rode, slowing Tormenta in order to fall back into place behind Invierno. The distance between them felt hard and cold and not nearly as comforting as he had hoped it would be. As much as he had resisted her attentions, he was surprised—and disheartened—to admit to himself that he now missed them.

Dawn was breaking to the east over the vast windswept desert plains, coloring the mountains burnt orange and saffron, when Onawa finally pointed at a barn in the distance, jutting upward, disrupting the flat clean line of the eastern horizon. It looked yellow in that rising light of morning, shimmered copper by the time they reached it.

Solitario dismounted first, followed by Onawa. He resisted the urge to storm the barn immediately, waiting for Blake to catch up. Huffing and puffing as he got down from his horse, he sauntered over with his gun drawn. Solitario's brow creased with worry. He wished he would not have the blood of these twins on his hands, on top of everyone else's. He also hoped that if they found Michael alive, he might hold some clue as to where his captors had taken the Boggs girls, which in turn was likely the place where Elena and the Tolbert girls were being held. This was an opportunity, he thought, but only if Michael was still alive.

Be alive, Michael Dobbs, Solitario nearly prayed, turning toward the barn doors with Onawa at his right side and Blake at his left. When he opened the doors and the light flooded the barn like stormwater filling a parched desert gully, they encountered a tightly bound body dangling from a beam high overhead.

There was nobody else in the barn, so Blake holstered his gun, scrambling toward his brother's motionless shape. "Michael," he called out, "are you alive?"

Solitario and Onawa followed him inside the structure, which appeared to have been abandoned some time ago. Solitario searched the ground for signs of any familiar boot prints, but nothing stood out to him in particular. Lying on the ground was what appeared to be a long rake handle. He examined it closely. He could see the point at which the metal rake had been sawed off from the handle. Whoever was in the process of slowly bludgeoning Michael Dobbs to death had used this tool.

Blake cut the rope and lowered his brother with Onawa and Solitario's help, gently laying him down on the straw.

"Michael, Michael, wake up," Blake begged, removing the blindfold and the gag wrapped through his twin's mouth.

Solitario cut the ropes at his wrists and ankles with the bowie knife he kept in a black leather sheath holstered above his right boot.

Onawa dribbled water from her canteen onto her hands and rubbed Michael's face with it, dampening his skin. As she did so, he stirred and his eyes opened, focusing on Blake's.

"Michael, you're alive. Thank God!" Blake smiled, hugging his brother.

Michael grunted from the pain as Blake squeezed him.

"Oh, I'm sorry," Blake said.

Solitario unbuttoned Michael's shirt, revealing his bruised torso. It seemed not an inch of his body had been spared. "He's in bad shape."

"We should take him to Dr. Ferris," Blake said. "I can carry him on my horse."

Solitario nodded. "Let's see if he can tell us anything first. Michael? Can you hear me?"

Michael moved his head in acknowledgment.

"Michael, you've been badly hurt. Do you remember what happened? How many men did this? Did you recognize anyone?"

Onawa gave him some water from her canteen, which he sipped slowly.

When he was ready, he cleared his throat and answered in a low, hoarse tone, "Jefe, I'm sorry I let you down. Is the Boggs family safe?"

"Don't you worry about that right now," Solitario answered. "Just tell me what you can remember."

"Somebody injected something into my neck from behind when I was out on the porch. They brought me here, blindfolded. I never saw a face. I did hear a voice." He paused, catching his breath and sipping some more water from Onawa's canteen. "It was just one man who did this to me."

"Did he sound familiar?" Solitario asked.

"I can't say. I don't think so."

"Did he say anything you remember, anything that stood out?"

"He seemed upset, like he wasn't too happy to be doing what he was doing, but he did it anyway. He said he'd be back again and again until his job was done."

Solitario nodded, patting Michael lightly on the shoulder so as not to cause him any pain but reassure him at the same time. "Good job, Michael. Now, you rest. The ride back to Olvido is going to hurt. Your brother will go slowly, but until Dr. Ferris can get some medicine in you, it's going to be rough."

Michael nodded. "And the Boggs family, Jefe? Are they okay? Mr. Boggs' sister-in-law, Georgina, is she safe?"

"Yes, she's safe, Michael," Solitario answered, choosing to omit the unfortunate details regarding the girl's mother and nieces. "Now, let's get you out of here before that man comes back."

Together, Solitario and Blake propped him up, looping his arms over their shoulders so they could help him walk outside. As they hoisted him onto the horse, Michael grimaced and groaned. When the Dobbs twins were ready to go, Solitario asked Onawa to accompany them back to town.

"Aren't you coming?" she asked, her expression toward him finally yielding from anger to concern.

"I will stay here and wait for the man who did this to return."

"You think he will?"

He nodded. "He has a job to finish. This must have been the sacrifice by bludgeoning that Alicia predicted."

"You shouldn't stay alone then," she said.

"I don't want to put you in danger. You go with them. If anyone comes after them, Blake won't be able to do much with his brother strapped to the horse behind him. You take my carabine just in case."

"I have my bow and arrows," she answered, glancing over to her horse, where her bow and quiver were strapped.

"Just in case," Solitario repeated.

She nodded as he pulled his rifle from the holster at Tormenta's side, handing it to her.

"And you?" she asked, her eyes betraying a flicker of fear. "You're not afraid to stay here alone?"

"I won't be alone. I have these." He patted the revolvers hanging below his hips.

Shaking her head, she mounted Invierno.

Just as she was about to put her horse into motion, he called her name, "Onawa."

She turned to look at him standing in front of the abandoned barn. "Yes?"

"Thanks for what you did. You saved the Dobbs boy."

For a fleeting instant, she smiled wistfully at him. Then she seemed to catch herself in the act, and her face turned to stone. She flicked her hair over her shoulder and patted her horse on its haunch, squeezing her thighs around his flanks to spur him forward.

Solitario watched as Onawa and the Dobbs twins rode away. *Poor Michael Dobbs*, he thought. Pobre muchacho. He blamed himself for placing too much responsibility on the boy's shoulders too soon. Without his old sergeant, though, what other options had been at his disposal? And now what? How would he face this band of violent criminals on his own? Michael would be laid up for days, if not weeks. Blake would probably want to be at his side. And Onawa? Her father's health was failing too. How could he keep her away from him now, when he needed her more than ever? Besides, he did not want to bring any harm upon her. How could he ask her to risk her life while at the same time denying her his love in order to protect her? He shook his head at the contradiction in his actions.

As the sun arced across the sky and the shadows shifted and lengthened in the barn, Solitario waited behind the closed doors, listening, expecting to hear the sound of a horse approaching from the distance, bringing perhaps the most important break in the case since he'd first spoken to Johnny Tolbert's spirit in the woods.

Come, coward, he thought. *It is easy to beat a man who has been tied up and strung upside down. Let's see how easy it is when you have to face a man with both hands free to fight back.*

TWENTY-NINE

Onawa rode ahead of the Dobbs twins, occasionally bringing Invierno to a stop to allow them to catch up. At first, she could hear poor Michael Dobbs moaning from the pain of each jostle and bump, but after a couple of hours, he fell silent. She worried that perhaps one of his broken ribs might have punctured a lung, or worse, that he was dying from internal bleeding.

Stopping on the desert road an hour or so outside of Olvido, she dismounted and approached Blake Dobbs' horse when he came near. "I want to check on your brother," she said.

He stopped and let her circle to the side of his horse. There, she stood on her tiptoes, pulled her hair back, and held her ear against his nose. He was still breathing. She wondered if it was better to keep riding or to lower him onto the ground so she could examine his internal wounds. Once she got him to town, the doctor would not permit her to do so. He did not believe in her ways. But if she checked on him now, she might be able to change the course of his suffering or gain enough insight to guide the doctor subtly in the right direction.

"Let's get him down on the ground, very carefully," Onawa told Blake Dobbs.

"Whatcha gonna do?" he asked, eyeing her through narrowed lids.

"I'm going to make sure he's not getting worse from being on the horse," she replied. Her philosophy was to always avoid giving the white man so much information that he could easily discount her intentions as superstitious or classify her abilities as "a wagonload of baloney," as she had once overheard someone dismissively refer to them.

Blake Dobbs descended slowly from his saddle. She could tell that he was distrustful of her intentions. She did not necessarily blame him for his caution. She knew the story about his parents' deaths during a violent confrontation between Olvido North's Anglo settlers and a band of displaced Apache fighters seeking retribution.

As he towered over her, she could not see the motive in his eyes in the shade of his Stetson. Just like she knew the story of his loss, she knew that he could exact his revenge at any moment. He was probably twice her weight. Of course, she was nimble and fast, but if they were to achieve any of the goals Solitario had outlined, they must not think in such terms. She urged herself to see beyond their differences. Could they not do more together than apart? Seeing past the conflicts of their ancestors, could they not find common ground? She waited, holding her breath against her will.

Finally, Blake brushed past her, untying the ropes that held his brother to the horse. Gently, he transferred Michael's body onto a colorfully striped sarape that Onawa spread by the side of the road in a sandy clearing between the cacti.

Michael remained unconscious as Onawa knelt next to him and leaned over his torso, her long, thick hair creating a natural drape between her face and a skeptical Blake Dobbs. She listened to his chest. His breathing was weak, but it sounded normal to her. The absence of a punctured lung was a good thing. She listened to his heartbeat, which also sounded faint but steady. Closing her eyes, she laid her hands over his torso. Within her mind she felt her consciousness travel through her arms into her hands, tingling as it passed through her fingers into his body. Like a miniature river of energy, she moved through him. She could sense there was much damage to the muscle tissue, but that could heal. Her concern was the state of his internal organs. Pushing further inside him, her body tensed as his pain radiated through her. His stomach was intact. His bladder and his liver were both fine. But when she examined his kidneys, she realized that the one on his right side was ruptured. Soon he would bleed to death, or the toxins being released by the organ would poison his bloodstream.

For a moment Onawa was overwhelmed by the daunting task at hand. She considered herself a seer, not a healer. Much more training was required to master such a complex skill. This was no doubt part of the mystery Alicia hoped to someday help her understand. But Michael Dobbs did not have time for her to retreat into the desert and study under the ancient bruja. And Dr. Ferris would be incapable of saving the poor, inquisitive twin from this lethal injury.

She turned to look at Blake, her mental vision still so immersed in Michael's anatomy that while her eyes stared blankly at the conscious twin, she actually still saw the other brother's innards spiraling toward certain death.

"What's wrong?" Blake asked, his voice trembling. "You look scared."

"His right kidney," she said. "It's terribly wounded."

"Can you do something?"

"I don't know."

"Can you try?"

She nodded, refocusing her thoughts on Michael, channeling and widening the rivulet of energy that had helped her see inside of him to envelop the bleeding organ, encase it, bathe it in healing light.

Suddenly, she felt the process take on a life of its own. It was as if something she had begun somehow managed to fulfill its own destiny according to a plan she could not fully understand. She felt like a conduit as the restorative power flowed through her from an unseen place. It swirled around the bean-shaped organ, repairing its structure, making it whole.

When she was finished, she removed her hands from Michael's flank.

Warily, Blake touched the red spot where Onawa's hands had just been. Flinching, he cried, "It's so hot!" Wide-eyed, he gaped at her. "What did you do?"

For an instant, she was not sure if he was grateful or angry, but she knew she should simply tell him the truth. "I did what I could."

"And?" he asked, appearing mystified as he sat back on his haunches.

"He will survive," she said, double-checking his inner state with her eyes closed. Assured they could safely continue carrying him to Olvido, she opened her eyes and rose, her head swimming as she did so. She nearly collapsed, but Blake steadied her.

"Are you okay?" he asked, genuine concern lacing his voice.

"Yes," she answered, regaining her equilibrium. The healing act had taken more energy out of her than she had initially realized. Clearing her mind, she took a step back from Blake, forcing herself to sound stronger than she felt. "We should keep moving," she said.

"You think he's going to make it?" he asked.

"Yes, I do."

Blake sighed in relief. Then the two of them hoisted Michael as carefully as they could back over the horse's loin, right behind the saddle, securing him into place with the same rope as before.

As she began to walk toward her horse, Blake reached out, gently grazing her elbow. "Wait."

She turned, looking up at him.

"Miss Onawa," Blake said, his piercing blue eyes reminding her of the sky on the clearest of days, "thank you."

He was the first white man to ever address her with this level of respect. Knowing how long a path he had traveled in so short a time, she suppressed a smile, nodded modestly, and hastily returned to Invierno. Mounting him in one quick motion, she led the way toward town. As she rode, she mulled over what a strange, new feeling it was to feel sympathy for anyone who came from that race that had systematically destroyed and dispersed her people. The Dobbs twins seemed different from most of the white men she had encountered throughout her life. Despite the hand they'd been dealt, they did not seem determined to hold a grudge against her or her people. Sure, they must harbor their suspicions, but they also seemed to keep an open mind. What more could one ask for in a land where every stranger was a possible enemy? Solitario must have seen something in them worthy of taking a chance. Was it something as simple as goodness?

She thought of Solitario as they neared Olvido. As infuriating as he was, she could not deny that he had keen instincts about people. She wondered if the darkness of la maldición lurking in his soul could truly threaten to overshadow his obvious goodness, so much so that her father would feel compelled to warn her about it?

It was difficult for her to stay angry at him. He was a wounded soul, one she longed to heal. If she could mend a ruptured kidney, might she be able to heal a broken heart? Might her power be enough to dispel la maldición?

In her visions, she yearned to see him at her side, but she rarely did. Might giving him more time, working with him, supporting him, change all that?

Spending all this time together had spurred a sense of urgency in her. She didn't just think about him. She wanted him, body and soul. What if by accepting his fear, she could help him transform it into courage?

She was tired of feeling alone. And with her father's deteriorating health, she feared her solitude would only grow. For some inexplicable reason, some great mystery of the heart, despite the countless men in the world, she could only picture Solitario keeping her company. She could only hope that—with her faith—his curse and his fear and his lingering sorrow could someday be overcome.

When they reached Dr. Ferris' house, Onawa helped Blake Dobbs carry his unconscious brother to the front porch. From there, she helped ease Michael onto a canvas stretcher. Dr. Ferris took one end and Blake grasped the other as she followed them into the house.

"We'll have to set him up in the room with Frankie Tolbert," Dr. Ferris grunted, struggling to hold up his end.

"He has some cracked ribs, but his lungs and organs seem fine," Onawa informed him.

The doctor stared at her oddly. No doubt he was wondering what she thought she knew about ribs and lungs and organs. "I'll examine him once we have him settled."

The doctor's wife prepared a second bed at the opposite end of the room, while the doctor and Blake held Michael aloft. As they did so, Onawa stood over Frankie Tolbert's pale, inert figure. *Why is this boy still asleep?* she wondered. It didn't make an ounce of sense. Her eyes landed on an array of empty vials on the nightstand next to Frankie's bed. Taking advantage of the fact that the doctor had his back turned to her, she picked up an open vial and sniffed it. Crinkling her nose in disgust, she thought, *This can't be helping him. What if it's keeping him asleep? What if the doctor doesn't want him to wake up?* She'd noticed Dr. Ferris' picture up on Solitario's board in the jailhouse among his other suspects. Glancing at the doctor's back as he helped transfer Michael Dobbs onto the freshly made bed, she closed her hand over the one remaining vial of amber liquid. She pressed it against her buckskin dress, concealing it in her palm, and slipped out through the front door.

THIRTY

Solitario waited in the shadowy confines of the musty barn. Tired of standing, he pulled an old bale of straw toward the entrance and sat on it, waiting to hear the approach of a horse bringing Michael Dobbs' would-be executioner.

As he sat there, his thoughts drifted to Onawa, despite his efforts to steer them otherwise. He could not expunge the image of her face, her long black hair, her slender figure, out of his mind, try as he might. He shook his head as if to cast off cobwebs. It was useless. He forced himself to go over the details of the case, the pieces of evidence he had collected, the eyewitness accounts Mr. and Mrs. Boggs and Georgina Lewis had provided. Still, none of it added up. Why would an Aztec-influenced high priest be working with Anglo henchmen wearing black hoods, injecting people with drugs, and performing gruesome ritual sacrifices? Who beyond these costumed performers was pulling the strings? Finding nothing but dead ends in these ruminations, his thoughts circled back to Onawa. Why could he not stop thinking about her? He replayed their argument. No woman, not even Luz, had ever spoken to him with such ferocity. Instead of being repulsed by her temperamental outburst, he found himself surprisingly unsettled. There was a fire in her that he suddenly yearned to be thawed by. He envisioned the wistful smile she'd briefly afforded him when he thanked her for saving the Dobbs boy. There was something about the way she looked at him, a melancholy that made him feel she knew more than she was letting on. But what could it be? It wasn't about the case. It was about him, about the two of them. Had she seen something in her visions? Did she know of something that was yet to happen, someday to come? Or was he simply imagining things, reading too much into them? Was she just a lonesome soul disillusioned by his hesitation, his reticence, his gnawing fear of ever loving again? Worse even, was it possible he cared too much already? If he allowed himself to feel more for Onawa, how could he face Luz's spirit when he finally made it back to El Escondido?

He shook his head despondently. It was difficult to have so many questions and yet so few answers. *I'm failing, Elias*, he thought. *I'm failing all around.*

In a far, dark corner of the barn, something stirred. Emerging from the shadows, Sergeant Elias became visible.

"How long have you been there?" Solitario asked without turning to look at his friend.

"I come when you need me, when your thoughts call me."

"You didn't have to ride El Caballo Sin Nombre to get here?"

"No. I just was pulled here by you."

"Some things seem easier in death than in life," Solitario observed.

Elias stood next to him, staring at the barn doors, his eyes glowering in the shaft of light that peeked through the crack between the two portals. "The killer is coming," Elias growled. "He knows where they are keeping my Elena."

"Sí, señor," agreed Solitario, at long last hearing a horse in the distance.

He stood slowly, his legs stiff from the long ride out to the desolate farm and from sitting on the bale of straw for so many hours.

"I wish I could fire a gun like I used to," Elias grumbled. "I'd fight beside you again."

"I'm glad you're here, amigo," Solitario patted him on the shoulder. "Now, let me do what I must do."

When the man opened the door, he froze in his tracks. Instead of finding a bound and bruised Michael Dobbs hanging from the ceiling, he was greeted by a seemingly empty barn.

"What in tarnation?" he exclaimed, walking to the spot where Michael had hung. As he bent down to pick up the severed rope, the telltale *click* of a pistol being cocked gave him pause mid-motion.

"Put your hands up," Solitario ordered, aiming at his back from a shadowy corner near the entrance.

The man, who wore cowboy garb and a frayed straw hat, raised his hands, muttering obscenities under his breath.

Approaching him from behind, Solitario disarmed the cowboy and was about to handcuff him, when the man surprised him by attempting to knock his pistol away. The gun nearly slipped out of Solitario's hand, but he quickly regained control of the weapon and butted the man's head with it. Blood trickled down the assailant's forehead as Solitario shoved him up against a wall and cuffed his hands behind his back. Then he pushed him to the ground in disgust. As the man lay there, Solitario scrutinized the sole of his boots. They bore the mark he'd seen at the Tolbert barn and outside Elias' outhouse: the *X*.

"Tell me who you're working for," Solitario demanded, incensed by the knowledge that this man had been present at the brutal murders. He must know who was behind them, who else was involved in perpetrating them, maybe even where the girls were being held captive.

The man looked away. His straw hat had fallen to the ground, and Solitario could now see the man was bald. "I ain't telling you shit. I ain't talking to no Mezcun sheriff."

Solitario scowled. "Unless you want to get treated the same way you treated my deputy"—Solitario's eyes flicked up to the ropes still dangling from the rafters—"you're going to talk to me, regardless of what kind of sheriff I am."

The bald man spat in disgust. "Go back where you came from, Mezcun."

Solitario shook his head. "Why did you come here? What were you here to do?"

The man lay silent, staring up at the ceiling.

"Do something, Solitario!" yelled Elias in anger. "Elena needs you to do something now!"

Solitario was taken aback by Elias' outburst. He was unaccustomed to his sergeant being irate and disrespectful. Perhaps now that he was dead, Elias no longer felt obliged to comply with the protocols of military rank. *Fine, so be it*, thought Solitario. Although he did not appreciate his subordinate's tone of voice, Solitario had to admit Elias made a valid point.

Solitario yanked the prisoner off the ground and heaved him hard against the wall. He punched him in the gut, grabbed him by the collar, and pulled him close. The bald cowboy stank of whiskey and tobacco. Solitario grimaced at the stench. "Who sent you? Do you work here? Why are you here?"

The man looked away.

Solitario struck him hard across the face, knocking a couple of teeth loose. Blood gushed from the man's mouth.

"Are you going to talk? Or do I have to knock the rest of your teeth out?" Solitario asked. "You'll be eating nothing but oatmeal and mashed potatoes the rest of your life if you don't cooperate."

Groaning in pain, the man spoke. "I was jis checking out the property for some buyers."

"Who do you work for?"

"I work for various . . . interested parties."

"Interested parties?"

"I'm a freelancer. I take jobs here and there for different folks."

Solitario frowned at him. "Who in particular sent you here?"

"Nobody in particular."

Solitario knew he was lying, but he did not want to cross the line between applying pressure and brutalizing his captive. "You're lucky I was taught to be humane to my prisoners. I guess that's one difference between the two of us, among many others." Solitario dragged the man out and helped him up onto his horse. "I'm taking you back to Olvido, Mister . . . what's your name?"

"Vance," he answered.

"Mr. Vance, you are under arrest," Solitario informed him. "Now, you ride in front of me so I can keep an eye on you. You'll be spending some time in jail until you're ready to be more forthcoming with the facts."

"No!" Elias shouted from the barn door as Solitario and Vance began to ride away. "You can't waste any more time."

Solitario looked back at his old friend, who stood in his tattered Republican Army uniform on the barn's threshold. "Paciencia," he whispered. "Poco a poco se llega lejos."

———————————

During the long ride back to town, Solitario worried that Elias was right. Time was running out. Michael Dobbs had signified the penultimate sacrifice, the bludgeoning. If the bruja Alicia was correct, and so far she had been right every time, next would come the mass sacrifice of all the captured girls, including Elena and Abigail and Beatrice Tolbert and the Boggs girls. What if he could not break Vance as deftly as he could break a horse?

When he reached the jailhouse, Solitario escorted the prisoner to the cell, uncuffed him, and shoved him brusquely to the floor for good measure. "Don't go getting too comfortable, Mr. Vance. If you don't cooperate, I'll ask the judge to hang you for obstruction."

"We'll see about that," Vance replied from the jail cell floor, favoring his arm. "I've got friends in high places. You jis wait and see."

Solitario stared at him, this lowly wretch. What friends could he have in high places? His employers? Would they deny any knowledge of him under the circumstances? Would he rat them out if they left him to rot in jail?

"Tell me who your employers are so I can see if they'll vouch for you," Solitario urged, thinking of Elias growing increasingly desperate and enraged by the pace of his investigation.

Vance looked up at Solitario, eyeing him suspiciously. "They ain't my employers, more like customers."

Words, Solitario mused. The gringos were prone to getting hung up on them. "Whatever you call them. Who do you work for?"

"I do work—like scouting properties for sale—for Mayor Stillman, Reverend Grimes, Mr. Dwight Grissom, and others," the man spat out, as if their names were supposed to impress Solitario and force him to back down. "You should let me go before they catch wind of this. If you do, I won't mention it to them."

"I bet you wouldn't," Solitario replied, "but that's not how the law works."

"What do Mezcuns know about no law?" Vance retorted in disgust.

"You forget . . ." Solitario said somberly, locking the cell.

"Forget what?"

"I'm an American now." Solitario stepped to his desk, where he discovered a hastily scrawled note from Blake Dobbs. It read: *Frankie Tolbert coming to.*

Without hesitation, Solitario dashed out the front door into the dark main street. He was in such a hurry he didn't even think about saddling Tormenta, who was resting after the long day of riding. He strode through the slumbering town toward Dr. Ferris' house, eager to speak with Frankie Tolbert. As he did so, he began to wonder, what if Reverend Grimes and Grissom were in league with each other? Both were interested in buying up land. Could both be scaring people out of town and using the Aztec ritual as a distraction to throw the authorities off their scent and blame the matter on the Mexican residents?

Deep in thought as he traversed the town, he was almost at Dr. Ferris' house when a tall, imposing figure approached him from a side street.

"Sheriff," Mayor Stillman said.

"Mr. Stillman." Solitario nodded. "Have you heard? The Tolbert boy might be regaining consciousness."

"Yes, indeed," Mayor Stillman answered.

As Solitario was about to continue toward his destination, he felt a sudden pinprick on the back of his neck, beneath his sombrero, right above where he'd cut his hair to present the clean image he believed a lawman should always project. Perhaps he'd chosen the wrong time to go to the barber, he thought as his vision blurred, his limbs went numb, and the ground spun. Landing sideways on the street, he stared at the mayor's highly polished shoes until everything went black.

For a moment Solitario thought he was waking from a bad dream. He sat up, unsure of his whereabouts. He was in a dark room. Was he home back at El Escondido? Had he been napping at Elias' house? No, as his vision adjusted to the darkness, he could make out the bars of the jail cell. He was at work? Had he dozed off while keeping an eye on his new prisoner, that bald Mr. Vance? He stood to light a lantern. As he did so, he was stunned to realize that he was actually inside the jail cell. Vance was nowhere in sight. On the floor was a body clad in black, a sombrero fallen by the wayside. He peered at it in the starlight filtering through the barred window high on the cell wall. The man looked familiar. He had a long mustache and wore a yellow bandanna. His belt buckle glowed faintly, turquoise blue. No puede ser, he thought. That was the buckle Onawa had given him years back. That was his sombrero and his yellow bandanna. Soy yo. That was himself, lying lifeless on the cell floor. He approached the cell door. Whoever had locked him in had left in a hurry; the keys still sat in the lock. Perhaps they'd known he would not be waking up soon, not waking up ever. Solitario walked right through the iron bars as if they were nothing but an illusion, a mirage. He was free. He turned and looked at himself lying there dead in jail. This was one place, and one way, he had never imagined it all ending. He'd spent so much time and energy worrying about how la maldición might affect those he dared to love, that he had never given much thought to his own state of impermanence, his own vulnerability. He'd become careless in his haste. Now, he had paid the price of his own incompetence. And so would Elena and all the other young girls. *All for what?* Solitario stepped through the closed jailhouse door onto the empty street. Tormenta whinnied upon seeing him. He looked into her eyes. Horses always appeared sad, mournful. Now was no different, but he could sense in their troubled depths her urgent concern. He touched her, and she nodded, turning to look down the street toward the edge of Olvido. Following her gaze, he knew what Tormenta was thinking, where she wanted him to go in search of help.

PART III

THIRTY-ONE

Luz stood on the back porch at El Escondido, bending down to admire the wrought-iron cages lined up against the wall, whistling to her attentive birds. Solitario observed her from his rocking chair, a gentle smile curved across his lips as he sipped his coffee. Luz wore a simple white linen frock, and her dark, wavy hair flowed in the breeze. Every morning since they had moved out to the ranch, this was their ritual. It was a refreshing way to start the day. The back porch faced the west and fell in the shade of the house as the sun rose on the other side. The still, cool morning wind sifted through the leafy mesquite trees as Luz taught her flock various short melodies. Her birds displayed an uncanny ability to mimic the tunes. They did not respond in the chaotic disarray one might expect from a motley collection of exotic birds, but rather in unison and harmony, like a finely tuned and expertly trained choir.

After the birds sang to the new day, Luz opened their cages and allowed them to roam about the porch and backyard.

The first time Solitario had seen her do this, he had been surprised, voicing his alarm, "Luz, mi amor, what are you doing? Won't they all fly away and die in the desert? This is not their natural climate."

"Oh, no," Luz smiled. "It warms my heart that you care, but my birds would never leave me."

Solitario watched in awe as the winged creatures sat on the porch railing and hopped about the wooden deck, happy simply to bask in her glow. After a while, some of them flew into the mesquite trees and pecked at the leaves, chirping happily.

As the birds played on the branches, Luz cleaned their cages. One by one, she carried them down the back porch steps, washing them beneath the trees. It was a laborious process, Solitario noted. As water spilled onto the porch steps, it also appeared somewhat treacherous. Worried that she would overexert herself or slip while lugging the cages back up to the porch, Solitario dutifully pitched in, helping Luz perform the chore.

When she finished the cleaning, Luz whistled a three-note signal for her feathered friends to return. They all flew straight back to their cages and climbed back inside, standing on their perches and studying her movements. Closing their gates, she gave them each tiny bits of whatever fruit she had in the kitchen, watermelon, apple, or even prickly pear from the cacti that surrounded the house.

Solitario had feared that she would not like living out on the ranch in the rustic house he had built, but—to the contrary—she had taken to it immediately. Her father had even offered his city house to them, but she had refused.

"I love nature and adore its creatures," Luz had responded to his generous offer. "Of course, we'll come visit you often, Papá, but it is time I make my own life with my husband."

Solitario was secretly thrilled because—although he appreciated the fineries of Don Miguel's house in Olvido as well as the splendor of the Spanish hacienda on his vast ranch—he preferred what he was accustomed to: a simple life.

"Would you like to bring your books? Your dresses?" he had asked Luz as they packed her things to move out to El Escondido after their wedding.

"Some books, yes, of course," she'd replied, "but forget the dresses. I'll have no use for those. We can leave them in the city, and if we come to an event I can get dressed in Papá's house."

"That's good, because I don't think we have room for another wardrobe in our bedroom," Solitario had answered.

The two had reveled in the newfound bliss of marital domesticity. While Luz tended to her canaries, lovebirds, parakeets, parrots, and conures, Solitario raised cattle and horses, venturing into town for a few hours each day to check on how the police headquarters was progressing. Olvido was booming under the peaceful order Solitario had established. And while he was at El Escondido with Luz, Sergeant Elias kept things running smoothly along with a well-trained phalanx of deputies.

Time flowed as swiftly and smoothly as the copious water the Rio Grande carried to the Gulf of Mexico. It was too easy to take such bounties for granted, Solitario realized as one wedding anniversary passed and then another. Everything was perfect, with one exception that had begun to perturb Luz's thoughts. She had not yet become pregnant, and this was her deepest desire.

"Mi amor," Solitario assured her during a horseback ride to survey their land, "it does not matter to me. I am content with you and you alone."

Luz wiped away a tear as they rode. "Even your horse, Oscuridad, has sired a filly since we moved out here. What if something is wrong with me? I so want to give you a child, a son with your laughing eyes."

Solitario patted Oscuridad so he would not feel guilty at making Luz feel inadequate. "Perhaps I am the one something is wrong with," he offered. After all, he was the one vexed by the maldición de Caja Pinta. Perhaps their inability to become pregnant was an echo of the dispelled maldición. "I never imagined myself having children for fear of passing la maldición on to them," he admitted, hoping that this insight would console her.

"Promise me we will keep trying," Luz said, smiling at him.

Smiling back, he answered, "We will never stop."

Galloping back to their ranch house, they could not even wait to get to their bedroom before disrobing each other. Hungrily, they caressed and kissed. He tasted the salt on her skin from the long horse ride in the desert heat as they made love on the steps to the porch. The birds sang in a frenzy that rose with their passions, subsiding as they rested quietly in the afterglow.

"I never dreamed I could be so happy," Solitario whispered, gazing lovingly at her.

"I will make you happier," Luz replied. "You'll see."

She did not make promises lightly, as he discovered. The next time they visited La Casa Colorada, she brought back a pile of tomes from the library, along with herbs and flowering plants from her old garden in the courtyard. On the back porch at El Escondido, she set up her laboratory, where she worked throughout the days, concocting herbal potions that were designed—she said—to enhance her fertility.

He knew that she had dabbled in herbs growing up, but he had never seen her so hard at work. Given the fringe benefits of her growing obsession, however, he was not about to protest. The more she desired a baby, the more she pined for him, and the more frenzied their lovemaking grew. He spent only a few hours in town each week, trusting Sergeant Elias to maintain order as he doted on Luz, immersed in his love for her, in her lust for him.

Until at last one night, during a particularly romantic candlelit dinner, Luz smiled knowingly at him from across the table and made her long-awaited announcement. "Solitario, tu Luz . . . va a dar luz."

It was a play on words. It meant she was with child. Solitario jumped to his feet and rushed to her side of the table, wrapping his arms around her. "Mi Luz, mi Luz, te quiero tanto," he blurted out.

Later, after they had feasted on each other and lay exhausted in bed, he replayed the scene in his mind as she slept. In that unrestrained moment of joy when she had informed him that she was pregnant, he had momentarily let down his guard and proclaimed aloud that he loved her. It was not something he had done before because of his respect for la maldición, for the possibility that he had not fully escaped its reach. A flicker of fear stirred within the dark recesses of his soul, like the lone candle that still burned on their nightstand, casting a faint glow through their otherwise pitch-black bedroom. He should have been more cautious. He should not have allowed those words to spill from his mouth.

He gazed anxiously at the candle as a draft floating through the room extinguished it, plunging them into absolute darkness.

———————

Solitario was at Olvido's jailhouse when Sergeant Elias burst into his office, sweaty and disheveled. "Jefe, there's something wrong with the river."

"What do you mean?" Solitario glanced up from his desk.

"You have to come see it with your own eyes," Elias said.

Riding Oscuridad and El Caballo Sin Nombre to the levee, Solitario and Elias wove their way through a mass of townspeople striding in the same direction. When they arrived at the river's edge, even Oscuridad seemed disconcerted, neighing in disbelief.

Solitario stared at the deepening river gorge. The crevice seemed to grow deeper before the crowd's astonished eyes.

Women fell to their knees in prayer. Children scrambled down the muddy ridge, laughing as they slid into the water. Whereas in the past their mothers had forbidden them to swim in the river for fear that the strong currents might drown them, now they could wade into the water, stand in the center of the Rio Grande, and still hold their heads above water.

The northern bank of the river was not as populated in those days, but a handful of settlers, both Anglo and Mexican, also gathered on the opposite side, gawking at the dwindling water level in dismay.

"What are we going to do, Jefe?" Sergeant Elias asked.

Solitario mulled over the question. There seemed to be only one thing to do: figure out what in the world was going on. Frowning, he answered, "Follow me."

Together, they rode west along the levee. In about an hour they reached El Escondido, where Solitario spied Luz standing at the river's edge. She waved as the men approached.

"What is happening, mi amor?" Luz asked Solitario.

"That is what we are going to find out," he answered. "It may be a late night. We must ride until we find some answers. Maybe somebody has dammed the flow upriver."

"I will light a candle and pray for you both," Luz said, reaching up to hold his hands.

He descended from Oscuridad to kiss her, running his fingers through her hair. "I'll be back as soon as I can be." He could see the worry in her eyes. Ever since she'd become pregnant, she had also become increasingly anxious that something would go wrong, with the baby, or with her own health, or with Solitario. She shared her gnawing ruminations with him regularly. His job was dangerous. What if he was shot by a bandido? What would she do then? He reassured her constantly as her belly bulged, but it required all of his willpower to keep the same worries at bay within his own mind.

As the sun began to sink toward the western horizon, Solitario and Elias reached a canyon with high, steep walls. Under normal circumstances, they would have had to search for a different way to follow the river from high above, but given the fact that the river had now transformed into a faltering creek, their horses were able to pass over the muddy shoals. It was a messy endeavor, mud flying everywhere as the horses' hooves sank into the soft banks, making sucking sounds as they rose back out of the sludge, flinging chunks of mud and bits of gravel onto each other and their riders.

Eventually, in the foothills of the mountain range, they came to an impasse. The canyon was blocked by a massive avalanche of boulders and rocks.

"The canyon caved in!" Elias remarked. "It's blocking the water. Maybe soon the water will back up, the level will rise, and it will spill over the barrier."

The boulders were too large and the climb too steep and uneven for the horses to proceed, so Solitario dismounted, stating flatly, "We continue on foot." He had to see this with his own eyes to be able to report back factual statements rather than assumptions and suppositions.

Solitario nimbly scaled the rocks blocking the passage. About half-way up, he paused and looked down. Elias huffed and puffed far below.

His belly had grown more than Luz's in the previous months. Solitario enjoyed ribbing his friend about the situation, but now his weight gain was proving more inefficient than comical.

"Ándale," Solitario encouraged his sergeant. "We must hurry so you can get back to Otila's tortillas for dinner."

"Not now, please," Elias gasped for air, struggling to catch up.

Solitario waited for a while, taking long gulps from his canteen. As Elias caught up, they continued the rest of the way in unison.

When they arrived at the top of the rockslide, they were met with an unwelcome, if memorable, sight. The water was not pooling and rising beyond the barrier, as Elias had hoped. What they saw instead was a confluence of the river into a broad low canyon to the south.

"When this avalanche happened, instead of pooling and rising to stay on its old course, the water found an easier way to flow," Solitario explained, pointing at the river's new course. "It shifted south through that canyon over there."

"So what does that mean?" Elias squinted into the setting sun beyond the wide expanse of water before them. It was as if the river now split in two, but the strong portion flowed swiftly through the other canyon to the south, whereas the part that flowed toward the dam they now stood on trickled feebly and stopped at the rocks.

"It means the river has abandoned us," Solitario summarized. "Soon, it will dig its groove completely in that new direction and this trickle below us will dry up completely."

Elias' eyes widened as he understood the magnitude of this occurrence. Solitario nodded glumly, staring out over the expanse of churning water interrupted by massive stones jutting out in various spots. Soon it would be dark. They should turn back, but Solitario could not stop gazing at the water. He had taken it for granted, just as they all had in Olvido. Now, who knew if they would witness its majesty—or be nourished by its precious contents—ever again.

The following day, Solitario delivered the unfortunate news to the towns-people of Olvido. He stood in the elevated gazebo in the old plaza, opposite the cathedral and adjacent to La Casa Colorada. He did not like speaking to crowds, but Don Miguel Santander had insisted that he be the one to share what he had witnessed upriver during his explor-atory trek with Sergeant Elias.

The crowd gasped and murmured as he spoke. As the severity of their new circumstances dawned on the community, the wind itself seemed to grow more arid, the leaves on the trees in the plaza turned brown and fell in waves across the audience like brown confetti. Some of the women cried. The men, especially the farmers who depended on the river for their crops, sat dumbfounded on the ground. The Catholic priest, Padre Esparza, consoled the abuelitas and abuelitos, whose lips moved in prayer for God to redirect the river back to its old trajectory.

After Solitario finished delivering the sobering facts, Padre Esparza climbed the steps to the gazebo and offered the people hope. "Mi gente, do not fear. The river may have abandoned us, but God will not do the same. Our city may be named 'Olvido,' but God will not forget us. We will not give up. We will build wells to draw our water, for it runs still through channels beneath the sand and rock. We will use that water to irrigate our crops, to drink and cook, and to wash ourselves. We will not surrender, for the Lord only gives us crosses which we are strong enough to bear."

The crowd nodded, chanting in rhythmic prayer to the Virgen de Guadalupe. Scanning the surroundings as Padre Esparza continued to rouse their spirits, Solitario spied an odd cluster of listeners gathered like a committee of vultures at a far corner of the plaza. It was a small group of Anglo men. He could tell they were from the other side of the old river due to their attire. They wore dark suits and ties, and their heads were crowned by black Stetson hats rather than sombreros. It appeared they were observing the proceedings with great interest. He wondered if they understood Spanish. That was when it first occurred to him that the scarcity of water caused by the disappearance of the river might not be the greatest of their problems, the heaviest of the crosses the people of Olvido might be forced to carry into the future.

As the multitude dispersed, Solitario wound his way through the packed plaza, following the Anglo men back to the levee. There, he watched them pay the ferryman a few centavos to essentially drag them across the squishy bed of mud on his raft. It was significantly more difficult than towing it across the water, but the ferryman now had the help of a mule. The entire process seemed absurd, but Solitario assumed that the men did not want to ruin their suits. Even with boots, walking across the muddy riverbed, one's legs would sink a couple of feet into the slime. Frogs and toads hopped about frantically as children chased them along the murky shoals. Weeds sprouted at an unnatural speed in the footprints left by the children, dotting the oozing wound in the ground in a luminescent green mesh. Solitario kept an eye on the Anglo men as they ascended the levee on the other side. The small cluster of buildings on the northern bank had long been an afterthought in the local community, an extension of Olvido, a handful of Anglo merchants to trade with, and Mexicans who had remained on that side to continue farming their lands when the Rio Grande had become the border nearly three decades earlier. *What now?* Solitario wondered as the Anglo men scrutinized the rapidly transforming riverbed and the Mexican children playing in the muck. He could sense they were planning something. Having fought in numerous battles during the French invasion of Mexico, he had a feeling that while the Mexican townsfolk were occupied ruing their fate and praying for salvation, the Anglo men were busy strategizing.

The very next day, Elias rushed into the jailhouse, startling Solitario at his desk. "Jefe, you have to come see this!"

"Sargento Elias, this is becoming a bad habit of yours," Solitario complained.

"I can't explain it," Elias replied. "Just come."

Solitario followed Elias to the river. The mud was beginning to cake and solidify. The once-frenetic frogs and toads had become petrified, miniature statues lining the banks. The children picked them up and hurled them at each other. Like snowballs, they exploded on impact, but instead of showering the targets with fresh white powder, they blanketed them in putrid dust.

"You brought me to witness the children's misplaced glee?" asked Solitario.

"No, this . . ." Elias pointed at a knot of women slightly downriver. They rocked back and forth on their knees, covered in dirt.

Solitario and Elias dismounted, stepping tentatively into the ravine. It was now dry enough that their boots remained on its surface rather than sinking into a quagmire. Solitario shook his head in dismay. Change came fast in the desert. The sun was baking the ground at an alarming pace. The wound was quickly becoming a scar.

As they approached the women, Solitario could tell that they were rocking back and forth on their knees, their hands clasped in prayer. They knelt before the steep river wall. On its surface, the earth had taken on a familiar shape, its curves, marks, and grooves resembling the outline of the Virgen de Guadalupe. Her cape was the only part of the chasm that still glowed green with the slick weeds that had inexplicably materialized the previous day. Tiny yellow blooms dotted her form like the golden stars on the image that hung in the Basilica in Mexico City.

"Es un milagro!" Padre Esparza proclaimed, his black robes turning a sandy brown as he descended into the gorge to join the women in worship. "Es Nuestra Señora del Olvido. She has come to save us, to comfort us."

Solitario knit his eyebrows together. He wasn't so sure about that particular interpretation, but he held his tongue, as was his preferred way.

"What do you think, Jefe?" Sergeant Elias asked. "Is she here to save us?"

Solitario climbed back into his saddle and turned Oscuridad back toward the center of town.

When Elias and El Caballo Sin Nombre caught up to Solitario, the sergeant repeated his question. "Is she, Jefe? Is our luck turning?"

Solitario frowned, riding slowly, deep in thought. "Who am I to say, Sargento? My job is to keep the peace, not to make prophecies or interpret signs from above. I'll leave that to the padre."

Elias seemed disappointed at the answer, falling behind as they neared the jailhouse. "But it can't hurt, can it? People need hope."

"Hope is good, but water is better," Solitario quipped. "We can subsist without hope, but we cannot survive without water."

"But we'll build wells, right, like the padre said?"

"Yes, I'm sure we will."

"So why are you so being so pessimistic? It is not like you, Jefe. You always find a way out of any jam."

As they passed through the plaza, the town already looked transformed. The billowing clouds of sandy dust were beginning to blanket the once-colorful buildings in a monochromatic desert hue. Even La Casa Colorada was beginning to fade. He did not want to further unsettle his sergeant, who still had a job to do, duties to perform, a family to raise. "You go home and have lunch with Otila and Elena and Oscarito," he told Elias.

Parting ways in the plaza, Solitario sat tall in his saddle surveying the changing cityscape. A ball of tumbleweeds rolled aimlessly across the deserted plaza, drifts of dead leaves chasing after it, rustling in the incessant wind. He squinted at the cathedral from beneath his broad sombrero. He saw cracks growing in it with every passing moment.

Yes, we will build wells, he thought in response to Elias' question. *The water may keep us alive, but it will no longer protect us from our neighbors to the north.*

Nobody had mentioned it openly yet, but surely others were thinking about it just as he was. With the river rerouted south, they were no longer in Mexico. Their fate rested not on La Virgen's apparition, but in America's hands.

––––––––––––

"Dwight Grissom, the Texan rancher, has offered to buy my lands," Don Miguel said as they sat together at dinner in his house overlooking the plaza.

"What did you say?" asked Luz, radiant in a silky green dress she kept in her wardrobe in the city.

Solitario's gaze shifted from her back to his father-in-law.

"I told him no, of course," Don Miguel waved his hand dismissively.

"This is our land. The river's change of heart does not change who we are or where we belong."

Solitario pondered the conundrum, staring down at his plate. Everything seemed different since the river had left. Even the food was less flavorful, as if it had been sculpted by an artist to look like chile relleno and guacamole and arroz Mexicano on the outside while being made of sand on the inside.

"Do you think we will be safe here?" asked Luz, placing her hands over her growing belly.

"Of course, we will be safe, m'ija," Don Miguel answered. "The reason Mr. Grissom desires our land is because it has become even more valuable now. He used to have river frontage, across the river from El Escondido, in fact. But now that the river shifted to the south, our ranch sits between Grissom's and the Rio Grande."

"Water is life," Luz murmured, still clutching her midriff.

"Yes, m'ija, it is," Don Miguel said. "Fortune has always smiled upon the Santander clan. Now, if Grissom wants water from the river, he will have to pay us for it."

Solitario listened attentively. He hoped Don Miguel was right, especially given his own family's experiences with the mercurial Rio Grande.

That night, after dinner, Solitario and Luz returned to El Escondido in Don Miguel's carriage. Lying in bed, Luz asked Solitario again, "So, you think we will be safe here, now that we are in America?"

Solitario turned sideways to gaze into her eyes. He did not want to lie to her, but he also did not wish to frighten her. She was already crippled by worry over the baby. "Maybe nothing will change," Solitario told her. "Maybe the Americans will forget about us, leave us be. After all, our name is Olvido."

She forced a tight smile.

The following day, Solitario arrived in the city to find a large group of Anglo men assembled in the plaza. They sat on their horses, staring impassively at the Mexican pedestrians going about their business. Some of them wore uniforms consisting of white shirts, dark pants, vests, ties, and shiny starlike badges. They wielded guns and rifles, brandishing them in the harsh sunlight as a growing throng of townspeople stopped to watch anxiously from the edges of the square.

As Solitario rode up to the heavily armed interlopers, he addressed them sternly. "Buen día, señores. What brings you to Olvido?" As he spoke, he heard El Caballo Sin Nombre trotting up next to Oscuridad. With a subtle sideways glance, he acknowledged Sergeant Elias.

One of the men, clearly the leader, angled his horse toward Solitario, replying, "I'm Captain MacDonald with the Texas Rangers. Who are you?"

"I'm Capitán Cisneros with the Rurales," Solitario answered. He had heard of the Texas Rangers. The fact that they were here was certainly not a welcome development, but it was also no surprise. He had hoped they'd forget about Olvido or at least take a lifetime to pay attention to it, but that was evidently not in the cards.

"If it's all the same to you," Captain MacDonald said, "it would be good to speak in private." He eyed the large crowd of townspeople gathering about the plaza.

Solitario nodded, gesturing for the Ranger to follow him to the jailhouse. Inside, Solitario showed Captain MacDonald to his small office and offered him a glass of tequila.

As they sat across the desk from each other, Solitario waited for the captain to speak.

"As you know, the river has changed course," Captain MacDonald stated the obvious.

Solitario nodded.

"We have been sent to secure the territory," Captain MacDonald explained. "There are more changes coming, Señor Cisneros. More people coming soon."

"What people?" Solitario asked.

"Settlers, merchants, what have you," Captain MacDonald answered. "When new land becomes available, people are drawn to it."

"And what of our people? The ones that are already here?"

"Well, they're welcome to stay, of course. There will be much work to be done. The town will grow and the road to the new border will have to be improved. Mr. Grissom, the rancher, has big plans for the area. Workers will be needed. Of course, anyone who wants to leave and go back to Mexico is also welcome to do so."

"Back to Mexico?" Solitario stared at Captain MacDonald. "For many of the people here, especially the ones born here, this is all they know of Mexico."

"But it ain't Mexico no more."

And that was the crux was of it, thought Solitario, his eyes landing on the shiny silver star Captain MacDonald wore on his vest.

"Like I said, lots of changes will be coming," Captain MacDonald said. "Soon, the new sheriff will arrive. Tolbert's his name. We Texas Rangers are just here to help with the transition. I'll be needing to collect your badge, of course."

Transition? Solitario wondered what the Texas Ranger had in mind. It was widely known that Texas Rangers had a fluid and often self-serving concept of the law. For them, keeping the peace and dispensing justice was as much a business as anything else. A Texas Ranger was just as likely to act as a gunslinging law enforcer as he was inclined to serve as judge, jury, and executioner. All one had to do was ask the Apache, which Solitario had indeed done on occasion, speaking with a chief of one of the tribes north of the river about the injustices his people had suffered at the hands of the Rangers in the name of so-called Texan progress.

"You don't talk much, do you?" Captain MacDonald observed. "I suppose your English probably ain't that good, so it shouldn't be a surprise to me that you're quiet. Plus, there's a lot to digest, kind of like eating too many jalapeños all at once, I suspect."

Solitario finished his tequila and placed it down on his desk, keeping his hand steady despite the rising tide of resentment swelling inside him. He heard the distant surf of the Gulf of Mexico, the sound of waves crashing on the beach at Caja Pinta where he had been raised. He heard the chanting of words he did not recognize, but he knew their sound. He knew they were Nahuatl. He had heard his abuela Minerva recite them when she worked on her spells in her jacal by the sea. He yearned to teach this man a lesson, send *him* back where he came from, but he knew that he would not be in the right, not in keeping with the law, not according to the Treaty of Guadalupe Hidalgo, which decreed that the border between the United States and Mexico would be the Rio Grande. If the river were to change course by natural means, then so would the border itself. He had already reviewed the terms of the treaty at length. Don Miguel kept a copy of it in his library. There was no denying that Captain MacDonald spoke the truth, as ugly as he made it sound. Change would be coming, like it or not. All Solitario could do was attempt to influence it to protect all of Olvido's residents.

Clearing his throat, Solitario finally replied, "You are correct that there is much to digest, Captain MacDonald, not just for me but for all of Olvido's inhabitants. This has been a peaceful town since I arrived, and we hope it stays that way. On the other hand, you are incorrect regarding my scarcity of words. I am a quiet man by nature. I always have been. My knowledge of your language is not the barrier, but rather my distaste for speaking in general. I find my actions to be more impactful than my words. As for a badge, I don't wear one. I have one here in a drawer, but everyone in this town knows who I am." Solitario opened the top drawer of his desk and pulled out a silver shield-shaped badge. It was embossed with the image of two swords crossed over three staffs of wheat. Below that, it read DEFENSAS RURALES. Between the two lines of text hovered a rising sun, and at the narrow bottom point of the shield sat the classic symbol of Mexico, the eagle perched on the cactus with a serpent in its beak. He placed his badge on the desk.

Captain MacDonald assessed it without moving to pick it up. "Tell you what, then, you keep your shield as a memento. It won't mean anything here anymore. But, hey, if you want to, you can always take it south of the river."

Solitario fumed. "Has it occurred to you, Captain MacDonald, that the people of Olvido might want to keep their lawman, even if we are now part of America?"

Taken aback, Captain MacDonald shifted in his chair, "Frankly, Cisneros, it doesn't matter to me what your people want. The war was fought and won a long time ago. It's just shit bad luck for the people of Olvido what's happened with the river. But what's bad luck for one is good for an-other. I'm being paid by that other. All's I can say"—Captain MacDonald rose to his feet—"is you'll need to refrain from attempting to enforce the law anymore, as you won't truly know what that law is now that Olvido falls under the jurisdiction of the laws of the Great State of Texas. My men and I will handle any disorder. And you should warn your old citizens that they heed our word or pay the price for disrespecting our laws. Now, we'll keep this jail here for the Mezcun criminals, and we'll be building another one on the other side of the gorge for the Anglo ones. I'll post some of my men here. You can gather your private belongings and clear on out."

The surging wave of anger threatened to drown Solitario's rational thoughts. He glowered at Captain MacDonald as the Texas Ranger exited the jailhouse. *This is madness, an outrage,* thought Solitario. *I'll show that prejudiced hijo de puta. There is no reason why I should not remain the lawman here, to protect my people.*

Solitario gathered his scant personal items, his Rurales badge, and strode outside, where Elias awaited him with a distressed expression etched on his face, his mustache drooping toward the ground.

"What is it?" Solitario demanded.

"That Captain MacDonald took my badge," Elias said, sounding like a child whose toy had been stolen by a bully.

"We'll see about that." Solitario set his jaw. "Follow me."

Standing in front of La Casa Colorada, Solitario and Elias saw the Texas Rangers lining up a large group of Mexican men and handcuffing them. Captain MacDonald barked orders at his men.

"What's he saying?" Elias asked Solitario.

"He's telling his Rangers to put those men in jail." Solitario spat on the ground in disgust.

"But why? They haven't done anything?" Elias' anxious eyes searched his jefe's for an answer.

"Because he wants to show everyone who is in charge now. He is intimidating our people. If they don't follow all of his commands, he'll beat them and throw them in jail. Once the jail is full, he'll just shoot them in the plaza."

They watched as an elderly man refused to march in line with the others toward the jailhouse, only to be butted in the head with a rifle and shot on the ground like a wounded dog.

Solitario could barely contain his urge to ride into the plaza firing. There were six Texas Rangers. He and Elias had beaten those kinds of odds while fighting the French imperialists. Who was to say they couldn't do it again? He looked at Elias, wondering if his companion would be up to the task. His eyes fell on his sergeant's bulging belly. He thought of Elias' wife and children back at home. And he couldn't bring himself to place him in harm's way. *Paciencia*, he urged himself. *Protect what is yours with patience. Do not squander it in haste. Vamos despacio que llevamos prisa. Let us go slowly that we are in a hurry.* He also recalled the legend of Juan Cortina, a Mexican gunslinger who had shot a Texan lawman for pistol-whipping an elderly vaquero in La Frontera back when Solitario was still learning how to crawl. The act had sparked a border war and cost countless lives. That was not the kind of future he wanted for Olvido and its people.

"Wait here," he commanded Elias, making up his mind. "Do not get involved. I can't have you getting shot by these men. If you do, then we won't be able to protect all the others, including your own family."

Elias nodded with a resigned look in his sad eyes. He waited outside with the horses as Solitario passed through La Casa Colorada's massive arched doors to confer with his father-in-law.

"Solitario, I understand you are angry, m'ijo," Don Miguel tried to soothe his son-in-law. "But it's no use fighting this. We must make our peace with shifting our roles here, just as the river has shifted its course. We must adapt in order to survive."

"What do you mean?" Solitario asked, incensed by the idea of simply surrendering and allowing the Texas Rangers to have their way with the people of Olvido.

"Look, m'ijo," Don Miguel said, motioning for Solitario to sit on one of the comfortable leather sofas in the library. "If we get along with the Anglos, we will succeed. We will prosper together. If we fight with them, we will fail. They have the upper hand."

"I will go to Austin and I will speak with the authorities. They will see that it makes sense for me to remain the lawman here. I brought order and peace and justice to this place, when it once was a lawless outpost for bandidos."

"What you say that you accomplished is true," Don Miguel conceded. "The people of Olvido will always respect you for what you have done, but now it is out of your hands."

"We'll see about that," Solitario said. "Don Miguel, you should not give in so easily. You are still the largest landholder in the region. Your word carries weight."

"My word only carries weight if the Anglos like what they hear."

Solitario shook his head in disappointment. Perhaps he had expected too much of the old man. Refusing to lounge on leather couches and surrender to a life of affluent contentment soothed by the elixir of tequila, he politely excused himself.

Outside, he instructed Elias, "Sargento Elias, you go home and take care of your family. Keep the children off the streets. Who knows what will unfold in the next few days. People may not react well to the Texas Rangers' ways. And the Texas Rangers may not have much patience with our people either."

"And where will you be? Why don't we protect the people?" Elias asked. "They just shot another man for refusing to go the jailhouse."

"We can't protect the people without the law on our side. If we try, then we will be no better than a couple of bandidos and we will end up shot dead on the street. We can't fight a war that has already been lost. I will go to Austin and I will defend my badge."

"But your badge, just like mine, was Mexican."

"I'll get you a new badge, Elias," Solitario answered. "Now go home. You're no longer a sergeant here. You're a civilian. Don't you forget that and go getting yourself killed."

Solitario galloped off on Oscuridad, hastening to El Escondido to pack a bag and let Luz know he was headed to Austin.

"No!" Luz cried, clinging to him as he packed his leather bag with a fresh set of clothes. "You cannot go. Please, forget about being a lawman. Be my husband. Be a father to our child. Don't risk your life for a badge."

"It is not the badge," Solitario snapped. "It's what is right. It's my honor." He heard the Nahuatl chants in the distance, beyond a wall of white noise that drowned out Luz's soothing words of wisdom, her futile attempts to convince him to stay by her side like a faithful, castrated dog.

On the front porch, she hung onto his jacket until he stormed down the steps and leaped up onto Oscuridad. At the top of the steps, she slid to her knees, weeping. "Don't go, Solitario, por favor. Stay with me. I need you here."

But he could not hear her pleas over the sound of the surf filling his ears like bubbling water itself, the water stolen by the river only to be poured into the Gulf of Mexico from where he'd come, waves sliding onto the slick sands of Caja Pinta, where the maldición he carried had been born.

"I'll be back soon," Solitario assured Luz from his mighty perch atop his black stallion. Oscuridad's muscular flanks tightened in anticipation of a purposeful journey the likes of which they had not shared since their days fighting for the Republic. "You'll see, Luz. What's right is right. I'll be back, and when I return, once again, my word will be the law."

He tightened his yellow bandanna around his neck, lowered the rim of his ornate sombrero to shield his eyes from the sun, and tore out of the clearing with a vengeance, leaving Luz crumpled in a heap of tears and shrouded behind a cloud of swirling dust.

Things in Austin did not go the way that Solitario had envisioned. After five days of arduous horseback travel across Texas, Solitario arrived at the headquarters of the Texas Rangers. There, he was told by an indifferent secretary that the head of the Rangers was too busy to see him. His typically distinguished charro uniform was caked in dirt and sweat. Only his distinctive sombrero seemed to perpetually shine as if it had just been purchased and taken out of its box. Solitario waited all day outside the office until the man emerged. At that point, the head Ranger told him that the Texas Rangers were in charge of Olvido until Sheriff

Tolbert arrived and that there was nothing to be done about it. All of Solitario's military commendations and his long list of law enforcement accomplishments were of no significance to the burly and brusque Texas Ranger, a man with shortly cropped silver hair and a matching goatee. He dismissed Solitario as if he were a lowly private.

Discouraged and exhausted from his journey, Solitario attempted to check into a hotel on Congress Avenue, only to be refused service. Following the imperious desk clerk's condescending directions, Solitario rode a ragged Oscuridad to the eastern outskirts of the city, where he found a lowly set of rooms above a gritty tavern far outside the long shadow of the majestically domed capitol building. Stepping up onto the rickety porch, he read a crudely carved sign by the door: "Negroes, Mezcuns, Injuns, & Dogs: Welcome one. Welcome all."

It was hard for him to resist the unfamiliar urge to slouch in defeat. He was fatigued from the trip, his ego was severely bruised, and he missed Luz. Maybe Captain MacDonald had been right, Solitario mused. Maybe he would be better off going "back where he came from." Not to La Frontera, no, that was a terrifying thought given the power of la maldición de Caja Pinta. He would never wish to expose Luz to the threat of the curse, especially in such close proximity to its birthplace. But there was always Chihuahua, where no doubt he could reestablish himself with the support of his old mentor, Governor Terrazas.

Avoiding the surly scene in the tavern, Solitario trudged up the creaky stairs to rest up for the following day's return trip to Olvido. In the early hours of the following morning, he was roused from a deep sleep by a rustling sound. Lying in bed, he turned toward the noise. In the darkness, he could not be certain what it was, but he could tell it was coming from the window. He reached for his gun in case it was an intruder, but soon he realized it must be a small animal. Lighting the candle on the nightstand, Solitario discerned a tiny bird on the windowsill. His first instinct was to smile, as the winged creature reminded him of Luz. But as he got a closer look, his smile quickly faded. This was no ordinary bird. It looked exactly like one of his wife's songbirds.

Es imposible, Solitario thought, his heart racing. He crept toward the bird. It looked like a miniature parrot. Its upper coat of feathers was emerald green, but underneath lurked turquoise-and-crimson plumes. It was one of Luz's conures. What did this mean? As he knelt at the window, the bird issued a familiar three-note call and took to its wings, flying southwest toward Olvido. It was precisely the same signal that Luz whistled when she wished for her birds to return home from the mesquite trees.

Solitario did not wait for the sun to rise. He hastily donned his fresh set of clothes and rushed out to where Oscuridad was stabled at the rear of the property.

"I'm sorry, amigo," Solitario patted Oscuridad as they began the five-hundred-mile odyssey back to Olvido. "We cannot rest any longer. We cannot wait." As he spurred Oscuridad through the darkness with a gnawing urgency, he began to dread that he had committed a terrible mistake.

Solitario rode as fast and as hard and as long as he could between brief stops to water and feed Oscuridad. After traversing the Texas Hill Country and spanning the vast plains that gave way to the deserts of West Texas, he was severely dehydrated. Oscuridad barely clung to life. The horse was foaming at the mouth, and his rib cage jutted from his flanks. Solitario's charro uniform was blanketed in layer upon layer of dust and sand. Only the singular sombrero Luz had bestowed upon him at their wedding remained impeccable through the journey.

As he arrived at El Escondido, he immediately sensed something was horribly wrong. Luz's white horse roamed loose in front of the house. The door hung open, flapping as if the home were waving goodbye. As he jumped off Oscuridad to bolt into the house, his numb legs collapsed beneath him, his pristine sombrero rolling black and blue across the dirt clearing. Scrambling, he crawled up the stairs until he could get back on his feet.

"Luz!" he called. "Luz, I'm home, mi amor."

But there was no response. He searched desperately through the empty house, finding the door to the back porch also open. It was what he saw there that brought him to his knees.

As Solitario knelt on the porch, his eyes widened in horror. Luz was sprawled across the back steps, her motionless shape covered by a lacy green cloak. Sitting at attention along the porch railing were her exotic birds, including the conure that had landed on his windowsill in Austin five nights earlier. Their cages all sat open. The post at the top of the steps was smeared with dry blood. Luz's feet were bare and white as alabaster. She looked like a sculpture at sleep beneath a delicately knit blanket. He crawled toward her, tears streaming down his face, dripping from the drooping tips of his mustache. "Luz, no," he whispered. "¿Porqué?"

As he reached her body, he could see that the lacy emerald quilt draped over her had been crafted by her birds. They had collected slender leaflets from the mesquite trees and knit them together with even thinner bark fibers. It was an impossibly fragile creation, just like her life had been. Noticing her dark hair was matted with dry blood, he deduced she had slipped on the slick steps during her morning chores, striking her skull against the post. Laying his head over her cold, hard belly, he wept for her and for their unborn child. *Never to be born*, he cried. He screamed, "No! No!" Startled by his outburst, the birds took flight, creating a dazzling rainbow across the clear blue sky.

"¿Porqué?" he asked again as the birds flew away, but he knew the answer all too well. He should have never left. La maldición had clouded his judgment, feeding his pride and ego. He had repeated the same terrible error that his father had committed a generation earlier. If he had been home, she would not have attempted to perform her morning chores all by herself. Since she'd started showing, he'd been carrying and cleaning the birdcages for her. If he had not run off in pursuit of his pride, his very presence would have prevented her from falling, but instead, she had perished alone.

Enraged, he stumbled through the house toward his horse. He'd ride into town. He'd fetch a doctor and a curandera and a priest and a shaman, anyone who might pray over her, heal her lifeless body, bring her and the baby back to him, even though he knew it was impossible. At the front porch, he found Oscuridad on his side in the clearing, white foam trailing from his open mouth, his eyes glassy and gawking toward the sky. He was dead, too. Returning to Luz, he lay down next to her, gently lowering the lacelike cloak to reveal her face. With his calloused and grimy fingers, he traced the curve of her cheek. Life was not worth living without her, he decided. It probably never had been.

That night, he buried her under the mesquite trees. The next morning, he rode Oscuridad's offspring, Tormenta, into town to deliver the news to Don Miguel, who fell to his knees in the library. He held Don Miguel tightly in his arms until the old man could sob no more. He then rode south to the newly baptized banks of the rerouted Rio Grande, determined to end his life.

There, perched precariously on a boulder by the rushing waters with his revolver in his hand, his plan was interrupted by Onawa during her coming-of-age ceremony. Her tribe had been exploring the new lands. Her father, who was familiar with Solitario, looked into his cursed and shattered soul and felt both fear and mercy for him. Aguila Brava insisted Solitario come to his home, providing some semblance of comfort to soothe his suffering.

"The road will be long," Aguila Brava cautioned Solitario as Onawa listened in a corner of their tepee. "But you must not relent. You have a purpose. Today, that purpose is not clear. It is hidden beyond dark clouds. But someday, those clouds will part, and the sun will illuminate your path. You must carry on in the shadows until that day arrives."

Solitario spent days with the tribe, witnessing the elaborate ceremonies surrounding Onawa's Rite of Passage. He understood it was an honor rarely shared with an outsider. He drank with Aguila Brava to ease his pain, and he wept with abandon as he watched the chief's daughter dance.

"Why have you and your daughter been so kind to me?" he asked the chief as they sat around the campfire on the last night of the ritual.

"My wife would have wanted one of her people here to represent her," Aguila Brava told him. "You see, Onawa's mother was Mexican."

Solitario nodded, sipping the fine tequila his host generously served. "I was ready to end it all," he confessed as Aguila Brava peered at his daughter through the sparks dancing over the flames.

"I know, but you cannot," he replied. "It is not for you to decide." He motioned for Onawa to approach them.

As the shy young woman came, her eyes flitted to the ground. She carried something in her hands, bringing it toward Solitario as a gift.

"My daughter has used her special abilities to craft this artifact for you," Aguila Brava said. "Tell him, daughter. You are coming of age. You can speak to this man. He will never harm you. He will always be in your debt."

Her voice was timid at first, but it grew more confident with each word she spoke. "I made this for you. My father says that your people are my people. That means you are one of us. This will restore your energy, renew your fire for life." Onawa placed a gleaming turquoise belt buckle shaped like an eagle in Solitario's weathered hands. It was smoothly polished and glowed deep blue in the firelight. He could sense it was otherworldly, pulsating with hidden power. "We are sorry for what you have lost," Onawa concluded.

Solitario stared somberly at the belt buckle in his hands.

"With each loss we gain a greater understanding of sorrow," Aguila Brava said. "We grow closer to our true selves, become more deeply connected to the spirit world where our loved ones go."

"Gracias," Solitario said, meeting Onawa's eyes with his. "I will treasure it always."

"Treasure not just this gift." Aguila Brava put his arm around Solitario's shoulders. "Treasure the greatest gift of all: your life."

As Onawa returned to her ceremonial dances, donning a feathered headdress and reenacting a revered ritual of independence, Solitario rubbed his thumbs over the smooth turquoise buckle, wondering what magic was stored inside its elegant encasement. The drums beat hard, and the tribe chanted in its language, a tongue foreign and alluring to Solitario. After knowing only suffering, he welcomed the unknown.

Beneath the glittering canopy of stars, gathered with Onawa's tribe in a half-moon around the raging fire, sparks floating on the breeze, he thought of Luz and of their unborn child and of all the dreams that had been dispelled by one imperceptible tremor of the ground in the remote wilderness, one avalanche of rocks, one swift river diverted, one city forgotten, one man's flaw, one persistent curse he now understood he could never outrun. Gazing with gratitude at Aguila Brava, he marveled at the resilience of the Apache, running, fighting, surviving, despite all their losses. Perhaps someday he might be more like them, but for now all he could do was lick his wounds and run from la maldición, hide in the desert, lurk in the shadows, disappear amid the spirits.

THIRTY-TWO

Onawa crouched over her father's withered frame. In the dark, it was hard to tell whether he was already asleep for the night. His chest rattled as it rose and fell in a steady rhythm. She yearned to speak to him but was hesitant to disturb him. He needed rest to carry on. She could sense the end was near and the fate of his fleeting existence on this plane would soon be determined by forces well beyond her ability to see. She peered at the vial she'd sneaked out of the doctor's house. She'd inhaled its musty scent and suspected it was not exactly what it seemed to be, but she wanted to hear her father's opinion. He'd lived a long life and earned much wisdom through those years.

I must wait, she decided, placing the vial back in her pocket. *I will ask him when the sun rises.*

As quietly as she could, she turned and began to tiptoe out of the bedroom.

"Onawa," he whispered in a raspy voice as she reached the doorway.

It was strange to hear him like this, to witness his once seemingly eternal strength eroding, like a great mountain slowly but surely reduced to rubble by the persistent wind. "Father," she replied softly, "you should sleep. We can speak tomorrow."

"What did you need, daughter?" Aguila Brava asked. "We must not leave for tomorrow what we can do today."

Reluctantly, she knelt at his side, stroking the long white wisps of hair that still clung defiantly to his head. "I am so worried about you."

"Do not worry for me," Aguila Brava said. "Worry for those who have yet to live their lives."

She nodded, producing the vial. "I was wondering if you might smell this and tell me what you think it might be. It is a medicine that is being given to the Tolbert boy. I am wondering if it might be keeping him asleep."

Unscrewing the small metal cap, she opened it and held the small container beneath her father's aquiline nose.

He sniffed it and then coughed lightly. "That is a powerful drug," he said, closing his eyes as he searched his bountiful memories. "It contains teonanacatl."

"Teonanacatl," Onawa repeated. "I've heard that word before."

"It is a type of sacred mushroom. It not only can make one sleep. It also sparks visions. It was used by the Aztec high priests in the ancient times to commune with the gods."

She nodded. "Yes, Alicia mentioned it to us." Stroking his hair admiringly, she added, "Thank you, Father. You know so many things."

He smiled weakly. "I am only beginning to know, daughter, but soon I will know more."

"I must tell Solitario."

"Go to him, child."

"Tomorrow," she answered, unsure if she was ready to see him again, whether to push him further away or simply embrace him as he was, with all his faults.

"Remember what I said about tomorrows." Aguila Brava's voice cracked.

As Onawa gave him a sip of warm tea to soothe his dry throat, a heavy knock on the front door startled her. "Who could it be at this late hour?"

"It is Solitario," her father predicted, shutting his eyes. "Hurry."

Onawa rushed to the door, knowing the moment she saw him standing outside in the dark that something was terribly wrong.

"What is it?" she asked.

"I need your help again," he answered without a hint of emotion in his voice.

She stared back at him, her eyes wide with apprehension. Why did his eyes appear dull and lifeless? "What is it?" she repeated.

"I need your help to find out who killed me."

Onawa glanced back toward her father's bedroom. Could he somehow be of help? When she turned back to better assess Solitario's state, he no longer stood before her. Stepping back into her father's room, she told him what she had seen. "What do I do, Father? Can you help me?"

"You do not need my help, Onawa," he answered. "You know what you must do. Go to him, now. There is not much time."

She ran to the front door, shutting it behind her back as she dashed into town. Where would he be? The jailhouse? Elias' home across the dry gulch? What if he was somewhere else altogether? What if something terrible had happened to him out at that abandoned barn where he had insisted on waiting for Michael Dobbs' tormentor? What if she could not reach him in time to change his fate?

Her heart pounding in her chest, she ran first toward the jailhouse, as it was the nearest of the sites that ran through her thoughts. As she approached, she saw Tormenta in the abandoned street. The horse paced restlessly in front of the building. Solitario had returned from the barn, she sighed with relief, but he had never gone to Elias' house to sleep. He must still be there, inside, dead, or close enough to it that his spirit had wandered from his increasingly inhospitable body. She burst into the jailhouse. Not seeing him in the dark office, she darted to the jail cell, wrapping her hands around the bars, finding him sprawled on the floor beyond the prison door.

Turning the key still in the lock, she knelt down next to him, pressing her fingers against his cold neck. In the deep, dark shadows, a sliver of moonlight filtered in through the barred window high above. The only other visible light was a faint blue glow pulsating at the center of Solitario's waist. She reached out and touched it, felt its hot surface. She knew it well, for she had forged it with her own hands. It was the belt buckle she had given him at the conclusion of her Rite of Passage. It had been designed precisely for a moment like this. At the time, she had assumed it might save him from himself, feed him life-preserving energy if he ever again attempted to end his own life. Regardless, it would be important now. As she touched the center of the turquoise eagle, a jolt of electricity rippled through Solitario's body, causing it to writhe wildly. A blue glow enveloped his form, tiny phosphorescent particles floating through the bluish haze like miniature fireflies drawn to a fire.

As his heart failed to respond, she poured water from her canteen over his face and slapped it hard. "Wake up," she urged. "Solitario, you cannot leave me now."

His body fell still again. She pressed the button hidden seamlessly at the center of the belt buckle once more, but this time she held it down, her other hand pushing down firmly on his chest. She closed her eyes and felt the energy emanating from the belt buckle surge through her as well. She focused on magnifying the flow of power and channeling it into his dormant heart. Suddenly, a scorching heat seared through her innards, her arms burning as if they were erupting in flames, her body shaking as she leaned over him, pleading for his heart to beat, his breathing to resume.

Solitario, don't go, she thought, the crackling cloud of turquoise energy swirling around and between them. *There is so much you still must do. I have not seen it, but I have wished for it. And I yearn for it still. I need you to live.*

Just as she thought she could bear the pain no longer, she felt his rib cage shake as his heart thundered back to life. His eyes snapping open, he gawked at her with great alarm as the blue ether dissipated into the darkness. Exhausted, she collapsed atop him, her tears soaking his shirt.

"I thought I was dead," Solitario murmured as she helped him up to his feet.

"You almost were," she replied, her quivering voice betraying her turbulent emotions.

"I saw myself lying here on the floor. Yet, I walked outside. I passed straight through the jailhouse door without even opening it, just as if I were the spirit of Sergeant Elias, and I walked straight to your house. Nobody noticed me, except for Tormenta."

"It was your spirit. Your body was essentially dead, but your belt buckle kept your soul tethered to it just long enough so I could revive it."

"But how?"

"The buckle contains a storehouse of energy. I am surprised it still worked all these years after I fashioned it with my childish imagination. I will need to replenish it for you."

He gazed at her, the meager beam from the moon falling between them like a faint curtain of light. "Your abilities are beyond what I could have imagined. Thank you, Onawa, for saving me. I would not mind dying, but not before I finish this job."

She stared at him, a multitude of thoughts rushing through her mind all at once. Having nearly lost him, she suddenly realized just to what extent she wanted him alive and well by her side. She yearned to hear him say not that he would not mind dying, but that he was desperate to live so he could be with her. How could someone so close also be so far away? She wanted to shake him and slap him and kiss him and hug him, but she knew they had important work to do. Children's lives were at stake. Her heart would have to wait so that her mind could focus on saving them.

"What happened at the barn after we left?" Onawa asked, wondering if Michael Dobbs' assailant had something to do with the attempt on Solitario's life.

"I captured a man. His name was Vance. I brought him here. Then I received a message that Frankie Tolbert was regaining consciousness. I was on my way to see him. I remember talking to the mayor on the street. And then, everything went black. Now the man I captured is gone. No matter what, I can't seem to make any progress. We are running out of time. Soon, Elena and the other girls will be dead."

"The Tolbert boy. We must help him," she told Solitario. "The medicine they have been giving him is keeping him asleep. It's probably the same thing that was given to you. I took the last vial from his nightstand, and my father confirmed it contains teonanacatl."

"If that's the case, I am not sure if it is the doctor or the apothecary who is behind this," Solitario muttered, retrieving his sombrero from the floor and dusting it off.

"What if it is both?" Onawa pondered, staring at the collection of images and notes that Solitario had arranged on the jailhouse wall opposite his desk.

As he stood next to her, she could sense that he was staring not at the wall, but at her.

When she faced him, she saw something different in his expression, something flickering like a newly ignited candle in the depth of his mournful eyes. It was as if, after meandering aimlessly with her through the shadowy labyrinth of a lonesome eternity, he had only now begun to recognize her in the glow of that feeble, nascent light.

"Your feet are bleeding," Solitario said, looking down.

Only then did Onawa realize that, in her haste to reach Solitario, she'd forgotten to put on her moccasins.

THIRTY-THREE

Solitario felt confused and off-kilter. His head was a heavy stone struggling to balance on his shoulders, but he did not have the luxury of time to recuperate from his near-death experience.

Only after binding Onawa's bloody feet did he manage to regain his focus.

"Come with me," he said, taking Onawa by the hand and heading outside.

The air was cool and the town silent as they made their way to Dr. Ferris' house. The kerosene lanterns were still on inside the home, the windows glowing warmly as they approached.

"Why are you here so late?" the doctor asked, a puzzled look on his face as he stood in the door in his long white pajama shirt.

"I heard Frankie Tolbert was coming to," Solitario said as Onawa stood behind him on the porch.

"He started rustling about, probably the dehydration bringing back his fever. I'd run out of medicine for him. I could have sworn I still had another dose." Dr. Ferris squinted suspiciously past Solitario's shoulder at Onawa. "Luckily the apothecary was able to bring me more vials."

"So he's not awake?" asked Solitario.

"No. He's resting again."

"I need to see him." Solitario edged his way through the door and stepped into the room where Frankie Tolbert lay listlessly on the bed.

Onawa followed him inside.

"What's going on, Jefe?" Blake Dobbs joined them. "Did you catch my brother's attacker? I've been sitting with him since we returned."

"Yes, but now he's gone."

"Damn it," Blake Dobbs grimaced, clutching his fists. "When I get ahold of him, he'll wish he'd never set eyes on us Dobbs twins."

"Right now we have to focus on Frankie Tolbert," Solitario replied. "Doctor, no more medicine for Frankie. Do you understand me? Do you know what is in those injections you are giving him?"

The doctor appeared taken aback. "Sheriff Tolbert never questioned my medical acuity. Who do you think you are to do so?"

Solitario glowered at him. "Answer the question."

"Like I told you before, I prescribed a hydrating substance and antibiotics to fight off infection," Dr. Ferris insisted.

"How well do you know the apothecary?" Solitario asked.

"He's been here for several years. I've never had any troubles with him. He understands my work."

"How's that?" said Solitario.

"Well, he spent some time in medical school himself, but he never finished," answered Dr. Ferris.

Solitario nodded. If the apothecary had attended medical school, then he would know the human anatomy, have experience removing skin and dissecting body parts. "No more medicine for Frankie, Doctor. Onawa will stay here to watch over him. Blake, you keep vigil over your brother. I have work to do."

"But, Sheriff," a flustered Dr. Ferris retorted, following Solitario to the door. "You can't turn my home into a boardinghouse."

Solitario turned and silenced the old medic with a fuming glare. "Just be thankful it hasn't become a morgue."

As Solitario strode through town, a familiar form came toward him, the portly silhouette of his old sergeant.

"Elias," he said, not slowing down.

"Where are you going, Jefe?" Sergeant Elias asked, struggling to catch up with him even in his spirit form.

"Haven't you learned how to move from one place to another without walking or exerting yourself?" Solitario asked.

"Otila would want me to exercise."

Solitario shook his head. "I don't think it will make a difference anymore."

"Where are you headed?"

"To the drugstore."

"Now?" puzzled Elias. "It is closed. Shouldn't you be looking for Elena?"

"That is precisely what I am doing, amigo. Although I must admit, I am driven mostly by the fear of failing you."

As they reached the pharmacy, Solitario knocked loudly on the door, peering up at the darkened windows over the store. There was no movement visible.

"Why are you afraid you will fail me?" Elias asked, trepidation lacing his voice. "You have never failed me before."

"Haven't I?" Solitario asked, knocking again. "You and your wife and son are dead, aren't you? Others have died now under my watch. I even died tonight. Nobody is safe. I fear I am no longer of much use."

"Nonsense," Elias replied, his voice hopeful as he gazed up at his old captain.

"What if I get Onawa killed? Or the Dobbs twins?" Solitario stared impatiently up at the dark windows behind which the apothecary resided. "People have a way of dying around me. Es la maldición maldita."

Elias firmly placed a hand on Solitario's shoulder, prompting him to turn and face his vanquished sergeant.

"Capitán, never stop fighting," Elias urged. "The only way you lose is if you give up. Save my Elena, Capitán, even if you die trying. You may be cursed by fate, but you are blessed with courage."

Solitario focused on Elias, the troubled emotions swirling through him at last settling like water coming to rest in a vessel after having been shaken and tossed. Sergeant Elias was right, he realized. He could not surrender. He could not allow fear to win out over the quest for justice. A current of anger bubbling up from deep within him, Solitario exploded into action, kicking the apothecary's door open. Drawing his guns, he stormed into the store.

"Druggist, show yourself," Solitario shouted, standing in the center of the darkened drugstore.

Behind the high counters, shelves bristled with glass jars glinting in the paltry light filtering through the storefront windows.

There was no response to Solitario's command. The floorboard creaked beneath his boots as he crept slowly through the store, checking around the counters to ensure the apothecary was not hiding behind them.

Moving slowly but methodically, Solitario climbed the rickety stairs to the rooms above the store. A simple kitchen and a rustic bedroom with scant decor yielded little of note. Returning to the ground floor, Solitario rifled through drawers, finding tattered anatomical atlases and dog-eared medical school textbooks. On a desk in the back, he discovered a book about compounding. It was open to a page on extracting essential oils from mushrooms and distilling these into their most potent form. Brown smudges in the shape of fingerprints lined the margins. Touching the powdery substance, he recognized it as trace amounts of the same teonanacatl he had found in the Jackson house near the beginning of this nightmarish quest.

Was the apothecary the familiar man Johnny Tolbert had spoken of? It would make sense. This would be motivation enough for the man to keep Frankie drugged and silent. And if so, where was he now? And with whom was he working? One man alone could not orchestrate all of these crimes, and the apothecary seemed like a pawn—perhaps a vital one—but nonetheless a pawn in a bigger game.

Stepping back outside, Solitario looked up at the lightening sky.

"You should rest," Elias said. "You'll need energy to keep going."

Solitario's hand moved instinctively to his turquoise eagle belt buckle, which glowed subtly, its tone matching the sky as the sun peeked over the horizon. "I have energy, amigo. I will not rest until I find your daughter."

As he said that, Blake Dobbs came running down the street. "Jefe, come!" he shouted, clutching his hat to keep it from falling off his head. "Frankie's awake."

———————

Solitario barely fit in the room with Dr. Ferris, his wife, Onawa, and Blake Dobbs gathered around Frankie Tolbert, who languished in his bed looking pale and weak.

"Frankie," Solitario said. "You've been asleep for a long time."

"I saw you in my dreams. I also saw her," he feebly raised a wavering finger, pointing at Onawa. "I dreamed you rescued me from the cave."

"They did, Frankie," Blake said, patting the boy gently on his shoulder. "You've done good, boy."

"Frankie, did you see anyone else?" asked Solitario.

"I saw my brother, Johnny, in the cave. And my sisters, Abigail and Beatrice, hiding with some other girls in what looked like a church."

Onawa whispered into Solitario's ear, "The teonanacatl made him walk like a spirit like you did last night when you came to my house."

Solitario nodded, gazing steadily at Frankie, speaking as calmly as anyone could given the circumstances. "Frankie, think back to the last night you had dinner at your house. It's been a long time. A man came knocking at your door. He asked your father and your brother to follow him out to the barn. Then he came back and asked for the rest of you to come too. Do you remember that?"

Fear crept into Frankie's tired eyes as he nodded.

"Do you remember the man at the door, Frankie?" asked Solitario. "Johnny told me that he had a familiar face. Do you remember who he was? If you do, that could help us find your sisters."

Frankie gazed past Solitario, looked out the window at the morning light. "There wasn't a familiar man."

Solitario turned to look at Onawa, his spirits wavering and threatening to sink.

"There were two," Frankie added.

"Two?" Solitario leaned in, his pulse quickening as he took the boy's cold and clammy hand into his own. "Do you remember who they were? Was one of them the apothecary?"

"Yes." Frankie nodded. "The apothecary . . . and one more."

"Who was the other man, Frankie?" asked Solitario.

Frankie gulped, his eyes opening wide as he recalled the man's face. "He was in the barn when it all happened. He was dressed in a fancy suit like he always is."

"Who was the other man, Frankie?" Solitario repeated.

"It was Mayor Stillman," Frankie whispered.

THIRTY-FOUR

At midmorning, Solitario gathered his forces at the jailhouse. Onawa stood next to him, along with both Dobbs twins. Michael was still nursing his injuries, but he insisted on getting out of bed and joining them.

Mr. Boggs was the last to arrive, flustered, flushed, and perspiring from the hasty morning ride, his suit rumpled and his tie poorly knotted. "What do you mean, Mayor Stillman is involved? That is ludicrous."

Solitario placed a sepia-toned image of the mayor, cut out from his most recent election poster, up on the wall next to the photographs of Dwight Grissom, the apothecary, Dr. Ferris, and Reverend Grimes. Note cards with names stood in for Vance and Captain Ringgold. "Frankie Tolbert has identified Mayor Stillman as one of the men who came to Sheriff Tolbert's house the night of the murders," Solitario stated. "On top of that, Vance mentioned he worked for Stillman on occasion. Vance wore boots with an X on the sole, just like the prints we found at the Tolbert barn and the Elias property. I figure when Stillman realized that Vance had been arrested and Frankie was about to wake up and identify him, he had to act fast to remove both me and Vance from the equation."

Boggs collapsed into a chair, his face betraying utter bafflement. "But how? Why? Where are they now?"

"Nobody knows where Mayor Stillman, Vance, or the apothecary are," Solitario answered. "Blake and I have already checked. The only suspects that have not fled town are Reverend Grimes and Dr. Ferris, which casts them in a better light at the moment."

"Why would the mayor do this?" Boggs shook his head in disbelief. "He's worked right alongside me to solve this from the beginning. He even suggested enlisting you to help."

Solitario pondered that question. "That is interesting indeed. Perhaps he expected me to fail. Or maybe he assumed if I figured out the truth, the townspeople might believe his word over mine." He glanced at Onawa, remembering her initial admonition not to trust the Anglos when they had asked him to take on the job. In retrospect, her instinct seemed prescient. After all, she was a seer. On the other hand, perhaps it should have been obvious to him, but in a moment of pride and vanity, he had chosen to believe that which made him feel better about himself.

"So what do we do, Jefe?" Michael Dobbs asked, clutching his flank as he spoke.

"You will do nothing," Solitario answered. "I will not have you in the field in your condition."

"I could stay in town and keep an eye on Frankie," Michael offered.

"Yes, he is still a very important witness," Solitario agreed. "When we apprehend the mayor, we will need Frankie's help to bring him to justice."

Boggs hung his head in shame. "I can't believe I trusted Mayor Stillman. He's had dinner in my home. He knows my daughters. If he is truly involved, I will see to it that he hangs for this."

"So you believe me?" asked Solitario.

"I believe Frankie Tolbert," Boggs answered. "Why would he lie about such a thing?"

"We need to figure out where the mayor, the apothecary, and Vance have all fled to," Onawa said, all heads turning in surprise. Never had she spoken so boldly to the whole group, but she was indisputably correct.

"They are not with Reverend Grimes," Blake said. "The church was empty, and only the reverend and his wife were in their home this morning when I visited."

"That leaves Grissom." Solitario pointed at the picture on the wall. "Vance also does work for him."

"Again, preposterous," Boggs shook his head. "He is Olvido's most wealthy landowner. He has the most to lose through all this. If Olvido is wiped off the map, what will the land be worth?"

"Perhaps he also has the most to gain," Solitario mused. "Blake, do me a favor, run down to the telegraph office and ask if anything has come in for me this morning. I am expecting to hear back from someone."

Blake grabbed his Stetson off the hook and dashed out into the brilliant sun. Onawa watched Solitario intently as they all waited for Blake to return. While Boggs and Michael wriggled in their chairs, Solitario rifled through the set of leather-bound tomes still piled on the worktable beneath the picture wall. His eyes followed his finger down a list of entries in an open ledger.

"I don't know, Sheriff," Boggs protested. "What if you're wrong? Dwight Grissom and Mayor Stillman will destroy you. And you'll take me down with you if I stand by your accusations."

"You are wrong to doubt that Mayor Stillman and Grissom would be capable of committing such atrocities simply because they are men of power," Solitario answered, his eyes still trained on the ledger he leaned over. "In my experience, once people get a taste for power, they'll do anything to keep it or grow it, including betraying their once cherished moral values. On the other hand, you were correct about one thing you said at the start of this investigation."

"What was that?" Boggs shuffled in his chair.

"When I suggested that there might be some obscure religious ritual at play, you insisted that we should follow the money. There is one thing that Mayor Stillman, Mr. Vance, and the apothecary all have in common. They all have received payments from Dwight Grissom. It says so right here in this bank ledger you shared with us."

"That's no surprise," huffed Boggs, rising to his feet and approaching the table. He placed his cracked eyeglasses on the bridge of his nose, squinting at the numbers neatly arrayed on the pages. "Grissom does business with everyone. I imagine anybody you name has sold him land or services or livestock at some point or another."

As Solitario looked up from the ledger, Blake Dobbs burst through the door clutching a telegram in his hand. "This came for you today," he panted, handing the document to Solitario.

All eyes were on him as he opened and scrutinized it. Slowly, he looked up from the paper in his hand, saying, "It is as I suspected."

"What is?" Onawa asked, drawing closer, trying to peek at the wire in Solitario's hand.

"I noticed a name in the bank ledger that seemed very unfamiliar to Olvido. It was not one of the town residents that, as Mr. Boggs has stated, would naturally do business with Dwight Grissom. The name was Mexican."

"There are plenty of people with Spanish surnames in Olvido, Sheriff. You know that," Mr. Boggs answered.

"Not Spanish, Mexican . . . Aztec. He wrote a substantial check to someone with the name Tezcatlipoca. The name was not one I'd heard in Olvido, but I felt that I had heard it years ago when I was still with the Rurales. I sent a telegram to one of my old colleagues in Mexico City to double-check. This . . ." he said as he handed the document to Onawa, "confirms my suspicion. Tezcatlipoca is a man wanted in Mexico for conducting sadistic rituals rooted in the ancient Aztec traditions. He has also been accused of using the hallucinogenic mushroom known as teonanacatl, of which we have found traces at various of the crime scenes and at the drugstore. He was likely the man wearing the mask and feathers at your house, Mr. Boggs, feathers which were also found in the Tolbert barn and in the cave with Frankie. He is working with Grissom on this, whatever *this* is. We must go to Grissom's ranch and put a stop to it . . . now."

Boggs' eyes widened. "But what if you're wrong? We will be ruined."

"Do you want to save your daughters, Mr. Boggs? Or do you want to save your fortune?" asked Solitario.

Boggs removed his battered glasses, placing them in his coat pocket. "I will come with you."

"So will I," Blake added.

"We will be outmanned and outgunned," Solitario warned.

"I will come as well," Onawa said.

"No." Solitario shook his head. He could not bear to endanger her life too.

"You cannot stop me," she replied. "I will follow you no matter what you say."

Solitario closed the ledger, handing it to Michael. "Put this in the safe, Deputy. Along with Frankie Tolbert's testimony, this evidence will be used in court." Assessing his team, Solitario fought back the swelling fear that he would get everybody who believed in him killed. It had been a very long time since he'd won a battle, but he did his best to muster every ounce of fight left in him to inspire them onward as he declared, "Let's ride.

THIRTY-FIVE

Elena held Abigail and Beatrice tightly, one on either side. The three of them had been taken as a group to bathe and change into fresh clothes. They wore simple white linen shifts that reached down to their ankles. Their hair had been brushed back and clung damply against the backs of their dresses. The Tolbert girls were dainty and pretty, thought Elena. This must have been the way they had looked every day when their mother watched over them and made sure they bathed and scrubbed and brushed regularly. Their skin glowed with cleanliness and innocence.

"Why are they being so nice to us today, Elena?" Abigail asked. "Are they letting us go back home? Are they taking us to a party?"

Elena feared that the truth was far from the young girl's naive suppositions. Despite her insistent prayers to the Virgen de Guadalupe, pleading for her to ease her worries and restore her faith in humanity, she could not erase the haunting image of the man with the feathered mask and jagged teeth sharpening his knives beneath the trees. She feared that she and the others were being prepared not for release, but for the end. At that very moment, the other captives were undergoing the same process that they had earlier. The Boggs sisters, Delphina and Eugenia, as well as the little green-eyed girl, Lavinia, were being cleansed and purified by a woman with long dark hair who also wore a mask with blue-green plumes. At least a woman had been chosen to perform the cleansing tasks. When Elena and the Tolbert girls had been led to the room with the claw-foot bathtub by the guards, she had feared that they would be further robbed of their dignity by being forced to undress in front of them. But the man with the mask and jagged teeth had arrived, shushing their snickers and abolishing their sneers. He had spoken in Spanish, saying the girls must be pure for the gods to accept them. Then he had ushered in the masked woman and instructed her to proceed with the preparations.

Preparations for what? Elena wondered, even though she suspected they would be sacrificed just as their families had been. At night, she awoke from her nightmares bathed in perspiration, only to realize that they were not dreams but memories. Night after night, she relived watching her father, mother, and brother burn at the stake. Would that be their fate as well? Fire? Hanging? Decapitation? If the knives were any indication, then decapitation seemed like the most likely route. She shuddered with fear as she held Abigail and Beatrice.

Papá, Mamá, will I be joining you soon? Elena thought. *Or will my padrino, Solitario, come to save us from these evil men?*

As she spoke to her parents in the sanctuary of her mind, the masked woman brought the other girls back into the chapel. They smiled ingenuously as she bent down to lace tiny white flowers into their hair. Their eyes twinkling with newfound merriment, Abigail and Beatrice released their fearful hold on Elena's waist and dashed toward the other girls to join in the festivities. They wanted flowers in their hair too, they chanted.

Elena wiped a single tear from her cheek as she sank onto the altar steps.

"You will look muy bonitas for the celebration tonight." The masked lady spoke in a sickly sweet tone. "The gods will be pleased."

Through an open window, a breeze eased the stifling heat in the chapel. At the same time, a familiar metallic, humming sound floated in on the wind. Elena recognized the musical tones, a shiver rippling up her spine. It was the sharpening of the knives again. How many times was he going to do this? She wished her father had not died so he could be there to defend them. He had always believed so thoroughly in his old captain, her padrino, Solitario, but he was yet to come, yet to find them. What if her father had been deluded? He was dead, after all. Had he been too trusting, too complacent, too content? Had both he and Solitario lost their edge after years away from the fields of battle?

As the younger girls pranced about the masked lady, relishing the clean clothes and floral adornments gracing their locks, Elena tiptoed to the open window and peered out, looking toward the sound of the sharpening.

There he was, the masked man with the skirt made of shells and dried corn husks, the mask crowned by aqua and cobalt plumes, the jagged teeth stolen from the jaws of coyotes. His raven hair hung down to his waist, tangled and matted. His torso, bare and dark, glistened with a coat of perspiration beneath the high noon sun. In his hands dazzling silver blades flashed in the brilliant light.

Elena's knees threatened to buckle beneath her as she stood at the window, watching him work. His movements were fluid as a dance choreographed to the music of his metalwork, his performance luminous and breathtaking. It could almost be inspiring, Elena thought, her skin crawling with a strange mixture of awe and fear, were it not a prelude to horrific pain and eternal darkness.

THIRTY-SIX

On the way out of Olvido, headed west along the dry ravine, Elias joined Solitario at the front of the pack, wedging his way between his captain and Onawa. He rode El Caballo Sin Nombre, which forced Solitario to do some explaining.

"Where'd that pinto come from?" Blake Dobbs asked from his position at the rear of the group. "Isn't that your old sergeant's horse?"

Solitario glanced at Onawa, who smiled knowingly at Elias. The retired sergeant, now more retired than he had ever thought possible, had reached a point at which he no longer cared who could—or could not—see him, nor did it matter to him what discomfort he might cause for his old jefe. All he wanted to do was help save his daughter. If it meant putting Solitario in an awkward situation, then so be it. He figured his jefe owed him, especially if he were to hold him responsible not only for the loss of his own life but also for the lives of Otila and Oscarito. He still had not seen them in the afterlife. All he had seen was desert and horse, Solitario and Onawa, the bruja Alicia, and more and more suffering and death. He simmered with a defiant rage he had never known while alive in the flesh. He thought that perhaps this was because of how he had died, watching his wife and son burn, consumed by fire himself, overwhelmed by a seemingly unquenchable thirst for revenge and an incessant desire to save his only surviving offspring, Elena.

Mr. Boggs echoed Blake Dobbs' inquiry, "Yes, indeed, why is that pinto horse accompanying us with no rider?"

"We will need a horse to help carry back the girls, when we rescue them," Solitario answered, staring ahead.

"Lies are more believable when they match up with what the listener wishes to hear," Elias said.

"I am glad you are here," Solitario whispered.

"Be careful what you say," Elias answered. "Don't reveal your true feelings for me. The others might overhear you and think you are speaking to Onawa."

"I'm relieved you haven't lost your sense of humor, even if you are more disrespectful than ever," muttered Solitario.

"Do not take personal offense, Jefe," Elias replied. "It is just that as a spirit I find it harder to contain my emotions and adhere to a sense of order."

He has nothing left to lose, Onawa thought as they rode on.

"You are usually correct, señorita," Elias retorted. "However, I have everything to lose. I have my daughter, Elena, to lose. That is why I have exceeded my limits."

"It's understandable," Solitario conceded.

"Why are we not riding faster?" Elias asked.

"It is best if we arrive in the dark. We do not know what to expect, and if they see us coming from afar, we will tip them off. If they fire on us, we will be out in the open. So we go slowly. Paciencia."

"Poco a poco se llega lejos," Elias recited.

"I like the old dichos," Onawa said.

"The Apache have them?" Elias asked.

"Remember, my mamá was Mexicana like you."

"Ah, sí. No wonder I like you so much," Elias grinned, forgetting his worries for an instant.

"Cuidado, Elias," Solitario admonished him. "Do not let your new-found freedom make you reckless. You must still be a gentleman."

Elias apologetically tipped his sombrero at Onawa, winking at her. It made him want to chuckle aloud that his old jefe might be jealous, but this was no time for distractions or jokes.

"Do you think we'll save Elena, Jefe?" he asked. He was not about to confess it, but he feared what his rage might compel him to do if they failed in their quest. He had heard of spirits becoming like demons, wreaking terror and vengeance on anyone in their path, even those who had nothing to do with their original loss or sorrow. Might he be doomed to such an eternal afterlife if Elena perished before her time?

Solitario gritted his teeth in a mixture of dread and determination, his jaw muscles flexing in silent response.

The sun was setting in front of them as they reached Dwight Grissom's vast ranch. The ocher light stung their eyes, rendering it difficult to see the dirt road ahead. Clouds of dust buffeted them, blanketing them in fine sandy powder.

"For an instant I could have sworn I saw your old sergeant riding on the pinto," Mr. Boggs coughed, raising his bandanna around his mouth and nose to filter out the dust. "What's the horse's name?"

"El Caballo Sin Nombre."

"Yes, what is it?

"That is it."

Perplexed, Mr. Boggs blinked behind his fractured glasses, now opaque as the lenses were covered in dust.

"We must stop here," Solitario instructed, bringing Tormenta to a halt at a cluster of cedar trees by the side of the road.

"Why?" Elias asked.

"We must wait for it to become darker. Water your horses. Drink. Restore your energies. Who knows what awaits us at Grissom's ranch?"

Onawa watered Invierno as well as El Caballo Sin Nombre.

Thanking her, Elias confessed, "I'm not too good at the daily chores."

"Were you ever?" Solitario asked.

"Otila would say no if you asked her." Elias grinned. "Maybe I'll get to see her again when this is over. Maybe I'll be allowed to rest once Elena is safe."

Onawa patted the pinto horse. Then she took a long draft from her canteen, her long smooth hair flowing in the breeze.

Elias admired her beauty and then glanced at Solitario, whom he caught staring at her.

When Solitario noticed Elias watching him, he turned away abruptly, his eyebrows knit together in a frown.

As the party sat beneath the trees, cleaning and loading their rifles, the sky began to darken, and a cool stillness settled over the land. Mr. Boggs asked if they could light a fire to stay warm. Winter was approaching, and the nights were growing colder.

"We must not let them know we are coming," Solitario said, handing Mr. Boggs his own sarape.

He walked down the road a bit by himself, squinting toward the horizon dissolving into inky darkness, his hand extending over the edge of his sombrero.

"Why do you keep her at bay?" Elias asked, appearing next to him. "Why do you keep them all at a distance?"

"I have to."

"Because of la maldición?"

"Sí."

"You didn't keep me away."

"Yes. And look how well that went for you."

"You can't blame yourself."

"Why not? You blame me."

Elias shuffled side to side, staring at the ground. Solitario was right. He did blame him, but not la maldición. "I thought the curse applied only to losing the women you love," he challenged.

"I don't know," Solitario admitted. "The more I live with la maldición, the less I understand it. All I know is that I fear for Onawa's life. Frankly, I fear for the life of anyone who might come to depend on me."

Elias nodded as the darkness enveloped them. On the northeastern horizon, the moon began to arc upward into the sky. It was a crescent, a sliver of silver, yet its subtle glow was magnified by the reflection of the expansive desert sands.

"I never had a maldición placed on me, Jefe, but I felt much the same way that you describe, as a husband and a father. Maybe it's the feeling not of being cursed, but of being blessed, of being human, of allowing yourself to love and to be loved. Anyway, try as we might to control these things, try as you might to isolate yourself . . . the human heart cannot be trained or commanded like a horse. Even when you think you have managed to become completely isolated, you are not. Look around you, Solitario. We are here because we believe in you. Try as you might to shut us all out, we are here with you."

Solitario arched an eyebrow as Elias called him by his name. Turning, he met his eyes. "Are you a sergeant or a philosopher?"

Elias grinned, his eyes glinting in the moonlight. "I am a ghost."

—————————

When they reached Grissom ranch, the gates loomed tall and imposing against the stars, their black wrought iron seeping into the cobalt sky above.

"In the dark, the gates are almost invisible," Elias murmured.

Solitario stared down the long road from the gates to the ranch house. The road was lined by mature cedar trees. At its terminus stood a graceful—if misplaced—southern plantation-style mansion, glowing white in the distance, its two-story columns visible in the dim light emanating from the windows.

Solitario picked the lock and pushed the gates quietly open.

"Remind me to keep an eye on you next time you're in my bank," Mr. Boggs remarked.

They traversed the shadowy lane to the front of the house, where instead of finding a guard posted, they found a body sprawled on the steps to the front porch.

Dismounting, Solitario drew one of his guns and approached the lifeless form. A trail of blood trickled down the steps. Glassy-eyed, the apothecary still wore a look of surprise on his gaunt face, his hollowed cheeks already rendering him a skeleton in the eerie light.

"Who is it?" whispered Mr. Boggs from his horse.

"The apothecary," Solitario answered. "He is dead."

"He must have been of no more use to them," Blake Dobbs surmised. "His cover was blown. He became a liability."

"He came out here to warn them and take shelter," Solitario guessed. "I reckon he only achieved the former."

"I expected a whole welcoming committee," Mr. Boggs said.

"It is not as I imagined it either," agreed Solitario, stepping over the dead druggist on his way to the front door.

After knocking and waiting for a couple of minutes, Solitario motioned for them to dismount and form a perimeter around the front porch, out of the way of the windows in case anyone were to shoot out at them. When the others were situated at the corners of the porch or behind the columns, Solitario tried the doorknob. Finding it unlocked, he pushed it, slowly and cautiously. The hinges groaned reluctantly as the weighty door swung open.

Inside, candles and lanterns flickered, but there was no sign of life. "Hello?" Solitario called out. "Grissom? This is the sheriff. I'm here to take you in. If anyone is here, show yourself at once."

There was no reply. The floorboards creaked beneath Solitario's boots as he passed through the elegantly decorated foyer into the dining room with its long table and crystal-laden vitrine. Ornate tapestries hung on the walls. Several plates containing a half-eaten meal still sat on the table. Solitario noted that, at the head of the table, the fork was stuck into a piece of steak that had been left hovering over the middle of the dish. The chairs were out of place. Grissom and his henchmen had left in a hurry after hearing what the apothecary had to say. In the kitchen, Solitario heard a rustling behind the pantry door. He extracted his second gun and cocked it, peering through the shadows as he approached.

When he reached the door, he extended his hand to turn the knob.

At that instant, Elias emerged through the pantry door, startling him and nearly causing him to shoot. "What are you doing?"

"Put your guns away," Elias said. "There's nobody here but the house-keeper. She's shaking with fear inside the pantry."

Solitario shook his head. "I nearly shot her through the door thanks to you."

Pulling the door open, he ducked and stepped into the low-ceilinged pantry, raising a lantern to illuminate a dark-skinned, middle-aged woman crouched on her knees in the back. She was shaking, indeed, as if she'd seen a ghost, which she probably had. Her eyes darted from Solitario to Elias lurking behind him, and back to Solitario again. He reached a hand out to her. "Venga, señora. Come with me."

Taking Solitario's hand, she followed him out into the kitchen. "Sit down," he instructed, motioning for her to sit at the small kitchen table. Opening the back door, he called out, "Onawa?"

Her slender silhouette appeared at the far corner of the back of the house.

"Onawa, you can all come inside. Nobody is here."

Back inside, Solitario asked the woman if she knew where her employer was.

She shook her head fearfully. "No, señor. I don't know anything. All I do is cook and clean."

"I believe you, señora," Solitario said. "What happened to the man on the front steps?"

"Somebody shot him." Her voice quivered.

"Did you see who shot him?" Solitario asked as the others in his group walked through the house searching for any other clues.

She shook her head. "No. I did not see."

"How long ago did everyone leave?" Solitario asked.

"A couple of hours, señor."

"Did they have the girls with them?"

"What girls?" the housekeeper asked, surprise evident in the tone of her voice. "Mr. Grissom has a daughter, but she grew up and moved away a long time ago. And his wife died not long after that. There are no girls here."

Solitario stopped, surprised by this revelation. If the girls weren't at Grissom's place, then where were they?

Mr. Boggs stepped into the kitchen, "She's lying. They took the girls with them. There's no sign of them here."

The woman shook her head frantically. "No. No. I swear to God, señor. There were no girls. Only men."

"How many men?" said Solitario.

"Four."

"Think back over the last several months. Are you absolutely certain that you have never noticed even a trace of a girl being kept here in the house?" asked Solitario, bringing his face so close to the woman's that his mustache nearly grazed her cheeks.

The woman searched her memory, her eyes scanning the ceiling. "Now that you mention it . . ."

"Yes?"

"A little while ago, Mr. Grissom gave me some time off. I went down to Chihuahua to visit family. When I returned, I noticed that his daughter's bedroom looked like it had been used. When I washed the linens, I found girls' hair on the pillowcases. Long dark strands and curly blond ones too. I thought it was strange but I had forgotten about it."

"That's it then," Solitario said, clapping his hands together. "They *were* here, but they were moved before you came back. This means we are on the right path. Bueno. You stay here. If you hear gunfire, you hide in the pantry again, you understand?"

As the woman busied herself cleaning up the dining room, Solitario motioned for the others to step outside with him. Behind the house, he used the kerosene lamp he'd taken from the kitchen to inspect the ground, his eyes following hoofprints headed south by southwest. He stared at the distant mountains, outlined in craggy black against the cobalt sky.

"They've headed that way," he said, gazing in the direction of Mexico.

"Would they take my daughters out of the country?" Mr. Boggs asked, his voice trembling.

Solitario squinted as if somehow this would help him see what was not there.

Elias knew what he was thinking. He suspected the kidnappers' motivations were far more sinister than a simple trip across the border.

"Pack some food from the pantry in case we need it," Solitario told Blake Dobbs. "There's a mountain pass down there. On the other side is part of the Santander ranch and then the river in its new place. We must keep going . . . we must get to the girls . . ."

He didn't finish the sentence, but Elias gazed somberly at Onawa. They both could finish his thoughts for him, they must keep going . . . must get to the girls . . . *before it's too late.*

THIRTY-SEVEN

Elena grabbed Abigail's and Beatrice's hands, and they in turn clutched onto Delphina's and Eugenia's hands, and Eugenia hung onto little green-eyed Lavinia. They made a sorry parade as they dragged their feet single file in their white frocks. The woman who had tended to their cleansing and attire guided them from the chapel as they were loaded into a shiny black carriage led by four horses. The carriage followed yet another more elegant one, rolling out of the hacienda's courtyard, over a bumpy ranch road toward the mountains in the north.

The sun was setting, and night was falling. Through the carriage windows, Elena could see cows dotting the landscape, cacti soaring toward the golden sky. Slowly, the view turned inky blue and then black as the carriage teetered upward, winding its way into a mountain pass.

When the horses finally pulled to a stop, the door was thrown open. It was the woman again. She had piercing charcoal eyes in which a fire seemed to dance, even though there were no flames to reflect. She instructed them to step down and follow her. The night air was cold, rippling through their frocks and chilling their skin. Elena felt goose bumps rising on her arms and legs, shivers tingling her spine. Was she afraid, or merely cold? She figured she was both as they followed the woman, who in turn trailed two men. Elena could not make out the men's faces. It was dark, and they were way in front, but she knew one of them wore the feathered mask. He was the one who no doubt carried the blades.

After trudging through the mountain pass, they reached a clearing. There, Elena saw the fire that she had divined in the woman's eyes. She heard one of the men, the one with the mask, call her Malina. Mal. That sounded bad. Evil. She was not cleansing them and dressing them for a party or a dance as the little ones hoped. Elena understood. Malina was preparing them for something far less desirable, a sacrifice like the one in which her parents and brother had been burned at the stake. The piñon wood filled the air with the scent of pine. A large bonfire had been erected in a clearing up in the mountain pass. From that elevated vantage point, Elena could glimpse the last glimmers of fading sunlight in the distant western horizon. She spotted four other men waiting in the clearing. Near them, six wooden poles stood equidistant around the fire.

Beyond the circle of poles and the raging fire at its center, a crude altar had been built with rocks. Behind the altar stood a gateway fashioned from two stone columns topped by a slab.

Malina and two of the men tied the girls to the poles with ropes at their hands and feet. The wind gusted, making them shiver and tremble with fear. Even the intermittent blasts of heat from the bonfire were not enough to provide comfort, only more worry. Would they soon be consumed by that fire? Elena scanned the girls as she was fastened to her stake. She had come to cherish each one of them in their own way. As different as they all were, would they meet a common end?

Her eyes drifted toward the altar. Standing behind its crudely hewn surface, the man with the mask unfurled a roll of leather across the tabletop. She could not see his expression behind the mask, but she could see his eyes. They filled her with dread as he raised one of his blades.

It was then that it dawned on her that they would not be dying by fire as her family had in the dry riverbed.

The woman donned her own feathered mask and danced around the fire, chanting in a language that Elena could not comprehend as sparks crackled and swirled chaotically in the vortex of wind created by the surrounding mountain walls.

The girls all looked at her expectantly. She could sense what they were thinking. *Elena, save us. Elena, stop this madness. Elena, please, you're the eldest. You said you'd keep us safe.* She tugged hard against the rough ropes binding her to the stake. She grunted and strained, but it was no use. The woman danced and chanted. The high priest raised not one but *two* long curved blades toward the sky. Their edges gleamed in the light from the wild flames. He, too, shouted alien words. It sounded like he was summoning someone. And suddenly, a ripple of cyan light filled the stone gateway behind the altar, like water turned on its side in defiance of gravity. Elena gawked at it, wide-eyed, not knowing whether she should feel more fear or simply awe at what was transpiring before her. The turquoise light filled the gate, like a translucent curtain beyond which the rock walls fell away and vanished. Straining her eyes to discern what lurked beyond the sheer fabric of light, Elena thought she could detect tree branches, leaves, tiny birds flitting about. It was a portal to a different world. Something—or someone—moved on the other side, gliding beneath the canopy of leaves, approaching the gate. Was it coming for them?

THIRTY-EIGHT

When they reached the mountain pass, Solitario smelled the piñon smoke wafting in the cold night breeze. They tethered their horses to mesquites and chaparral in the foothills so that they could climb more quietly in the dark.

"Hijos de puta," cried Elias, struggling to keep pace with Solitario, despite the fact that he could have simply shifted location without any physical exertion. "They aim to set Elena on fire, just as they did to me, Otila, and Oscarito. We can't let them hurt her, Solitario."

Solitario pushed himself harder, climbing up the trail to the mountain pass. "They do not plan on burning her and the other girls."

"Then what?" Elias asked. "What did the bruja Alicia tell you?"

"You don't want to know."

"What?" he demanded. "I deserve to know."

Elias was right, thought Solitario. He did deserve to know. In death he seemed determined to claim his equality with Solitario. He no longer acted like his sergeant. He acted like his compadre, which he was. "Alicia said that in this final sacrifice, they will cut the girls' hearts out and offer them to Huitzilopochtli."

Elias scrambled frantically ahead as Onawa caught up to Solitario.

"What is our plan?" she asked. "We can't just burst in there out-numbered."

"No, we can't," Solitario agreed. "Maybe you could take them all out with your bow and arrow."

"It crossed my mind," Onawa said.

"No, I have to first try to arrest them peacefully, give them a chance to go with us and stand on trial."

"That is the white man's way," she answered. "It's an unnecessary risk. You know they are guilty. And you also know they will not go without a fight."

"It is the law."

"Out here the law writes itself. Isn't Mayor Stillman also the judge? Do you think he'll issue an arrest warrant for himself?" Onawa said as they climbed, a steely determination growing harder in her eyes. "Let me try. I can probably drop two of them before they even know what's happening."

"No," Solitario answered.

"Let her," Boggs huffed on their heels. "I don't care what it takes to save my daughters."

"There's a right way and a wrong way to do things, Mr. Boggs. That's why you hired me."

"Not really," Boggs protested. "We hired you because Mayor Stillman said we should. Now I have my doubts about why he suggested it in the first place."

Solitario frowned, glancing at Onawa, wondering—as no doubt she was—if her initial suspicions had been correct all along. Why *had* Mayor Stillman insisted on hiring him instead of bringing in a Texas Ranger?

By the time they reached the boulders surrounding the clearing in the mountain pass, Solitario had formulated a plan. From beyond the crest of the rocks, he surveyed the situation. Stillman stood at one northern corner of the clearing; Grissom was at the other. Along the southern edge, Vance and Captain Ringgold stood guard at opposite ends. In the center, tied to posts arranged around a bonfire, were the six girls. A madwoman danced around the flames, which whipped wildly in the mountain winds. She could not be discounted, he thought. Beyond an altar on the eastern edge of the clearing stood the high priest in his mask and ceremonial garments. He brandished long knives in each of his hands.

Solitario gestured for the others to lean in toward him. In hushed tones, he outlined his plan. Each of them would take one of the guards from behind in silence, and then on Solitario's command, they would move slowly into the center of the clearing. Solitario assigned himself Grissom. "Once we have them under our control, I will instruct Grissom to tell everyone to drop their weapons and turn themselves in."

"What of the high priest and the dancing woman?" asked Onawa.

"Keep your bow and arrows ready," Solitario replied. "Hopefully, they won't take any action. They are not there to defend Grissom. They are being paid by him to conduct this macabre sacrifice. Once the game is up, they might try to run south to Mexico, but I doubt they'll want to stand and fight."

As they fanned out, stealthily circling the rock outcroppings toward their targets, Elias put his hand on Solitario's shoulder. "What about me? What do I do?"

"Can you wield a weapon?"

"No."

"Then wait for your chance. When you sense an opening, untie Elena and tell her to run."

Even though it was dark, Solitario could see the faint starlight reflected in his friend's eyes. Deep within them, he felt the lust for revenge, but underneath that, he sensed a volatile mixture of fear and hope. If his heart could beat, it would surely race.

———————

Solitario suspected that Mr. Boggs was the weakest link in his chain. Might the man's motivation to save his daughters compensate for his lack of experience and strength? As Solitario sneaked up on Grissom and placed the nose of his revolver close to the back of his head, he saw Mr. Boggs do the same to Mayor Stillman. They waited for Onawa and Blake to circle the clearing and respectively restrain Vance and Captain Ringgold.

When Onawa nodded at him across the clearing, her oval face aglow in the firelight, Solitario cleared his throat and interrupted the chants rising from the high priest at the altar and the masked woman dancing around the flames. "You are all under arrest. Bring this abomination to an end."

Grissom lurched forward, but Solitario held him in place with an arm around his neck and the gun pressed hard against the base of his skull. The woman performing by the bonfire stopped and peered at him through her mask, but the high priest seemed deeply entranced, continuing his incantations in Nahuatl.

Mr. Boggs had Mayor Stillman under control, his hands up in the air. Onawa held a knife against Vance's jugular, his eyes bulging in fear.

Captain Ringgold, however, was not intimidated by Blake Dobbs' rifle nuzzled against the base of his skull. Dropping to the ground, he swiftly swept Blake's legs out from under him, disarming him in the process and knocking him unconscious with the butt of his own rifle. He then pointed the gun squarely at Solitario. "You bring this to an end, Sheriff Cisneros. Or I'll bring you to an end right now."

"If you shoot me with that rifle, we both know I won't be the only one that gets it. So will your boss," Solitario shouted back. "Now, drop it, Ringgold. Slowly, all of you lower your weapons to the ground. We will not settle this here. We will take you in, and you will be treated in accordance with the law."

"You don't know who you're dealing with," Grissom snarled at Solitario, straining against his choke hold.

"I've got a pretty good idea," Solitario said. "Tell them to drop their weapons."

"Solitario," came a hauntingly familiar voice from the shadows beyond the altar, behind the masked priest with the blades, to the side of the stone portal glowing blue. "This is why you were chosen. So at this moment, you could tell your own followers to drop their weapons."

Solitario peered into the murky darkness. Who was that speaking? What was he talking about?

"I told you . . . you don't know who you're dealing with . . ." Grissom whispered, trying to wriggle free of Solitario's grasp.

That was when Solitario finally saw the man, stepping out from darkness into the flickering light of the fire, outlined in a blue haze from the stone gate's rippling energy. His white hair and dignified demeanor gave him away. It was Don Miguel Santander, his father-in-law.

"Don Miguel?" Solitario said, his surprise evident in the unsteady tone of his voice.

"Sí, m'ijo," Don Miguel answered, stepping closer, everyone's anxious eyes upon his elegant figure in his dark suit and tie. "I chose you. Because I knew that you, and only you, would appreciate what I am trying to accomplish."

"But Don Miguel, this is madness. All the people that have perished. You are a good man. How could this be? How could you wish to bring more suffering to these children and their families? You must stop this now. Perhaps the courts will take mercy on your soul and imprison you for the rest of your days rather than hanging you . . . I am not so sure about your conspirators, but you must stop this bloodshed here and now."

"Aren't you curious?" Don Miguel asked, approaching Solitario, who now held Grissom almost as a human shield between him and this least suspected of all the possible offenders.

"Curious about what?"

"Why I've done all this?"

Solitario stared back at him, muted by his own confusion. "Why?"

"To bring her back, m'ijo. To bring Luz back. Your Luz. My Luz. She is right there, on the other side of that blue curtain of dazzling energy. The gods can return her to us, make her whole again, even erase that foul curse your own abuela placed on you and the men in your family, la maldición de Caja Pinta. Imagine, having another chance with her. Imagine, bringing a child into the world with her, and being free to live outside the shadow of that hex."

Solitario gazed longingly at the glowing blue portal. The high priest was still chanting. Beyond the shimmering curtain of light, he saw a woman's outline. She wore a flowing dress. He could make out her long wavy hair. As she stepped right up to the translucent barrier, he could discern her elegant facial features. Don Miguel was not lying. The woman beyond the gate was Luz.

He suddenly felt his heart pounding in his chest, blood whooshing in his ears, an internal Nahuatl chant of his own ringing in his mind. He felt love and desire and rage swirling in one turbulent nexus, like the place in the Rio Grande's delta where the river's water flowed into the sea. He kept his face calm and controlled, as placid as the surface of those waters near his birthplace, despite the fact that underneath he was being pulled in opposing directions. His heart yearned for Luz. His mind knew that this was an ungodly act. His soul understood that it was a preposterous tragedy to take innocent lives in order to undo what had already been written. But still, his love knew no reason. He dropped his gun to the ground, allowing Grissom to wrestle free of his grip. As his followers gasped in dismay, the tables turned. Mayor Stillman whirled about, knocking Boggs' pistol from his hand and overpowering him. Vance turned to pounce on Onawa, but in doing so, sliced his own throat on the razor-sharp edge of her blade. He fell to his knees, clutching at his neck as blood streamed down his hands, his eyes wide with horror as he stared at her standing over him. Captain Ringgold fired at Onawa, but she ducked behind a boulder as the shot ricocheted away.

"Tell the Apache woman to drop her weapons and come on out into the light," Don Miguel commanded.

Solitario shook his head solemnly. "Leave her out of it. This is between you and me now."

"So you will cooperate?" Don Miguel asked. "You will help us finish the ritual to bring Luz back?"

Solitario stared at Luz, trapped beyond the blue veil. He could feel Onawa's eyes on him, along with Mr. Boggs' and Blake Dobbs' and Sergeant Elias'. Maintaining his poker face, he answered, "Let me see her up close."

Don Miguel swept his arm toward the glowing portal to the other plane. "Be my guest. She awaits us, Solitario."

Slowly, he walked up to the gate, entranced. He stared at her through the sheer field of energy. "How could this be?"

"It is," Don Miguel assured him. "I found the most powerful

sorcerers in Mexico City, descendants of the high priests of Tenochtitlan, and I brought them here. Tezcatlipoca and Malina. They have
communed with the gods, and in exchange for these sacrifices, they will
bring Luz back to us and undo your maldición."

Solitario stood directly in front of Luz at the blue gate. He gazed into
her eyes. He raised his hand and touched the curtain of light, watching
her do the same on the opposite side.

He could not hear her, but he could see her lips move and understood what she was saying. "Te quiero," she whispered.

He loved her, too. He had always loved her. He could never stop.
Now he felt that love dragging him beneath the waves, like the under-
tow of the ocean.

"Don Miguel," he asked, hearing his own voice as if he were under-
water listening to somebody else speak above the surface, in the land of
the breathing, "why has Grissom helped you do this?"

"In exchange for my lands," Don Miguel explained. "He had long
wanted me to sell, especially since the river moved and he lost his position
on the border. He offered to help me with this if I agreed to sell him my
lands at a fair value. M'ijo, with the money, you and Luz and I, we can go
back south to Mexico and start a new life. Forget all of this. Forget Olvido."

Forget Olvido, thought Solitario. How he wished he could. He could
not bear to detach his eyes from the gravitational pull of Luz's gaze, which
was more powerful than he could recall despite the fact she stood only in
another dimension. Summoning all of his inner strength and willpower,
however, he did pull his eyes away from her. He saw Onawa peeking at
him from beyond a boulder across the clearing. He observed Mr. Boggs
crying on his knees, peering through his glasses at his daughters tied to
the stakes. He watched as Elias untied the rope around Elena's wrists. His
eyes shifting downward, he noticed that the knot around her ankles was
already undone, the rope curled like a dead serpent at her feet. "I wish I
could forget Olvido, Don Miguel," Solitario said at last. "Because that way I
could forget what you have done. You have brought shame to Luz's memory.
You have dishonored her. While I can bear to lose love, I cannot bear to
lose honor. Take my life instead of these innocent children's. Let them go."

"It won't work," Don Miguel replied. "But if that's what you want, we'll take your life. I will not be denied my daughter again."

Grissom and Captain Ringgold grabbed Solitario, one on each side.

"Adios," he whispered, glancing at Luz one last time as they pulled him toward the fire.

"Start with him," Don Miguel ordered. "And then the children."

"Cut his head off," Malina laughed wickedly. "The gods will like that."

The girls shrieked and looked away as Captain Ringgold brandished his bowie knife, ripped the yellow bandanna off Solitario's neck, and plunged the blade toward his jugular.

———————

Elena's lone scream pierced the night as Ringgold's blade splintered in half, repelled by Solitario's enchanted necklace. The jagged shards shot backward into Ringgold's eyes, burrowing into his brain. Stumbling, he fell into the bonfire.

As the stench of burned flesh filled the air, Onawa leaped onto her boulder and began firing arrows. She struck Grissom squarely in the chest, dropping him to his knees. She struck Mayor Stillman in his right thigh. As he knelt in pain, Mr. Boggs wrestled the gun away from him and hurried to untie his daughters.

In that moment, Solitario watched what unfolded as if time had slowed and they were all moving sluggishly through a viscous material. A liberated Elena shoved Malina into the fire, her body bursting into flames atop Ringgold's. Crying in horror, the high priest, Tezcatlipoca, finally stopped his incantations. Rushing toward the flames, he swung his blades in a fury, light flashing blindingly from them. Solitario realized between two beats of his racing heart that the high priest was coming now not to provide tributes to the gods but to exact his own vengeance against Elena. Malina was his lover. His eyes ablaze with the reflection of the bonfire, he swung both swords ferociously, aiming to detach Elena's head from her body.

At the last second, Solitario stepped between Tezcatlipoca and his target. The high priest's blades shattered as they touched his necklace strung with fragile seashells collected on the beach by his abuela, la bruja Minerva.

As the metal shards fell to the ground, Solitario drew and fired the gun that remained in his left holster. The high priest collapsed in a motionless heap.

"Papá!" Elena shouted at the sight of her father. "You came. You saved us."

Elias smiled gratefully at Solitario through the smoke. Solitario nodded solemnly, turning to look back at the stone gate. The sheer curtain of blue light had vanished and then there was nothing left in its place but air and stone, cold and stillness, only death. Nearing the gate, Solitario noticed a movement in its shadows. Peering through the darkness, he found a hummingbird perched on a rock at the foot of the gate. He'd never seen such a creature sit still. As he stared at it, its wings blurred and it rose, disappearing into the night sky.

As Onawa freed the other girls, Blake Dobbs handcuffed Mayor Stillman and Dwight Grissom, who were injured but still very much alive. The Boggs girls cried, embracing their father. Abigail and Beatrice Tolbert dashed toward Blake, the only face familiar to them. And Lavinia held Onawa's hand, a melancholy expression etched on the young girl's face, sorrow glittering in her green eyes as she stared through the fire at the reunions unfolding around her.

"My family burned in a fire," she told Onawa.

"I know."

"I thought I might join them tonight," Lavinia added.

"Not tonight, child." Onawa stroked her hair. "Life goes on."

Tears streamed down Lavinia's rosy cheeks.

Solitario picked up his bandanna and walked slowly toward Don Miguel Santander, who sat now on a boulder by the altar, his head cradled in his hands.

"You are under arrest, Don Miguel. Extend your hands so I can cuff them."

"Nunca." A distraught Don Miguel looked up at him. "I knew when I met you, you would be the end of us. You and your pride and your honor and your maldición. Burn in hell, Solitario Cisneros. Someday, you'll get what you deserve. That will be justice."

Before Solitario could intervene, the old man pointed the revolver hidden in his lap at his own right temple, pulling the trigger.

The shot echoed through the canyon as Don Miguel's body crumpled to the ground.

THIRTY-NINE

It was Christmas, and Frankie Tolbert had been granted his wish—well, at least, the best he could hope for, given the circumstances. He knew he could not bring back his mother or father, or his brother, Johnny. But here he was again, at the dinner table with his sisters, Abigail and Beatrice. A large turkey graced the center of the table, along with sides of mashed potatoes and gravy and roasted carrots. The feast even included a heap of steaming Mexican tamales stuffed with shredded pork and raisins that Sheriff Solitario and Elena had brought along. The Dobbs twins had moved in with Frankie and his sisters, tending to the farm and watching over them.

After dinner, the Boggs family showed up on the front porch, bringing gifts. The Boggs girls ran around the house, playing with Abigail and Beatrice. Their aunt, Georgina, who was still visiting from Boston, flirted with Michael Dobbs by the fireplace as Blake and Elena cleaned up.

Frankie, who was finally walking again, took Solitario's hand and headed outside. "Walk with me, Sheriff," Frankie said.

Solitario allowed the boy to tow him onto the porch and down into the neighboring field. It was night already. Most people would have thought Frankie was crazy, but Frankie knew that the sheriff was different. He wasn't the same kind of lawman his own father had been, but that wasn't necessarily all bad either.

He led Solitario across the field toward the edge of the woods. "Sometimes I still have nightmares," he confessed, "about the familiar-faced man."

"It is hard to forget such things as you and your sisters have seen," Solitario soothed. "But with time and friends, you will heal. As for the apothecary, he is gone forever. And the other familiar-faced man, Mr. Stillman, along with Grissom, they are gone too. They've been taken to a jail far from here."

Frankie sighed thankfully. It was a relief to know that the evil men were gone.

"On a happier note, Frankie," Solitario added as they strolled across the field, "Reverend Grimes finally dropped his land dispute. He didn't think it would look good in the eyes of his congregation for him to continue bickering with you and your sisters over the property line in the woods."

"Since we're orphans?"

Solitario nodded. "I was an orphan too."

When they reached the boulder upon which Solitario had long ago waited for Johnny, Frankie patted the cold rock. "Johnny said he would meet us here."

In the pale moonlight, Frankie saw the familiar flash of his older brother's golden hair moving swiftly through the woods. Then, he stood in front of them, still in his dungarees and white T-shirt.

"Merry Christmas, Frankie," Johnny Tolbert said, smiling wistfully as he hugged his brother. "Merry Christmas, Sheriff."

"Feliz Navidad."

"You kept your promise," Johnny said. "I wanted to thank you before I go."

"You won't be in the woods anymore?" Solitario asked.

"Like I told Frankie, I'm tired. I need to go rest. Our mother and father are waiting for me. They need me now."

"We'll be okay here, Johnny. Tell them we'll be okay." Frankie squeezed his brother's hand.

Johnny smiled and dashed into the woods, fading into the darkness.

As Frankie and Solitario walked slowly back to the house, the boy looked up at the sheriff and asked him, "*Will* we be okay, Sheriff? I just said that to make Johnny feel better about leaving."

"I'll keep an eye on you. Don't you worry," Solitario answered.

Frankie missed his father and mother. He missed his brother. But it made him feel ever so slightly better knowing that somebody had his back. "I just don't know if I'll ever be able to get those terrible things I saw that night out of mind," he confessed. "I wish I could forget."

"There are many things I wish I could forget as well," admitted Solitario.

"Is that because we're both orphans?" Frankie asked as they walked up the stairs to the front door.

"No," Solitario answered. "It is because we are humans."

FORTY

The day after Christmas, Solitario rode to Onawa's house. He had visited Aguila Brava every morning since rescuing the children. Tormenta whinnied with sorrow. She knew that Aguila Brava was nearing the inevitable next step in his journey. She could sense the universe opening up, the membrane between this plane and the next softening, clarifying, like it had that night in the mountain pass. She had known Aguila Brava, felt his calming presence, gone on long rides and arduous hunts with Solitario at the chief's side. She knew Solitario felt a heavy burden of guilt, like he owed Onawa's dying father something, yet it was a debt he was either unable or unwilling to repay. And now Aguila Brava would exit this earth with that debt uncollected. Solitario would have to live on, endlessly carrying that burden. In Tormenta's mind, the prospect loomed like a load of cargo that would have to be transported for an eternity with the gnawing knowledge that the destination where it would be unloaded could never truly be reached.

While she waited for Solitario, Tormenta communed with Invierno beneath the clump of mesquites out front of Onawa's adobe house. When Solitario finally emerged, his sadness engulfed her. Onawa accompanied him slowly to the horses. Tormenta could tell that the young woman was moving her feet with more hesitation than usual. She did not wish for Solitario to leave.

"Won't you stay with us?" Onawa asked him.

"I cannot," he answered. "I must return to my ranch. I have neglected my cattle for too long in the pursuit of justice."

Onawa looked away, holding back her tears. She took a deep breath, straightening her back, her hair flowing in the cold winter wind. "Will you come when he passes?"

"Sí, of course." Solitario mounted, touching the brim of his sombrero as he nodded at her.

At his sudden urging, Tormenta moved abruptly, glancing back at Onawa, who stood watching them as they left. Escaping Olvido, Tormenta felt a droplet of water on her neck. She surmised Solitario had not wanted Onawa to see him shed a tear.

Following the dry riverbed, they rode over its snow-covered surface in the shadows of the canyons. Halfway back to El Escondido, Solitario dismounted beneath a towering outcropping. There, he shared the last drops from his canteen with Tormenta.

She whinnied in gratitude as the snowflakes that floated through the canyon landed lightly on her mane.

As Solitario sat on a rock, Tormenta noticed Elias approaching.

"You're leaving?" Elias said.

"My work is done," Solitario replied.

"Gracias, amigo. Elena seems as happy as I could hope, given the circumstances. She likes helping take care of the Tolbert children and that little green-eyed orphan."

"Elena has much love in her heart, just like her parents."

"You'll watch over her?"

"Of course. That is my sacred duty as her padrino."

"I made a good choice."

"Was there any other option?"

"Not really," Elias conceded, shrugging.

They both stared in silence at the swirling snow.

"So will you accept Mayor Boggs' offer to stay on as sheriff?"

"I don't know."

"What about Onawa? Will you accept her offer?"

"She has made no offer."

"You know her heart is yours for the taking."

Solitario stared into Elias' eyes.

"You can't go on alone," Elias said. "Nobody can."

"We are born alone and we die alone," Solitario recited.

"You were a twin. You were not born alone."

Solitario frowned at his friend. "Look at you. Death has changed you too much. Will you be staying in town or joining Otila and Oscarito?"

"I'm going to keep Elena company for a while. So if you need me, you know where to find me."

Solitario nodded. He stroked Tormenta's neck gently, brushing off a layer of freshly fallen snow. Then, he slipped his left boot into her stirrup, rising effortlessly into the saddle.

As they rode west, Elias called out after them, "Solitario, live while you're still alive."

Without turning around, Solitario waved adios.

As they reached El Escondido, the sun was setting behind the ranch house. He dismounted to open the gate. Then they rode to the clearing, where he unsaddled her and led her to the water trough, pumping fresh water from the well into it. It was cool and she drank it gratefully.

After he dunked a bucket of cold water over himself and changed into his cotton pajamas, he relaxed into one of the two rocking chairs out back, watching the sun set over the distant desert horizon.

After she drank and ate her fill, Tormenta kept him company beneath the cluster of mesquite trees, resting by Luz's tombstone.

As he sat on the porch flanked by the empty birdcages, Solitario sipped his tequila and thought of things only he could remember, but Tormenta knew he was thinking of Luz.

Savoring the cactus liquor, Solitario squinted toward the amber sky. And when that sky turned turquoise and then purple, and pinpricks of light poked through it, Tormenta's form faded into the darkness. It was then that, for the first time in Tormenta's memory of this ritual, Luz's delicate figure draped in flowing white gauze did not appear. Her raven tresses did not hang like vines over her shoulders and breasts. Her lips did not gleam like rubies in the rising moonlight. Solitario's eyes could not meet hers through the ink of night, and he did not smile wistfully as she stood there gazing at him. Solitario was indeed, finally, alone.

––––––––––––

The following morning, after drinking his morning coffee while watching the sun rise from the front porch, Solitario sat at a rustic table beneath a particularly tall mesquite. The sun shone brightly, melting the previous day's snowfall. Tormenta observed quietly as Solitario hammered at something that flashed in the sunlight. He cut a strip of leather from a piece of cured cowhide, looping it through a hole he had punched in the metal, knotting its ends together with care and precision.

What is he doing? Tormenta wondered, stomping her front hooves impatiently on the ground. She was eager to ride out with him and check on the cattle.

Solitario looked up at her from the table, smiling faintly. "Paciencia, Tormenta. Paciencia."

FORTY-ONE

Onawa had learned the meaning of patience from her father, but it was always harder to put into practice than it was to embrace in the mind and heart. Still, she tended to him diligently as he succumbed to the weight of his years. His body withered and his breath rattled in his chest.

"I have loved you, child, more than I had ever thought was possible," he said, closing his eyes as she clung to his feeble, bony hand. "You taught me that being a father is a more noble task than being a chief."

"You were always a chief, my chief," Onawa whispered, caressing his forehead and white hair. "And you will always be my father."

"I wish I could have seen you married, but I had you late in life. I am sorry to leave you alone. You know how I wish that . . ."

"Yes, I know." She placed one finger delicately on his cold lips. "Do not say it. We must be grateful for what we have, not sad for that which eludes us. You taught me that."

He nodded. "Don't give up . . . on him . . . or yourself."

She rested her head on his chest, listening as his breathing slowed. Paciencia, she recalled her mother saying. Dying took longer than it should sometimes. Between each breath, a longer interval stretched. But his spirit was so strong that each time she thought he was gone, he inhaled yet again. Each time, the breath was shallower, shorter. Each time, his chest rose ever more slightly. And when at last—in the middle of the long, dark night—his labored breathing came to an end, she raised her head, opened a window, and wailed in grief.

Outside, she heard a horse departing. Solitario had instructed Blake Dobbs to stand watch and retrieve him when the time came.

While waiting for her father to pass had been a slow and seemingly interminable process, now she must make haste, for it was the way of his people to waste no time disposing of the dead. Her father had been a Mescalero Apache. In accordance with the rituals he had taught her, she tore her clothes off and cast them aside, wearing only the oldest, most dilapidated dress she could find, a tattered remnant from her teenage days. She grabbed a flint knife and roughly cut her hair, shortening it to her bare shoulders. She hung the long cuttings from the trees in front of the house, shivering as her legs and arms were exposed to the cold. Weeping as she continued, she set aside a couple of sentimental items for her father's burial and destroyed the rest of his meager belongings in a roaring fire behind the house they had shared since he left the tribe to raise her in relative isolation. As the fire burned outside, Onawa cleansed her father's body, face, and hair. She dressed him in his finest traditional Apache attire, strung his necklaces and carefully arranged them across his chest, neatly parted and combed his hair, and crowned him with his feathered headdress. From her kitchen, she brought a bowl filled with golden pollen. Dipping her finger in it, she anointed his forehead, making a yellow cross on his mottled skin. She lit the candles on the altar to her mother, and she knelt next to Aguila Brava in silent prayer throughout the rest of the night.

As the sun rose, she heard a horse approaching before the roosters crowed. Opening the front door, she saw Solitario dismounting. Familiar with the traditions of her people, he took her hand and drew one of his silver revolvers. Pointing it toward the heavens, he discharged a single shot to alert the neighbors of Aguila Brava's passing. Then he followed her inside, where he knelt next to Aguila Brava and prayed.

With Solitario's help, Onawa placed the few possessions of his she had kept, alongside a pair of fading family photographs, upon his body, wrapping him tightly in a colorful sarape that had belonged to her mother.

"I will carry him on Tormenta," Solitario insisted.

Onawa was relieved that her father no longer owned a horse, for if he had, tradition would have required her to use the animal to ferry her father's body to its final resting place, ending the horse's life at the grave site.

Locking up the house and strapping a small bundle to Invierno's back, Onawa led the way toward the foothills south of Olvido. It was a long day's ride. When they reached the mountains, they climbed until they could see the new location of the Rio Grande winding majestically below them, sparkling like a river of gold in the setting sun.

Solitario unstrapped his shovel from Tormenta's side and dug a shallow grave two feet deep and six feet long as Onawa wailed and wept at Aguila Brava's side, soaking the colorful blanket that encased him with her tears.

When the digging was done, they each took one end of his body, lowering it gently into the cavity. They gathered branches, twigs, and stones to cover him. Then Onawa produced a sprig of sage to make imaginary crosses over both of their foreheads.

"Ghost medicine." She smiled faintly at Solitario as she brushed it over him. She knew neither one of them was afraid of ghosts. And she did not expect her father's spirit to return now that it was free to soar through the skies while still watching over her. But traditions were meant to be respected. When she was finished, she placed the sage on her father's grave.

Afterward, Onawa again led the way down toward the river. In the cobalt shadows of dusk, she stripped and bathed in the river as Solitario fed and watered the horses. Cleansing her skin and washing her hair, she prayed for her father, she thanked him, and she allowed her body to shake with grief. She wailed in mourning one final time and then completely immersed herself in the icy cold water.

By the fire that Solitario made on the banks of the river, they sat quietly on a soft blanket. They ate some bean tamales that Solitario had brought along, sipping an aged tequila. When she kept shivering from the cold, he wrapped another sarape around her shoulders. She took hold of his hand so that he would let his arm rest around her. And when he did so, she nestled up against him.

"You should have worn warmer clothes," Solitario said.

"Our tradition is to wear something that's falling apart, the worst article of clothing we possess."

Peeking out from beneath the blanket, her legs glowed amber in the flames. Sensing his gaze on them, she drew him closer. She ran her hand through his hair, gently pulling his face toward hers, their eyes locking. In that moment, she saw him naked even though he was clothed and wrapped in the colorfully striped blanket with her. She saw his sorrow and his desire, his yearning and his solitude. She kissed him. As his lips pressed back against hers, she rolled onto him, her hair dangling down and brushing against his rough cheeks. She kissed him again and again, desperately trying to make up for all the times she had yearned to touch him and feel his lips on hers. She tore at his clothes, feeling him harden beneath her as she straddled him. His hands were on her hips as she oscillated gently over him, moaning with desire and pleasure.

"No," Solitario panted, hesitating. "I cannot take advantage of you."

She clasped his face in her hands as she leaned over him. "I am the one taking advantage."

"I cannot be with you."

"I love you. I have always loved you."

His eyes searched hers, melting with emotion. "I . . . I . . . feel . . . I cannot hurt you."

"Just be with me now. Here." She moved slowly again as the fire crackled.

Embracing her tightly, he thrust in unison with her until both their bodies shuddered together.

Falling silent, she lay on top of him, resting her head on his chest. When their breathing had slowed along with their hearts, she reached up and caressed his face, surprised to find it wet with warm tears.

"Why are you weeping?" she asked.

"I long to give you what you want but I cannot. I wish to be with you but I cannot."

"Because of la maldición?"

He nodded.

She resented him for not throwing caution to the wind, but she loved him even more for denying his desires in order to protect her. This was honor. And to love a man of honor was to accept the sacrifices that honor demanded.

"I am sorry if I have made your pain worse," she said, holding him tightly, "but I would rather have this memory than nothing at all."

When they awoke, ate, and packed, they rode back up through the mountains. Once in the desert valley, Solitario began to lead the way back north to Olvido. When he noticed she was no longer following, he paused and turned back, gazing at her from his saddle atop Tormenta.

"What is happening?"

"I am not going back," she said.

"Why?"

"Now that my father is gone, I have no reason to be there. I have brought what I need." She glanced at the bundle strapped to Invierno's back.

"But," he said, swallowing hard, apprehension filling his eyes, "where will you go? It is not safe for you alone, outside of Olvido."

"There is an Apache reservation opening in New Mexico. I can start a new life there."

"That is so far away." His voice cracked with emotion. The outer corners of his eyes drooping in concert with his mustache.

"I cannot go on living close to you yet kept at a distance." What she didn't tell him was that she had not yet given up on him, that she still hoped to learn how to break la maldición.

He looked away, squinting toward the rising blaze on the horizon, his majestic sombrero failing to shield his eyes and face at the sun's morning angle. "I understand."

"Goodbye, Solitario," Onawa said.

"Let me accompany you to the reservation. I can help keep you safe along the way."

She shook her head. "I am going to the bruja Alicia's house first. I promised her I would return. When I am finished training with her, I will head to New Mexico."

"Can I take you to Alicia's then?"

"It is not necessary. It is near. Go," she said, fighting back a wave of emotion that threatened to spill over as tears gushed from her eyes. "Go, now." She waved him away.

He hung his head and turned, spurring a reluctant Tormenta north toward Olvido. She could tell he was riding harder and faster than he needed to, but she figured he had to escape his emotions as rapidly as possible to prevent himself from changing his mind . . . or hers.

Over the brilliant desert sands, Onawa rode Invierno through the harsh, cold winds of winter. After a couple of hours riding—and weeping for her father, for Solitario, for herself—she paused for a drink of water. She knew what lay ahead would be difficult, but her father had once told her that if something was easy, it wasn't worth doing.

When she reached for her canteen, she felt something unusual in the pouch containing it. It was a hard, flat object. As she pulled it out, it flashed brightly in the sun. It was a star, Solitario's sheriff badge. He had punched a hole in its top center point and threaded a leather loop through it to create a necklace. Smiling, she raised it over her newly cropped hair and let it fall around her neck. As it flashed in the white winter sun, she mused that the only thing that could shine brighter was the sliver of hope she now carried inside herself.

EPILOGUE

1884

Solitario rose with the sun, as he did every day, alone on his ranch, El Escondido. Spring was at hand and the desert exhibited all of the signs of another rebirth. The cacti bloomed yellow and pink. The mesquite trees sprouted fresh green leaves, spindly, fragile, and new.

He donned his black charro uniform, the polished silver buckles along the outer seams of his pants jingling as he stepped outside into the newborn day. He drank his bitter coffee on the front porch, squinting into the growing light, watching the sky change colors from deep blue to aquamarine. He fastened his turquoise eagle belt buckle at his waist, slung his ammunition belts across his chest, and adjusted his holsters at his hips. Around his delicate necklace strung with shells, he knotted his yellow bandanna. And as he marched toward Tormenta, he placed his sombrero on his head.

He had agreed to return to work in Olvido. It was better than slowly dying in hiding. At least this way, he could put his talents to good use. There had been a time when he wondered if he still had them at all. Now when he rode through town and the children chased him laughing, he drew some modicum of pleasure from checking in on Elena and Elias, the Tolberts, and the Dobbs. Working with Mayor Boggs was a welcome new experience. He had never collaborated with a gringo before, but Mr. Boggs was fair, smart, and eternally grateful to him for rescuing his daughters from the jaws of death. Perhaps, together, they might also succeed in saving Olvido from itself.

Mounting Tormenta, Solitario rushed through El Escondido's wrought-iron gates, kicking up a trail of churning dust in his wake. His heart pounded as he leaned over Tormenta's thick neck, her muscles glistening in the light as she galloped without restraint. That day, instead of following the dry riverbed, which reminded him of death and desolation, he decided to take a totally different route. It was longer, but the scenery was well worth the effort. They streaked with the speed of Tormenta's namesake desert storms, thundering through the vast valley, steadily ascending to a desert mesa where Solitario swore it felt like he could practically reach up and touch the sky.

Perched high on the elevated crest of a prominent butte, Tormenta paused. Solitario gazed out over the sprawling, creosote-dotted valley below. The setting reminded him of the spot where he and Onawa had watched the sunrise months ago and shared a coffee. He wondered what she was doing at that moment. Was she learning powerful magic with Alicia? Would he ever see her again? And if she gave him another chance, would he still pull away from her as their skin touched?

In the distance Olvido stirred from its slumber. He could make out its telltale scar in the earth, the ephemeral source of life that had drawn the settlers to begin with, winding through the collection of buildings. A sprinkling of white plumes rose defiantly from fires burning in the stoves and hearths of those determined to stay, those committed to keep toiling despite the obstacles aligned against them in this increasingly inhospitable environment north of the border. To the south of the town, beyond a spine of weathered hills, the Rio Grande uncoiled like a capricious snake, glittering copper in the growing light. It had forsaken its people and its natural duty to nourish and unite them, yet it persisted obstinately in its assigned task of splicing nations. As the sun rose beyond the mountains to the east, the range's long shadows stretched through the yawning canyon. There was not another living being in sight, but Solitario felt comforted by a presence greater than his own.

ACKNOWLEDGMENTS

No matter how isolated and lost we might feel—we are never truly alone. At its core, this is the spirit of *Valley of Shadows*.

Sometimes we must cross a border to be reunited with those we love or with our home. Sometimes that border is a river, other times it is a geographic distance or an emotional divide.

All too often what keeps us apart and alone is of our own making as humans: war, racism, xenophobia, contagion, and fear. Other times, it is the invisible wall between the living and the dead, between us and our God, between our fate and our free will, or between the extant and the imaginary.

All of us live this truth in some way or another. We exist alone, yet not alone.

Writing itself is a solitary craft, yet it reminds me that—again—we can achieve nothing by ourselves. For words to be made real, they must be read. For thoughts to become more than figments of one's imagination, they must be expressed, they must be heard. Storytelling should be called *storysharing* because it comes alive through the connection made in the process of writing and reading, telling and listening, creating and remembering.

In my case, I am keenly aware that my lifelong dream of writing and sharing my stories with readers would not be possible without the love and support of my family, starting with my wife, Heather, my daughter, Paloma, and my son, Lorenzo. They are constant sources of inspiration as well as encouragement. I would like to thank them for cheering me on as I worked on *Valley of Shadows* during our shared pandemic quarantine. Hiding from the rest of the world deepened my appreciation of our own little universe. And a very special thank-you to Lorenzo for asking me a few years ago to "write a Western horror novel" so he could read it. I've never been able to say no when my children have asked me to tell them a story. And I so enjoyed writing this one. Also, speaking of family, I have to express my gratitude to my own mother and father, my brothers, my abuelos and abuelas, and even those ancestors I only know as names and places and years inscribed in barely legible script on ancient documents unearthed by my wife during her genealogical research. Their daring struggles and passion for handing down family fables from generation to generation have long inspired me to be a storyteller and bequeathed me a treasure trove of material on which to draw in spinning my yarns. To them I must say: Etérnamente, y de todo corazón, muchas gracias.

Without my family, I couldn't begin—or sustain—my writing, but without my partners and collaborators, I could not get that writing out into the world. With that in mind, I am forever grateful to Blackstone Publishing, its founders and leadership. It is a true pleasure to work with a publisher that shares the same values that my wife and I have held dear in our own endeavors. When I learned that Blackstone was created by a husband-and-wife team, I had a hunch my writing had finally found its home. This is a publishing house that puts people first, one that treats each project not simply like a disposable product to be sold and forgotten, but like a living work of art, a craft diligently made for sharing, and a form of vital and enduring human expression and connection. The process is as magical and special as the end product, which is ultimately, hopefully, a rewarding, memorable, and transformative reader experience. I have found the entire collaborative experience particularly unique and rewarding. A special thanks to Rick Bleiweiss, who introduced and championed my work at Blackstone, and to Josie

Woodbridge, Naomi Hynes, Lauren Maturo, Hannah Ohlmann, Kathryn English, Ciera Cox, and everyone else at the publishing house for the personal attention and care they instill into all they do to delicately place each book as a cherished gift in the readers' hands. Likewise, a sincere thank-you to Laura Strachan, my literary agent. Laura is a constant and savvy guide, who often helps me remain grounded and focused as not only a creative writer but also a strategic and patient one, qualities that are essential to keeping one's sanity as an artist of any kind. In writing this book, I also benefited greatly from the advice of Sarah Cortez, a published author and editor, who collaborated with me on the editing process. Sarah's help in adding depth and nuance to the characters' journeys taught me to further appreciate the richness and the rewards that a thoughtful and open-minded approach to developmental editing can bring to the entire writing experience and hopefully the final product and the reader's immersion and enjoyment.

Most importantly, one of my most genuine aspirations in writing *Valley of Shadows* was to be respectful to the context and authenticity of the key characters, some of whom are displaced Apache, Mexican, and other Indigenous people who struggled for survival and a peaceful place to call home in the face of great persecution, oppression, violence, and injustice. I am deeply aware that I could never fully understand or capture their suffering and resilience, but I felt compelled to craft this story with them and their lives at its heart, at times—no doubt—imagining a magical realism past with an optimistic outlook rooted in the future. I am eternally grateful for all of the contributions that the peoples and unsung heroes these characters represent have made to their—and my—own families and communities as well as to our ever-evolving understanding of the American identity, what it means, and what it *could* mean to be a part of it, both in its atrocious failures and its alluring potential to live up to its ideals of equality and freedom for all people, including those of diverse backgrounds and origins.

In the end, if *Valley of Shadows* is about loneliness and companionship, it is also about life and death, fear and hope, the eternal balance we must strive to maintain as we journey onward. And it is about a sense of place, how sometimes what keeps us company is the very soil we stand on, the air we breathe, the trees we shelter beneath, the caves in which we seek refuge. In these places, some of which our ancestors have inhabited for generations and centuries, we create our dreams, our histories, our mythologies, the very ether that feeds our souls. We become tied to place, one with it. A border, a river, a desert, a mountain, a cluster of homes holding each other up in the face of harsh winters, brutal summers, and unwelcome invaders. When we walk in this valley of shadows, we are never truly alone. Whether we believe in a higher power that protects us, or the very land that envelops us, we walk through the darkness together, all of us, and for that comfort I am most grateful.

—Rudy Ruiz

11-22

CU